BLOCK

XX/XX
2020

Written by

DrGooseX

BLOCK XX/XX
BLOCK 2020

© Copyright 2019, DrGooseX LLC

ISBN: 978-1-7340689-0-0 (Book);
ISBN: 978-1-7340689-1-7 (E-Book);
ISBN: 978-1-7340689-2-4 (Audio).

Library of Congress Control Number: 2019915584

The book consists of works of fiction. Names, characters, places, and incidents are the product of the author's imagination or are used fictitiously. Any resemblance or similarities to actual events or locales, and characters (living or dead) in this book are fictitious and purely coincidental.

Although many characters in the following story are based on actual historical figures, and some events are a matter of record, this is a fictional account about BLOCK XX/XX - otherwise known as BLOCK 2020.

www.BLOCKXXXX.com

Dedication

Dedicated to Mr. G

Table of Contents

BOOK ONE

BOOK TWO

BOOK THREE

BOOK FOUR

BOOK FIVE

BOOK SIX

BOOK SEVEN

BOOK EIGHT

BOOK NINE

BOOK TEN

Preface to BLOCK XX/XX

BLOCK XX/XX was inspired by true events. No matter what your faith, your belief, your level of spirituality... Everybody is different. No faith or beliefs at all... no worries. We are all one, under the same sun. This book is a religious writing based on various viewpoints. **BLOCK XX/XX** follows many different cultures and beliefs from the past to present.

<pause>

BLOCK XX/XX is a triple touch tale, meaning that you can have a whimsical experience, think at a higher level, or read and reveal secrets. Expand the experience and let yourself be affected.

This is an intentional read: Follow your intuitive thinking and look for something sacred. Imagine yourself in the scene with your senses. Use your spiritual imagination through meditation or discuss the book with friends who have also read it.

<pause>

Ponder one, two, three times... Pause to think. Absorb the book's contents. You are a sponge in water.

Others may ask you what the book is about, and you might honestly answer, "I don't know. You have to read it for yourself." Each person will react differently. Or you could just say, "Some things cannot be told." Keep the contents a mystery. Do not spoil it for them... that would be cruel and mean.

<pause>

The unique literary style creates the new "Hybrid Fiction" genre. You can have an entertaining or informative read, depending on the depth you wish to reach. Each chapter can be read leisurely at a fast or slow pace. To assist and aid the reader:

- Between each thought is a cartoon graphic.
- **Life's lessons learned are bolded texts.**
- Quotes from "Mr. G" are in red (red letter edition).

Read carefully. Give yourself space to grow, be reflective. The goal is to "Chew your food before swallowing." Time is not important here. But if you read a book (10 chapters) in less than an hour, you ate too quickly. Savor the flavor.

<pause>

BLOCK XX/XX consists of a ten-book set. Each book has 10 chapters, therefore 100 chapters total. At the end of each book is a "Test of Understanding" that must be passed before proceeding forward. (No cheating!)

x

After completing the set, readers are given an invitation to a website wherein they can interact with the book and others. Here they can contribute their own videos, graphics, short stories, suggestions and comments. We suggest your character be fictitious (game mode). After you set up a character, you can log in and contribute. (Please be kind online.) This is especially special for those enjoying this book on Audio. Sometimes it is easier to see a picture or take the tests here.

BLOCKXXX.com

(Constantly changing and under construction.)

<pause>

Somebody better explained this book as an off-road read. Do not get lost... You need to drive slowly. You will find yourself cruising along and enjoying the beautiful scenery only to suddenly get stuck in a spot that requires shifting into four by four for extra traction. The bumps in the road are well placed and wake you up on the journey. Oh, and to warn you, in some places trespassing is forbidden.

Lost? Stop and circle around. Re-read or retrace your steps. Read it more than once to expand your enlightenment.

<pause>

Parts of this book intend to offend. Give it no mind. Based on real life:

Rated M, for immature minds; Rated R, readers discretion is advised.

Because of this it is banned in some countries.

<pause>

To conclude the preface with a prelude, imagine if heaven was here on earth. **BLOCK XX/XX** teaches a path for people to live as people. Live with compassion, diversity, honesty, impartiality, respect, insight and understanding, and without discrimination. Most importantly, live with love. From this Foreword on, I wish for you to keep moving forward.

Let your spirit guide you.

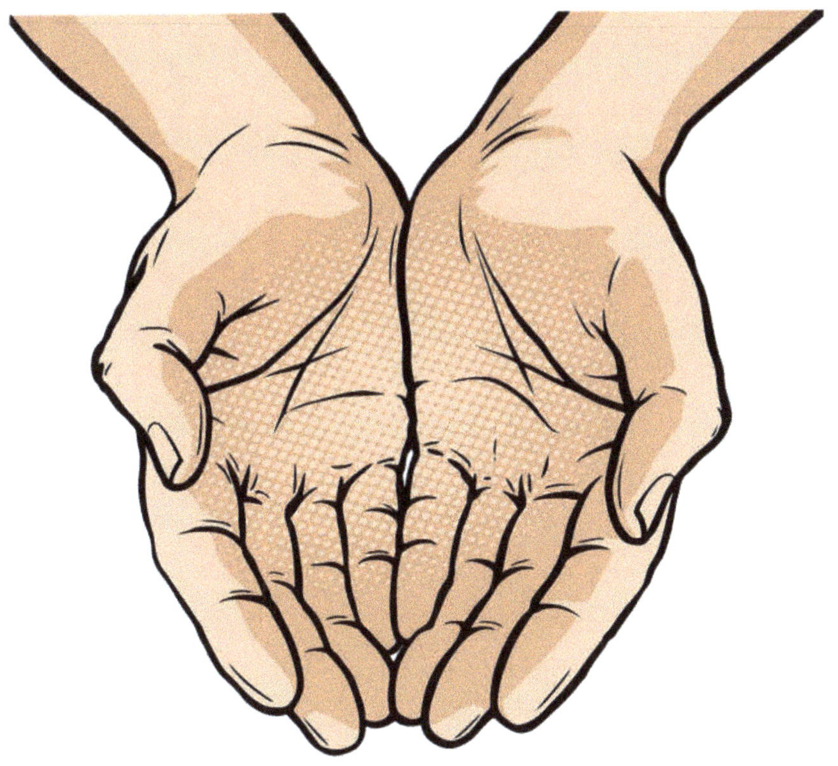

Chapter 0
Bubble

Zero, none, nothing... Before anything, there was nothing...
Imagine a bubble. An air bubble is magic. It is a translucent film of water... A rainbow of light bounces off its shimmering surface... radiant and shining. Air is enclosed in an empty sphere with internal pressure pushing out as an equal force holds it delicately from the outside. The bubble is symbolic. Simple, yet complex.

Let's imagine a bubble floating through the air, drifting with the soft breeze. A gentle touch can make it disappear. And sometimes not even a touch is needed for some to vanish. They are interesting to observe.

Breathe in deeply... Relax... Enjoy the tranquility and peace... Feel your heartbeat.

Deep breath and go! Your heart quickens as you explore the source of the energy in the room.

A 360-degree view: The spray of bubbles came from the four corners. All aimed at the middle, the bubbles filled the center with a whimsical cloud of suds. Children danced and played as they bathed themselves in the foam clouds. Enjoy the excitement and feeling of fun.

Breathe in... Breathe out. Your heightened senses notice the concentric circles of people in the room. Youngest to oldest, wildest to calmest. You want to look. As we view the room from the midpoint, notice the next age cycle of teens and parents watching with amusement. Their heads were actively moving, their bodies animated with laughter.

The ring of chairs and tables were mostly abandoned as the room focused on the nucleus of entertainment. The elder group remained furthest from the energetic center. Older couples moved their chairs closer. Taking advantage of the moment, a gentleman reaches out to put his arm around his lady. The woman sneaks a sweet kiss on the cheek of her love quickly enough so as not to be noticed. Yet others leisurely take small morsels of the cake set before them on the table. Smiles emerge.

Breathe in... Breathe out... Relax totally. Slowly, Breathe in... Breathe out. Do you notice it? Can you feel it? Plug yourself into the environment and the sensations. A feeling of love... and the calmest of emotions... As light as a bubble, love and harmony is softening you. It is your natural state of being. A relaxed, calm, emotion of love is responding. Can you feel it now?

The clothing styles are as diverse as the people in the room. Solid colors, no patterns. Scattered observations: Women wear one or more silk scarves. (Generally, the older women wear one scarf and the younger prefer two or more colors.) Men choose heavier natural fibers, but this was not always true, just as most women prefer light or sheer fabrics. "Sexy" was a style, just as "natural" or "relaxed" – there is no "code."

Interestingly, no hats or glasses. **Clothes were not worn for status, but more for reflecting their feelings.** Having said all this, most chose to wear bright colors and today the color red was the fashion. You feel like you want to explore further. As we orbit the room, you feel the cohesion of the crowd. Feel the moment. Your senses become heightened. Fill your lungs with fresh air... then slowly exhale.

However, more important than the bubbles were the five chairs on the outside edge, backs against the wall. Perhaps the most significant sight was the two women and two men sitting stoically, still, facing forward. A few errant bubbles floated by.

From left to right: A young and exotic dark-skinned woman next to a much older, Aryan man. In the center was an empty chair. To the right – a tanned and rough Native American man whose rustic looks contrasted the refined elegance of the Asian woman to his side. He raised his arm to wrap around her, but she swiftly stopped him and gently held his hand. This seemed to be a more subtle, but deeper connection or bond. Without looking at each other, they simultaneously smiled.

Scanning back to the left, the young, dark-skinned woman holds the hand of an elder man. In an instant, energy was exchanged, and both sets of eyes sparkled. Holding hands, these four were unified despite the missing center person.

Now... inflate your lungs with more fresh air.

A bubble is simple and complex. A combination of science and art. A contradiction of strength and weakness. The bubble is the center of the universe. Inside the bubble is nothing.

In sociology, a "bubble" occurs when fiction is repeated again and again until you feel it is true.

Chapter 1
Block

Towards the beginning of the twentieth century, a group of wealthy investors decided to claim land and build what was later known as the "BLOCK". The BLOCK consisted of only square structures. Each cube was identical – 100 meters long, 100 meters wide, and 100 meters tall. **Upon its completion in the late 1920s (exact date unknown), when urban renewal and planned neighborhoods were in full swing, the project was abandoned.** Some said about the BLOCK, "The world created the infant that was to be ignored."

Elsewhere things moved quickly: World War 1 ended in 1918. In 1920, the Nazi party was founded and by 1933 Adolf Hitler became Chancellor of war whipped Germany. In 1931, the Empire of Japan conquered Manchuria. Mussolini entered Ethiopia in 1933 and began his revolts across Africa against the British Commonwealth and the North African people. By 1937, the Emperor of Japan invaded China, pushing his way into Mongolia by 1939 and preparing for expansion westward into the Soviet Union. The great depression began in 1939, about the same time Germany invaded Poland and Stalin's republic entered the war.

One hundred million soldiers from 30 different countries fought in World War II which came to a climatic end with the atomic bombing of Japan, leaving a million dead in two quick attacks. Elsewhere, 11 million Jews had died in concentration camps. A total of more than 75 million people, many innocent, were gone by 1949.

So, it's no surprise that this social experiment, called "**The BLOCK**", was ignored during these twenty years. Doors were locked and life continued in the outside world. In addition, Communism became a dirty word and the world grew cold.

The winter snow swirled through the streets as cars rarely moved past the BLOCK.

"Papa, what is that?" A young child sat staring out the window at the eight white stone structures. Snow was scraped off the streets and piled on the sidewalk against the vacant buildings.

"I do not know. I remember when my grandfather worked to build this. It seems the same now as it did when I was your age. The size may be different, or maybe it is just me."

"I don't see any windows... no trees... no people..." the youngster observed in a mixture of wonderment and confusion.

"No windows and doors..." Thinking, "Yes dear, it is actually quite well designed not to waste a single piece of space. Well designed... Eight identical buildings spaced equally apart." Reflecting, "There are no streetlights because the white of the building reflects the light of the day and the fluorescent façade glows like warm neon at night..."

Moments later the elder man continued, "I think it is some type of artistic monument with a meaning I do not understand."

The little one remarked, "Papa, they look nice... but..." Stopping and then, "**Nobody talks about it.**" After that the two remained quiet during the rest of their journey.

Nobody else took notice. Nobody else said anything.

The BLOCK consisted of identical cubes that were perfectly aligned and spaced. Starting at the north, the four buildings were titled A, B, C, and D. The next four buildings to the south were E, F, G, and H. West to East (or left to right) were A, B, C, D, followed by E, F, G, H.

If buildings have feelings... wait.

Researching the city records, you can find the original plans. Each floor was partitioned into 100 squares (10 tall, 10 long, 10 wide) ... 100 square meters in size (a 10 by 10 grid) ... totaling 1000 square meters each. Ten floors. Overall, 10,000 square meters inside each Cube.

The gap between each building was 40 meters wide, ample space for a street and sidewalks. The concept was for the loop around the BLOCK to be a mile (a 1600-meter perimeter). This was a design ahead of its time.

Meshing the amazing buildings together was an invisible rooftop. For structural support and protection of the space below was a full, flat surface. Flying over, a camouflage effect was created.

The winter storm threw a blanket of pure snow over everything. Tracks got covered quickly... During a whiteout, your main concern is yourself... If you do not look, you will never notice.

Chapter 2
Balance

The pace was a peaceful calm. A clear mind and limber body were the result. There was a surreal sensation while inside the BLOCK. It was as if you were watching a movie slowed down 10%: gliding movements with fading pauses and gaps of silence. It takes time to adjust to this speed.

Was distortion of time a reality? Could there be more than 24 hours in a day? No dimension of time except for the rhythm of your body? Without the sun, perhaps energy was naturally strengthened? Without the moon, was there a weakened gravitational pull?

One must surrender. The sensation was relaxing, but the reason was beyond understanding. Feel your heartbeat within you and let your mind ease.

It is normal for us to criticize things that are new or different or that we do not understand. When dropped into a foreign culture, we instinctively make comparisons. We look for similarities that ground us and make us comfortable. We also look for flaws to compensate for our own discomforts. Suppress your thoughts. Delay your normal instincts. Float along with everybody around you.

Forces in motion seek balance... The law of nature is a guiding force and cannot be changed. The laws of nature prevail both inside and outside the walls of each cube and the entire BLOCK.

Within the BLOCK, within each cube, within each person was a "sun" that fueled everything. Unlimited love energized each person to share and give. In return, receiving love generated gratitude and thankfulness. **The law of seven: for every one that you give, you will get back seven fold.** For every gift of a dollar you give, you get back $7, somehow, somewhere. One smile equals seven smiles. One hug eventually is seven extra hugs, etc.

The basic law of scarcity states, **"Man has limited needs and unlimited wants."** What are the basic needs of man? Air, water, food, sleep, safety/security, physical/emotional Health, and love. We only need a limited amount of these to survive. As it was explained to me, anything beyond this is our desire for more.

Outside the BLOCK: There is a feeling of not enough resources to satisfy unlimited wishes. The hunger for more creates a competition amongst people, the feeling of vanity and envy that leads to greed.

Primitive man was satisfied with meeting his or her basic requirements. Each gift Mother Nature gave was a joy.

Inside the walls, there was **a feeling of gratitude and thankfulness.** All basic requirements were met...

Love brings happiness. **Helping, aiding, and caring for others creates a warm energy within the giver.** Those weak and tired gain stability and strength. The reward grows as you share more of yourself. Love is addictive and in unlimited supply.

The desire to give more replaced the desire to want more... **An infinite amount of giving begat infinite receiving.** A limitless amount of love replaced limitless desires. It is possible to love without limits. (For example, a mother can love more than one child.) This is the basic law of abundance.

Man evolved. Energy is exchanged, not currency.

Simple yet complex. Understanding in theory, but when faced with reality there was confusion. For example, history...

History imprints itself on us. What we did yesterday makes us what we are today. Last week, last month, or last year is tattooed into our minds. We cannot control what happened to us in the past. That time is gone. Truth be told, humans easily forget most things.

History imprints itself on our traditions and culture. What happened to us as children makes us what we are today. Our family, parents, grandparents, and our ancestors developed customs based on their experiences. Truth be told, however, civilization easily forgets the sources and true meanings.

From our memories within... and interactions with others... today's thoughts and actions are formed. By understanding history, we can see reality without confusion. Life's lesson is that we do not know what happened most of the time. Accept it... learn and embrace it... But **do not dwell on time that has past at the expense of the present.**

Within the cube was a balance of nature: Magic is only an illusion. A miracle is something unexplained. Within the cube there seemed to be a balance of magic and miracles.

Life was much easier, fun, and satisfying within the walls. Effortless joy... Goodness. The BLOCK brought balance, stabilizing what would otherwise be out of control in the world.

Chapter 3
Magic

Slowly and gently she became aware. She could feel the air move around her and into her lungs. The smell was sweet. She heard a soft voice.

"Relax... pumzika... 放鬆 (fàngsōng)... relájese... relaxat... расслабьтесь (rasslab'tes')... आराम करें (aaraam karen)... se détendre... du entspannst ... **relax**..."

She tried to open her eyes, but they were heavy. The only image she could see was a blur. It was only a second or two... Then abruptly it went dark and she fell into a slumber.

She melted into consciousness with the feeling of a hundred hands moving across and touching her skin. Hot, cold...soft, smooth.... heavy, light...fast and slow.

Her mind was no longer petrified but had loosened into clouds.

The scent was clean and a little minty, fresh.

She deliberately kept her eyes closed this time, but a sliver of light came in like a snapshot. The image was not recognizable.

Sounds? I do not know. "Is comfort a sound?" she thought just before the switch turned off.

No dreams... just blank nothing. The smooth introduction into awakening was followed by random senses attaching themselves to her coherent mind. But without any notice, the darkness always came back.

As these episodes repeated, they became longer in duration. Numb... Clouded judgement... Mind fog may also express it. It felt like... It felt like there was something or someone there with her each moment. Someone who smelled like... soil. A good smell. Other times she heard the windy sounds of a flute and smelled a woman's scent of sweetness mixed with something blooming. Breezes brought in the manly scent of musk and wood.

As her senses unlocked, she bravely made a plan to open her eyes.

Eyes open. **Light immediately replaced darkness.** She saw the face of a man. She could not focus on the face as a whole, but small details like the shape of his nose, the texture of his skin, or the blue color of his eyes were absorbed into her thoughts.

Then it happened! She felt his hand touched hers. The instant of contact created a surge of energy, a lightning bolt hit her! She felt alive! It felt wonderful! He smiled.

Frustrating! Confusing! The flashes of lucidity... Seconds seemed like hours or maybe hours seemed like seconds... Finalized with the unpredictable flip of the switch to darkness and a dreamless sleep... Aggravating! These flutters in and out of consciousness were annoying. This sensation inside her needed to be released. **No more floating in the water of nothingness.** It had to stop!

"Hello." The voice of a woman... a soft voice of a woman... the soft voice of an Asian woman. Yes! She was correct! When she opened her heavy eyes, she perceived a woman.

She sat up. Moving into the sitting position created a rush of blood from her head. A moment of dizziness enveloped her, and then faded... She could not talk...

The woman moved to her right side and sat down. ...The right side? The man she saw earlier was on her left side... Erratic and uncontrollable thoughts such as this slithered in her brain.

The woman gingerly moved the waft of hair from her face. "I care you... I care for you." She smiled and seemed full of happiness. Then she gracefully poured water into a cup, presented it with two hands, and moved it forward. "Water. Try ..." Sipping the water as you would the most expensive drink ever tasted.

Hurriedly, she took another sip. "Water. More..." The woman kept the cup to the girl's lips and this time seemed to pour it into her mouth. The bedridden girl lifted her hands to the cup.

"Yes... I love you." The caregiver moved her hands away as the patient shakily held the cup to her lips. Swallowing and breathing in alternating motions. Then she had to move the cup away and rest. She had finished half the water. But when the Asian woman looked into the cup, she said, "Water. Finish." The caregiver abruptly poured the remaining liquid into her mouth, forcing her to fiercely swallow as quickly as she could.

"Water... Good!"

"I hug you. I care for you please." said the woman with an embrace that lingered.

The facial expressions were tender as her almond eyes glistened, soon to weep. The young female looked into loving eyes and smiled. Then she heard,

"Good. Tomorrow you walk."

"What?" she thought in horror.

Her eyes closed and locked shut into darkness again.

Chapter 4

J'me eXquisite

Slowly and gently she became aware. She could feel the air move around her and into her lungs. The smell was sweet.

Softly she heard, "Relax."

The dazed girl was pulled forward and pillows pushed behind her back. There must have been four or five attendants bouncing around. A moment of rest and clarity in her eyes, and then the next step. Her feet were swung to the side of the bed and her legs dropped.

A moment later, she was jerked forward onto her feet. If done a moment too soon the clarity in her eyes would be replace with a glaze. The group of attending women closely monitored her.

"Walk. Try." Then... "Walk. More." Then... "Walk. Finish." Then... "Walk. Good."

The girl had gotten out of bed and made her way to a chair. Then the attendants left as if vacuumed out of the room. She sat in the chair, alone, in silence. She felt tired and closed her eyes.

"Hello. Did you miss me? How are you?" The sunshine woman's voice raised her from a warm slumber.

"Arrgh ...   Hello." She took breaths between each word. The caregiver was very excited, but also very patient when she heard her speak for the first time.

"Hello. I missed you. I am happy now." The Asian woman was singing her words.

Responding with more like grunts than speech, "Arrgh, hello... **I am...**" Then silence.

With an Asian accent, "M?" (Alphabetically) "A, B, C, D, E, F, G, H, I, J, K, L... M!" she uncoded, then "Oh, am I. M. U. N..." (This was going to be fun.) **"My name is Juan Li."** (The Chinese pronunciation of her name sounded like the letters U and N.) She giggled.

From the bed, "U....N...? Ahh... Juan." Followed by a pause, then, **"Je m'appelle..."** (Her words faded with her strength but meaning, "My name is..." in French.) She said as she pointed to herself.

Hurriedly, **"Oh, J'me! Nice name."** Juan was bouncing up and down uncontrollably in pleasure.

"I... I do not... know. Arrgh ..." J'me looked down to the floor as she was blinded by her memory loss. The fun had disappeared.

"Relax. I care you please. My English not so good now... Water?"

"Arrgh ... I am sorry... I do not... Yes... water please." Moving from grunts to mimicking her caregiver's poor English.

"Take my hand. We will go." With that, J'me stood up with the help of Juan and walked out of the room.

The days following were filled with joy, as the two became best friends. Juan was careful with her recovery yet pushed J'me every day beyond points she thought physically possible. Their communication had improved as well.

"Hello. Have you eaten? Did you miss me?" Juan said as she opened the door to J'me's room.

"Arrgh. What will we do today?" replied the once lifeless patient.

"I brought you clothes. Blue and green... Comfortable. Here... my white scarf."

Juan helped her change into a loose fitting aqua blue dress with a rich green colored sash belt. She felt different in these clothes, a good or better feeling. J'me draped the white scarf around her neck and the ends dropped down to camouflage the prominent breasts beneath.

Juan usually chose to wear a shiny red silk dress that was so form fitting you could see the contours of her nipples when she got aroused. **Juan easily got aroused.** She preferred extremely short hems and extremely tall high heels that elongated her legs. She was firm in shape, but demure in height. Today she pulled out a gold cape to wrap around her. The length of the cape fell below her dress.

Clap! "Let's go. Zou Ba!"

They left the room and entered a corridor where people were walking about at different paces. Some slow, others more quickly. They all looked strikingly beautiful; exotic and naturally healthy. The contrast of colors was exquisite!

Large and small. The little children swirled around J'me and Juan, reaching out their arms to touch them. It was like a friendly "Hello." Juan reached out her arm to touch a friend as they passed by.

They arrived at the center of the fifth floor... the dining center. It was a huge room with an array of round tables and chrome chairs. Immaculately clean!

"Follow me." said Miss Juan as she took J'me's hand and guided her to the center table. When they arrived, a voice from behind J'me bellowed, "Exquisite!" (Sudden and abrupt, this alert was like J'me's lungs were being inflated.)

Chapter 5
Grace

Entering dining hall E155 was a treat. The delicious aromas drifted up the nose making you so hungry your mouth watered. The sights were entertaining to the eyes. Everything looked shiny and new. Servers pushing chrome carts moved in an orderly fashion delivering food and clearing tables.

The round tables were unique. Three concentric circles: The center circle housed a hot plate. About twice the diameter was a swivel top where food was place for sharing. The outer circle was stationary. Black center, gray spinning surface, and a wide white rim for eating. This table had four chairs set equal distances from each other making four imaginary corners.

You could hear happiness as people leisurely enjoyed food and fellowship with their friends.

"Follow me." said Miss Juan as she took J'me's hand and guided her to the center of the dining hall.

J'me followed the woman and then felt a large man hug her from behind. "Exquisite!" he said.

The voice matched the indigenous man. A wild man whose uncombed hair was thick and indigo black. His attire added to his masculine presence... The brown poncho was made of rough wool. His head, arms, and waist were encircled with thick gold ropes. Not a belt, the braided cord around his midsection was beneath the brown cloth hanging from his wide shoulders. Evenly bronzed skin stretched over chiseled muscles beneath.

This man's deep voice was pleasant and distinctive. Soft spoken, yet strong. His glowing grin seemed a noticeable contradiction. His manners were polite, in contrast to his appearance. "Please, allow me…" The grizzled man sat the eldest woman across from him and then J'me to his right. The hemp satchel from his shoulder dropped to the floor next to his chair when he sat down.

A clear water kettle was placed at the center of the table with two glass bowls at opposite sides. Four small cups were set before Auntie Juan.

"My name is Juan (pronounced "wan" in his deep manly voice). You can call me 'Tio' (meaning "Uncle" in Spanish). Nice to meet you my little flower. I hear your name is J'me… eXquisite!"

Miss Juan (U.N.) stood up, flung the sides of her sheer gold cape behind her, and grasped the boiling water. She effortlessly raised the pot and looked through the glass for a second. In her other hand she took each small cup and rinsed it over the larger bowls. It was a beautiful sight to see her delicate movements. Careful hands cleansed each cup with hot water over the glass bowl. The clear kettle was then returned to the hot table center.

"We have no rules." said Tio Juan, "freedom… no bonds…" Miss Juan dropped a pinch of tealeaves into the four small cups. J'me moved her head from left to right, right to left, back and forth.

"There is no right or wrong, no good or bad… no judgement."

Miss Juan poured more hot water into each cup.

"We are followers…" Looking back and forth…

"Do what you want."

The water was swirled in each cup, cleansing the leaves, then adeptly drained into the glass receptacle. Fresh water was again added to each cup then placed on the swivel circle as an attendant replaced the filled glass bowl and clear kettle.

"Love yourself and others."

At the end of the tea ceremony, Tio Juan took one of the cups as it spun before him. Then the teacups swirled passed J'me and drifted back to the gracious host. Miss Juan took one cup and set it to her right (in front of an empty chair); she gave a cup to J'me, and then sat down and placed the last cup in front of herself.

Tio Juan concluded with, **"We are thankful."**

J'me nudged herself into the conversation. "Tio Juan and Auntie Juan... Thank you."

"Don't think too much." interjected Auntie Juan.

Agreeing, Tio Juan said, "Just feel mucho!"

Ugh." was the only response J'me could make.

Across from J'me a man took the empty metal chair. He was the same person who visited her bedside while she was in her deep sleep. His face mesmerized her and his touch electrified her.

"Hair clog, just in time! Let's drink tea." said Tio Juan.

They all raised their cups. The new guest closed his eyes and lip-synced a few words, then took a sip as the others were lowering their cups from their mouths. A slight delay then eyes looked across the table. Auntie Juan giggled.

Chapter 6

Love

In the center of the dining room, the mysterious man shared tea with J'me and Juan at Auntie Juan's table.

"My little love... I would like to have the pleasure to introduce to you, Doctor Melvin K. Klug. I call him Herr Klug." J'me only heard part of what Tio Juan said... Her eyes were mesmerized on the face of the elder gentleman dressed all in grey. She did not notice the food being served. She was thankful to be with friends.

Yogurt, six almonds, and a spoon. That was what she had. The others shared food from the rotisserie. Auntie used chopsticks, Klug had a knife and fork, and Tio Juan chose to eat with his hands. But it was more than satisfying as she soon noticed her food was gone and she felt a slight pang in her stomach as though it was a feast.

"My love. Are you ok?" Asked Auntie. These were the first words J'me had discerned since the introduction to Herr Klug.

A little girl came silently up from behind J'me and stood next to her, unnoticed. She gazed up at J'me for a moment but said nothing. When J'me sensed the little stare, she looked down. Quickly, the mini miss put an orange in her hand and ran away. Her parents were not far away. They coaxed her to stay, but the cute girl in the yellow dress and white scarf was too shy. She ran behind her mother and hid. She wrapped her arms around her mother's leg and shuffle-stepped to her side. At that moment, the proud parents smiled and the father crouched down to wrap his arms around his daughter.

An orange. The little girl gave her a gift but was too shy to speak. **So sweet.**

J'me leaned towards the girl and smiled. "Thank you." The cute girl grasped her mother's leg tighter for comfort. The three then left as the parents mouthed the words, "Thank you" back to J'me. Everyone smiled.

Klug never spoke... He only glanced around the corners of the room. When Auntie filled Klug's teacup, he tapped his fingers on the table three times. Eliciting smiles.

Tio stood, "We will be back, excuse us." Tio walked around the table and Auntie drew her cape around her and punched out her hand to grasp Tio's inner elbow as they strolled the room together.

Sitting across from each other, Klug and J'me made eye contact. Thinking to move quickly J'me took Tio's empty seat... Klug slid closer and laid his palm upward on the table. She reached to touch it but recoiled when she felt an energy flutter tickling her hand like the wings of a fairy. In that fraction of a second, she was immersed with emotions... Her hand hovered above his as the feeling became more pleasant and controlled.

The messages that were sent came too rapidly, despite avoiding Klug's touch. J'me's head slumped down as she intently tried to discern. She could only receive and did not have the ability to respond or question or speak.

Suddenly Auntie pinched the nape of J'me's neck... This brought J'me out of her altered state and back to reality. Auntie pulled back the hair from J'me's face and massaged her temples. J'me tried to unscramble the messages from Klug, but they were a dream that vanished like little memories. **Vanished into vapors... like the steam from the boiling pot.**

Auntie allowed J'me some time, then said, "We go and rest." Both her head and her stomach were full as she stood up and assembled herself.

A memory lag moved into her consciousness as J'me exited the room:

Tio Juan came into focus with his arms around two women. Melting through the meaning... Tio Juan had earlier noticed the beginning of an argument and took Auntie Juan with him. They startled the two women as they stepped between them. Raising his arms wide, Tio gently held opposing shoulders.

"Oh, this is wonderful!" he said, startling the two even more. "I need your help. I have a mission only you can do." He brought the women closer into a private huddle and then whispered, "The valley of the six seasons... I need you two to travel there." Auntie Juan touched their cheeks before excusing herself to leave.

Off focus, J'me remembered to take her orange and then later realized she was already somewhere else.

Chapter 7
Soul

Vanished into vapors... J'me was weak. Her first taste of real food and the mental exercise with Klug had beaten her. It was a warm feeling.

J'me was now in a shaded room with other women preparing to rest. She mimicked the actions of others – disrobed, laid herself down, and covered her nakedness with her white scarf as a blanket. She smelled the citrusy vape as...

Three...

Two...

One...

Eyes closed... lights out.

J'me eXquisite woke from her nap and felt a sensation against her face. Next to her was the little girl she had met earlier in the cafeteria. Her little friend had disrobed and was also covered with a scarf. Apparently, she laid down when J'me was slumbering.

J'me gently moved aside and cautiously sat up. The little person had fallen asleep with one arm outstretched to touch her new friend for comfort. Around the perimeter of the room were sleeping pads and pillows. At the center of the room women had congregated to preen each other. Several motioned her to join in.

Her face and hands were washed as she chewed on a licorice root to cleanse her teeth and mouth. The chew stick was at first hard... but eventually the end softened in her mouth. She used this twig to brush her teeth.

She reached for a spray but lost the competition to somebody who was more alert. J'me scooted back to her mat to put on her aqua blue dress and green sash. She pressed out the wrinkles as she stood up...

Gently, J'me reached down, pulling up and shaking out the wrinkles of the girl's little yellow dress. She noticed her move. Tiny lips stretched to form a smile — pulling open her eyes. Both arms stretched out from beneath the scarf and she gave out a cute squeal.

Women moved forward to wash the little hands and face while slithering her small frame into a miniature dress and scarf. Then the women sprayed, brushed, and braided both their hair in matching styles (like sisters). Another little girl came over with the fibrous stick for her schoolmate to clean her teeth. Refreshed.

Lastly, J'me took her gifts – the white scarf from Auntie Juan was around her neck. She picked up the orange and safely cradled it in her green sash (forming a little bubble). Giggling, the two girls dressed in yellow reached up their hands to touch the bulge.

Hand in hand, they took J'me with them on their walk.

When they met Tio Juan, he greeted J'me and the two dandelion girls ran off to play. "Welcome! May I guide you through the learning area?"

"There is no schedule for education. No grades.. No tests. Everybody is different and unique... so we have different systems when we are receptive. **You can learn anything at any time. The only limit is you... yourself."**

"There are three layers." Touching J'me's forehead he said, **"The conscious, thinking and knowledge."** Touching the top of her head, **"The subconscious, feelings and memory."** And, as if pulling up a zipper, Tio traced a line from her womb to her heart and said, **"the sensing soul."**

Then, with inward perspective, he said, "The spirit rides on roadways to the brain. Now... I take little journeys... or as my ancestors would call them, spirit walks. **I listen to whispers..."**

Calmly, they started their walk around the classroom. **"There is also a mind and body balance.** If I take in too much too quickly – I am not at peace. These are the times I visit Miss Juan because my body is out of balance. Miss Juan and I have many things in common."

"Like how you spell your names?" quipped J'me.

"We exchange services. Separate souls, yet when combined, we complete each other." (complementary)

The children were well behaved and content. Nobody noticed the woman mastered in the art of reading micro-expressions and discerning vocal tones. She had heightened her senses to feel the emotions of the children. Other helpers with special gifts were also stationed about.

The two continued their chat as they moved around the room. "Both 'nature' and 'nurture' together. **We learn in both cognitive and intuitive ways.** We never stop learning." Quickly Tio Juan deflected, "Oh, children have a big appetite and are very curious! They seem to be playing, but they are learning. As we get older, **we must balance our desires.** Play and work. Work and play. We cannot have just one for very long."

At this point J'me stopped Tio Juan and said, "I think I know what you are saying."

"Have you been to the C3 cleansing room?" Tio Juan asked with glee.

Chapter 8

Infinite

"Infinite capabilities... **Within everybody is greatness!** I am not just saying that, I mean it! **Everybody has a "gift."**

"Do you see that woman sitting on the floor in the corner? One of her two jobs is as a nurturer. She appears old and her body weak, but she has this tremendous gift. Whenever the children feel tired or out of balance, they go to her. She comforts the little ones. She has a power that draws the children to her."

J'me listened intently, thinking that perhaps she was as a child learning and seeking the blessing she had hidden within her. They exited and trekked into the maze of walkways.

"**Many people are searching for their magic powers. Others just try to manage them.** We evolve similarly. There is at first a fear when they are discovered. Then, like the physical body, these powers need to be exercised and strengthened. This is draining but must be done to achieve mastery."

This was a longer walk... giving J'me time to reflect. Auntie had the healing touch... Herr Klug was a genius... Tio Juan was different... (J'me was not sure what blessing her Tio Juan possessed.) J'me was not sure what blessing she held...

"eXquisite, we are in building D, the cleansing and creation floors. Very popular! This is one of many types of cleaning rooms. The family rooms are much different." Tio Juan spoke again with glee. "There are people very important for you to meet, but first... let's enjoy a nice washing."

"Infinite choices...If you have any preferences, please let me or the others know, ok? The first room is the rain room." As they entered the large room, a cloud greeted them. Moving forward they walked into heavier showers. "This is when we take off our wet clothes and place them in the baskets. Everybody is naked."

"I have no opinion." was J'me's initial response followed by a sincere, "Ok."

"Good. For some it is uncomfortable at first... **I enjoy natural.**"

An attendant approached and asked, "May I help you?" This happened often during their visit.

Many people joined. "Notice the large pool surrounded by several small ponds? Outside ponds are warmer and infused with herbs, minerals, and oils." Along with new friends, Tio Juan guided J'me into the center pool to relax.

Somebody pointed to the ceiling and showed J'me the clouds. "Look closely. The clouds are moving."

"Look, I see a flower!" Soon everybody started to share his or her imaginary finds.

Tio left her and was sitting in a bubbling therapy bath. The water felt comfortable and J'me often swam below the surface. It felt good to have every part of her touched by the water.

"After we are finished here, we have many more choices. Remember, this is called the cleansing and creativity center." A couple she befriended remarked, "What is your wish? Please let us know."

"Would you like to go to the grooming area or meditation rooms? May we help you?"

"Ugh, I think..." overwhelmed, J'me could not answer.

"The grooming area is where we can modify our appearance."

"Aww, that sounds good!" purred J'me.

"Other C&C centers have massage and various medical rooms... some have playrooms.

From behind her, J'me was surprised to hear Tio say, "I always elect for the creative meditation rooms." Tio Juan was only moments ago in the hot bath. "The rooms are very quiet... intimate-private, or you can join small groups. There are many choices here."

The couple concluded, "The grooming room for us. We will explain the beauty options they offer."

"After grooming there will be somebody to assist you with your clothes (they will have been cleaned and prepared fresh for you). Somebody in the lounge will escort you. OK?"

The grooming room seemed more carnal for those craving something more lustful. There was blunt openness in the room; nothing was off limits. It seemed more honest, relaxed, maybe crass, but definitely more fun. Today they spoke about undergarments.

Apparently, bras were seen as an adornment. Bottoms were another story. Bothersome for men, it was something for women. Young girls with their randomly damp thighs and shy virginity felt more modest in panties. When a woman was high tide in her menstrual cycle, she also sported knickers. The topic regressed to mention women wearing crotch less panties (as the whispers revealed, for convenience during intimate moments).

"Infinite greatness! I am not just saying that... Everybody has a "gift."

Chapter 9
Return

J'me went to pick up her laundered clothes and noticed a mistake. She was given a soft gray dress, three Aryan blue scarves, black heels and a purse. "Oh, I am sorry. These are not mine."

"Oh, you got gifts!" The assistant placed the personal items she came with into her new purse (scarves, dress, licorice stick, and an orange). Then she helped J'me with her new outfit.

"First, wrap this around your bodice." J'me then noticed the ribbons in her hair matched the light blue hue of the three scarves.

"Let's see... There are four overlapping panels joined at the waist and an apron top... step into this dress here..." J'me noticed the fabric was denser than what she had previously worn. The length was to her ankles. The top half had open sides and back. She used one of the scarves as a belt and the other was wrapped around her bouncing bosoms. The shoes, although slender and steep, were comfortable. As she walked, the four panels opened and exposed her loins. Shy, yet suggestive.

The assistant waved his hand and squealed, "**Beautiful inside and out, within and without.**" J'me was escorted to the C&C Center lounge.

J'me did not want to crease her dress by sitting, enjoying how it moved, and she loved the loftiness of her new shoes. Then she saw it! J'me moved with a purpose. A primitive wooden sphere just had to be touched!

The lounge was a good sized room with a view of the pools, stationary lounge chairs arranged in tidy rows and columns, and various visual arts scattered about. Some people chose to relax or sleep in the chairs, while others mingled in small groups. The largest group was centered around a couple who just returned from their mission from Angel Falls in Venezuela. Another couple had reminisced about Iguazu Falls (Brazil/Argentina), adding life to the conversation.

With both hands, J'me rubbed the surface of the wooden sphere. Deep within her she felt the sounds of tribal drums and soft chanting intermixed with wood flute tones. It was as if she had returned to a place she had been before... It was enchanting. Her heart rate increased to the rhythmic percussion of the drums.

She was to meet somebody. Who?

A young man reached forth to place his hand on the sphere. While imbibing she felt the cushion of energy from the wooden sphere and sensed the young man's touch, as well. "J'me, would you like something to drink? You should have a glass of something. There is an infinite selection." J'me thought of water and a server immediately handed it to her.

J'me finished her water and lifted her hands off the primitive artifact. "This way please." said the helpful stranger. Moments later, they were in motion through wide corridors. The brisk walk took them to another building, Cube C... first floor.

She came upon a museum, science exhibit, displays, or was it an organized collection? Despite not being able to define the space, the room was filled with many unique and different things. As she entered the room, there was a sense of gravity. Gravity... A force pushed down on her head, shoulders, and feet. There was a feeling of friction in the air similar to her earlier swim in the pool. After taking a few steps, J'me had to stop. She wondered if she had just become tired from her day's activities. An overload, perhaps?

"This happens sometimes... You may need to adjust." said the escort. "Wait!" He held J'me's hand and stood closer to her.

There was a huge, bright sphere that looked like a ball of fire! Three silhouettes of older men emerged from it and moved towards her. The escort darted out of the room!

"Whew!" exclaimed J'me... then she heard, "Super!", "Toll!", and "Ho, ho, ho!" Hearty laughs came from the three men. One was Melvin Klug!

"A grand entrance?" asked one of the elder men. Then, "I think so... did you see the young man's eyes? Success!"

Their laughing stopped as sparkles disappeared behind them. They looked more like three children in identical grey pajamas. Their pockets were filled and bulging with little treasures.

"I can't wait to see Miss Juan!" said the man on the left.

"Oh, for our adjustment and alignment?" said the second man.

"No, I miss her food!" he laughed.

Klug said nothing, as J'me thought of tea, yoghurt, six almonds... and an uneaten orange.

QUIZ

0

Summary Quiz

Test your understanding of what you read. Pick the best answer for the following ten questions. After completing all ten questions, check your answers on the next page.

If you score a 70% or above (answer seven or more questions correctly) you may proceed to the following chapters. However, if you score below 70%, read the previous chapters again.

Please take your time reading and meditating to unlock the next chapters.

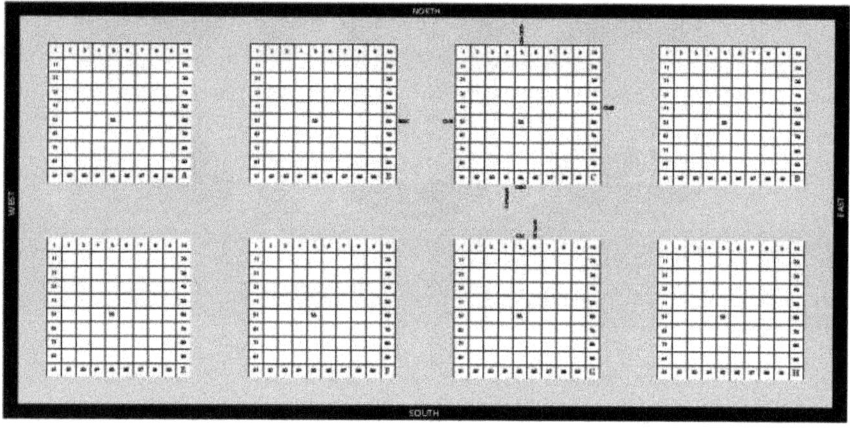

1.   What is the name for the room in Cube E, first floor, room 55?

    a.   李娟 (Juan Li's) 的亚洲餐厅 (Asian Restaurant)

    b.   E155, The Tea Room

    c.   N.T.U.N.'s T Room

    d.   All of the above

2.   B-110C and C-101B are:

    a.   B2C and C2B

    b.   Across the street, between Cubes B and C

    c.   The North Exit Ramp, parking level (Sublevel One)

    d.   All of the above

3.   What is the (above ground) area of each building in the BLOCK?
     a.   103 M/cube
     b.   1002 Meters per cube
     c.   10,000 Meters (excluding the rooftop)
     d.   All of the above

4.   Who was able to awaken J'me eXquisite from her long sleep?
     a.   Juan Li (Auntie Juan)
     b.   Tio Juan (Uncle Juan)
     c.   Dr. Melvin K. Klug (Herr Klug)
     d.   J'me released herself from unconsciousness.

5.   TO1, NTUN, and J'me are:
     a.   The leaders of the BLOCK
     b.   Acronyms for Tio Juan, Auntie Juan, and J'me eXquisite
     c.   Dr. K's BFF
     d.   All of the above

6.   Who had sex with Li Juan?
     a.   Nobody talks about it, DK (don't know)
     b.   Tio Juan and Klug
     c.   Juan's husband
     d.   Nobody, she is a virgin

7.   According to Tio Juan, what are the guidelines within the BLOCK?
     a.   Forces in motion seek balance
     b.   The Law of Seven
     c.   Don't dwell on the past at the expense of the present
     d.   All of the above

8.   Auntie Juan is to physical care as...
     a.   Tio Juan is the mind and spirit wellness
     b.   Klug is to care, repair, and prepare for things

    c.   J'me is to love and happiness

    d.   All of the above

9.   What choices did J'me make within the C&C center?

    a.   To be naked and later meditate

    b.   To wear panties and sit in the hot baths

    c.   To swim and go to the grooming room

    d.   To visit the massage and medical rooms

10.   On what continent do you think J'me's family originated?

    a.   Asia

    b.   America

    c.   Europe

    d.   Africa

Quiz 0 – Answers

1. Prior to the "BLOCK" being abandoned, Li Yuan ran a successful restaurant. When the buildings became closed off from the public, many acronyms or symbols were developed by the inhabitants to make life simpler. Answer: D. All of the above.

2. The best answer is The North Exit Ramp, parking level (Sublevel One). In this case, you did not know there are four underground ramps below the BLOCK. Originally there was a North, South, East, and West ramp (currently the Southern ramp is blocked closed). The secured entrance to the BLOCK is from the East Ramp. Both the North and West ramps are exit only. If you did not know about the ramps and the underground spaces, you could strategize that the other three answers were not as precise.

3. If you know math, the answer is simple: D. All of the above.

4. You could argue that one person was the most instrumental to J'me's awakening. You could argue that each person caused J'me's awakening. However, the truth is that J'me had to want to awake. The best answer: D. J'me released herself from unconsciousness. (I got that one wrong myself.)

5. Life was much easier and fun within the walls. There is less effort by using common symbols. And although Klug was friends with everybody, his Best Friend Forever (BFF) was not any of those mentioned. Answer: C. Acronyms for Tio Juan, Auntie Juan, and J'me eXquisite

6. **Sex is one of the basic needs of man and therefore not taboo.** But you are curious about it nonetheless. **Sexual intimacy is the highest form of showing physical love.** Juan Li also knows through thousands of years of research that women require frequent sex to improve their physical and emotional health. (Juan easily got aroused.) But in this case, we do not know because nobody talked about it, Answer A.

7.   There are no rules inside the BLOCK, except the innate laws of nature that nobody can escape. Tio Juan tried to explain this and give his suggestions to somebody new to the environment. Best answer: D. All of the above.

8.   There are no rules inside the BLOCK, but everybody works. If Auntie Juan was an expert about the body, and Tio Juan was concerned about mental and spiritual health, then we could understand that the intellectual Klug was about "things" and making life easier through the three stages of care, repair, and replacing. J'me was a blend of all three, using emotions; she tried to seek her way. Therefore, you can deduce the correct answer to be D. Love and happiness.

9.   Did you remember that the correct answer would be choosing to swim and go to the grooming room? Answer C.

10. You may have guessed the answer to this question. Although never mentioned, we believe that Li Juan was Asian, Tio Juan was an original American, and "Herr Klug" was a blending of European ancestry. There is a great amount of diversity; to complete the small group, J'me eXquisite was probably African. But it probably does not matter to the people within the BLOCK. (We are curious about it nevertheless.) Answer D.

Chapter 10
Root

A great tree, before it is born, is just a seed hidden in dirt. It grows roots before we can identify it... It is not until it breaks the surface that we call it a plant.

It began with a dream... traveling the world, noticing many strange and odd things. His work required him to explore and meet people. But there were always diversions entertaining to the traveler. **Before the beginning** of the 21st century, **life was very different from now**. The 20th century was the age of ideas that exploded from everywhere. Rapid transit was not yet a reality, so much time was spent traveling. This allowed him much time to think. Mr. G had much time to dream.

The vision of the **BLOCK** was actually a series of visions. He shared his ideas with his friends who were very interested in his concept. Actually, **it was not a single concept, but a series of concepts, interwoven like a beautiful tapestry.**

Everything was meticulously planned before it began. The dream became the fantasy of many people. It would be misleading to further define this project as one person's vision.

The notion was not to build a utopia or a perfect world. That would not be true, though some had envisioned a Shangri-La. Perhaps they only saw one big idea and could not see how it would evolve.

Throughout his travels, Mr. G made many special friendships. These special people also had the special skills needed to build this conglomerate. Further recollection... some people did not have the talents required, but shared his desire and were just as special. For example, a dozen wealthy followers financed the operation. **Everybody brought something!**

With help, locations were first found: mountains for mining, flat lands for farming, populous places for production, central points for distribution, and safe havens for storage. The core center, called "The BLOCK." was the last location chosen.

The feeling of warmth on a cold day... He, Mr. G, was the sun

Who was He? Although not pertinent, people who met him said he looked like Clark Gable (Clark Gable, 1901-1960, was an American actor referred to as the "King of Hollywood").   Nothing more than the appearance of the man can be validated... discovered second-hand.

What we do know is...   The names of the original dozen philanthropists still remains **confidential**. The location of the sites remain **hidden**. The number of people involved is **unknown**. This is what we know...

At the turn of the century, excavation and building began on the BLOCK. Skilled experts had plotted every detail to produce the desired effect. Efficiency was already seen in the farms, mines, and factories that were producing goods. Distribution networks and storage hubs were growing. Everything was still decentralized and required a single location, the BLOCK.

Those that were lost were now found. Those souls once scattered, were now settling in. From all corners of creation people came together for the first time. **Everybody was happy!**

Exploring further, there were two underground levels with outside access – a parking garage and underground delivery. This subterranean space was one huge cavern beneath all eight structures. Four entrance/exit ramps were located on the north, south, east, and western sides. The southern exit (Exit FG) was blocked closed... All entered through the east ramp (Entrance DH), with smaller vehicles departing the north ramp (Exit BC) and bigger loads exiting the west ramp (Exit AE). Generally, for every three trucks entering the east ramp, one left full.

The trucks were nondescript, all white. Two by two, every hour, they entered from the east and two trailers left the opposite side... turned right and in tandem headed north. This was a different dance from the routine daily deliveries to the BLOCK.

Interesting... The original floorplans did not show the existence of "Sublevel Three." A storage area? A secret place for people to safely congregate?

Exit FG was blocked... Cubes F and G were vacant... If buildings could have feelings... wait.

"Papa, what is that?" A young child pointed at the eight stone structures.

"I do not know. Remember we spoke about this before?" the older man remarked. "Nobody talks about it."

"Not true. WE talk about it... I think it is beautiful!" Looking more surreptitiously at the glowing exteriors.

(Nobody said anything about the steam/smoke rising from across the street.) **The more they saw, the more they neglected to see...**

"Thank you...   Thank you...   Enjoy yourself. Please drink responsibly. Stay clear.... Thank you for visiting and have a happy every day!"

Chapter 11
Together

Something new was happening inside the BLOCK... There was a feeling in the air, similar to that before a weather change. Push the pause button.

Deep breathe and go! Your heart quickens as you explore the source of the energy from the BLOCK...

Deep breathe in... Breathe out. Feel the moment...

Your senses are heightened. Fill your lungs with fresh air.... then slowly exhale.

Meditating... thinking... putting the pieces together and braiding the loose ends.

Alone, J'me entered the large dining hall. A rush of oomph excited her senses. It smelled of fresh baked bread. Men sang. The sound in the room was boisterous. Immaculately clean... it seemed that everyone skated on polished ice. **Together it created a captivating feeling.**

Using the **80% rule (true to define eight of ten occurrences, with a couple of exception**s,) we simplify the diverse crowds into clusters... there were three age groups: children, adults, and older. Subgroupings would be male and female. For example, children generally sat at one table, adults at another, elders **grouped together**, men **sat together**, and women generally sat near the children... Many seemed large in size.

Youngsters cheerfully prepared the tables for dining and also removed the clutter afterward (**Work was considered a reward for the children... a good and wholesome activity!**). Just as with the inner workings of a complex watch, there were efficiencies to every movement.

More detailed observations of the staff: **The workers moved together in synchrony.** Women marched in straight paths, equal distance apart, predictably turning at exact angles and matching exact steps. It was not robotic, but similar to a dance with spins and twirls.

J'me **sat down at a table together** with the wise men she had first seen emerging from a ball of fire. The "three wise men" were:

- Doctor Melvin K. Klug (an old friend),
- Doctor E. Lyja (half of the Dr. E^2 duo),
- Doctor E. Noch-Nicht (half of the Dr. E^2 duo, nicknamed "Nick").

The table was rectangular with seating on two sides. It could be described as a rustic park bench or picnic table if not for its crystal composition. Ten centimeters thick, the clear glass held fine wires meshed inside, together forming a golden grid.

"Watch this!" said both the Dr. E.s. They gently nudged their plates and saw them skid along the table.

"Slicker than saliva!" said Dr. Lyja.

"Yes, it takes a bit of practice." said Dr. Noch-Nicht, moving the plates back into position.

With this J'me turned and saw one child tilting a table and two children on the opposite end catching all that slid off the edge. **Together,** quick hands sorted scraps into carts and completely cleaned the large table with little effort. They laughed as if they were playing, not working.

An overtly buxom woman served the drinks. Six large glass steins with golden ambrosia were placed on the table and spun to center. Everybody picked up their glass, raised them, and **together exclaimed,** "Here's to Mo!" (Klug only muttered the words.) "To friends gone!" and then they took large gulps of god's elixir.

A disjointed observation: The three men's eyes seem a glowing blue and hair an electric blonde/gray.

Two women came to the table and sat warmly on both Dr. Es' laps.... grabbed the two extra steins from table center, kissed the men, and swallowed all the contents.

Nick said with much effort, "We are... rock stars." The words "rock" and "stars" combined was an enigma to those at the table, but everyone laughed. The new words and women were noticeably awkward for Klug. The women sang a deep-throated melody and then moved on to another gathering.

The sights, the sounds, the savory food and limitless drink together were well crafted. J'me noticed that she had slid closer to M. K. Klug at meal's end. It was at this point that Nick pulled an oversized pearl from his pocket and rolled it across the table to J'me.

"Here, for you." said both Dr. E's **simultaneously, working together.**

J'me captured the oversized white pearl and asked, "What is it?"

"Try this..." Nick cupped his hand and placed it parallel to the table, knuckles down.

As J'me opened her hand, the orb looked as if it was spinning and lifted off the surface of her palm. J'me's eyes widened with glee. It felt wonderful!

"That's it!" said Dr. Lyja as J'me noticed Klug's hand move and hover above, palms down. Lowering his hand... **their hands clasped together**... and then, J'me sensed inside Klug, "I loved your grandmother."

Chapter 12
Equilibrium

Africa! After trekking for over a month, he had all but given up hope of home. He had almost given up on finding any place familiar. Then he came upon a hilltop and looked at the valley below. It was a fertile basin with a surplus of fruit trees and berry bushes. This created a beautiful canopy of green hues, glittering with bright colors – red, orange, yellow, blue... As the cool breeze crossed his face, he noticed the scent was floral and fruity... fresh!

He faced the afternoon sun that stretched out through the edges of the clouds. White fluff played in the sapphire sky. The fog looked like flowers. To his left he saw a waterfall and a small pond reflecting the aqua sunlight. He headed in that direction, south.

The valley was immense. He thought himself observant, but it was not until a kilometer into his descent that he realized he was not in a valley, but a crater (Perhaps created by an ancient meteor or a now extinct volcano?). He stopped to snack on some berries.

He was fascinated by how dark and fertile the soil was. And he also became curious about the sharp crystals embedded in the soil he had to avoid. He stooped down to observe them more closely.

He felt himself being watched, however he had not seen a bird in the sky nor witnessed even an insect, for days. He heard a waterfall softly splash and moved closer to its source. Inside himself — he did not sense danger; however, he was cautious.

It was not until he reached for an unfamiliar fruit from a tree that two naked children, a boy and a girl, immediately ran to him, frantically motioning for him to stop. They waved their hands like the words, "stop" and "no."

Behind the naked children, more nudists exposed themselves to him. This land was inhabited. They all were naked.

Soon he was the center of a large circle of uncovered people. They kept a distance between him and the feared fruit tree. "No, do not touch!" "Stop, do not eat that!" sounded a choir of voices. Their speech was very melodic, expressive (making up for what they lacked in diction). The original little boy and girl moved closer and carefully reached out to him. "Please!" Soon a throng of children grabbed his hands and grappled his legs, moving him in a different direction – away from the forbidden fruit.

As quickly as they had appeared, these beautiful people smiled and came forth to touch him. It felt odd, being swarmed by naked people, but their touch was light and gentle. They were friendly.

The tribe was vast. They dwelled in large caverns below the surface. This perhaps explained their unique skin color. Their features were slightly "African," but since they were rarely exposed to the sun, they had a lighter complexion. They emitted a healthy radiance.

They seemed to understand that the foreigner was heading towards the pond and **they guided him along the best paths**. They often pointed to the clear gems that protruded from the ground, so as not to step on them. They were barefooted, but even his boots did not seem a match for the crystals' edges.

Immediately after arriving at the pond's edge, he released his packs, disrobed, and bathed in the invigorating water. A few people joined him in the swim. Some wanted to feed him and put different fruits, berries, and herbs in his mouth to eat. He was even given a dry powder that had a metallic, spicy flavor.

Soon the sounds of the waterfall went away, and he began to hear percussion coming from people stomping and pounding. The youngest were the first to dance, but eventually everybody was overcome with the spirit and chanted sounds that had no meaning to the traveler. They harmonized perfectly!

He was refreshed.

The entrance into the cave was hidden and unmarked. A bubble of molten rock may have burst before cooling, forming a glassy, large circular opening.

It took a moment to become balanced... Your senses and your mind needed to adjust as you entered the caverns. The refracting light affected the members' eyes making their normally black iris' become orange, red, green, and blue rainbow auras. The crystals dispersed light into every corner; however, there was also a magnifying affect (wherein you could focus on a single hair from a distance).

Chapter 13
Remainder

Inside the cave the man felt unplugged from the rest of the universe. It took a moment for him to regain his equilibrium. Even so, his vision was drawn to a man across the room. Their eyes locked in recognition; the foreigner and the leader.

Both were striking; both with symmetrical appearances. Their eyes were distinct — the whites of which glowed. The leader, however, had a full beard.

People between the two stunning men parted. As the two moved nearer, they grew more certain. The leader raised his hands in the air and shouted, "Praise you!" He could not control himself. "Lucky me!" He finally collapsed in front of the man and began crying on the feet of the stranger. Despite the excitement this caused in the room, the guest was calm.

"Do not cry." He reached down to raise his old friend to his feet. "Mo, come."

Mo was filled with emotions. "You heard my boys, wife, and I passed through the veils of death. It was true. My sons and wife died, but I remained alive. Now I no longer travel or write my poems that you liked so well. **If you consider yourself dead, and only living in the present time; the remaining time is relished.** I am totally submissive and no longer struggle."

After sundown, they sat at one end of the largest cavern. Music was playing. The center of the room was open for dancing. The stranger sat with the leader's family.

The first selection was a cup of honey in warm water. Then they were bathed in fruit with baskets of berries, dates, figs, raisins, and prunes surrounding them. Adding yet another basket that contained only persimmons. A drink of fruity vinegar came with two large baskets of apples, pears, peaches, plums, and grapes. To the side were nuts and olives. After the melons, the third cup contained wine, which the stranger only sipped.

"This is my second wife... my divine four daughters..." His wife lovingly reproached him for talking so much and not allowing their guest to speak. She remained busy all the time graciously serving and finally took this opportunity to sit down and delight in the music, dance, food, and drink.

"Enjoy the now!" The stranger responded. **Everyone felt at ease.**

Their nest was still bright although it had become dark outside. The embedded crystals continued reflecting the days' light. While others danced and sang, the two men ate, drank, and talked.

The guest grew tired from the activity and wine and excused himself to rest. The light from the clear gemstones daintily dimmed.

"My daughters have taken your things and prepared a place for you." Then he leaned closer to whisper in his ear, "You will sleep with four of our most beautiful virgins. It is our custom."

The four girls took him to a secluded room within the caves. He knelt on a mat of flower pedals to meditate while the tribal princesses anxiously waited for him in the bed. He stood up, took the position in the middle, two on each side... laid himself face down... and then slept. (The girls were not yet to know what it was like to be a woman... as was his custom.)

The stranger was invited to stay. Dedicated discussions were held five times a day, like clockwork. Interlacing history with present day gave them many interesting topics. One of which was the crystals... They were like the thorns on a rose to the clan. The stranger was encouraged to "Take them all."

The diet of fresh fruits detoxified the wandering traveler. In a short time, he felt his skin cleansed, his energy return, and his head more clear. It was a temptation to stay, but he was inspired to take the enchanted crystals to a friend in Egypt.

"Egypt?" said the first lady (actually the second wife of the leader). "I am from Egypt. I can take you."

"I will remain here. I have many things to ponder." That was the reaction when the leader heard of the plan. His daughters would care for and accompany them.

Remarking simultaneously, the stranger and wife said in unison, "We need to wear clothes."

Egypt was yet to be modernized, but it did not take long to find his friend... Melvin K. Klug's eyes doubled in size at the sight of the crystals and exotic companions.

Unplugging from the universe is a good method of discovery to see what is removed and what remains... and then see how what is left behaves.

Chapter 14
Melvin K. Klug

"Zero."

Slowly and gently she became aware...

"One times zero."

J'me could feel the thoughts of Melvin K Klug...

"My favorite equation is 1 x 0 = 0." This was the image.

"Anything times zero is nothing." Was the message J'me shaped in her mind. "Nothing cannot become stronger or weaker no matter how much energy you exert. It remains nothing."

J'me also thought... **"If it is not important, it does not exist."**

Klug laughed.

"I am one. You are one." Her mind was being nudged in a different direction.

J'me reflexed, "1 + 1." but was surprised to learn it was not that simple.

"No. 1, 2, 4, 8, 16, 32, 64..." the impression solidified.

"128, 256, 612... accumulative!" J'me answered.

The idea accelerated forward, "By itself one is only one... **One is the beginning of exponential growth and decay.**" was Klug's response. "Fun isn't it?"

It was not individual notes being played, but a powerful symphony. They shared thoughts, feelings, and secrets. The opus infinite was beautiful. Today's inspiration was the importance of zero, one, two... and infinity! This was the autobiography of Melvin K. Klug.

It was a little like taking huge gulps of water as quickly as possible so as not to choke. Her mind was always on the edge of confusion, but Klug made the mental journey feel effortless.

Their hands unclasped... J'me was in the dining hall sitting with the three wise men. Then... then... she looked down through the crystal table and voiced the words from within, "Arrgh... Hello." Obvious... the men were aroused (showing erections pushing against their garments). J'me repositioned her dress to better cover herself.

Simultaneously, a group of saucy grandmothers stopped singing and stood in unison. They had a duty they were eager to perform. Like a mechanized unit, they approached the men. Their bodies were large and well padded. They jutted their chests forward unashamed, scuffing their breasts against the faces of the men and then roughly yanked the dazed men from the table. They seemed surprised, but did not resist. One woman asked, "Have you ever had your toes sucked?" With that, J'me was alone and her companions were swept out of the dining hall.

She felt a light tug on the back of her dress. J'me looked behind her from both sides but saw nothing. She swiveled and looked down to see a charming fair-haired boy with short strawberry-gold fuzz making him almost bald in appearance. She leaned forward. His stubby little fingers reached to pull her face closer. He put his cheek to her face and fluttered his long eyelashes... butterfly kisses. He repeated this several times.

"Archibald R, there you are." Yodeled a giant young woman coming towards them. The miniature man jumped up and down, swinging his arms in unrestrained glee... Then ran around his imaginary circle chanting "Nanna, Nanna, Nanna!"

"It is his birth day." excused the young yet oversized frau.

"It is alright Archie R." said J'me sweetly, rubbing the boy's head.

From an oversize hand, J'me was given a rare white snow apple. "My name is Frija-Frig G. Have you come for the exhibition, also?" Frija's braided brown hair glistened with white, gold, and red sparkles.

Moments later, Frija and J'me held hands as they entered the great hall. The people in the room were rather huge, a race of light skinned titans, clans from outside the BLOCK. At first, J'me seemed a foreigner... But her clothes were the same color, similar in style to everybody's. She matched. Soon they were greeted by those who had already arrived; **they were not strangers, but longtime friends. It felt heavenly.**

It was a magical exhibit. Near the center of the room was a metal ball spinning aloft. The sphere stayed in place by itself, unattached. The crowd seemed a bit cautious and created a vacant space, an empty circle, around the ball. As J'me and Frija-Frig G moved closer, they found themselves part of the guard, the circle of people nearest the orb. **She felt a peculiar tingling inside her. It felt odd, but good.**

At this phase, J'me experienced irregular senses – clouded vision, the feeling of wind, colors and shapes appeared in curious patterns. At her feet she saw two metal balls that matched the spinning sphere at room center. Frija's people hushed.

"**It is easy, if you know how.**" said J'me. The two leaned forward to pick up a ball and found themselves inside the circle.

For reassurance, Frija looked at J'me and questioned, "**Size does not matter?**"

"**Our powers are exponential!**" replied J'me with a wink.

Chapter 15
Exponent

"Exponential energy!"

In preparation, J'me only needed to close her eyes... and relax... extend her arms forward... In her mind she thought of powerful feelings such as love and comfort... open hands (placed parallel to the ground, knuckles down) ... subtle vibrations... extending her reach further and further...

Rather than giving step-by-step instructions, let's explain what happened.

Gradually the metal ball in her cupped hands moved, spinning (so it seemed). The gyrations increased in speed, lifting the sphere above her extended hands. Up... up... up...

It was not an illusion... It was a display of unseen energy... ignoring the basic laws of gravity.

J'me began the demonstration with elevating a single sphere and then moved it in a circular motion around the stationary globe in the center of the room. Then she returned the ball back to her palms to rest.

Next was the quad corner trip. This entailed moving the ball to each of the four corners of the room. The ball stopped and changed course at each joint before moving on.

Lastly, she took two balls and lifted them simultaneously. One ball orbited clockwise, the other counterclockwise around the secure center sphere. The two metal orbs took flight around the room to eventually bounce off the smooth stonewalls, creating angular designs. This formed a "ping" sound, followed by a "purr." Music could be made.

All the time, the sphere spinning at room center did not shake, wobble, or move. It stayed spinning.

J'me repeated the show, each time improving her skills. It was draining, but her endurance developed... She enhanced her skills with each demonstration.

Originally, the agenda included a workshop for those interested to stay and learn. However, during an early exhibit one student accidently bounced their sphere into the center ball creating an uncontrolled ricochet that produced a frenzy! More than one tall guest got a hit in the head. For this reason, it was wiser to schedule the practice sessions with fewer people in the room.

About 80% of the students could get their spheres to move, simple elevation. They improved quickly. Strange, but true, **successful students were mainly females**. Another observation was that **the best were men.**

With each practice session there were new creative discoveries. For example,

- Spin brought stability to the object. Theoretically, a ball could stay suspended indefinitely if the correct gyration was created. However, the whirling motion was not necessary.

- After mastering the skill, hands were not needed to elevate and move objects. A walking stick, a wand, a wink. Some people could elevate and levitate just by closing their eyes.

- With the correct amount of concentration, anything could be moved (no matter the matter).

Cube F (of the BLOCK), once vacant, now temporarily lodged the visiting clans. But many enjoyed Sublevel Three because the ceilings were taller with only four walls... a giant-sized room.

Everybody seemed to adjust well. But there came a point where some guests wanted to go home for various reasons. Some were leaders of their clans and felt it their responsibility to stay with their people. Others thought of the upcoming spring plantings. Some missed their friends and loved ones back home. **Their reasons were not to leave, but to go back.**

Although compelled to return to her clan, Frija said, "Archie has grown quickly. I feel these surroundings are the safest for my son." In all, 20% stayed. But before the exodus, it was time for a celebration!

Women wore their traditional ribbons and skirts. Space was made for the young ones to pirouette, increasing speed, which lifted their hems to create the image of a blooming flower. The slimmer girls danced alone because **the gentlemen Giants preferred the pleasure of plump ladies.** A man would take two women, one for each arm, then pivot in circles, increasing their speed and the arm strength needed to lift the women from their feet. Imagine flowers blooming.

J'me's slim frame did not lend itself to this style of dancing. However, she enjoyed watching as inhibitions faded into rough sport and the party became exponentially wild. "Whew, I like it loose!" J'me exclaimed as she threw her scarf off.

Note: When the Giants came to the BLOCK, they brought their music. This was the first time J'me was aware of music. **Music affects your mood and works better than any food or drink to liven a moment.**

Hosting the Giants was a giant risk that not only worked, but also infused the BLOCK with new energy and inspired creativity.

Chapter 16

$$(-2)^4$$

Two by two, deliveries entered the East Ramp (DH) and two trailers left the opposite side (AE)... exiting west and immediately turned right and in tandem headed north into the fog.

When the Giants visited, there was joy. Differences were entertaining. The Giants marveled at the smaller sized people in the BLOCK; the people in the BLOCK were amazed at their larger size. The honest nature of each other affected everyone. The Giants were rough compared to the graceful little people. The little people saw the power of Giants as an advantage, wherein the Giants saw the delicate ability to move small objects with detailed efficiency as equally inspiring.

Just as everybody is different, each person had their special memory. **Their spirits affected each other in a special way.** Everything affected J'me more... She was still raw and sensitive to life.

J'me sat motionless on the floor. Her eyes were open yet she was blind to what was around her. She heard nothing... She sensed nothing... She felt nothing... She had no emotions... She felt one times zero equals zero...

Dr. Klug, Dr. Lyja, and Dr. Noch-Nicht approached the motionless J'me. It only took a moment for them to realize... "Bring in the women!"

The doctors understood they needed what some call the "mid-wives," masters of the medical and spiritual arts. (They were also called "enchantress" or "priestess" or "nurse". For obvious reasons, "women" was used to identify these specialists.) From grandmother to mother to daughter, they were trained from birth through death.

Like a mechanized unit, large and well-padded women entered the room. They had a duty they were eager to perform. They encircled J'me on the floor, sitting with their satchels on their laps. They responded to the doctors' orders.

"Open her purse."

With that, the women began to joke. "What is wrong with men? You cannot even open a woman's purse? Just do it! There is no lock on her purse. Are you afraid your nose will be bit off?"

But none-the-less, they opened J'me's purse. The men feared to peer inside.

"Ahh, do you see a filter? It looks like..." He was cut off.

One woman pulled out J'me's licorice root she used to clean her teeth... Shaking it in their faces, two women said almost simultaneously, "Afraid it is going to bite you?" Then, another woman said, "Here... here is a white ball."

Klug took the pearl, sat down, and connected with J'me...

Channeling their thoughts amongst themselves, the doctors then explained that it was negative two to the third power (-2 x -2 x -2 = -8) situation, and must be made **negative two to the fourth power (the product of which is a positive number 16).**

Then it happened! She felt his hand touch hers. The instant of contact created a surge of energy, a lightning bolt hit her! She felt alive! It felt wonderful! Eyes opened. Light replaced darkness immediately. She saw the faces around her and focused only on Klug.

"Negative two to the fourth power!" J'me blurted out, like being the first to solve a puzzle. Klug smiled.

The women laughed, but demanded the men leave them in privacy. Then Klug stood and dropped the pearl into J'me's open purse. Concurrently the men left, not needing to be escorted.

"She is ready." The women said in unison. (J'me started her period.)

Math is symbolic logic... For many, the symbol $(-2)^4$ is how to make money gambling. It is simple — for every bet you lose, you double the wager. Begin with a $2 parlay. Bet $2, lose, and then bet $4, lose, and then bet $8, lose, and then bet $16. If the odds fare as they should, you will make money along the way. **If you lose four consecutive times, stop**. But if you win along the way, you will make money. When you win, reset, start again with a $2 parlay.

In this context, the wise men were speaking of something not simple. It took J'me a moment... Let's explain the symbolism slowly (not at quick Klug speed).

$x\text{-}1$ = you harm yourself.

$x\text{-}2$ = somebody harms you.

$(-2x)^2 = (-2)(-2)$ = two wrongs creates a stronger balance, **an eye for an eye.**

$(-2x)^3 = (-2)(-2)(-2)$ = **learn, then turn the other cheek.** ...But do not stop; avoid a negative outcome.

$(-2x)^4 = (-2)(-2)(-2)(-2)$ = outcome finished positively, reset and start again.

There is no such thing as good or bad luck. From bad comes good. And from good comes bad. Not everything is bad. Not everything is good.

THWAP

Chapter 17

Past

From chaos and conflict and confusion comes creativity. From creativity comes innovation (A quote from the three wise men).

From Auntie Juan: **Creativeness creates a beautiful balance.**

From Tio Juan: **Everybody is creative to some degree.** You make your own choices and follow your desires.

From J'me: A child was given the task to color a picture of a cow. The cow was blue. When asked, "Why did you paint the cow blue?" the child replied, "I have never seen a cow. But I know cows are big, so I painted it blue because the Giants wear blue." With that J'me replied, "That is a lovely cow!"

"May I help you? the young man asked J'me.

"Uhm, I think... maybe... I am looking for Frija-Frig G, the Giant woman. She is in Cube B... or C... She is taking the show and tell tour."

"My name is Naz. Please follow me." responded the new friend.

Moments later J'me entered the reception room. It was familiar to her **(from the past)**. She had to adjust to the Cube C change in the air. This time she was not alone, many people were wandering through the displays. Soon she noticed an old friend.

"See you later." J'me departed from the escort and pushed her body through the pressurized room.

"No chariot or ball of fire?" J'me said, surprising E. Noch-Nicht.

Nick twinkled, and then busted **out in** laughter. **"Sometimes the best moments are those not planned."** (Like inventions, this idea unfolds in the future for J'me). He went on to speak through his chuckling, "I spend my life predicting, but I have learned that we cannot work, work, work. **We need to think less and play more!"**

"I will remember that." replied J'me.

"Oh, do not step!" Nick exclaimed. "In these buildings you can slide and glide. Watch this!" He slid his foot forward on the floor. "Push off and fly!" Soon his feet were together, and he was floating around the room.

J'me followed his lead, but was not yet as graceful. Even though she wobbled and bumped about, she was having fun. He was a waltz; she was a polka.

"I am here for the tour, but it seems it has already begun." J'me finally said to Nick.

"Unplanned pleasures... I can be your guide until mealtime. Then I must leave."

J'me thought about his words and also about the first time they ate together **(from the past)** ... and his quick abduction... and getting his toes sucked. "I will remember that." responded J'me **(She was definitely not saying all that she was thinking but thinking what all she was saying)**.

"Cube C is now dedicated almost entirely to innovations and improvements. In actuality, the air is not heavier here... less cohesion... less friction... Creating a dream-like state. Please follow me."

With that, J'me and Nick skated through an adventure of science and technology. Like nerds skating through a science fair... Interacting with the inventors and exchanging clues...

**** Due to non-disclosure (patents pending), the contents of the tour cannot be shared. ****

"Care, repair, and prepare – these are the ways to wise maintenance" **(The fourth is fun).** J'me said goodbye to her old friend Nick and glided into the dining hall. Breathless, she looked around the crowd in the large room. This was the same dining hall that she shared a meal with the three wise men **(from the past)**.

Her head felt like gears shifting downward. Third, second, first gear, neutral, reverse...

Summary, **from the past:** Let's see if this is correct. An old man is so smart he cannot speak. He communicates using symbols. His two friends are connected telepathically with him. J'me must use a pearl to receive his thoughts.

The peaceful, almost predictable life inside the BLOCK was altered when a race of Giants, hidden away, comes to visit. This changed the environment. But after a while, most Giants decided to go home... some stayed.

Oh, do not forget the discovery on how to break the laws of gravity using the exponential method. It is simple, if you know how (and remember size does not matter) ... Something like that, right?

After four fails, you start again $(-2)^4$. There is no such thing as failure and that is the secret to (roulette and real life) success... Alternatively, perhaps J'me was just having to wear panties (period)?

The show and tell tour turned out to be the no show and no tell. **It had passed... ended.**

Chapter 18
Variance

Something new was happening inside the BLOCK... There was a feeling in the air, similar to that before a weather change.

"May I help you?" said Aarov Naz, J'me's earlier escort.

"F'Frig G, the Giant woman, is now in Cube C with the show and tell tour. You are welcome to eat with us. We are sitting at that table over there."

J'me followed Aarov to the table where she was introduced to his family. "These are my brothers, Arjun, Arnav, and Arush Naz..." From behind her J'me felt two tugs. "I am Mari!" Twin sisters introduced themselves in unison.

"Mari! Please have a seat Mariah and Maribeth, (Mari A and Mari B)." chortled J'me, embarrassed by her surprise snort. The younger sisters sat on both sides of J'me during the meal. They adjusted the hems of their skirts.

The feast of knowledge was about to begin. Two conversations interacted simultaneously.

Mari A: "We call this 'Sweet Celebration'."

Mari B: "It reminds us to be thankful."

Mari A: "We invented it!"

Plates were made of crunch cookie and the spork was crystalline sugar. Gingerbread bowls with pies, puddings, and pastries were served by the twins.

Aarov: "We researched the 'lag effect'..."

Arjun: "That is the time from efforts to rewards..."

Arnav: "There is a natural delay or decay rate..."

Arush: "How long between putting your hand in the fire and pulling it away?"

The speed of speech seemed to increase with every mouthful eaten.

J'me: "Delicious!"

Mari A: "What is your favorite?"

Mari B: "I like them all!"

Aarov: "Everything can be calculated... It is like a chain..."

Arjun: "A multi-variate chain that leads to multiple results..."

Arnav: "But the norms are consistent, therefore we identified the correct algorithm."

Arush: "Can I have another spork? I ate mine."

J'me: "I like the pies, puddings, and pastries!"

Mari A: "Me too. Each has unique flavors and textures."

Mari B: "There's more."

The speed of eating increased. As they ate faster, they spoke faster.

J'me: "The butterfly effect can be calculated?"

Arush: "Not fully, that is still an enigma..."

Arnav: "But we can isolate many variables and results."

Arjun: "Girls, the fruit has a delicate flavor that I love!"

Mari B: "We infused the fruits with many subtle blends of flavor."

Mari A: "Save room for dessert."

Adding to the clutter, trays of cookies, cakes, and candies were served. Their sugar buzz was like bees around the hive. Note: To an outsider, the rate of speech was almost beyond comprehension.

Aarov: "There are many anomalies..."

J'me: "They look beautiful. I love how you decorate them."

Arjun: "Response varies..."

Arnav: "The lag can range from a lifetime or even generations..."

Arush: "The lag can be immediate."

Aarov: "Many covariates to explore and explain. Focus on norms."

Mari A: "Thank you. But Mari is the artist."

Mari B: "Thank you, but Mari is the artist."

A slight skirmish ensued between the two artists. This led J'me to make her next comment.

J'me: "Positive energy yields positive responses."

Aarov: "Very simply... Cause and expect an effect."

Arjun: "Action... then reaction."

Arnav: "Expect rewards, not consequences."

Arush: "My mouth is tired."

This triggered the two Maris to stop bantering and start bartending. Crystal goblets were half filled with a golden milk.

J'me: "What is this?"

Mari[2]: "HoSuCaJuWa" "HonSuCan J-Wash" (Their pronunciation was fast and not clear.) We invented it!

Mari A: "Lick the glass first."

Mari B: "The glass is made of salt."

Mari[2]: "Then chug the honey and sugar cane juice as fast as you can!"

Everybody picked up their glass, raised them, and together exclaimed, "Here's to Mo.", then took large gulps.

An explosion of sweetness! Each reacted differently. J'me squeezed her eyes, her lips, and then her throat. She squeezed her face so hard that it tickled her sphincter and she rocketed out of the room.

The show and tell tour had concluded when J'me entered the grand hall of Cube C.

"Three things to remember:

    1. Top down then circle around.

    2. Organize, then multitask once.

    3. Worst first, trash last."

That was the summation of the presentation J'me had missed.

"Next is the pairing of partners."

J'me heard her name from the commotion in the room. It was Frija-Frig G waving at her.

But what the three wise men saw was a massive mess! "What in the world happened down here?"

The three men shared the same expression. **"Now is the time."**

Chapter 19

Tau

"F?"   Mumbled an elderly Asian gent with braided beard and queue...

"F? F?" (It was difficult to understand him.) His bald forehead looked shiny...

"F? F? F?" He was an instructor without students.

Finally, it clicked with Fija-Frig G, "Yes, Cube F... That is us!" she exclaimed.

Very proudly he slowly introduced himself, "I am Kung Tau Fu Z!" His grin grew across his face, forcing his eyes to close.

"Kung Fu?" Frija was confused.

"Kung Tau Fu Z ... Fuzzy!" responded the man with pride.

"Fuzzy is a lovely name." comforted J'me. His height reached between J'me's breasts and Frija's navel.

"This is J'me and you can call me Fridge." They exchanged bows.

Fuzzy became animated and lively. A bit too much perhaps for the moment.

"Shhh... Let me share with you my secret... stealth." With that, Fuzzy vanished and reappeared behind the two. "Do not be seen when you clean." The last words were sung in a strained melody that covered many notes, tones, and octaves. "Do not be seen when you clean. Do you know what I mean?" He sang again after he reappeared.

J'me looked at Frija. Frija looked at J'me then said, "Sounds like a gay leprechaun having an orgasm. Hah!" J'me laughed despite not fully understanding the meaning of her joke (This happened often when she was with somebody more advanced, such as Frija-Frig G... a.k.a. the Fridge).

Cube F was once fully occupied by the Giants... now only 20% remained. (Also, many secluded themselves to Sublevel Three.) Therefore, the task of cleaning Cube F would be relatively easy.

The top floor was empty. This was their training site. They received their tools and began the process of cleaning from the top down... trash last. But at the end, there was only dust to show for their efforts.

Maximum efficiency with minimum effort... blend in... be invisible... **Moving with their natural rhythm was relaxing. A blend between energetic focus and tempered concentration allowed them to "flow."** The word used by Fuzzy was "artistry." He wept...

The task became more difficult as they progressed down from floor to floor... The Fridge did not do too badly for her size — she was quick yet careful. J'me started slowly but improved. Fuzzy disappeared somewhere in the lower floors... They would do better the next time.

The Sublevel docks were different... J'me had never ventured "outside" to a new world.

"Ahh." Frija-Frig G felt similarities to home.

"Gaaasp!" A triple explosion of air disconnected J'me. The difference in air temperature, pressure, and quality shocked her. She immediately began to lose the feeling in her fingers, toes, and nose. J'me began to shake and shiver. F'frig G scuttled her behind boxes. Moving from inwardly focused to outwardly aware... reset... then J'me began to acclimate.

The pair found a hiding spot near the closed ramp FG. They climbed on top of stacked crates and scouted.

Their eyes scanned the activities on the docks. **They noticed everything**: trucks morphing in, being packed, being unpacked, and moving out. Workers were well organized and efficient. Rarely did they speak.

J'me was curious about the shape of the workers and guards. Their torsos were enlarged. Frija explained that the clothing covering their upper bodies was called a "jacket."

Nearby, a nondescript white trailer was parked. Men seemed to loiter and linger while others worked. Some of the packed items J'me recognized from her tour with Nick.

There was one thing in particular that captured their attention. A man... A man in a silver jacket... A man in a silver jacket emerging from the white trailer.

The man was odd in the best of ways. He seemed to have an aura of power... magnetic. He emoted a feeling of love. J'me was in a trance. Her stare was broken only when **the man looked in her direction and winked**. He then got into the truck and drove away. After the rear lights vanished, the women went back inside the Cubes.

"What the frack?" Tio Juan and Auntie Juan saw a hole along the southernmost wall. Extracted from this was various rubble that was strewn on the floor of Sublevel Three. "What happened?"

After a slightly elongated pause, Tio replied, "The Giant people unblocked the barrier. They removed the loose bricks to discover the building beyond."

They stared into the space. Both broke the silence by saying, **"Now is the time."**

QUIZ

I

Quiz One

Test your understanding of what you read. Pick the *best* answer for the following ten questions. After completing all ten questions, check your answers on the next page.

Unlock the next chapters: If you score a 70% or above (answer seven or more questions correctly) you may proceed to the following chapters. However, if you score below 70%, read the previous chapters again.

1. The BLOCK was originally planned as
    a. A single person's vision/fantasy/dream
    b. An utopia/perfect world/Shangri-La
    c. A single concept/idea
    d. A core/centralized area for planning

2. What is the formula for exponential growth?
    a. 1x0=0
    b. 80% + 20% = 100%
    c. a(1+r)t
    d. $(-2)^4 = 16$

3. Klug's autobiography excludes...
    a. a love song
    b. ignore the meaningless of nothing
    c. 1 is the beginning
    d. the power of exponential growth/decay

4. Who was the young Giant woman with braided hair?
    a. Frija-Frig G
    b. F'frig

     c.   The Fridge

     d.   All of the above

5.   What was not below the surface of the BLOCK?
   a. Two levels of underground parking and storage
   b. Partitions
   c. Sublevel Three
   d. Four exit/entrance ramps, with one blocked

6.   Who took J'me on the Show and Tell Tour?
   a. Nick or Dr. E. Noch-Nicht
   b. Auntie Juan and Kung Tau Fu Z
   c. Tio Juan and Melvin Klug
   d. Frija-Frig G and Dr. E. Lyja

7.   What was not at J'me's first feast of thanksgiving?
   a. Sweet inventions by Mari[2]
   b. "Reap what you sow" research
   c. Part of the Naz family
   d. Pilgrims and Indigenous people

8.   What key to janitorial work did Tau Fu give to J'me and Frija?
   a. Top down... circle around
   b. Multivariate thinking then multitasking
   c. Worst first... trash last
   d. Super stealth

9.   Who noticed everything in Sublevels 1 and 2?
   a. The workers and the guards
   b. J'me and Frija, plus the man in the silver jacket
   c. The three Doc's, plus Juan[2]
   d. Everybody outside, it was an open area

10. What happened in Sublevel Three?
   a. The Giants unblocked a barrier making a mess

   b.   Leprechauns hid their pots of gold
   c.   Deliveries were made, trucks were loaded
   d.   It was used as a secret storage area for the BLOCK

Q1 – Answers

1.   Answer: D. It is the center of a much larger network. That was the beginning, but over time it has become something more. We're still trying to unravel everything about the BLOCK.

1.   Note: The next best answer, A, is also acceptable. But we know the BLOCK was more than one man's dream. He had much help.

2.   The formula for exponential growth is

      Growth: $a(1+r)^t$

        a = starting amount
        r = growth rate
        t = time intervals.

Therefore, you need to know where you are beginning (a), how fast you are growing (r), and for how long (t) to get a bigger number. So today it is 1, doubled daily, would be 2 tomorrow.
f=art can also be written as the function (y=2x).

3.   A... A love song. Klug finds is easiest to express himself symbolically using numbers. He shared with J'me his thoughts and feelings. We know Klug loved J'me's grandmother, but love songs were not his style.

4.   Who was the young Giant woman with braided hair? There were many, but you must pick the best answer. All of those names are the same person. Answer: D. It goes to show that names are not important and are just a tag we use to identify something/somebody.

5.   The best answer is B — Partitions. OK, if you want to get technical, there are three sublevels separated by floors/ceilings. Within each sublevel, there were no rooms or even pillars for support, just a lot of open space! That would be the *best answer* of those to choose. (This is a test of your understanding... not a law exam.)

6.   Easy! Nick was her personal escort and skating partner (Answer: A).

7.   Silly question... No pilgrims or indigenous people (Answer D).

8.   Master Fu brought the stealth of a ninja or a leprechaun to the chore of cleaning. (Answer: D).

9.   That would be B — J'me eXquisite and Frija-Frig G, plus the man in the silver jacket (as they were surprised to see him wink at them before he drove away).

10. **It is crazy how things happen and at the time you do not see the significance of it.** For example, where were you Thursday, March 13, 1986 when Microsoft stock sold for only $21 a share? If you bought $10,000 worth of shares, then you would be a multimillionaire today. Answer A - Sublevel Three was unblocked and this crack in the dike changed the world.

Chapter 20

XX

XX stop... ◀◀ rewind...

Back, back, back... when there was only one continent. The "Tree of Life" was the center of civilization.

Surrounding the magnificent tree was a garden that provided more than what was needed.

Mr. G lived at the continent's center, never wandering. He loved his job and worked six days straight, and then rested but one. At this point, he delegated most duties to his support staff. Mr. G did not consider himself a leader, per se, but most people followed him.

Most people freely followed Mr. G, but not all. One in particular actually despised his good deeds. Whining, "I work harder than you! I work every day without rest. I make my people do the same. Nothing is free! They don't have a choice but to succeed!" He called himself a deity and coerced cohorts, usually through trickery... He was a dirty deity.

"Life is not a game." said Mr. G.

"True, rather it being a game of chance, take away the gamble. Everybody wins!"

"That is not how it shall be. People should be free to choose. Give them the freedom to decide for themselves. Stop playing with them."

Mr. G had the numbers, most followed him. However, his opponent had grit, tenacity, and they cheated. It was a war that some say has not concluded. Others believe in the Big Bang Theory, wherein an asteroid hit the tree of life with such force that it split the continent apart.

The garden was gone; all that was left of the tree was a stump. For many millennia the primitives rubbed it for good luck. Eventually it became smooth and then round, like a sphere. It became known as the (wooden) "Bubble of Balance". Based on the number of years that have passed, it is probably petrified by now.

Some believe that the original tree of life and the garden were in current day Philippines. More than 7,000 islands? And why do you often see Mr. G there on vacation?

Nobody knows for sure. Even the name of the evil opponent(s) is not available to us.

▶▶ Fast forward, ▶▶ fast forward, ▶▶ fast forward... oops, ◀ back up just a little...to the end of the last millennium, the last century... Years 1900 to 1999 were the twentieth century. That was when the bubble burst.

History repeats itself. In the past we had border wars, civil wars, religious wars, wars of aggression, wars of independence, and wars of succession. Man's inhumanity to man has been well documented.

Now new wars: economic rivalries, electronic warfare, information wars, nuclear war, psychological warfare, and wars of mass destruction. We now have more words for killing each other: battles, campaigns, clashes, conflicts, disruptions, disturbances, engagements, ethnic cleansing, forced famine, insurgence, interventions, invasions, offenses, police actions, pre-emptive strikes, skirmishes, terrorism, and weaponizing. Wew!

Man-made wars are done in groups; the will of the people was violence and destruction. Their goals were good, usually serving some or one's self-interest. Fighting is both moral and immoral (depending on which side you are on) with reasoning such as: the ends justify the means, the best defense is a good offense, or this is for our future security.

Perhaps you can take solace from the animal kingdom? When overpopulated, there would be a natural readjustment. Perhaps it was diseases, fires, floods, outbreaks, or maybe famines that cut back their numbers? Occasionally, the bubble had to pop as part of natural evolution.

But the twentieth century was unique. We have yet to see a true 360-degree bubble view. If you combine ALL the genocides of the twentieth century, they pale in comparison to the 45 million deaths during the "Great Leap Forward" by Chairman Mao Zedon or the 40 million murders "Movement" by the General Secretary Joseph Stalin. People were forced into believing in one unified continent again.

The dirty deity was working overtime. **The most innocent people suffered most. Bad things happen to good people. And there were good people doing bad things.** Stop playing with them!

While part of the world was off the bubble crazy, the BLOCK was balanced. There was also absolution, forgiveness, mercy, and innocence. Earthly communism was based on fear and force; the heavenly commune inside the BLOCK was based on feelings and freedom. The BLOCK did not have leaders, only followers.

Time to update the computers, the year 2000 was a new millennium. It was a new time and a new beginning.

Chapter 21

New Millennia

Spring was coming, nudging nature out of its hibernation. Nighttime temperatures could go as low as 21 degrees Fahrenheit (-6 º C) and the daytime peaked at 70 º F (21 º C). The bright mid-day haze was nature's gift.   People moved at a slower, hazy pace. Icy streets and slippery sidewalks required focus and finesse and a sense of balance. One slip could be a graceful slide or painful impact. **Everybody "cared" in one way or another: carefully or carelessly.**

The floral sky touched the earth and frolicked with the light. Either a dense fog or an occasional brightness blinded you. Everyone moved unpredictably, carefully and carelessly onward.

The rhythmic sound of the wipers, clearing the dew off the glass, broke the silence.

"Papa, can we stop and eat our lunch in the car? I think we are near the BLOCK..." said the young passenger.

After a slight pause, Papa flicked his signal light to blink right and pulled to the side. His arms ached from grasping tightly to the steering wheel. When completely stopped, he wriggled his fingers, stretched his palms, and shook his hands. As he tilted his head left and right his shoulders sunk in relaxation.

The wipers and blinkers played two out of sync tempos. He shut them both off and immediately calm enclosed them.

They finished their relaxing lunch and put away the remnants... then sat quietly sipping their drinks. Breaking the silence, the lad said, "Do you see the bubbles?" He squirmed to look out all the windows. "If you look you can see bubbles floating..."

"Do you see the bubbles?" he said again with great joy. "Can we get out?"

Papa said, **"It is a perfect day to play outside."**

Without saying a further word, they both had an ominous feeling that going outside here was like being the first two people to walk on the moon. Minutes later they emerged and carefully shuffled closer to each other while keeping one hand on the car at all times. Moments later they decided to unleash themselves from the car and start their exploration... One small step...

A man emerged bathed in bright light. They squinted to see him. They gazed upon his face. He was smiling. "May I help you?"

Dumbfounded they did not know how to answer that question. The elder man finally said, "Hello." and the youngster followed with a "Hi." and then there was silence as the man in the light waited for the answer to his simple question.

XX stop... ◀◀ rewind...

The two soon noticed the ground was wet, but not icy. **They moved freely.** The temperature was **perfect.** It seems the sun's warmth made the clouds feel like a puffy insulation from the cold. An occasional breeze pushed the fog away. This frequently allowed shafts of sunshine to break through. It was a **perfect** light show.

Moving patches of light appeared and disappeared on the ground. In the distance, the two could see an aura moving towards them. They were filled with curiosity at what seemed an unexplainable illusion. Through the dense vapors they recognized the silhouette of a person... a person coming nearer.

Of all the senses, their sixth sense (balance/intuition/subconscious thought) seemed the strongest. This pleasant feeling grew as the man moved closer... He was magnetic, with unlimited energy and power. **A feeling of love was absorbed in toto to the center of their brains.**

Gradually, their five physical senses absorbed into their awareness. They noticed he was very clean... shiny. This glare affected them. He had striking features, symmetrical in shape. The man's eyes were distinct with the purest of white... almost glowing.

"We finished our lunch and decided to take a walk." Papa said. Again, not an answer to the man's question. The man continued to smile. They noticed his black hair reflected a spectrum of blues and reds.

"Uhm... We wanted to look at the BLOCK." the young lad said.

"The BLOCK?" The stranger was amused.

"Yes, we call it the BLOCK." Papa said innocently.

Chuckling, the mysterious stranger responded, "Great! I will be your guide, but today we are doing renovations and cannot go inside. I apologize. When your grandfather worked here we did not have these walls..."

"This way please. The tour is about to begin...

Welcome. Hello everyone! My name is Mr. G, your guide. If you have any questions, please ask.

I would like to remind you to stay with the group and do not wander... Also, be kind to one another."

Chapter 22
Catch

J'me eXquisite opened her eyes. There were blur bubbles moving across her view. These floaters stayed when she blinked, only changing position and direction. She sat up and rubbed her eyes. Her lashes were wet.

J'me had slept with her clothes on. Her back was solidly pressed against the stone floor. She'd slept hard and was lightheaded. She had just woken up... but felt tired. Did I sleep too much or not enough? Dazed... Her mind moved slowly... J'me stretched her arms out first, and then twisted her neck and back before standing up. These body movements also energized her mind. J'me sensed she was alone. She yawned, bringing in new air to inflate her lungs.

J'me slowly rubbed her palms across her face then quickly brushed her clothes to smooth out the wrinkles. No water. The room was empty.

She reached down to the floor to pick up her purse and as she rose, her face fashioned a smile... a dry and dusty smile that formed slowly. Reaching inside her bag, she grabbed her licorice root brush to clean her teeth. Ah, better. No water... but a smooth smile.

A new perspective and a heightened sense of her surroundings — J'me now saw things with a new set of eyes... She noticed things clearly for the first time. She had an **amplified awareness** that allowed her to notice details previously overlooked.

J'me stepped outside then abruptly stopped. The room she had just left seemed duller. Curious... She moved her face close to the wall. It sparkled. The walls glittered. As she moved her hand across the smooth surface, she noticed a glowing trail. The walls responded to her.

She paused for a moment to look around, and then stepped back into the room in which she slept and noticed a change from dark to dim to day. She walked to the center of the room and closed her eyes. Waited... and opened her eyes again quickly. Nothing had changed.

In the past, J'me ignored trying to reason. **But she now felt inquisitive.**

She closed her eyes again and imagined the grand celebration the Giants had hosted. **The feeling in that room was festive.** Comparing that feeling to the dining hall... the science labs... the vacant floor... **Each room had its own "feelings".** When J'me was with friends, walls brightened.

J'me was learning how to discover... learning how to learn.

Miss eXquisite moved out from her room in Cube F towards the Cleansing and Creation Center (C³) in Cube D.

Goodness! Was everything white? Inside... White floors, white walls, and a white ceiling with the corners being the only break in the hue. It seemed disorienting at first... White, white everywhere! Now she was like a tourist looking up at the ceiling and moving her head about to see each wall. How had she not noticed this in the past?

Her mind was moving. J'me understood that learning was a new source of happiness. She adored this feeling of discovery!

Catch 22 – When her consciousness was opened, she startled her instinct to discover.

When J'me awakened her awareness, she also started to question. **The more she learned the less she knew.**

The pace of her thoughts moved faster and faster. Her mind was multiplying ideas. Her body was moving slower and slower.

She was soon oblivious to where she was. She had escaped inward. She had to capture herself before she reached infinite exponential thinking. J'me filtered:

Remove meaningless thoughts... $1 \times 0 = 0$

Exponential growth and decline...

You have infinite choices...

J'me began to **prioritize her thoughts based on only two criteria:**

Is it urgent?

What's important?

She felt a little shaky, but commanded herself to move forward. **As J'me was able to simplify, she regained control.**

J'me needed a mind and body balance. Knowledge and thinking came from the brain... and from her core was her soul. She remembered the path the two little dandelion girls had taught her earlier. She headed towards the learning center.

Once inside the woman with the heightened senses motioned J'me to the opposite side of the room. There sat a man waiting for her. He was Mediterranean, with an olive complexion, dark hair and dark eyes, chiseled cheeks, strong nose, full lips, muscles rippling, and oiled skin glistening. The second thing she recognized was that he was Harrius, and **he came from an ancient time when a beautiful body meant a beautiful mind.**

Chapter 23
Blessed or Cursed

How is it possible to live forever, immortality, eternal life? That was her goal, her inquisitive mind wanted to know. A complex question answered simply by Harrius.

"This 'gift' can either be given to you or you can achieve it. For example, if you are 'chosen', **you may be blessed with a wonderful life without end, or cursed with it and suffer.** Some people purely performed a spell or used magic for a deathless life. But most of those were summoned to fulfill a mission – to toil and tarry, remaining on earth: earthly angels. No matter the method or the goal, these were all done through a higher energy."

"Theoretically and not proven... yet... there are other ways people will be able to live forever. There will be people that are now alive and will witness the entire thousand-year millennium. Science will discover first an electronic connection to your brain using replacement body parts. Later will be a chemical discovery (DNA repair) that reverses the aging process itself." He paused... "To be technical, there are immortals that can die. Their gifts are taken away, quickly. But we won't go through the morbid details of this surrender."

J'me was satisfied with this answer but needed to ask another question. "Harrius?" asked J'me. "How do we know who?"

With that he reached out his hand to be merged using the oversized pearl that allowed him to communicate beyond words alone. Connected, J'me would understand earthbound angels.

"Around the year 523 there were twelve divisions on the sunset side of the Eurasian continent. Each had their own leader to "make things right", called 'ritter richter' in German, they were knight-judges. They were protectors, both political and religious leaders for their land. They were sometimes cleric, sometimes executioner. Note: There was also a thirteenth knight, without land, called the "Dark Knight" who came from the bowels of hell as explained in lore."

"Not the largest or wealthiest in terms of land or possessions, the Judge of the Giants, Richter der Riesen, was held in the highest esteem by the people he served. He maintained fairness and balance. He was the largest in stature among the twelve... thirteen knights. Constantly tested, he was almost always the victor."

"One day Richter der Riesen was blessed for his good deeds by Mr. G, put fresh beef under his saddle, and rode away. **He was chosen.**"

Harrius was a historian of people, not places or events. He traced the lineage of everybody who ever existed. Alpha begat beta, beta begat gamma, gamma begat... back from the beginning. However, Harrius made genealogy easy for J'me to grasp. For example, he often used abbreviations, contractions, or symbols for individuals.

Earthly angels are usually related, following a family line. "Almost 1500 years later, unaware he was special, Richard Ritter Richter G (R3G) benefitted from this knights' blood line, but also as a male descendant of Mr. G. ███████████████████

████████████████████████████████

████████████████████████████████
████████████████████

████████████████████████ he was just a babe when his father left him. Growing up was a struggle. Bullied and beaten, he   had   to   fight   to   survive.
████████████████████████████████
████████████████████████████████
████████████████████████████████
████████████████ As he said, 'He put a burger under his butt."

"R3G struggled to succeed ██████████████████████
████████████████████████████████
██████████████████████████████
████████████████████████████
████████████████████████████ Nothing in life is perfect; there is no such thing as "fair".

Life is both a blessing and a curse. The eternals were different not by whom they were or what they did... It was usually determined by somebody else. Perhaps we think of it as random, but in the end, they were chosen.

In life there are both blessings and curses that cannot be foreseen. The root of which may come from the past."

Parts of this have been blacked out and blocked from our view. (This omission was deliberate.) It is for the protection of others and possibly yourself that you do not know.

Chapter 24
Promises Kept

You share 25% of each of your grandparent's DNA. Because of this shuffle, siblings only share 50% of the same DNA.

However, most Y-chromosomes are passed father to son with few changes.

If you go back over 250 years, about eight generations, it is unlikely that all have contributed to your genetics. There are 256 ancestors to factor.

It is said we are 150 generations from Adam and Eve... The Sciences say more. Depending on what you believe, it is still a big number. But spirits are not science, and are not connected to your DNA or genetics.

Earthly Angels follow a genealogy chart. Alpha begat Beta, Beta begat Gamma, Gamma begat Delta... begat, begat, begat, begat... and ultimately... hey, you begot J'me eXquisite!

We know there are those who walk among us who have never died. Chances are that you have seen at least one. Their names, as well as your name, have been omitted from the BLOCK book.

There are many good people who wish to remain anonymous. **You may even know an actual eternal!**

Some secrets are secret and cannot be disclosed. Deliberately deleted with our safety in mind.... **Accept that some things are not for us to understand.** Some things cannot be written. Somethings cannot be told. Somethings we are not to know. Empty and unknown...

This page is deliberately left blank

103

BLOCK XX/XX

This page is deliberately left blank

This page is deliberately left blank

Dear Mr. G,

As you can see, I kept my covenant with thee.

We are all, in some part, descendants of ancient families. We are special!

Clear the clouds of confusion and grant clarity to those who follow.

Please bestow your blessings on us all.

Amen

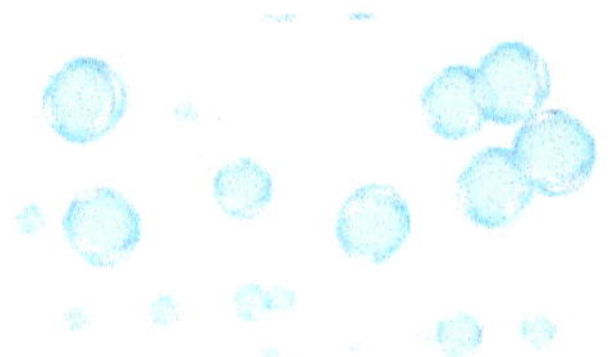

Chapter 25

Cognitive C^3

Then Harrius suddenly stopped. "Past, present, future... Perhaps I went too far? I must protect the privacy of others." Implied was that these were sacred spirits, honored and eternal. This was the first time Harrius shared at such a level.

J'me reassured him that his intentions were pure and that no harm was done. With that they parted ways onto different paths. J'me was off to C^3! Her mind and body needed balance.

Then she thought, "Oh no! I should have asked Harrius **who am I**?"

J'me eXquisite recalled the first time she entered C^3 and the cloud that became a washing rain. It was magical! Again, it felt wonderful... as she breathed in the moisture and felt herself absorbing water. She moved slowly through the process of disrobing before entering the bathing area.

She held her breath and submerged herself. Her mind melted from something solid to soft to liquid. When she stood up to get air, she felt fresh.

Her eyes explored the soaking pools around the center bathing area. She decided to try something new, to discover how the rehabilitating waters affected her. She glided through the water towards an edge to exit, but she never got the chance as she heard her name called. "eXquisite!" It was a deep voice. "Tio!" J'me screeched as she felt the hug of a large man from behind her.

J'me was caught. Tio Juan kept his hands clasped around her diaphragm. She could not move. From behind her he whispered, "White... Yellow... Orange... Red." More slowly he repeated it in a normal voice, "White... Yellow... Orange... Red..."

This was the **cognitive color code**: "White is inwardly focused and unaware to what is around you. White..." he paused. "Yellow is aware..., Yellow," again pausing, "Orange is alert..., The color orange." Then finally, "Red is responding! Red."

J'me repeated it as follows: **"Red is reacting... Orange is ready... Being aware of what is around you is yellow, and ... White is your head is in the clouds."** Then she was tickled by Tio as he released his firm grasp.

J'me and Tio Juan emerged from the edge of the pool and stood a moment. Then Tio walked towards one of the many healing ponds. J'me held his inner elbow as they waded into a warm salt bath. They squatted down so their shoulders were submerged. A wave splashed their faces as a young grandmother and two older gentlemen exited... leaving them alone.

With only their heads above water, the conversation started when J'me explained her morning. "I have so many questions!" she concluded.

"That is great!" responded Tio Juan. J'me had to strain to listen, as if hearing underwater with aqua ears. There was a long pause...

"I do not know what I don't know." There was another pause.

Slowly Tio Juan responded... **"Nobody knows everything."** This echoed inside J'me.

Listening intently and not moving, she found herself staring at Tio Juan's face, partially lip reading his words because of the fuzzy noise around them. "Relajada... You will learn new things... Relax..." His voice was muffled.

After a long silence, J'me submerged her head below the surface, squeezing her eyes shut as tightly as possible. She emerged and removed the water from her face. J'me allowed both hands and her shoulders to remain above water.

The teacher instructed the intent student... **"Sometimes you do not know what you see... until somebody tells you."**

"Your gift, for example." Juan revealed to J'me, "You know how to make people happy and feel love."

Although the Cleansing and Creation Centers (C^3s) were very popular inside the BLOCK, they were not the most important centers. From the single self-serve, to the larger centers, there was diversity in the C^3s.

J'me entered the "Creation" center of C^3. She enjoyed feeling submissive. She was willing to do whatever Tio Juan wished. Conversely, Juan went to the grooming rooms. Tio Juan accepted this service but passed on his hair trim. Neither participated in the bawdy topic of toilets.

The cleansing area was simple to understand, it worked from the outside in. **Clean and fresh, people feel better when they look better.** The creation portion works from the inside out. **Happy and healthy, people look better when they feel better.** For example, the meditation area inside

C^3 in Cube D was Tio Juan's favorite place. Here he built his mental and spiritual strength.

The last portion of the Cleansing and Creation Centers were congregation chambers. This created a relaxing climax.

Chapter 26
Creating Meditating

In the robing room, J'me was caught pleasantly surprised. Her new wardrobe matched the style and colors of Tio Juan (TO1). Secondly, she found a gift inside her satchel. It was a gold robe. The delicate fabric reminded her of Auntie Juan (NTUN), but when she tried it on, she noticed a hood.

A perfect fit! She moved her hands over the contrasting course undergarments and silky cloak and found a tag. She would not have seen it if it had not caught the light. It was a message that J'me did not understand... Then she realized it was her concealment cloak, a gift from her previous mentor, Tau Fu, a.k.a. Fuzzy.

"Where did you go?" Tio asked after J'me took off the cloak and neatly placed it inside her satchel. "I could not find you."

TO1 explained, "Next is the meditation area... a place to ponder. **Everything starts with the spirit.** It is something not seen — a feeling, a knowing, an intuition. This life force is your existence."

They walked through a maze of veils that created separate sections. Some had small groups, couples, single people meditating, and some were empty.

"Our spirit powers our thoughts... Our thoughts guide our feelings and mood... And this controls our actions."

J'me reasoned out the logic to this progression. Then it was followed by an incongruous thought in another direction...

"**You will have failures...** Realizing I made a mistake, first I apologize, then try to fix it, hoping for forgiveness, and finally am full of care not to do it again: **Rolling through recognition, remorse, rectify/resolve/repair, reform, and then to reset.**" (J'me simplified this evolution: first notice your mistakes, fix them, and then learn... Repentance equals -2^4?)

Continuing to speak in metaphors, "When I get knocked down, as fast as possible I get on my feet and move on. **Try to recover quickly.** It is our normal nature to enjoy."

"**The purpose of the mind is to forget, not remember.**" Tio Juan's accent and his light airy tone made this phrase poetic, a verse to a song.

TO1 said softly, "**They say there is no such thing as a pink sun...**" (The sun is either red, orange, yellow, or bright white.)

As J'me thought about it, there was a deeper symbolism to this statement. One cannot be a blend of red and white; it is not possible.

The past and the future blend simply into today. But we respond to what is now, not mixing white and red in your head.

Meditation cleans a messy mind... The movement of Juan's thoughts went to many places, making J'me dizzy! "Let's sit down." The room was dim, filled with smoke. Subtle mellow tones mixed with spiced scents.

J'me kicked off her sandals, then dropped her pouch. The two sat with their legs crossed directly in front of each other. When TO1 exhaled, J'me inhaled and vice versa.

A clear ball of air was created between them in the murky room. The pure bubble expanded as they relaxed and flowed together as one. They not only exchanged breaths, but also each other's energy.

J'me thought ... then opened her purse and pulled out an oversized white pearl, her communications sphere she had been given to understand Dr. Melvin K. Klug. The gemstone was powerful, working at a deeper level than words (for example, Banana: You did not just see the yellow banana, but everything including the fruit inside the peel.) J'me and TO1 now clasped hands with the pearl in their palms.

"**Do not dwell on history.** It imprints itself on us without knowing. But the past is weak.

History is based on more than one perspective... based on the number of eyes. Our memory fades. Don't dwell on the past at the expense of the now."

When communicating through the sphere it was as clear as the dream ball between them. This broke the barrier inside Tio Juan, to places others were forbidden to visit.

"**I am many spirits.** Mud and blood...I was a farmer in my first life, a fighter in my second life, then an emperor... and now I am here."

J'me heard, "Use your spirit to explore, take a journey, a spirit walk."

When was the last time you meditated? I mean, really meditated. It takes purpose... patience... a small place and a short time. Set aside a quiet, comfortable place where you won't be distracted. Start by relaxing and then let your mind loose. Let it go...

Chapter 27

TO1

Wonder full... **Life is filled with "What in the world?" distractions that are impossible to understand...** Be a bubble floating in the air. Ignore the urge to filter what you follow.

In a different place, at a different time, important events occur that affect the future. **Most of the time we are unaware; sometimes we wonder why they are significant.**

A lone man wandered down a worn path in the woods. Suddenly he heard — Roar! Thwit, thwit.

Efficient arrow shots through the heart and head of the bear... Instant, painless death.

Emerging from the trees came the tanned hunter who saved a white man's life. A teen with hardly hair on his loins. Born a farmer, he was forced to hunt due to bad weather and poor crops. Hunting was better than starving. He was modest, not yet in his prime. Ashamed, he was not given a name.

The young hunter chanted as they tied the carcass between two trees. It was a vulgar sight to see the bear gutted and skinned. Its remains were stretched over a smoking fire to be cured.

The two men shared the heart for dinner. There is a legend that states those who eat a bear's heart will be brave.

They were both on their own now. The young hunter and his elder companion were to go the same way. They trekked the "straight path crooked river" to the capital city of "water meets sky".

When they reached the base of the mesa, guards were stationed to control entrance into the capital city. Because neither of the two travelers had status, they were not allowed in during the celebration. The only way for them to enter was to forfeit the bear pelt and participate in the contest. The ultimate winner would marry the princess and have a chance to someday be chief.

The tournament was a series of fights spanning the week of celebration. Daily winners would be invited to the nightly feasts/fiesta.

This was more difficult than originally thought as they were only two (the foreigner and local) outnumbered by larger teams with more experience in battle games. The two compadres were only equipped with a bow, arrows, a hunter's knife, and their wits.

Nobody was familiar with their form of fighting. They were defensive and used their opponents force and weapons against them. This was done with only non-lethal maneuvers. Rather than executing their foe, they offered surrender. Rather than basking in their victories, after each battle, the two men tended to the injured.

The men soon amassed quite a following. The crowds were amazed. How was it possible? Two could overcome ten... leaving them to submit and ask for mercy. In addition, they gained the admiration of the other fighters. In the bowels of the arena, they gave aid to the wounded warriors. The two chose to stay here away from the pageantry. They were only required to fight and attend the evening banquets.

Barely a man, a simple boy with no name, faced death daily. During the celebratory dinners he wandered away to rid himself of the crowds. He was not alone... Crouched in the shadows in a storage area was a girl, younger than he, her body had not yet begun to blossom. The princess prize was crying.

Hidden away, the young man sat and held her hand. He was an empathic listener and calmed her emotions. Before returning to the party, the lad tickled her and forced a smile. The couple entered laughing.

The final show would be the tandem versus the General and his hardened officers. The General was as ruthless as he was arrogant. They hacked their foes and made a vulgar sport of death. This time the loyal soldiers were commanded to stand down. The General boasted that he alone could defeat two tiny combatants.

What ensued was almost a comedy. The General was humiliated with every failed attempt. The longer this went on, the louder the crowd laughed. He was furious! His anger built into a frenzy when the General next did something unpredictable. The General leaped with outstretched sword to kill the Chief.

Roar! Thwit, thwit. — Efficient arrow shots through the heart and head of the General...

Instant, painless death.

Postlude: This tale is based on a true story. It can be found in the lore of many Indigenous peoples. Only recently it has been authenticated. This is an excerpt from the Princess Glyphs:

"My eternal love, Mr. G is gracious.

I give you (the) name, Juan."

Chapter 28
De-Stress or Distress

Nowadays books follow formulas: conflict, rising tension, climax, and conclusion. Yet, that is not realistic. This is not the formula for life. In fact, there was no conflict or tension within the BLOCK. There was not a climactic moment that needed to conclude. For the same purpose as those who pay attention to the news, they want to read books. **Without these prescribed pieces, you may feel bored. But so is life... sometimes.**

For this reason, the next topics of conflict and rising tension are just for you. To be able to appreciate life in the BLOCK, you must change your mind. **De-stress not distress.** Otherwise, you are only reading words you cannot feel... meaningless to you. **If people with less do not stress, so can you.**

Stress is self-induced; it originates from within or as an unavoidable reaction to your actions. That feeling of emotional or physical tension is your body's response to a challenge. In short bursts, stress can be positive, such as when it helps you avoid danger or gives rise to a sense of urgency... or motivates you.

Pressure is what you put on yourself. Sometimes we think exponentially, and it spirals. For example, "If I am late to work, I will lose my job. If I lose my job, I won't have money. If I don't have money, I cannot buy food. If I do not eat, I will die. If I am late to work, I will die!" **Bad ideas bubble up...** "What will they think of me? (You think of the worst possible outcome.) This anxiety can kill you.

Everybody makes mistakes and nobody is perfect. **You made mistakes, you are making mistakes, and you will make more mistakes! It has and had consequences.** You worry and fear... This escalates into something bigger when you reflect on your future... Doom and gloom is just a mind trick.

There are intentional and unintentional mistakes. You need to know your errors. It is an added burden to wonder why. Living with secrets can cause stress. It is best to hear what you fear.

Your first step is to stop being stupid. Start by removing the rotten eggs. Rid yourself of negative thoughts and stinking thinking. **You underestimate your good values.** Is it really that important? Are you going to live in pain and die? Let your mind release and relax... clear your mind of these thoughts. **If you cannot change it, accept it and move on.** Worrying never solved problems. Am I right?

Gone are the days of people responsible for you. There are no more gurus and guides who share their life skills. Without experiences, you can only do your best. You are on your own and nobody is helping you.

Not only learn from your mistakes but share them and help others. This is part of your problem and part of your solution. "When I was your age" stories are annoying, but with the best of intentions. Listen and learn from others: **You are not the first, nor will you be the last, to have this pass.**

It must be said, be careful, because even with the best intentions, good advice can be bad for you. **Do not blindly follow all things recommended.** Sometimes the advice will not work for you. Listen with both ears, see with both eyes, and use that one brain in-between them.

This is all good for those "before" and "after" moments. But those moments in the middle are stressful. You care and you suffer. If not, you fail to see what is important. There are three types of people, those that complain yet do nothing, those who don't do anything and have the habit of waiting for others' help. These two types relive this cycle to only start over again... But there is a third type of person who sees life as a learning process. They know better than to do nothing or think somebody will solve their problems for them.

In summary, **clean your mind, be open to advice, but ultimately know you are in control of your thoughts and feelings. Ultimately you are responsible for your actions.** Accept or reject.

Be boring! Pick your own prescription. There are many formulas you can follow. But be willing to change. When I was your age... wait. Never mind.

They say the difference between humans and animals is their ability to think. Animals act on instinct, whereas humans can process thoughts and plan ahead. **We should thank our ancestors for thinking.** Because of them we are alive.

What do you think?

Chapter 29
Intentionally Meditating

For a moment J'me felt regret, but quickly stopped herself. After finishing their journey from within, the two moved out of the meditation area to the congregation room exiting the Cleansing and Creation Center in Cube D.

"Enjoy!" Tio Juan told J'me. "Keep it casual. Stay simple and take it easy..."

Auntie Juan appeared and J'me asked her to translate the note she had received earlier. Auntie looked at it and read, "This is your concealment cloak." After swiveling her head around, she added, "Fu is somewhere... I cannot see him."

Later, she ran into the Naz brothers carrying empty cups. "We were remiss earlier. Our original goal was to recreate fate... at a later date. The lag affect is just part of the process we are researching.

Do you believe in fate? We must wait..."

J'me felt like a dark goose among white swans. She remembered to touch the wooden sphere sculpture and rub her hands across it. This made her feel good!

J'me donned her concealment cloak and disappeared. Where did she go? She went back to the center of the center, back to the meditation rooms. She found a secluded spot and sat down, alone.

Straining her ears to hear the soft popping of suds...J'me was a frothy liquid calm. First, bubbles melted into the air, as sediment settled to the bottom. Next was seen purity growing between the layers. In her mind,

sentiment/sediment was covered in clarity and clarity lifted the foaming surface. Over time, the froth in her head vanished in a slow, calm celebratory way. Time and movement combined cures the mind. At the end, foam forms clarity. J'me was calmed, reaching a clearer state of mind.

She allowed her mind to wander, not fixed in one direction. This was just her first try at intentional meditation. Not a meditation, but a vision occurred. J'me had her very first

original dream... so it seems. In contrast to the clarity she had before, this was something more messy... buttery, blurry, busy, bubbly.

Something... something... A big church...Three sets of doors were opened. Inside and under... a room filled with treasures and a wooden crate with "Do not touch" painted on the exterior. Something... something...

In her dream, J'me discovered this was a missing master key of some sort. D.I.K.E.? A. I., 5G, Mr. G... (Gibberish).

"Into the heavens!" Something... something...

There was a five-minute free fall... somewhat relaxing.

Something... something... Then it vanished and J'me was awake and willing.

Let's introduce our dream expert, messenger Mori, teacher of morals, to help us decrypt and decipher J'me's vision. Not that this matters, but Mori was a tranny, with three bumps: two on top, and a bulge down below.

"One third of our lives we sleep. One third of our sleep we dream. A few minutes after a dream we forget half of it. A few minutes more and half of that is lost. Did you know that your brain is more alive when you are dreaming than when awake? To prove it, **your brain works better when your eyes are closed.**"

"Can you translate for us, please?"

"There are many meanings, but you are the best interpreter." Mori replied. "But I will try. The feeling of falling is probably one of the most common dreams people have. For example, falling can relate to anything from insecurities, loss of control, or the fear of hitting hard when you land. Sigmund Freud suggests sinking is sexual, giving in to your inner impulses. But in this case, it may be more like flying and the feeling of freedom. I'm not sure... I will take a pass on that."

Mori continued, "The dream of doors is when something is blocking progress or the ending of a phase... But by entering there are new opportunities, moving to a new level.

Your positive attitude, your potential, the possibilities, and your drive for success could possibly be the wooden crate.

A master key answers many problems. If you find a key, you have found a solution.

To dream that you are touching something indicates you are trying to communicate your feelings and your needs. It could also be about gathering information.

Opposite to this is the meaning of being touched. Now this is sweet. It is closeness, being connected, and in tune.

Heaven is your desire to find perfect happiness. Outer space means boundless creativity. Combined, this may mean faith, optimism, and hope.

Something... Something like that." messenger Mori mimicked with a laugh.

QUIZ

Quiz Two

Test your understanding of what you read. Pick the *best* answer for the following ten questions. After completing all ten questions, check your answers on the next page.

If you score a 70% or above (answer seven or more questions correctly) you may proceed to the following chapters. However, if you score below 70%, read the previous chapters again.

Please take your time reading and meditating to unlock the next chapters.

1. In the Twentieth Century, more deaths occurred from:
    a. World War I and II combined
    b. All the communist revolutions combined
    c. All the genocides combined
    d. HIV/AIDS

2. The grandfather and grandson that visit the BLOCK met Mr. G. What did Mr. G offer?

    a. Be their guide
    b. Work for him
    c. Play a game
    d. A cup of pure water

3. A dual edged sword, a paradox with no good solution to a problem is a "Catch 22" situation. Which of the following is a Catch 22?

   a. Vote for the right to vote
   b. Denied a job because you do not have work experience
   c. The more you know, the less you know
   d. You need money to make money

4. Prioritizing is based on which of the following two questions? ___ and ___.

   a. Is it urgent?
   b. How much time will it take?
   c. Is it important?
   d. Who does it help?

5. How are earth bound angels, sacred spirits, eternals created?
   a. Blessed or cursed
   b. "Chosen" for a mission
   c. Magic spell
   d. All of the above

6. Why are parts of this book blocked, omitted?
   a. People want to remain anonymous
   b. This protects others (and possibly yourself) from harm
   c. There was a promise made to Mr. G. by the author, DrGooseX
   d. Some things are not for us to understand

7. The Cognitive Color Code: Match the letter to the number, the explanation to the color.

   a. Act, Respond, React   1. Red
   b. Alert, Be Ready   2. Orange
   c. Aware of what is around you 3. Yellow
   d. Inwardly focused in thought 4. White

8. The Cleansing and Creation Chambers in Cube D have many choices. What was Tio Juan's favorite area?

    a. Rain room entrance with soaking pools in the Cleansing Area
    b. Partitioned Meditation Rooms (Creation Area)
    c. Grooming and Robing Rooms (Creation Area)
    d. Congregation Area with the "Bubble of Balance" and refreshments

9. Conflict, rising tension, climax and conclusion are elements of the cookie-cutter formula for books. What ingredients are in the formula to avoid this in life?

    a. Avoid conflicts
    b. Avoid tension and stress
    c. Be boring
    d. All of the above

10. What is the first step you must take to de-stress?
    a. Stop being stupid
    b. Stop worrying
    c. Be aware of unintentional mistakes (and secrets)
    d. If you cannot change it, accept it

Q2 – Answers

1.   HIV/AIDS has a death toll of approximately 36 million people to date. Although it was first seen in the 1980s, it still persists. However, if you add China and Russia together, HIV/AIDS had the highest casualty count in the 20th Century. The sad answer is, "All the communist revolutions combined." B. Man's inhumanity to man, oh my.

2.   The answer is A: Welcome. Hello everyone! My name is Mr. G, your guide. If you have any questions, please ask.

3.   The answer is any of those situations. J'me felt that the more she knew, the less she knew. However, this was a trick question, a freebie. You could not get it wrong. A, B, C, and D are all Catch 22 situations.

4.   KISS = Keep It Simple, Stupid. There are only two questions you need to ask yourself when prioritizing your time. Is it urgent and is it important? The rest does not matter. A, C.

5.   All of the above. People that will forever be in our world, without death, are special. But also note that Harrius said that in this next century science will catch up and we will have replacement parts and DNA that will allow us to keep our bodies alive longer.

6.   I must first apologize. It was not my intent to deceive you. The book was finished, but there was... Well, as you can see, **some things are not allowed to tell and some things are not allowed for others to know.** For this reason, another freebie. All the answers are correct: A, B, C, D. Plus, even if it was fully explained to you, you still may not understand and it may not be worth your struggle.

7.   The Cognitive Color Code is as follows A=1, B=2, C=3, and D=4. Easy.

8.   Each of the C^3's in the BLOCK is different. However, the C^3 in Cube D was Tio Juan's favorite spot. More specifically, he enjoyed meditating and taking "spirit walks" in the veiled rooms within the Creation Center.

It was a bit of a surprise that he went with J'me to the Grooming Room. (Do not expect that to happen often.) Answer B.

9.   **When writing your life story, will you have this formula?** I hope not. This book was based on real world, authentic situations. Pre-prescribed plots are not real. So the answer is D: All of the above.

10. The first step is not so easy for some: The answer is stop being stupid, being blunt. **Some people bring stress upon themselves by thinking or acting stupid. Avoid storms and dangerous situations. Find and remedy your mistakes quickly and be more careful. Dedicate time; make an appointment to remove stress you have built up.** Today, heart disease is the number one killer of people. It beat out infections from the century before. So the first step is stupidity, Answer A.

Chapter 30
Harmonic Sensation

Wandering with or without a purpose? Are you a lost soul? Do you march through mud every day? If that is what you choose, you lose.

Wandering is a wonderful way to exchange energy, mixing harmonies, and synchronizing your soul. Conclude to exude optimism and absorb the harmonic sensations that echo back to you. **You give and get what you interact with.**

Visually amazing! Inside the BLOCK the walls, floors, and ceiling are a pure white. This could be a bit overwhelming... But then there is the diversity of clothes and colors that are... amazing! Also, there was the peaceful time distortion (movement that is about 10% slower than outside). You should be accustomed to this by now, not surprised. It is always visually entertaining and always fun.

There are short and longer adjustment periods. It takes longer to adapt to the noise or vibrations resonating about. You see, inside the BLOCK, **there was also a special harmony that affected the sense of sound and individual intuition.**

Overall, the BLOCK was filled with pure sounds. Occasionally, a breeze of soft noise floated by.

Language was no barrier, everybody understood each other perfectly. There was another layer to the spoken word and that was the feeling that resonated from the speaker: **Perfect communication was possible through the harmonies that transferred feelings.** If you thought, "I am thirsty..." somebody was soon by your side with a drink. Before you could complete the thought of "coconut water", coconut water was offered. **Life is magical!**

Back to the beginning. When the BLOCK was being built, radio was a scientific infant. Scientist s knew sound traveled by invisible waves naked to the eye. The transfer of thoughts and feelings (vibes) was the fantasy of fools. More sensitive, rare spiritualists could communicate via the notes that break glass and raise the ears of dogs.

So... Vibrations could not be seen or heard; they were sensed. The slightest touch was felt from within. Sensations moved constantly within the walls of the BLOCK, sensing feelings was common.

This may not be clear when simplified like this, but in summary, **inside the BLOCK everybody was connected**. The sensation was relaxing, but the reason was beyond understanding.

Feel your heartbeat within you and let your mind ease. Suppress your power to resist. Surrender and float along with everybody around you.

Glitter... Sparkling light... sheets of shimmer to behold. In front of this was a film of what looked like glossy bubbles that reflected both light and color. When a bubble popped, it created a spit of a spark (just a spit). Closest was the neon fog that surrounded the boy. Blinking did not distort the fantasy; it was real.

He pressed his hand forward. The fog moved away lightly. The lad quickly looked down to assure himself he was standing on solid ground and balanced. Left foot: stomp. Both feet: Stomp, stomp. Yes, it was real. This was the closest he had ever been to the BLOCK.

He heard the words, "May I help you?" but felt the words, "I love you." He hesitated to answer and just said "Hi". A man emerged and appeared so clearly from the haze that surrounded them. His grandfather, standing next to him told the stranger, "We finished our lunch and decided to take a walk."

The boy revealed that they wanted to see the BLOCK, but they found they could not go inside now. The older men were happy discussing his grandfather, who they both knew.

When the boy touched the silver jacket of the stranger... he noticed something odd, he was getting healthy. Wait, "healthy" was not the best word... He matured quickly, passing through layers or gradients of time. He felt stronger. His muscles started to inflate; his bones grew. His strides became longer as he grew taller. He was more acute mentally. Everything about him was growing!

By the time the three reached the car, the youngster now older, had hunger pangs. He interrupted the adults to say, "I am hungry. Let's go." and concluded with a stomp, stomp, stomp.

Restrooms to your left... and the gift shop is to your right. The exit is on the other side of the room past the cashier's stand. Just look for the tall security scanners.

Thank you and come back soon... I hope you have a great day!

Chapter 31
Phoenix Therapy

Corpses were strewn on the floor in a tangled mess. The pale, skinny bodies could not be recognized as man or woman. The figures were entirely shaved naked and covered in only light spreads of fabric woven throughout. It looked unnatural, as if they were thrown into the room in a careless fashion. Arms and legs overlapped, and faces pressed firmly against whatever they landed on.

A single hand clap was heard outside the entrance. Three stout matrons shuffled in, heads bowed. Their feet cleared a pathway to the center of the room. The three crouched down and started gathering the fabric, unlacing it from the bodies. This was done quickly and without concern to how they had to toss the frail figures about to complete their task. After all was collected, each of the three held similar sized heaps of fabric. They turned, and exited in unison.

Two quick claps were heard from outside. Again, matrons shuffled in. This time they carried a metal container of water suspended between two long poles. The pot emitted a peculiar fog (from ice warming into steam). Its frosted sides now sweated and spit droplets.

They lowered the misting container to the floor. The handling poles were removed from the kettle rings and one woman exited as the other stayed positioned near the pot. She grasped handfuls of dried herbs from her satchel and released them elbow deep below the water's surface. When her bag was empty, she crouched with her head kept down. Her arms slumped to her sides, dripping.

Three claps were heard from outside, but these were distinctively different, as if they were made by the banging of two hard objects together. There was a slight lingering echo.

Two matrons returned, carrying tall stacks of towels. The heather fabric was made of natural fibers that gave it a clean, light color.

As if serpents, the bodies on the floor slid and slithered in odd movements. Slipping themselves free of each other, the animated frames moved apart. They made a few grunts, groans, or slight squeaks. Their eyes opened as they carefully poised themselves to stand. Reaching, stretching, and balancing upward to their feet. (You found yourself looking closely for toppling or even a wobbling mistake, but their effort exceeded your desire.) Over time, they moved their bodies more easily... in a less jerky and clumsy manner... nimble, almost graceful. There was something in the air.

Before something new can be created, it must be destroyed.

Only two tasks remained. Next was the exo-cleansing, "guasha", better known as "skin scraping". This opened the outer layer, exposing the inner layer. Damp towels were scrubbed across the same surface path 50 times. The number of strokes, 50, was not as important as the effect: raw, bruised, weeping skin. Each helped the person in front of them to rub their backside. This marked open trails along the flesh of their neck, shoulders, arms, backs, buttocks, and legs.

The brushing looked painful at first, based on the facial expressions of those in the room. Ache eventually numbed by the monotony of the continuous rubbing. Pain morphed into pleasure... a little fatigue gave way to a rush of energy. Their bodies seemed to glow and radiate out of something previously mistaken as a lifeless corpse.

Meditation was the last cleansing step. **From chaos comes clarity.** This was an internally driven meditation. Melting mind and body as one, each individual sat on the floor. As a group, they were symmetrical – all facing the same direction, legs crossed, hands cupped, heads lowered, eyes closed. They now looked like an artist's creation.

During this moment of silence, the matrons moved the large kettle and scattered towels out. The haze created in the room seemed to exit with them. A wind without source? The combined breathing of each person? Maybe something as simple as suction coming from the doorway evacuated the dampness.

Just as you wanted to believe what you saw was magical, Auntie Juan walked in with an oversized bag on her back. She dropped it on the floor and a cloud of soft white silk robes and gowns escaped.

"Water. Try ..." Juan added a clap, clap... clap, clap. "Water, more..."

J'me ate a quick snack with Frija-Frig G ... It was one of the smaller foraging places scattered throughout building D, the Cube in the northeast corner of the BLOCK.

She sensed she was being watched from a distance. Her awareness was increasing.

Chapter 32
Triple Change

Three... two... now, one!

J'me enjoyed her time with Frija-Frig G. They often practiced their levitation and also cleaned building F together. Although they were unique individuals, they were most compatible.

J'me had developed a new skill, **comparing**. She noticed Frija changed. The first time J'me saw her, she had a baby bulge, a mommy tummy... just given birth to Archibald R inside the BLOCK. Now her stomach was flat and firm. She had a glow about her. **A new dimension, change over time, was another perception added to J'me's skills**.

Maybe not apparent, but J'me eXquisite knew she had traveled a long way since she first met Frija. J'me had observed and explored; she also had gained insight from others within the BLOCK. Despite all the quirky inward changes, Frija-Frig G remained her most reliable friend.

She continued to sense that she was being watched. They walked to the docks. The two separated when Frija headed towards the sublevels. J'me knew the BLOCK well and took a surreptitious route to the first floors of Cubes B and C. She meandered through the displays then darted out. This time she was on her way to an area in Cube E. Perhaps she could lose her stalkers there.

It was to no avail. Mingling within the crowds had not shaken her feeling of being followed. She had one more plan. This time she headed to Building F, her home cube. Her plot was to catch them on one of the upper floors. She knew this area best.

When she walked into the top floor of Cube F, J'me immediately pulled her invisibility cloak from her satchel and put it on. Then she moved to one corner of the room and waited.

It did not take long... Three teenaged African girls wearing black oversized one-piece dresses and yellow scarves, scurried into the room. Not just their faces, but their whole bodies expressed their disappointment to find the room empty.

J'me silently watched. The three girls held hands and then circled together for comfort. Their yellow scarves almost drooped off their black dresses. All the while J'me was thinking how it was possible for them to have followed her that distance without being caught? Amongst the heavy room with the exhibits, they kept track of her. Even moving among people was no deterrent. Then she sensed something...)

She removed her cloak and revealed herself.

"Oh! Oh! Oh!' the girls screamed in surprise! Then they ran to J'me and began to give her heartfelt hugs. "J'me eXquisite! I cannot believe it! It is you!" J'me only had time to stuff her cloak back into her bag before she was mobbed. "We are holding J'me!" the girls fanatically shrieked. It took a moment before they un-groped J'me and gave her a chance to breathe.

The three girls were joyfully crying. "Stop crying." J'me cautiously coaxed them. "It is just me." The three reached to grasp J'me's hands, but they were still bouncing in delight.

"Who are you?" J'me asked sweetly. She immediately sensed them... "What are your names?" With this the girls stopped moving and quickly looked at each other. Concerned, J'me asked, "Who are your father and mother?" And then the girls' tone turned somber and they looked downward. There was silence, like it was the quiet game. Nobody spoke first.

Finally, one asked, "Can we braid your hair?" It was not an inquiry, but more of a life-long fantasy.

"Sure!" J'me said, and immediately smiles came from their dark complexions.

They sat down on the floor. The girls pulled out a flat shaving stone and combs. At first they only used their hands and ran their fingers through her hair. They pulled it in different directions to shave the fluff they found around the edges. Then there was some firm tugging.

"It is true... you can become invisible?" "You are friends with Dr. E. Lyja, Dr. E. Noch-Nicht, and Dr. Melvin K. Klug?" "You can talk to Dr. Klug?" "Can you lift me up without touching me?" "You know all the Giant's names?" Then the girls said, "Teacher (Tio) Juan said we are like you." They moved their arms to show that their skin color was the same.

"Um, yes, but I do not know everybody... I did not know you." J'me replied. It seems that the girls were secluded within the BLOCK. She was able to get them to open up as they expertly preened J'me's braids.

Chapter 33
Sub Three

When J'me stood up she brushed her hand across the bundles of smooth locks on her head. She had never had braids tied so tightly. To her surprise, her scalp was not sore from the vigorous tugging and pulling, but tingly.

She faced all three of the teens at the same time and noticed that they did look like her. They were identical to each other and similar to J'me. They all exuded a strong feeling of love.

"Are you sisters?" J'me whispered, as if exposing their secret... then she wrapped her arms around their shoulders. It was a huddle hug.

They were born outside the BLOCK but grew up primarily within the learning center. Without parents, they often retreated together, alone. Their story became interesting when they said, "Teacher Tio says **everybody has a special gift**. Do you want to see ours?"

"Ok, we are new at this... We work better as a team... Actually, we are inseparable." The three girls were anxious to show off their abilities.

The middle girl reached for J'me's hand and held her arm. Another brought out the shaving stone. The third opened J'me's hand. Just before they were about to cut her, one girl said, "I hope this works." J'me's hand pulled back immediately. The three girls laughed, "She is joking!" When everybody stopped laughing, they settled down and began again.

With her hand open, the shaving stone was pushed deeply across it. The sound of scraping bone would make anybody wince. J'me looked at it and asked, "Is this for real?" Then the girl unclasped her arm and she felt the horrific pain. When she regained her grasping touch, the pain disappeared again. Next, a girl placed her hand over the gaping gash. When removed, the cut disappeared, leaving a pinkish wound. J'me moved her fingers; moving from paper to rock, rock to paper, open and closed. The third girl moved her hand across to remove the scar and evidence of blood. It was better than new.

J'me exclaimed, "You are women!" which elicited the girls to broaden their eyes and move their hands over their stomachs. "No, no! We have not...!" they shyly responded.

"No, no... a woman... a priestess, enchantress, mid-wife, nurse..." J'me explained. "You have been trained in the medical and spiritual arts."

"Mother" (This was the first time the girls called her this. It felt good, so J'me did not correct them.) "Mother, we have learned this ourselves. Teacher Juan only knows a little of this."

J'me took a moment to collect everything that had just happened. Then she had an idea!
"You are ready... There is somebody you should meet...   I hope this works." And they laughed again.

Frija-Frig G, the Giant woman also known as F'frig to most (and to one spritely Asian man, Fridge) was as elusive as a Titan woman could be in the BLOCK. Being a mother was her priority. She was away, and when she returned Archibald R had grown the girth of an oak and the height of a spruce tree. She was the first to admit that she had help from her fellow community of Giants. Everyone took part in his care and training. They did their best to impart wisdom onto Archibald R.

The Giants were industrious people. It seems when they were not working, they were working. They washed their own work clothes, which many wore except when they were mingling outside their familiar Cube F. The clothes they came with had sturdy leather and strong metal fasteners. But their ornate aqua blue garb they all chose to wear were impressive and made them distinguishable as much as their size.

Like most of the Giants residing in the BLOCK, Frija and Archibald R spent a large portion of her time in Sublevel Three. This was the informal gathering area below the BLOCK with the most space. People thought that their zest for laughter, loud singing, and rowdy play was the reason they chose this space. But they were only partially correct.

Along the southwest wall (below Cubes E and F) of Sublevel Three the Giants discovered a crack in the wall. Innocently, after loosening the stones, they started pulling them out. Noticing something behind the wall, they continued to take more of the wall down and remove the loose rubble behind it. It was a mess!

As Dr. Nick says, **"Sometimes the best moments are those not planned."**

Chapter 34
NTUN

There are moments when things happen like a well-choreographed dance. They could not have been planned better. This was one of those indescribable moments.

J'me's plan was to take the girls to Cube H, home of Auntie Juan and the infirmary. Auntie Juan, the healer, was responsible for the health of those in the BLOCK. Knocking down two birds with one stone, Auntie Juan was also the person who gave J'me her name. She certainly would know what to do.

The three inseparables were now four with J'me. They played and laughed so hard that their cheeks got hot. It seemed they all had a similar healthy sense of humor.

What was in her mind was the now. There was no other good excuse to explain it... It seemed she had been overcome with the excitement of the moment. Before she noticed, they had descended below the docks to Sublevel Three. It became apparent when they entered the open space.

Let's for now skip the part where we learn the impact of the room on the five (or six) senses... Instinctively, they held each other's hands and Momma eXquisite scuttled her daughters safely to the side, out of view. They hid behind some debris like rats at a trash dump. They squatted quietly, hoping not to be seen.

J'me admitted her mistake. She had planned to take the girls to Building H, not a hell hole. She wanted to introduce them to Auntie Juan, the healer.

The girls asked, "You mean the elegant woman who wears the tight red dress and golden scarves? She is over there."

Sitting in one corner of the cavern was Auntie Juan, smoking a cigarette and snacking on strawberries. She was at a table with a miniature triage area behind her. Attendants prepared the workers like elite athletes before rough labor. They also had a few on beds with minor needs.

Before moving forward from their protected position, they reset. Moving from inwardly focused to outwardly aware (cognitive code orange, melting between red and yellow). The four girls were ignored by everybody who saw them.

Finally they were discovered. "J'me!" It was Auntie Juan, followed by "I C A B, O A B! R U A B? G A B!" She seemed to be playfully referring to the black dressed, yellow scarfed trio holding J'me's hand.

Auntie jumped from her mood to give J'me a hug and say, "You miss me. I love you." Then she began to examine the bumble bees. With one hand she grabbed the wrist of one girl and with her other hand, pushed back on her forehead and looked into her gaping mouth. "Hmmm". Then she grabbed the next girl in a similar manner and tilted her head back to examine her open mouth. She poked out her tongue. "Hmmm." And finally, the third... wrist, forehead, mouth, and tongue... followed by a "Hmmm." Juan looked a bit confused. She clasped her hands together and said, "**Need balance**. Hmmm..." then said nothing.

Juan thought for a moment and then clasped the breasts of each of the three girls, comparing it to her own breast that she was also squeezing. Further confusion... further silence.

The awkward moment concluded when Auntie Juan dropped a large framed man to the floor with a single slap. Immediately, J'me's trio rushed to the victim and overlaid their hands on his cheek. "Are you ok? How do you feel?" they quickly asked. He began getting to his feet. "Great! Never felt better!"

Then the biggest smile came from Auntie Juan's face... "You like me."

A laborer standing on top of a rubble pile lost their footing and slid to the bottom. Crystal shards imbedded in the stone not only shredded his clothing, they sliced deep layers of flesh from the bone. Work stopped.

Briskly, a nearby Giant woman lifted the injured worker. The gentle way in which she did this was impressive... as if she was not touching the person. They maneuvered quickly to the corner aid station. All eyes were on them... if you blinked, you may have missed it.

The patient was laid on a makeshift bed. Auntie Juan stood nearest the gaping wounds with two attendants on her right and left wing, standing behind her shoulders. Juan's hands moved gracefully, assessing the damage. An open artery spurted blood on Juan's red dress. She moved her hand to cover the spray.

The Giant woman stepped back from the bed, mixing in with the semi-circle of curious onlookers. From the crowd came J'me's daughters, moving forward without forethought.

Chapter 35
Hope United

"Madam Juan Li, help me!" the injured man begged.

The first of J'me's daughters found a spot to place both hands directly on the victim. This allowed him to relax, pain-free. The next girl did a washing with bare hands across the wounded area. She repeatedly brushed her hands over the surface making it new.

Juan directed the areas which needed attention. Some internal maladies were not as obvious as the exterior wound. When the third girl stepped in to administer aid Juan and her assistants stepped back. Auntie Juan Li looked like a maestro conducting a symphony, flamboyantly waving her arms and pointing to different areas that needed care.

When everything was cleaned, all three girls removed their hands. They approached Juan and overlaid their hands down the front of her spotted dress. Auntie Juan gave off a couple of deep coughs, then stood straight up on her high heels.

J'me focused on her followers, her adopted girls. They snuck off to the nearest wall and formed a circle, holding hands. She moved through the crowd to be near them. The young women were sweating and breathing heavily. "Are you ok?" J'me asked with the deepest concern.

The girls bobbed their heads up and down and muttered, "Tired." She stayed by their side. Moments later, they all squatted down.

Frija came over and slid her back down the wall, sprawling her legs out in front of her. She was also sweating. "Can you believe it? He is back out there working! At least he's over in the sorting area with the women... Still wearing his tattered clothes. Showing it off like a badge of honor." J'me sensed she was about to say the word, "stupid", but she knew Frija better.

J'me asked, "Where you the one who carried him over here?" She paused... "If I was not mistaken, it looked like you were levitating." She looked directly at Frija whose head popped up at her question.

Frija replied, "I was not sure that was you, J'me. Your hair..." she said, and then looked at the three young women holding hands beside her. "I have never..."

J'me interrupted her friend, "I would like to introduce you to my daughters!"

The three girls unclasped their hands and used their scarves to wipe their faces and around their necks. They knew who Frija-Frig G was. This would be their first time to meet her. "Oh! Oh! Oh! It is Frija!' the girls said in surprise! They did their best to give her a hug.

J'me explained that they were really not her daughters; but they really were sisters; they really idolized her (for lack of better words); and they really got lost (for lack of better words) and ended up in Sublevel Three. J'me wished for the girls to meet Auntie Juan, possibly work in the infirmary, and to get real names and happiness. Frija understood this.

Auntie Juan walked up from behind J'me as she finished explaining all this to Frija.

"You are in the right place. They call me the giver of names. Let me see... Usually they come straight into my mind... Ahh..." Pointing to each girl, "Freeze... Froze... Frozen."

That seemed pretty simple, but when Juan said with her accent, "Fleas... Flows... Zen..." they knew there was something wrong.

J'me suggested, "Wait... Just a minor adjustment. "Ease" (The young girl repeated it but with a wave of her hand, like a dance move). "Rose" (The second girl moved her hands like a blooming flower). "Zen" (Her hands reached out, cupping her palms, then brought them back to her chest... with a slight head tilt). "That's it!"

Frija excused herself to go back to her responsibilities, but before she did she gave one giant sized hug to all three of the young women. **She had renewed happiness.**

"You must eat!" Auntie Juan demanded. She departed with two attendants on each wing behind her. "Let's go." the sisters said with a stomp, stomp, stomp.

J'me, Ease, Rose, and Zen followed the procession.

They had no problem finding dining hall E155. The delicious aromas made their mouths water. Juan withdrew to the kitchen while the four aides arranged a table for them to share. They wanted to sit between each of their guests. The vacant seat to the right of J'me was soon occupied by an older woman. She sat down without a word, patted the back of J'me's hand and smiled. Soon afterward Juan Li came back from the kitchen.

Chapter 36
Bottoms Up

First, two servers carried a large soup bowl to the center of the table. Each guest got a small plate, two bowls, chopsticks, and a spoon. Auntie Juan and the four attendants stood up and ladled bowls of soup for everyone. Juan Li made sure "grandmother" was the first served.

"Ok?" Juan asked, not sure if it was directed towards the eldest, J'me, her daughters (Ease, Rose, and Zen) or the four medical attendants. The once betel nut beauty, now a "nai nai", responded by petting/tapping the glass top a few times with her fingers. J'me and her daughters said, "Yes, thank you." in unison, and the attendants just smiled.

The servers returned shortly carrying ten small saucers and a large ceramic jug of wine. Another group came with large plates of food and set them on the rotisserie. As the food was spun around each person took a portion for themselves.

"Here's to Mo." everybody said in unison.

Auntie Juan was attentive to the older woman sitting between them and always served her first. Each time the woman graciously tapped the table, thanking her. She never said a single word, just ate, drank, and thanked.

After a few morsels were eaten, the saucers were filled and spun around the table. Each guest took their drink. J'me and the three girls did their best to mimic their host. Then Auntie Juan raised her saucer first and said, "I love you." Each person lifted their saucers and gulped down the rice wine. They looked at each other's saucer to make sure they were empty (If not, you had to raise it again and finish it).

Before the bowls of rice could be served, the four attendants had replenished everybody's wine and moved to the other side of the table. They tilted their drinks in the direction of Auntie Juan and "nai nai" (grandmother), said "gan bay" and drank the strong elixir. J'me thought this second gulp was smoother, but noticed the girls were still squeezing their faces and felt the burn.

In between the toasts, more food was brought to the table. It became a game to eat as much delicious food as possible before the large serving plates were empty and taken away. Not as proficient with chopsticks, the Asians out-ate the Africans at about four to one. But to be fair, the Africans out-drank the Asians at about five to one (arrgh, forget the math).

Just for fun, let's count the number of times a drink was raised for **health, happiness, and good cheer.**

1 – "I love you" from Tio Juan to the entire table

2 – "Gan bay" (bottoms up, Chinese) from the attendants

3 – "Kanpai" (bottoms up, Japanese) from the table to the left of J'me

4 – "Gun bae" (bottoms up, Korean) from the table behind J'me

5, 6, 7 and more... – "Cheers", "Prost", Salud", "Salute", "L'chaim", and more "Here's to Mo!" ...

After about the 12th or 24th or 36th chug (Arrgh, I don't know! Forget the math!), J'me saw two cooks from across the room beckoning her to come. As smooth as possible, she got up from her seat and wobbled the distance of the room. Her three daughters were doing the same behind

her. When she got closer the cooks removed their scarves from their heads and she noticed Mariah and Maribeth Naz (Mari A and Mari B).

The two Mari's were younger than Ease, Rose, and Zen... but they had a good question for J'me. **"Moderation... Do not exceed your bounds... Balance everything...** Remember?"

J'me slurred, **"More is too much.** Hmmm..." With this the three girls held hands in a curing circle. Quickly, their heads and stomachs were fresh.

"Oh, oh, oh, we need to use the toilet!" everyone cried.

Mari² respectfully went to the table to explain the guests were in the restroom but would be back.

When the four returned, everyone was in a festive mood. Even the older woman had a wide grin and a little drool of wine down the side of her mouth. She was given fruit from the tray by Auntie Juan. It was a beautiful watermelon carving; a decorative display too beautiful to eat from.

The conversation was loose women talk. The topic was menstruation and their reoccurring cycle. **"Nature has a rhythm... Go with the rhythm of the body."** started the conversation.

"Women have low and high tides." added an attendant.

"Do all women bleed?" asked Zen.

"We can cure ourselves." explained Rose

"No pain." added Ease.

"None is not enough. Hmmm..." said J'me.

Chapter 37
Prime Path

J'me, Ease, Rose, and Zen slept long and well. They comfortably cuddled together like pups against their mother. They had bonded. Everything was perfect.

Here are selections from mother/daughter discussions:

Before their first time to the infirmary, J'me shared this with her daughters. She wished to say something monumental and unforgettable. But she felt like she had too much to say.

"Some people choose to follow tradition, a straight path, while others meander through unlimited choices trying to choose the best one.

I have been fortunate to have friends who imparted wisdom that I needed. For example, there are no leaders or followers here... You have many choices... If you choose to follow Auntie Juan, you are not breaking any rules... There are no rules to break."

After learning and working in the infirmary, Ease, Rose, and Zen each told J'me how happy they were.

"Muscular, skeletal, circulatory, respiratory, nervous system... Lymphatic, renal/urinary, endocrine, and the exocrine/integumentary (outer covering) systems we already knew." Then they asked, "Can you teach us about the reproductive system?"

J'me did her best. But she had to admit her lack of expertise... **"There are some things we must learn on our own."**

Which made her think. Maybe J'me should go to the Cleansing and Creativity Center more often. Isn't that the place to learn?

Here are more excerpts from later mother/daughter talks:

J'me shared the tip she had learned, "I have heard... the first time you are harmed... wait. Maybe it was an accident. The second time somebody harms you, be defensive, protect yourself, but again wait... Maybe it was not their intention. Yet, study your opponent. The third time somebody tries to hurt you it is time to fight back. By now you know your enemy and you will win." After pausing, **"It is not an eye for eye... or turn the other cheek. You must always protect yourself. It is a three-strike rule."**

"Remember the man who comes to visit patients?" The girls began their discussion....

"You mean Mr. Most? (An acronym for **Mission, Objectives, Strategy, Tactics**.) He comes to play games to occupy the minds and lift the spirits..."

"Yes! That's his mission. **His objectives are SMART... Specific, Measurable, Attainable, Relevant, and Time bound.**"

"Mission is his main motivator, wherein his objectives are to distract sufferers from boredom...and make them feel happier. His strategy is how he does it..."

"Playing games... Mr. Most used this method as his strategy, part of his objectives that lead to his mission."

"Mr. **M...O... S...T.... mission, objectives, strategy, and tactics**.... From the simple purpose to the specific action. Tactics are the details of what he did."

J'me was caught up in this. "What were his tactics?"

"He was simple, generic, so only speaking in general terms... He lost every game!"

J'me shared something she learned on her own. "When I first started to learn to levitate, I felt tired afterwards... as if I had exercised. After resting, I would practice again, each time getting stronger. **Eventually you can run without being weary.**"

The young girls understood. From then on they were more careful and controlled themselves... and they grew stronger. **"Balance work with play and rest.**"

J'me wanted to see how Ease, Rose, and Zen had adapted. Her mothering mind was curious. How did the girls fit in? Did they stay independent or become interdependent? Had they proven themselves? Their lives were changing.

Cube H was the "Health Building". It was easy to find the triplets. She followed the braids... Apparently, her daughters had made many friends. Braids became popular. When she entered the infirmary, she found herself surrounded.

There was one hand that pulled her out of the crowd. He had masculine features and a feminine demeanor. "Momma eXquisite!" he shrieked as he flamboyantly waved his other hand to scatter the crowd. "Come with me, please." He pulled her out of the reception area of the infirmary.

Next she met a curvy girl who gave her a cushioned hug and kissed her cheeks. The girl was packing plenty of comfort with a shapely, full figure. "Momma eXquisite." She smiled a beautiful smile. "Come with us, please."

She was escorted right, left, right... into a room where sat the older Asian woman she had previously dined beside. She approached J'me, smiled a wide grin that seemed to make her eyes close, and then rubbed the back of her hand. Moments later, Ease, Rose, and Zen entered the room, in that order.

Chapter 38
Love Pranks

J'me continued her introductions to her daughters' medical team. "Mx. eXquisite, I am Ota Menté. (pronounced Oh-tah Men-tay) a name easy to forget." (Remember her name using strong vowel sounds that match the roundness of her body.)

"Ota is like us, but her powers are not yet developed." explained Zen.

In a manly voice, "Don't forget me! I'm Patrich." With that he cupped his palms together at his chest and gave a head bow.

"Patrich has many talents. He is here because he is not sure what to pursue. He keeps us straight and organized." This was explained by Rose.

Ease spoke next. "And you met Chi Nü (or Zhinu) before. She is ancient, but lovely and likes to assist Auntie." Chi Nü, sometimes called "The Jade Princess" by Juan Li, held J'me's hand and rubbed it.

"We are the attendants!" said Patrich, with an effeminate flair. (Was Patrich gay, or just acting that way?)

"No, do not say that! We are a team!" softly scolded J'me's girls.

"Ease, Rose, and Zen... then Patrich, Chi Nü, and uh, uhm, Ola, uh... It's... Ota Menté ... got it." smiled J'me.

"Why don't you have braided hair?" asked J'me, half-jokingly.

Patrich flipped his hair back, "I have done just about everything!"

Ease and Rose said, "We got to pick our own attendants... We did not choose them because of their differences. Then Zen followed, "**We chose them because of what we have in common...** Each is full of compassion!"

The group chatted and joked. J'me felt herself being pulled in, like arms embracing her and comforting her mood.

You could both see and feel the unity of the six as a team.

- As one, you have the strength of one...
- As two, ... three...
- As three... five...
- As four... seven...
- As five, you have the strength of nine... (Another Dr. Klug math equation.) Thus unified, a team of six equals 11 individuals! "Team power!"

The older woman, Chi Nü excused herself as the others moved from the hallway to a small sitting room. Moments later, she returned with Juan Li (Auntie Juan), Kung Tau Fu Z (Fuzzy), and refreshments.

There were a few things going on at the same time. First, Chi Nü made a brew especially for J'me. It had an earthy taste like a strong tea... But there were other flavors present. After a few swallows, she felt a pleasing peppery zing that moved upward to her head. This made her face feel warm. She noted a bit of carbonation during her second cup. This made her chest and stomach calm down. The fruity aftertaste was noticed later. This made her hips and groin tingle.

The third cup...   There was a dash of some unknown flavor that loosened up her joints – she felt it first in her neck and shoulders, then down to her ankles and toes. Perhaps there was a hallucinating affect? She fantasized finishing the fourth or fifth cup? J'me was practical joked drugged by Chi Nü.

From J'me's perspective, the next thing she noticed was that it seemed like Auntie Juan was always eating. She made mention of this... It became a topic starter for a lesson.

Auntie Juan explained, **"Our body is energy.** This energy is called Chi, Qi, Ki, or Prana...." She paused, thinking. "Chi is a balance of Yin and Yang (male and female, positive and negative), which flows through everything..." J'me understood.

"This energy circulates through our body and gives us life..." She made circular motions tracing many pathways within her body and along Ota Menté. **"We replenish our xi energy by breathing, sleeping, and eating... primarily."** This time Juan Li stopped to rub Ota's lucky belly.

She concluded, "I must always try to keep my energy moving... **The amount I eat is equal to the amount I use."**

J'me was able to reach beyond her five senses... She could feel the mood and feelings of everybody... She knew their intentions by enhanced communications. This was the power of the elixir taking effect.

A tap then J'me could not move! But her eyes sparkled, giving hint to her inward laughing. Kung Tau Fu Z played a paralysis prank on J'me before leaving.

Ota Menté came forward and explained, **"When you block or slow down the movement of energy, you create disorder."** Wrapping her arms around J'me, she gently tapped her back to normal. J'me stood erect. **"You must release your energy, use it, not keep it inside you.** Too much energy stored for your body to process causes fatigue."

Chapter 39
Energy Arts

The power of the elixir took full effect... Her feelings were aligned with her physical body. J'me felt a release of compression from within. She was balanced.

The room immediately went silent. Everybody was receiving an intuition.

"We must go!" they said and quickly departed.

J'me looked around the cluttered room and started cleaning.

When everything was tidy, she felt the urge to explore. She was going to see what was on the upper levels of Cube H.

J'me loved new things. On the second and third floors were semi-private rooms around the outside perimeter filled with various pieces of medical machinery. In the center were empty beds. There were no patients... maybe these were replacements?

The fourth floor looked like a research laboratory. It was a mixture of old and new equipment. J'me was not sure of its purpose but was fascinated by the details.

The fifth floor was in the process of renovation. Perhaps it was once a cafeteria but was being converted to a recovery area. Beds raised above the floor had soft mattresses for comfort. This was a great place to rest.

In a dream state, half numb, out of nowhere, J'me heard, "Your body is a BLOCK. **Prepare, care, and repair your body and your brain as you would a building…"**

"Next floor, you will see the building of healthy minds."

J'me pulled her invisibility cloak over herself. She did not want to disturb the concentration of others.

These floors were filled with artists, creatives. These people seemed more obsessed with transferring what was in their mind into something tangible.

One… two… three floors were crowded with various types of projects, ranging from music to masonry. She was enchanted by some of the works. They made her think.

The top floors were the C^3 sections of health Cube H. The Cleansing and Creation Center was organized almost opposite of the one she was most familiar with, the center that J'me and Tio Juan enjoyed. For example, men and women were separated at the door. J'me was taken aside to private rooms, disrobed, and then given a soapy shower, scrubbed, then rinsed.

Next was an interactive massage and yoga with meditation. J'me unleashed her core chakras, spiraling energy disks that ran through the center of her body. **She learned to balance herself. Each energy center was unblocked and J'me felt spirited.**

She was laid face down on a padded table while one attendant brushed her hair and tied it back. She began to relax, drifting away... J'me felt well-oiled hands slide across her skin with pleasing pressure. Her mind wandered from music to memories, then calmed.

They log rolled J'me onto her back, face up, and began to cover her with more penetrating oils. The massage did not miss any spots and focused on more tender, erogenous areas. **Her tensions drifted away. She decided to go with the flow.**

Afterwards she was escorted to a corridor with other women. She moved slowly while others passed her in a rush. Then J'me entered the very large lounge area. The open room was divided, men on one side, women on the other... in the center was a shared area to mingle. Being oiled during the massage, people were playing on the floor... Playing not as children, but as adults giving and receiving physical pleasure. J'me saw this as visual artistry.

There was a young Giant moving towards her, making his way to the center of the room. They approached each other and lovingly embraced.

J'me released her love juices... and it felt good.

He whispered in her ear, "J'me, remember me? I am Archibald R."

Suddenly Auntie pinched the nape of J'me's neck... She raised her head up to notice everybody was still in the room. They had thrown a weighted blanket over her while she slept.

To be openly honest: A pearl is not just a calcium carbonate crystal, it is nature's living gemstone. It does not come from the depths of the earth, but from the bottom of the sea. It is a hard object produced from the soft tissues and the juices excreted by a living mollusk.

J'me had a powerful translation pearl, a perfect conduit for vibrations. It worked at a deeper energy level by rushing feelings to the touch.

Anything bigger could be brutal. Too hazardous to handle... Masters of the Energy Arts knew its strength. **Energy can be released at different weights and in different ways.**

QUIZ

III

Quiz Three

Test your understanding of what you read. Pick the *best* answer for the following ten questions. After completing all ten questions, check your answers on the next page.

If you score a 70% or above (answer seven or more questions correctly) you may proceed to the following chapters. However, if you score below 70%, read the previous chapters again.

Please take your time reading and meditating to unlock the next chapters.

1. When the little boy touched Mr. G's hand outside the BLOCK, the boy...

    a. Grew stronger and taller
    b. Became smarter
    c. Got hungry
    d. All of the above

2. The cleansing therapy, also called the Phoenix Ritual, recharged people through...

   a. Acupuncture
   b. Body scraping
   c. Cupping
   d. Massage

3. Who was stalking J'me through the BLOCK?
   a. Frija-Frig G and Archibald R
   b. The eXquisite Sisters (Ease, Rose, Zen)
   c. Dr3 (E. Lyja, Nick, M. Klug)
   d. Attendants3 (Patrich, Ota Menté, Chi Nü)

4. Besides laugh, play, dance and sing, what else did the Giants do?
   a. Washed their own clothes
   b. Cared for, educated, trained their children
   c. Opened the Southwest wall of Sublevel Three
   d. All the above

5. Communications was felt through...
   a. Vibes or vibrations
   b. Resonating feelings, harmonies
   c. Feelings from within, intuition
   d. All of the above

6. Who has healing powers?
   a. Auntie Juan Li (Li Juan)
   b. Ota Menté, but not Patrich
   c. The eXquisite Sisters
   d. Everybody has healing powers

7. At this point, what best describes J'me's view on "No Rules" in the BLOCK?

   a. Excitement from adventurous choices

    b.   Guided by intuition

    c.   Happiness from working

    d.   Comfort in tradition, routine

8. When working as a team, your productivity grows. A team of seven has the potential power of ___ individuals.

    a.   13

    b.   17

    c.   22

    d.   70

9. Which is not related with the energy that flows through our bodies?

    a.   Chi or Xi

    b.   Waterfalls

    c.   Yin and Yang

    d.   Chakra

10. Who had sex with J'me?

    a.   Nobody talks about it, **NADK** (no answer, don't know)

    b.   Tio Juan and Melvin Klug

    c.   Archibald R

    d.   Nobody, she is a virgin

Q3 – Answers

1.   Nowadays we rush our child to the Doctor after a growth spurt. Maybe he has a disease? Rest assured, he is fine. Answer: D. All of the above.

2.   The answer is B: Body Scraping, otherwise known as "gua sha". This treatment removes toxins, increases blood flow, and re-energizes the body to fight off sickness. It is more extreme than acupuncture. This has become popular as a remedy for drug addiction.

3.   B. The eXquisiteSisters. But their names have evolved... Freeze, Fleas, Ease (eventually Alice); Froze, Flows, then Rose; and Frozen then Zen (eventually Jen).

4.   The Giants came from a "closed community", so they preferred to do their own cleaning and child care. Even when they broke the wall in Sublevel Three, they chose to fix it. Answer: D. All the above.

5.   Has there been a time in your life that you sensed something? You got a certain vibe, or felt something? Maybe an intuition of some sort? This is real. Answer D: All of the above. Although this was common inside the BLOCK, you can train yourself to be more receptive to this communication.

6.   You have an immune system as part of the standard package when you got your body. (Most admit this was a natural add-on that came with their bodies.) Answer D: Everybody has healing powers. Now, if you want to upgrade to a healer, it is difficult to learn. Be careful what you wish for... After a healing session, you will feel completely exhausted!

7.   At this point, J'me enjoys the excitement of adventure and learning new things. Answer A. As with everybody in the BLOCK, work provides a feeling of happiness. J'me has only a few routines, but mixes those with activities she enjoys with others. She is just now learning to tap into her intuition... but she will get better?

The equation is:

    2 people = (2 people + 1 person) = 3
    3 people = (3 people + 2 people) = 4
    4 people = (4 people + 3 people) = 7
    5 people = (5 people + 4 people) = 9
    6 people = (6 people + 5 people) = 11
    7 people = (7 people + 6 people) = 13... the answer is A: 13

8.   This is due to **the "division and specialization of labor" that takes advantage of each other's skills and abilities.**

9.   Answer B: Waterfalls. Although you can argue that waterfalls are a great source of energy, they are exterior, not interior. But think about it. Rain falls and water seeks its lowest level. The movement of water is nature's renewable energy source.

10. Sex is one of the basic needs of man and therefore not taboo. But you are curious about it nonetheless. Sexual intimacy is the highest form of showing physical love. But in this case, we do not know because nobody talked about it, Answer A.

Chapter 40
20/20 Acuity

Everybody has 20/20 hindsight into the past. Nobody has 20/20, perfect vision into the future. Therefore, see what is happening now.

The BLOCK was easily ignored for a century. The world experienced so many changes. People became more and more focused on themselves, or things in their control. The outside world never noticed buildings without doors, windows, signs or artwork attached. **People couldn't have cared less...**

Things change... The original plan changed for the hub and all its supporting pieces. It was hard to ignore the factories producing superior goods. Those were the first to be absorbed into the outside world. The mines and farms were remote and hidden, but they too were also claimed. The same was the case for the massive storage and distribution centers located globally. In each case, one entity, St. Wx, now controlled most of the original operations.

St. Wx defined itself as a religious organization, therefore non-taxable, non-profit, and non-disclosure. It was very close knit and tightly managed. It was a religion that did not reach out. It never needed to publish or promote... it kept itself private. If you search for information about St. Wx, as many people have, you would eventually give up.

Although the value cannot be proven, some claim St. Wx is wealthier than entire countries. During a time when money meant more than anything, St. Wx had the funds to do anything it wanted.

Although things changed... The BLOCK still had adequate support for its limited needs. Daily, large white trucks continued to enter from the East and exit Sublevel One out the West.

It was a beautiful Sunday morning! The streets were empty. As they drove towards the BLOCK, they could see two large white trucks in the distance. Then they vanished. (Actually, they dropped down the East Ramp DH into the Sublevel of the BLOCK).

"Wow! Did you see that? Those trucks disappeared like magic!" said the grandson.

"We must be getting close to the BLOCK... Maybe we will find the guide again." said the grandfather, squinting his eyes.

They drove a circular tour around the perimeter of the BLOCK (north, west, south, east; in a counterclockwise direction). As they turned the corner of Cube E they headed directly into the rising sun. They pulled over and parked the car.

When they emerged, the energy level changed immediately. A man approached with rays of light and radiance.

"Good morning! The sun is a bit bright... Let's walk." said the guide as he met and moved the two so they had their backs to the sun.

The guide continued his dialogue. "The original BLOCK was a larger grid... many cubes... with letters representing each structure."

"Things do not stay constant, forever in motion. It grew... it changed... it is living."

The two visitors were speechless and felt overwhelmed.

"Our newest addition is a cathedral where Cubes I, J, M, and N used to sit in the southwest corner of our BLOCK."

Then the guide stopped walking as they stood in front of two huge doors (or gates). The building was the size of four cubes without space between them. It was massive!

"This was where the bubbles came from..." they reasoned aloud. **"Seek, knock, and it shall open."**

"Constructed from the materials we were able to salvage from the original Cubes, this building was excavated using bubble mining... from the bottom up." The large doors then opened and the three stepped inside.

A spray of lights, millions of stretching slivers invited them. The brightest of lights froze them. Sensory surplus... Everything rushed to their attention. Stimulus overload...

The large doors automatically closed behind them.

Peaceful... It was a time when confusion gave way to clarity... It was like warmth when you are cold. Distant and removed, the two now felt enveloped in love. They were not alone... With each breath they calmed themselves.

"Born again!" They walked to the center of the empty tower. "In order to be new, the old must die."

"Cathedral IJMN," said the old man. "In J's mighty name... we are blessed."

Chapter 41
The King Returns

J'me was awake! She had a special glow about her. She felt alive with energy. She was always cheerful, but it seemed her smile was brighter than before. A small change... an improvement. **Eventually, after many small improvements, comes something enormous.**

While her three daughters were getting dressed for the Giants' party, J'me went to grab a quick meal. She was already wearing her three scarves, overlapping blue paneled dress, ribbons, high heels, purse, and, (of course) her hair was braided.

She entered the new dining hall in her building (Cube F). Its claim to fame was its coffee. Once a hobby of a chemist working in Cube C, this coffee was individually tailored to each person's taste preferences. After the third visit, he would have blended the perfect cup of coffee just for you. The food was delicious also.

This time she noticed somebody new, sitting alone. He had a stoic expression on his face. As she approached him, he continued to gaze forward, focusing at a distance.

"Hello." J'me said with a smile. But the newcomer did not respond.

"First time here? I recommend the coffee." J'me added politely. He then looked at her.

"May I sit with you?" asked J'me. This time the man gestured to the open seat across from him.

"My name is J'me eXquisite. What is yours?" she asked as she sat herself at the table.

"I was the CEO/COO..." muttered the man.

"Key-Oh-Coo?" (sounding Japanese).

"What work do you do?" asked the stranger.

J'me hesitated. It seemed like an odd question... then answered, "I clean this building."

A uniformed waitress slid a strudel and a cup of Café Vienne (with extra cream) to the man and a shot of Cuban Expresso and a large Jamaican Blue Mountain with a squeeze of cane juice to J'me.

The two stared into each other's' eyes. Neither blinked. Then a slight upturn of the corner of their lips... Then full smiles followed by laughter. They slid their cups around and said simultaneously, "I think you have my order."

"I am meeting my daughters, Mr. Key-Oh-Coo, after this. The Giants are having a party. Would you like to join us?"

"No..." responded the gentleman. "My name is Snowden White.

"Like Snow White and the little people?" J'me mused.

His lip curled as he breathed in the aroma of his Jamaican coffee, and then took a slurp.

J'me and her daughters reached the entrance to Sublevel Three at the same time. They glanced at each other and noticed they looked beautiful in the traditional ribbons and skirts of the Giants. They were ready to play.

However, after taking a few steps into the cavern, they froze in place, overcome by cheer-fullness... A surplus of joy! Everything rushed to their attention. Momentary overload... Things were vastly different from the last time they had been here. Delight – full.

The dancers had already begun to make their flower show. The spinning and twirling of the dresses were in full bloom. They felt a breeze.

J'me was teaching her daughters **the art of "working a room."** First, the four walked the perimeter of the room in a clockwise direction. They just gave quick smiles, waves, or hugs to the people they met. They only stopped to pick up a beverage. The second lap was more casual, and they often stopped to talk, reminisce, and tell jokes. Just as each person is different, each person had a special memory of the Giants. Their spirits gave new life to those in the BLOCK.

Once a vacant space, made into a playground by the Giants, renovated, and was now an impressive hall for the people of the BLOCK – Sublevel Three. But to J'me, **people were more important than the place.**

From behind her, she heard her name being called, "J'me! It was Frija and Archibald R. They exchanged hugs, but it seemed like longer embraces than usual for J'me. A difficult moment followed.

"Our work here is done... It is time we leave." It took a moment for this to settle in. "Archibald R must lead his people." sadly said Frija.

Not everything is bad, not everything is good. True, it is sad that her forever friends were leaving her – that is bad. But they were going to their home – that is good. J'me will not have to clean up after the Giants are gone – that is good also. But J'me will be alone in the Cube – that is bad. **What's bad is good and what's good is bad.**

Chapter 42
The Ultimate Answer

J'me was in a deep sleep... **Extra sleep was her cure.**

The girls quietly left for breakfast and the clinic. J'me awoke slowly, put back on her traditional dress and a smile, and then walked down to the Sublevel One's departure area. When she arrived, the last Giant had already departed. A feeling of separation... **Eventually, after many small sorrows, comes change from within.**

The air felt cooler on the docks. J'me sat comfortably alone, thinking, before going back to Cube F.

Without thought, J'me wandered the empty floors that once were the home of her Giant friends. She was now alone... she saw nobody. She continued her dazed white walk.

Eventually she reached the new dining hall. It too was empty except for Key-Oh-Coo.

"Hello." J'me said, as she sat to the right of the newcomer. He continued to stare ahead... Moments later he turned his head and slightly smiled in response. Then he continued to face forward. His coffee was already served; he took in a large slurp, and then swallowed.

J'me looked around the vacant room, not sure what to do next. She moved herself directly across from him at the table to watch his face. J'me waited patiently.

Her coffee was served. Today it seemed more bitter. J'me calmly sat while enjoying the small nuances in flavor. Her brain fog began to clear when she had almost finished her first cup.

The man faced J'me with his eyes focused far away. It seemed she could not make out his eye color... The light affected his eyes making their normally black irises become... orange, red, green, and blue rainbow auras.

J'me said the words, "How are you?" but felt the words, **"I love you."**

She was at peace. She knew he was thinking, converting. His mind was moving. J'me said, "They say, there is no such thing as a pink sun." (This was a roundabout way of explaining Tio Juan's color code because the sun is bright red, orange, yellow, or white.) "Red is reacting... Orange is ready... Read what is happening around you is yellow, and ... White is your head is in the clouds."

"Your mind sometimes meanders on the meaningless." Snowden White finally broke his silence by mumbling. **"If you are not cutting the tree, you should be sharpening the saw."** (Do not waste time.) His intent was to give helpful advice. J'me listened empathically and understood him.

A stack of pancakes with syrup cascading over the edges was delivered to J'me. She began to eat straightaway.

This time he was watching J'me as she ate and was deep in thought, listening to his inner voice. He contemplated out loud, **"Optimize every moment. Strive, drive, and push for maximal efficiency! There is always improvement."**

A cold glass of milk was then served and she enjoyed its creamy taste. Both then smiled.

She could not finish the stack of pancakes and noticed an extra fork was given to Snowden. He helped her finish, leaving nothing to waste.

They spoke at the pace of a slow golf game on a bad weather day. They bogeyed the first hole. Not too bad since it was a long par 4. On to the next tee.

"Can you get paper and a pen?" Snowden asked.

J'me was bewildered by this question, but then understood that Key-Oh-Coo was recently from the outside world. He was adjusting to life in the BLOCK. He had not yet "synced".

"Sure Key-Oh-Coo. Why?" asked J'me.

"If you wish to learn about the outside world, **you must mind your business.** You will need a guru." The newcomer had finally connected. She was pleased at the progress. She made a new friend, uhm, guru.

J'me wished for paper and pen. Then she waited... One waitress cleared the dishes as another wiped the table clean. A third arrived with paper and pen.

Next was the question, "What is money?" was written on the paper for J'me to see. She didn't know how to respond, so he wrote, "God is money." J'me looked perplexed and then took the pen and wrote, "God is love." Just as quickly, Snowden said, "Ok... Ok."

Snowden thought deeply. Either thinking out loud or talking to himself he said, "In the outside world **people love money... But money has no feelings.**"

Snowden White wished...

Angel Number 42 heard and responded positively with resonating energy. The 42nd Angel **blessed them BOTH with a nurturing approach that was ideal yet practical.**

Chapter 43
Coffee, Classes, and Commandos

J'me believed she knew the basics of life outside the BLOCK. Tio Juan taught her many things, plus she had heard the stories from the people who had ventured out.

However, the religion of business, huh? **Income should exceed expenses** was something easy for her to understand. Some things took a leap of faith. For example, buy something for seven, sell it for ten, and you profit three. Why?

The hush of time was a secret for J'me to fully understand. Earning money generally took time and effort. There was often a boss to measure and manage your time. Crazy!

 Most of the people became slaves to their jobs. They worked to get money... so they could spend the money...

Without money, people did not have food or homes. Beyond this level, people worked to have more comfortable lives. **"Man has limited needs but unlimited wants."** The enigma, according to Key-Oh-Coo was, **"Time is money and money is time." A slave to money, a slave to time?**

Key-Oh-Coo had been around the BLOCK before. He was one of the first to reside in the BLOCK before construction was completed.

Back then, people did not know his name and didn't even call him Mister. Now he did not want to be noticed.

He continued to stare ahead, his face withdrawn, in a white void. The rainbow auras of his eyes continually changed, affected by the light in the room. His mind had been multi-tasking since he arrived. Sometimes he would scribble something he thought was important on papers.

Key-Oh-Coo had not yet connected... He preferred to be alone but found himself enjoying the friendship from J'me. Everything was free inside the BLOCK. This made it hard for him to adapt, to crack the shell he created.

They say **time heals all wounds**, yet there was no concept of time inside the BLOCK. Time was only relative.

'Quick and efficient. A different method for learning: **Lecture, Listen, and Learn**. The coffee shop classroom was perfect.

They sat at Café F, or "Café Jefe", the Spanish description for Boss's Cafe. Key-Oh-Coo and J'me were intense in studies. During the momentary lulls, J'me pondered what she had learned. During one of these silences, something hastily happened!

A man entered the doorway and moved to the right, "Despajado." Another man entered and moved to the left, "Despajado." Rapidly, a third man came in, moving the first entrant to the next corner, "Despajado", "Despajado". Before you could count them, one— two— three— four... there were seven men anchored around the room's perimeter with their backs to the walls. "Libre!"

Key-Oh-Coo immediately recognized it as a military maneuver, **clearing the room**. He ducked under the table.

This took J'me by surprise; she blurted loudly, "Pan dulce y chocolate caliente!"

J'me next heard her daughters entering the room, slowly and rhythmically chanting. "Respira... aspira... respira... aspira..." The men's rigid stances relaxed. They were then invited to sit at a table using a hand gesture.

"Momma!" The three girls gave J'me hugs and cheek kisses before sitting down next to her. They had missed her deeply.

A tray of sweet breads and cups of hot chocolate, with a hint of cinnamon, were soon served. The seven men sat like automatons around the table, still on duty.

"These men came to our clinic from outside. We mended many wounds." shared Ease.

"They speak Spanish. The call themselves (mimicking a deep voice full of pride), "Los Guerroros Águilas!" said Rose.

J'me added, "Eagles. The Eagle Warriors?"

"They have come to see Tio." said Zen. With that the girls went to the table to swipe a sweet bread and chocolate drink. The men then started eating and Key-Oh-Coo crawled out from under the table.

Using a golf analogy, you just scored a snowman, eight strokes on a difficult hole.

TAKE your time... Take YOUR time. (Perhaps look back at Chapter Two now and reread it? Movements are 10% slower with the feeling of vibrations and pureness. Feel a deeper penetration.) Remember the BLOCK was a different atmosphere. Over time it is normal to become desensitized.

Adjust...

Adapt...

Attach...

Chapter 44
Fairy Number 44

Imagine a fourth dimension. One we cannot see. The fourth dimension is not time, it is a non-physical force. At this time, it is trying to get your attention. Try to sense it.

This was the most people J'me had seen in Café F. She almost forgot this former feeling of comfort as her daughters snuggled closely beside her.

"Momma, you work too much."

"All work and no play makes you Melvin." they said, laughing.

"Work, work, work." The way she said that evoked laughter even out of Key-Oh-Coo.

J'me defended herself, **"But I enjoy this change. I am learning new things.** Have you met Key-Oh-Coo?"

Snowden White stood and shook hands with the girls. He was smiling and very friendly. This was a change from his brooding self J'me had become accustomed to.

"Oh... speaking of work... Can you take these men to see Tio for us please?" The girls asked of J'me, pointing to the seven indigenous men carrying long blades. "We want to return to the clinic."

"Guaranteed, go ahead." replied J'me, pleased.

As her daughters departed, they left her with **"Have some fun!** Take them to C³. Plus, that is usually where you will find Tio Juan."

J'me felt a tiny finger tickling her back. She turned around and noticed a little lady with wings. Making her more unique was her sparkle, a spectral sensation (like a rainbow). J'me leaned forward but decided to levitate her to the table. This made the woman smile brightly.

Everybody in the room took notice. "Hello, my name is J'me eXquisite, this is Snowden White, and my new friends over there are..." she stopped herself.

The tiny tinkling woman spoke in a soft squeaky voice into J'me's ear.

"Oh, your name is фея (pronounced "Feya" in Russian).

The fairy queen shook her head yes as the Spanish speaking warriors shook their heads no.

"¡No fea! Ella es una hermosa hada." They shouted, "Not ugly; she is a beautiful fairy!" in Spanish. "¡No fea!"

Fairy Feya unlocked the urges in the room. The comatose Key-Oh-Coo was no longer glaring at the walls, the soldiers felt vibrant, and J'me felt something stir inside her. Everything was made magical by the glittered fairy with rainbows flowing from her. She turned to the haplogroup QM3 Y-DNA men, cupped her hands together, and blew. It looked like spirals of stars cascading across the room and falling on the men with square heads, round faces, and ear to ear smiles... "¡Jaaa! Ahora entiendo." They soothingly understood. It was as if a looming question had been answered and their paths ahead foretold.

Immediately, the men stood up in unison and headed towards J'me. "Orale" (an expression meaning to go in a hurry, in a positive tone). With that, J'me took them to see Tio Juan in the Cleansing and Creativity Center.

The men were hesitant to give up their blades, but disrobed without reluctance. When they made eye contact with Juan in the pool, they tilted their heads down in respect. It was not until Juan reached out that the men moved closer to touch the first few pads of their fingers with his. This seemed most earnest with the head nod. They were old friends reunited. Square heads, round faces, and ear to ear smiles... It was a heartwarming moment.

J'me started to feel "normal" again. She had not realized the toll her trade training had taken on her. It was true what Key-Oh-Coo said, **"Everything has a price."** Her daughters' prescription "Have fun!" was the remedy. Or perhaps a reimbursement? She had distracted herself from **something more important, love.**

Now she was submerged in the comfortable water, surrounded by positive sensations. **She forgot what she had forgotten.** J'me was exchanging smiles again.

A flutter of feelings... This is how it began. Like the ripples from the moving water, she knew something was going to happen. J'me stood as the waves seemed to push her over like a tsunami. Lightening had hit the water! The epicenter or strike point was... wait... it was Juan. As if the sun's energy was turned on like a switch, Juan emitted a great amount of spiritual energy!

As with everybody, J'me moved closer. She had a strong desire to have Juan submerge her underwater and purify her, to cleanse her and make her new again. Moments later, it happened. Deep breath in.... Tio Juan tilted J'me backwards under the water and when she arose, **she saw the light. She was pure.**

Chapter 45
Magic Number 45

- Add $1, plus $2, plus $3... all the way up to $9. (1+2+3+4+5+6+7+8+9 = 45). You get the sum of $45. Remember it goes both ways. Add to $9 another $8, then $7... down to $1 and you get $45!

- Subtract $123,456,789 from the larger number $987,654,321... and you get a set of numbers that add up to 45 ($864,197,532 converts to 8+6+4+1+9+7+5+3+2 = 45)

- The magic cube is a box with nine squares, three by three. Take 45; divide it into equal parts so the perimeter equals the sum of 15. Each row and each column adds up to 15...Now you made the magic cube!

2	9	4	15
7	5	3	15
6	1	8	15
15	15	15	45

By the time J'me returned to Café F, it was empty. When she entered, the magical Fairy Feya fluttered past her. No Key-Oh-Coo... However, she noticed things were left for her on the table where she habitually sat.

Seven identical sapphires were lying next to a blank book. What made these heart-shaped gems rare were their bright blue color, saturated evenly throughout, and their size (all seven stones, when adjusted properly, were just the right size to fit in both hands). They appeared to glow when touched. She carefully placed the sapphires into her purse and paused before reaching for the book.

When J'me opened the pages, they were blank. Except for the first page which had her handwritten note: **"God is love."**

Then it struck her... Like the mysterious marble Melvin Klug gave J'me to communicate, the book was enchanted similarly. J'me had wished she knew everything that Key-Oh-Coo knew about business, both the science and the art. All his knowledge and experience... All was transmitted from the book. She held it close to her because she knew Key-Oh-Coo was gone. Then she absorbed the contents of the book inside her. **Everything made cents.**

Many years ago, a stranger traveled to uncharted lands to explore. During the heat of the summer he ventured into an immense stone city. The people there were in awe of his appearance. They knelt before him.

"Get up, get up." he said, waving to the cowering crowd. "Do not be afraid."

As he walked, people reached out to touch him. This was done partially out of curiosity, but also to get good luck. Beautiful smiles overtook the people. Happiness, joy, tranquility, peace, and love were combined into one sensation. This feeling amplified.

The stranger was escorted to the leader of the vast city, Raja Paintaalees. Here the wanderer was given a regal welcome, befitting of a Lord. "What do you desire? Ask for anything! I will do as you wish." said the Raja in all earnestness.

"May I have water to drink?" was the reply. Astonished, a soft gasp escaped from the mass assembled.

"No, you don't understand." replied the Raja. "You can have ANYTHING! If it is possible, I would pull the sun from the sky for you."

Equally astonished, the traveler just said, "Water please."

The stone walls of the palace created a contrasting coolness from the heat outside. The stranger sat on the floor with his back against the wall, relaxed, and sipped his fresh water quietly.

An elderly woman approached him. She was worn thin. "Please come with me to rest."

How bold? Offering a cottage when a castle could be had? The man accepted the offer and thanked Raja Paintaalees for his gracious hospitality.

The elderly woman and the man walked slowly, turning down one street and up another, away from the city center. The crowds that had amassed were thinning. Eventually, it was just he and the elderly woman on the outskirts of town.

She pointed to her home without a door, "Your house."

Inside was only a small cooking area, a hammock, and handmade containers lining the walls. Not a single table or chair was seen. The man noticed the woman was weak from the journey and begged her to lie down.

She was submissive and immediately wrapped herself in the webbed hammock. "I have been waiting for you." she said, before falling quickly asleep.

This story does not end here. In 2010, India renamed their highways. All east-west oriented highways have odd numbers increasing from the north to the south.

They say from June to mid-July you may see an elderly woman walking Highway 45 in the Tamil Nadu Province. Sometimes she walks alone, but if you are lucky you may see her walking with a man.

Chapter 46
Beyond the Chromosomes

The wanderer reclined against a soft wall of satchels. He, too, was resting. Moments later, a man rushed through the doorway. He was covered in dirt; his hands were caked in mud. "Who are you?" he asked in a strong voice.

The traveler put one hand to his mouth and used the other to point at the old woman asleep in the hammock.

The man's eyes caught sight of the woman and then waved to the traveler to step outside. He took the stranger to the shaded side of the shack. Then he stood in awe, just as the villagers had done earlier.

"Namaste, do you know who she is?" asked the man covered in dirt. "She is the Mother of All, Sabhee Kee Maan... Hamaaree Maan... our Mother." He was thinking deeply, trying to find another way to explain. Then he said, "She was the first person to live here... everybody is a descendent of Mother."

The stranger responded with neither an expression of surprise nor disbelief.

"Yesterday she asked me to dig up her heart stones. They were buried beneath a large tree." With this he pulled out clumps of mud from his bag. "I have them here." labored the man to speak, referring to the dirt clusters.

The worker then noticed his soiled appearance, "While she rests, we should clean ourselves for Mother."

The two became friends as they cleaned their clothes and then soaped up themselves while swimming. Then they sat under a tree on the bank. Their clothes were stretched over dark rocks nearby to dry.

"My clothes are white." Laughing, he continued, "I was in a hurry. I ran to the other side of the forest, cut down the tree, split the wood into pieces, dug up the stones, dropped some seeds, filled the hole, stacked the wood, and ran back."

The stranger asked, "Aren't you tired?"

"No!" he said, proud of his answer, "I did this for Mother."

As the cleaned men approached the simple shelter, they smelled something delicious. They became hungry. Inside, the men saw a large variety of foods prepared and... Sabhee Kee Maan... Hamaaree Maan... looked younger! Sleep had done wonders.

The Master of Mothers blessed the food, "Men, sit and eat. May the food give you good health."

Before they began eating, the laborer chanted a mantra. The traveler added, "The love from the cook gives flavor to the food."

They all agreed, amen, but the stranger noticed that the cook was not eating. "Sit down and share food with us."

She blushed and smiled, "You eat. I am fine." The now spry woman poured the men cool fruit water and restocked their bowls with more food. Next, hot earthen bread covered in a cloth was served. Finally, Mother filled her bowl, then sat on the floor to eat with them. This made her happy.

The worker did not intend to be impolite, but there was still food in his mouth when he said, "Hamaaree Maan, I brought the stones you asked for."

With this he pulled out seven heart shaped crystals, blue sapphires, from his pocket. They were clean, shiny and polished. As the sapphires neared the older woman, and passed before the traveler, they began to glow. She just took them in her hand and reached behind her, dropping them into the pocket of a travel bag.

"Thank you, my son." She leaned forward to touch the cheek of the man who was now bubbling with pleasure.

In the morning, the old woman arose... She looked lively, as if she was younger still. The worker was still asleep on the floor. The stranger watched as she gently laid the sapphires on the sleeping soul. The stones changed colors!

Mother explained that she was awakening his chakras: "Red is the root chakra, orange is the sacral chakra, yellow is the navel chakra, green is the heart chakra, light blue is the throat chakra, and indigo is the third eye."

The stranger watched and listened intently, then hesitated. "You have one more stone."

The woman laughed, "It is an extra." Then Mother placed the last stone on the top of his head, "The violet crown chakra is for wisdom."

The worker was still in a deep sleep on the floor when Mother picked up each stone from his seven chakras. Then she placed the now radiant sapphires into one of the bags she had loaded on herself. She no longer was a frail, old woman.

"**Do the needful.**" she said to the stranger, who picked up his pack and chased behind her.

Chapter 47
Friends, Family, Fun

Cube F was filling up with color. They were beautiful people. Everybody was an individual with the most diverse dyes of clothing. The variety of cheerful color combinations was beyond description. Remember, inside the BLOCK clothing was worn as an outward expression.

Individually they were creative, but collectively they were art. She had more than enough help to keep the Cube tidy. J'me and her three daughters connected quickly. **"You can never have too many friends."**

They all had something in common, their darker skin shade. (This was not a form of segregation at Cube F; they chose to be together.)

The feeling was beyond friendship, they were like a family. **The love from "family" never goes away.** When you are with family you feel the oneness, the wholeness. You feel secure. Even in errs, disappointment does not diminish love.

There are some times when the family gathers together to settle issues regarding life's consequences. But then when you are with your family, all of you stay together and talk together. Because you are one, you believe in one another, no matter the size of the situation. Everyone adds creativity to the question resulting in the right solution. At the end, there is happiness and contentment because they are with you.

Cooing: **"Oh, just a hug or a kiss makes you feel exalted!"**

They served each other, getting a warm feeling from service. Unselfishly, this gave them deeper happiness. **"If you are happy, I am happy."** There was a fulfillment from feeling useful, gratifying and grateful. Both the giver and the receiver were thankful, again and again, and again. It lingered.

There was an empathy, sympathy, and compassion connection that became a considerate cycle. Meaning, the more you gave the more you were given. It was an exponential explosion of caring. This evolved into people anticipating your needs and wishes without question. The result was a glowing spirit about them.

J'me was not the creator of this vibe. More or less, she was the example used within the Cube. By the way, this did not differ from the rest of the BLOCK, but since it started from almost nothing, it was just more noticeable.

Cube F was unique from the others in the BLOCK. Since it was the newest Cube, it took advantages of many of the latest technologies from Klug's Cube C. The most obvious was that it was self-sustained; everything was within the Cube and you never had to venture out (if that is what you wished). It was more convenient. For example, food was delivered. People served each other's needs. They had their own school, storage, clinic, an arts and crafts area, and of course their special Cleansing and Creativity Center.

This C^3 revolved around recreation and gaming. There was both active sports and inactive gaming. Of course, team sports were without scores. It was more leisurely, less competitive. **Everybody was a winner!** You could say that Cube F was livelier and more entertaining. There was an attitude of **fun** in Cube F!

There were many forms of entertainment in Cube F. Each person was an individual, liking some things less than others. J'me, for example, did not appreciate the joy of taking a bouncing ball and throwing it through a horizontal hole. It did not seem productive. What was the benefit to this? Many people missed the hole and the ball bounced back. Just to try to throw it again for a chance to make it through the hole. And then there were the people who did not participate, but enjoyed watching this. J'me's girls loved to play this game, while their friend Patrich was just an amused observer.

J'me did not judge, but for her the best forms of entertainment were those that produced something positive, like cleaning the Cube. To her, that was fun. But why didn't people sit to watch her with her sport?

There is nothing like something. That is, there is nothing like something handmade. There is no such thing as imperfection. The slip of a stitch or the fingerprint on pottery makes it one of a kind.

In the arts and crafts area, J'me enjoyed just watching the masters at their craft. Every movement had meaning. And from nothing, something tangible appeared. This was less serious, more social, than the artisans/creatives in Cube H's three upper floors. **It was not for the goal of perfection that she enjoyed practicing, it was in the doing.**

Chapter 48
Celebrate Good Times

Patrich's words rhymed when he spoke to J'me and her daughters. "Have you met the tattooed storyteller named Blue? His tattoos overlapped, giving his skin a special hue."

They flew to a floor that was newly occupied. Blue took a long draw from his pipe, inhaling deeply, held it in, and then blew out a fragrant scent over his guests.

Next, he placed a wooden plate on the floor in front of him, rubbing the surface lightly. He inhaled from the pipe again, but this time blew the smoke over the plate.

They observed him pulling out obsidian stones, each irregular in shape. He passed this before them to view and touch, took a toke from his pipe, and then rattled the stones within his hands, exhaling this time without smoke.

Opening his hands, the stones shone like dark diamonds. They made clicking sounds when he dropped them on the plate.

"Oh, I have more than one story for you." he finally said in an altered state.

Pointing to a tattoo that now stood out like a branding scar he said, "Can you see it?" Looking around the room he then whispered, "**The great spirits of the past, present and future are with us**."

This time when he took another long draw from his pipe smoke came from both his nose and mouth as he said, "You are not orphans. You were conceived with love."

Closing his eyes, Blue listened intently. It seemed as if he was trying to hear more than one person at a time. "**Each one of you is special. The future is foretold**." He then placed a mask over his face...

It is ok to feel skeptical at this point, everything seemed a bit generic, other than the ritual. Blue never really revealed anything to prove otherwise. (Spoiler alert: J'me, Patrich, and her three daughters really were special and play a pivotal part to the future.)

"No, that is not important." said Blue, seemingly to the skies.

"What's not important?" they sat on the edge of their seats.

"They want me to tell you that you look like your mothers... Patrich, you look like your father.

Moments passed while Blue was intent on listening to the voices he was hearing. He finally said out of frustration. "Hey, let's try this... I cannot talk that fast."

To his guests before him Blue commanded, "Make a circle, holding hands." He then sprawled his arms outward, reaching, exposing scars.

When united, they heard so many sounds and voices!

J'me liked how they pronounced her name correctly. A soft "J", light and nasally (like a French lover), followed by the stressed, upward accent of "Mah". "Je m'appelle" were the first words out of J'me's mouth.

Blue raised his hands and broke the grip of the circle... "Wait!" said Blue to the spirits. "I don't care." was his response to the voices in his head. "Ok, that's fair. Sure, you can introduce yourselves, but don't go on about their beauty and birthrights, I mentioned that already." They clasped their hands together again... After silence, a single voice was heard.

"I am the oldest and wisest one here. Play the song Celebration by Kool and the Gang!"

https://www.youtube.com/watch?v=3GwjfUFyY6M

When the tune played, they stood up, danced in a circle, and were able to receive all the positive messages from the many spirits. **There is magic to music.**

Cube F was a family. The duties of the mother, the duties of the father, were shared even though it was not their child. Everybody was related, even those from different tribes.

A closer bond was built between J'me, Ease, Rose, Zen, and Patrich. They would often practice their gifts together.

Then there were the sporting events. The girls participated; Patrich and J'me were side spectators.

Patrich and J'me both enjoyed the Arts and Crafts Center. J'me liked working with thread because it was more intricate.

J'me was not materialistic in any way, but had acquired many things. Most gifts were "from the heart", such as wisdom shared, but some were materials. Friends in Cube C created a special pouch that was so futuristic it seemed like a magician's bag. But what made this purse special was that J'me had woven the outer shell of the satchel. Its value was priceless, one of a kind.

People did not hoard, they shared. The storage area was merely a convenient place for the hunter and gatherers to organize the items they collected for the Cube.

Chapter 49
Beyond the BLOCK

For J'me, the gift had many special meanings. Each letter, each word, each sentence... each thought was golden. The book without words was absorbed by J'me. But it was also absorbing her. The contents were interesting. It made her mind move into new paradigms.

The entire book was a big puzzle that created a picture from little pieces. It was a challenge sometimes to understand. There was one phrase that was helpful for her: **"It seemed the right thing to do at the time."** Eventually the "book without words" made J'me stronger. She knew the writer's intentions were pure.

Why would people lie?

What was the advantage of hurting others?

Was it false or was it real? Fact or fiction?

If based on truth, was it twisted with embellishments and extra exaggerations? A tall tale?

Alone, there was nowhere for J'me to go for help with these trusted secrets. Not that anybody else could solve them. She had to put things together herself.

To some, J'me had a reclusive nature about herself now. She was becoming like Tio Juan who often liked his secluded meditations. Oh goodness, not as extreme as Key-Oh-Coo! Laughing...but she had changed.

It was an intentional read, meaning deliberately and delicately she pondered once, twice, three times. Then J'me paused to think further. Eventually, things that were confusing became clear. When her mind was weary, she put it away.

Approaching it as a sacred text, routinely and repeatedly, J'me absorbed the meaning of the manuscript to herself. Following her intuitive thinking, searching for something special, through spiritual meditation she could imagine herself in the scene with her senses. J'me was expanding her experiences and letting the book affect her.

The "book without words" by Key-Oh-Coo first exalted St. Wx, and then his regrets.

Next, was the subject of wealth. **Wealth has no limits, but there are four kinds:**

- **What you have,**
- **What you do,**
- **What you know, and**
- **Richness of character, what you are.**

Here is a selection of proverbs from the book:

Be trusted, respected, honorable, and ethical.
Be fair, do the rigGht things, otherwise you will not be happy.

MoOney can't buy everything.

Rich or poor is a mindset, you can be rich yet poor and poor yet rich.
Never be afraid or ashamedD to be rich;
but remember, your wealth comes from others around you and before you.

A wealthy tree never stops producing fruit; be grateful.
Give away your surplus; be generous and do not demand it back.
Wise men save and share, while fools spend whatever they get.
Perish through fooliISshness.
Do not look at a poor person as a fool, they just have other fortunes not found.

Wealth is a reward.
MeaningfulL wealth is only obtained O from good objectives.
The best part of wealth is what you make of it.

There is nothing wrong with a little profit.
Always be a lender, never be a borrower. A borrower is a servant to the lender.
Pay what you owe.
Owe nothing to anyone, your only obligation is to love them.

Have faith that you will be supplied what you need (except a fool).

Have confidence, not hopeE. This is stability.

Success is how you define it; it is different for everybody. Successful is feeling grateful.

Admittedly, most of the book covered the basics, and then went to the advanced, interspersed with the mystics of money.

Imbedded within the writing were random letters and numbers. For example, if you reread the previous seven passages, you would notice extra letters were intentionally placed to form a hidden message. There were nine extra letters, no numbers, placed in the text: G O D I S L O V E. The book was riddled with these junkets. Some messages J'me could not immediately solve.

Supposedly, the BLOCK was much bigger at one time. But then there was something like an un-civil war that split the BLOCK? The BLOCK was broken up into pieces?

Key-Oh-Coo was just one of many who committed mutiny. Is that possible? Well, according to the book, it did happen. One-third of the group fell away. Just as the BLOCK was not one man's idea, St. Wx was the combination of many people's dreams.

St. Wx was driven by people power (both powerful and powerless). Key-Oh-Coo knew that St. Wx could manipulate weak people on any day to do any deed...at any time... for any task.

QUIZ

IV

Quiz Four

Test your understanding of what you read. Pick the *best* answer for the following ten questions. After completing all ten questions, check your answers on the next page.

If you score a 70% or above (answer seven or more questions correctly) you may proceed to the following chapters. However, if you score below 70%, read the previous chapters again.

Please take your time reading and meditating to unlock the next chapters.

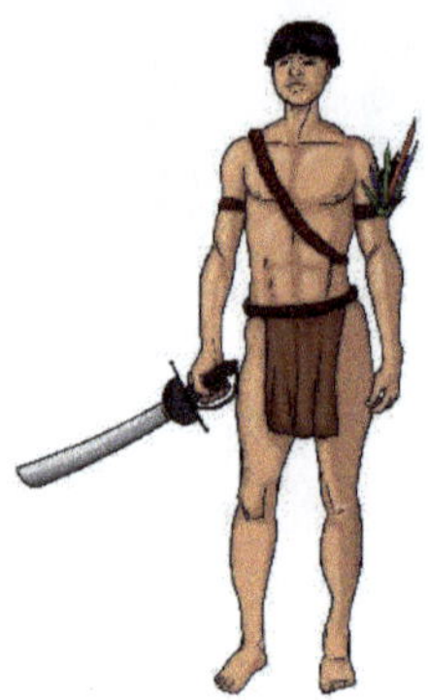

1. Where did the grandfather and grandson go?
    a. St. Wx
    b. Cubes A thru H
    c. Cathedral IJMN
    d. Heaven

2. How do you say, "Breath in... breath out...."? in Spanish?
    a. Despejado
    b. Libre
    c. Respira... Aspira...
    d. Pan dulce y chocolate caliente

3. The "tricky par 3 hole" was actually:
    a. God is not money – God is love
    b. Sharpen your saw

    c. You must mind your business

    d. Always improve

4. A typical 9-hole course is 35 strokes. What was J'me's golf score?

    a. Of course, 35!

    b. 8 strokes over, or 43

    c. The business to golf analogy confused me. I do not know.

    d. No score, but she recorded a snowman, 8 strokes on the last hole

5. Who was the last person to see the stranger in Café F?

    a. Fairy Number 42 (Messenger telling you change is coming)

    b. Angel Number 43 (Guides, inspires, gives clarity)

    c. Fairy Number 44 (Folklore fairy that does random good deeds)

    d. Angel Number 45 (Work hard and work smart and you will do it!)

6. Who did the traveler chose to stay with?

    a. Rajah Paintaalees

    b. Tamil Nadu

    c. Master of Mothers/Mother of All

    d. In the home of the laborer

7. In Cube F, the letter "F" is symbolic of:

    a. Jefe (Boss in Spanish)

    b. Fairy Feya

    c. Friends, Family, and Fun

    d. A FOREVER expanding spiral of caring

8. Mr. Blue had many tattoos,

His many tattoos could talk,

When asked Mr. Blue, "What shall we do?"

What did the spirits say?

    a. You were conceived in Love

    b.   Each person had a special future

    c.   Play "Celebration" by Kool and the Gang

    d.   All of the above

9. What was contained in the Book without Words?

    a.   Descriptions beyond the BLOCK

    b.   Secret Code

    c.   The mystics of money

    d.   All of the above

10. Using the Key-Oh-Coo Code, what hidden message is found in this passage?

Thou shalLt love thy neighboOr as thyself. (Jesus Christ)

AbovVe all, love each other deEeply, because love coOvers a multitude of sins. (John the Apostle)

My commanNdment is this: Love Eeach other as I haAve loved you. (God)

Love is a gift of one's inNner most soul toO another so both can be whole. (Buddha)

So compeTte with each othHer in doing good. (Allah) Only those who havEe love, will attain God. (GurRu Gobind Singh Ji)

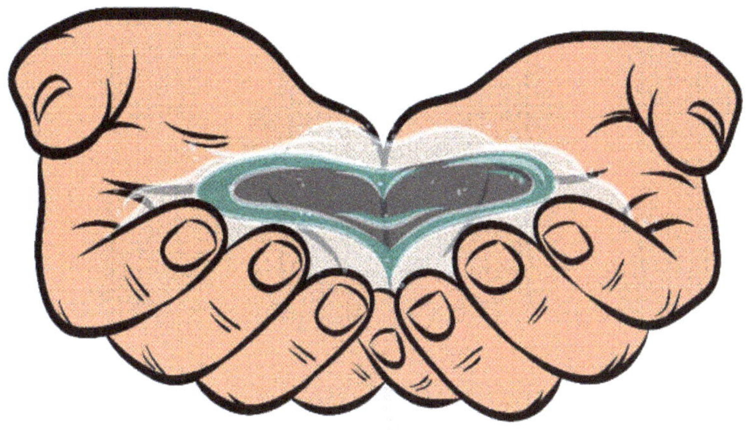

Q4 – Answers

1.   When the grandfather and grandson entered Cathedral IJMN, it was like those who have experienced leaving their bodies and going to heaven. The best answer is C: IJMN, but D: Heaven is also acceptable.

2.   Originally there was only one language. Floods and famines required people to disperse, they became diverse. Now there are over 7,000 languages spoken in the world today. However, inside the BLOCK you do not need a translator. But the Eagle Warriors just came directly from the outside world and were still using Spanish. They will adjust...
If you are not fluent in Spanish, you probably guessed the answer: C. "Respira... Aspira..." is "Breath in... breath out..."
Here are some other translations:

- "Despejado" means the area is clear, open, or literally dismissed.
- "Libre" is "free", but it also means vacant or unoccupied.
- "Pan dulce y chocolate caliente" is bread sweet and chocolate hot... or sweet bread and hot chocolate.
- "Ahora entiendo" is "Now I understand."
- "Orale" depends on the tone or inflection in which it is spoken. It is informal interjection like "wow", but here it was used as "Let's go" or "Hurry up"
- Bonus: "Cuando" is where and "Cuanto" is how much. (Tricky)

3.   A: God is Love... The book is laced with subliminal messages. Just like golf, business cannot be mastered. So just enjoy it. Learn to be happy when you hit a good shot or make some money.

4.   Deliberate distractions, like the air travel interruptions, are scattered throughout. This requires you to dig deeper to understand...
You may have never played golf, and others do not appreciate the game. What are your chances of getting a hole in one (hit the ball once and it goes into the hole)? What are the odds of business success?

What golfers do to their mind; mixed martial artists do to their bodies. Try it! It is fun! C and D are the correct answers: we are not certain what her score was on the course.

5.   There are more Angels than there are Fairies, but the numbering system has been used to help identify each one based on their special abilities.
   A.   Fairy 42 is a messenger. Your wishes have been heard and change is coming.
   B.   Angel 43 provides direction, motivation, and precision. This gift is sent from the Gods.
   C.   Folklore Fairy 44, Fairy Feya, randomly does good deeds. (Nice to have, Cinderella.)
   D.   Angel 44 is big! This angel has got your back and will help you succeed.
   E.   Fairy Feya was the last one to see Key-Oh-Coo. Think about it. Fairy 42 came earlier to let them know changes were coming. Angel 43 and Fairy 44 were not needed at that moment.

6.   Who did Mr. G, the traveler, chose to stay with? His Mother... Answer C.

7.   Oh, it has got to be fun... and family... and friends! Answer: C, maybe.

8.   Did you notice the question rhymed? It has got to be... answer D!

9.   An impossible question, because even J'me does not know everything that is in the book written by the CEO/COO of St. Wx! D: All of the Above is the best answer.

10.   Check for the capital letters. They are in order in the passage. Three words: LOVE ONE ANOTHER (J'me eXquisite).

How did you do? Did you score a 70? Did you get seven of the ten questions correct? Are you ready to move onto the next book, Chapters 50 through 59?

Chapter 50
50/50 Chance

J'me found herself on the docks again. This became her favorite place to sit alone and think. She was meditating about love. **Love can take you to the highest of highs and the lowest of lows.** J'me's thoughts took on added dimensions when she added her own perspective and creativity to what she had learned and experienced during her time in the BLOCK.

She quickly scuttled behind some wooden crates when she saw the elusive Mr. G emerge from the back of a white semi-trailer. He paused for a moment, then started walking in her direction. As if to hide herself, J'me looked down only to hear, "I love you." He said each word slowly with emphasis and meaning... in a voice that was pleasing to hear. She hesitated, bobbing her head, and then looked up to see Mr. G standing over her, glowing in his silver jacket.

J'me felt the ultimate in humility and reached inside her purse for the concealment cloak. Just then, Mr. G touched the top of her head. She felt overwhelmed with emotions extruding throughout every pore of her skin. When J'me had clutched the communications sphere to the hand of Dr. Melvin Klug, she felt a rush of thoughts and ideas. **This time she felt feelings.**

Without thought or words, J'me followed Mr. G to the cab of the truck. He opened the door to his super single and guided her inside to a soft seat. She was in a fresh fantasy as the fully automated, self-guided 14-wheeler sped down the roadway.

The seats turned so they could chat better. They were deep in discussion, gleaning truth from tradition; answers were given before questions were asked. This was something between sacred and secret. We cannot disclose the full conversation, but it began with... let's see... "I love you." And it... well, it never really ended.

Mr. G was not Oz, he was omnipotent. He was well traveled and explored many places and met many people along the way. **Time flew.**

When Mr. G and J'me arrived at their destination, **she was enlightened**. She understood his ideas and how everything interacted beautifully. It was not a single concept, but a series of visions made by many, interwoven like a beautiful tapestry. J'me envisioned paradise.

J'me learned that the BLOCK was the center of the creation. It started as a four by four grid of 16 Cubes or buildings. The BLOCK had expanded and collapsed and changed over time as a living entity. There were also areas outside for farming, mining, production, storage, distribution, and later, offices. **But the BLOCK was not about the buildings, it was about the people.**

Camp KLOP was originally Cubes K, L, O, and P. They were later moved to a secluded valley location. It became the wayside to the world: A transitory stay for people coming to and leaving the BLOCK.

J'me realized that **not all things are good or bad. There are different levels. For example, there is good, better, and best.** The BLOCK was the best. She was going to someplace better.

A tall West Texas cowboy with a wife half his size approached. "Hello, I am Harold von Viehzüchtermännerstamm (this pronunciation was so thick it was hard to decipher his name) and this is my wife Mar'Ann. It is nice to meet you." He reached out to shake hands. His face did not match his build; his grin was like a child's.

"I'm a hugger!" Mar'Ann exclaimed, and lavished J'me in a lingering embrace.

"My friends call me Mac." he said to J'me with a slower Texas twang.

Mr. G had vanished to the back of the trailer he was pulling. In the distance you could hear a large group of people cheering while watching a football game. It was a game of no rules football, sometimes called "street soccer".

"Let's take a lookie." said Mar'Ann spryly while taking J'me's hand. Mar'Ann's other hand reached for Mac's elbow as they walked towards where the crowd had congregated. J'me noticed that the braids in Mar'Ann's hair were pinned up to form a flat bun on the back of her head. And Mac wore a large brimmed stiff straw hat that she also admired. J'me took her shoes off a few strides into the walk and dangled them next to her purse. The ground was green and soft... she was walking barefoot in the grass for the first time.

Chapter 51
Welcome to Camp

J'me's head was on a swivel, looking at all the green plants at Camp KLOP. Trees, bushes, flowers, and of course the grass she enjoyed walking on. Up, down, and around; everything was covered in plants. She walked past a patch of flowers and had to stop to take in their delicate beauty. Mar'Ann put her arm around J'me's waist and squeezed; affirming that she liked the flowers too. Mac came back with pecans to snack on.

They finally meandered their way to the football field. J'me's eyes spied old friends. They were dressed identically, all wearing khaki fatigues and sleeveless cotton shirts, no shoes. She could understand now why they were called the Eagle Warriors. They flew like luche libre wrestlers around the black and white patterned ball.

J'me blinked... Just then there was a long and loud scream of "Goooooooooalllllll!"

It would take time for J'me to speak and become acclimated to her new surroundings. J'me was soft. She needed to adapt. Mac and Mar'Ann had seen this many times before and they were the most hospitable. **Those coming to the camp from the outside world needed to decompress, destress, and become their natural selves again. Simplify...**

They needed to be healed internally. Those coming from the BLOCK needed to harden externally and become prepared for the customs beyond the BLOCK. J'me learned that **education does not replace experience**. Through meditation, education, and now experience, J'me was to evolve.

There were many things to like about living in the camp, but for J'me, she first fell in love with the soft beds. She found herself sleeping more than normal. But this changed one morning when Mar'Ann woke J'me up. "You have visitors." she said. "They are outside waiting for you now. Here are some clothes they gave you to wear." With that, a stack of folded fatigues with boots were placed at the foot of her bed.

Moments later she emerged from her room with a new wardrobe, holding the boots with a look of confusion. Mac looked up from his morning reading ritual and noticed the problem. "I served in World War II. Let me help you." J'me gave the boots to Mac while Mar'Ann placed a breakfast casserole before her to eat.

For 20 minutes and 51 seconds, the Warriors were outside waiting. This was the first day of training. A long walk to the lake, a swim, and then a walk back. It felt good to be active.

The next few days, she did better. Besides the hikes, they developed their skill not to kill, a special combative technique from the Ancient Mayans and Aztecs wherein they would capture their enemies and bring them back as a slave or sacrifice.

Day and night... night and day. The first lesson J'me learned was time.

One morning, the Warriors did not show. J'me saw Mac sitting alone. "Once a week we rest. We rest our bodies and reenergize our spirits.

Mar'Ann went to early service; I will go this afternoon... She made a delicious cobbler... I think I will have another piece."

J'me had the day to herself. She decided to clean their home first. She felt like she had not contributed to the family. Then she went out to explore. She walked around the complex, seeing new things and making new friends. She even heard people talking about Archibald R and Frija. This made her reminisce about life in the BLOCK.

From behind a tree, J'me heard music. It was the sounds of a bamboo flute. She approached to find two men, a younger and an elder, listening to the music that came from a portable player. It was Master Wushi Yi and his apprentice. They welcomed her and were happy to have her join them. She sat and listened to the relaxing melodies. For J'me, this renewed her spiritual energy.

They noticed she looked weary. The apprentice massaged her adeptly, applying pressure to release all pains and strains. He also inserted acupuncture needles into her chi pathways to allow her energy to naturally flow.

J'me could feel the breeze better when she closed her eyes. The soft sound of the flute soon put her to sleep. When she awoke they, and the needles, were gone.

The following weeks were filled with gradually more intense physical conditioning: Blisters, bug bites, snake bite, cuts, cramps, dehydration, diarrhea, rash, splinters, sprains, sunburn and rope burn. Did I fail to mention, infection, fever, flu, a fracture, and... **fun**?

THWAP

Chapter 52
Compulsory Discretion

J'me's intense day long workouts were coming to an end, because now she had mandatory classes. Her transition was to attend school, something not necessary for those who knew what life was like in the real world and the BLOCK. History and current events were taught through technology, not a teacher. Once connected, you were implanted with significant events, after that was mind wandering wherein you could get answers from different perspectives and branch out from there.

J'me finished quickly and later caught up to her comrades. However, one day before changing into her fatigues, she saw a white semi-trailer truck parking and she seemed to recognize two old friends... Mac was already there with Mar'Ann grasping his elbow.

When J'me saw the Dr. E's, she exclaimed, "They are rock stars!" trying to evoke a laugh like she had heard earlier in the BLOCK.

"We do not listen to rock" replied Mac and Mar'Ann, "We like blue grass." They said, smiling, but not laughing.

J'me was now even more confused. Quick witted, she replied, "Have you ever seen a blue cow? They are beautiful."

No response... she explained the punchline, "The Giants are big and they wear blue." She was the only one to laugh.

Mar'Ann just tilted her head and then Mac explained, "The Giants are a New York football team."

Lesson: Imagine our minds as a bowl of water with bubbles underneath. The bubbles are ideas attained and retained in our minds.

Our goal is to express our thoughts out of the water to the listener. **We should connect our thoughts**.

"We came only to give you a gift... We got it from Charles at Fort Bennett... Do you have your ball?" asked both Dr. E's simultaneously, working together.

J'me placed the oversized pearl into the hands of the doctors and they clutched it together. Her eye's widened with excitement!

"You mean...? J'me tried to imagine the unimaginable.

"Ho, ho!" they said with guttural glee.

"And I can...?" asked J'me.

"Ho, ho, ho!" again.

"Can I try it? Can I try it now?" J'me acted as if she had learned the secret to a magic trick.

Ever so carefully, J'me cupped her hands together, placed them slowly in front of her... began to bow her head... then stopped.

"Wait! Let me try this again." J'me shook her hands outward and then cupped them once again. She closed her eyes and lightly lowered her head.

J'me made Mac and Mar'Ann appear next to her. "What in tarnation?" was all the two could say.

"Quantum teleportation... **It is easy if you know how.**" said Dr. Lyja. **"Ach, it is all in your head. Mind over matter!** Try it again!"

"Watch this!" J'me stepped forward and held out her hands in fervent prayer...

Then appeared Ease, Rose, and Zen. Behind Rose was Patrich, who was in the process of braiding her hair. "Oops." he said as if to apologize.

"Momma!" They screamed in unison and rushed to give J'me a group hug. Brief introductions were exchanged...

Then J'me did it again! However, this time she captured the Eagle Warriors with their trousers down to their knees in a circle, as if they were urinating on the same shrub (with J'me in the center). Before they could yell, "Exquisita!" she hurriedly made the men vanish.

Fort Bennett, (1869 – 1889): before the turn of the century in an abandoned fort in South Dakota. Once home of the U.S. Calvary during the Indian Wars, it was now vacant except for one soldier, Charles. He was stationed there to maintain fortifications. Located next to a river, his sustenance was mainly fish and any edible vegetables he found. Charles never ventured more than a walk away.

When he signed up to join the Army he believed in the promise of exotic excursions to faraway places. This was false. His first and only assignment was a ride to an unfilled fortress.

Charles was a scholarly man, a full-time student. **From everything there was a lesson.** They called the stone storehouse the "Church of Charles". People said he spent his time in meditation, prayer, and talking to the angels. They whispered that he found God.

Fast forward to the 1900 World's Fair in Paris. We find a young man named Charles walking the exhibits alone, lost in the crowd. Fast forward further to the 2020 World's Fair in Dubai. An older man named Charles walked the exhibits alone, again lost in the crowd.

Chapter 53
Giddem'up N Moo'em'out

Giddem'up N Moo'em'out (A melodic phrase belted out at the beginning of a trail ride; Get them up and move them out!).

Mac and Mar'Ann proved that love is not a glass of water. The more love you give, the glass is still full. **Love is infinite and never empties, never ending, with no limits.** To their guests Mac merely said, **"Mi casa es su casa"** (my home is your home). Mar'Ann would add, **"There is beauty all around when there is love at home."**

United again, **no matter where you call home, you are still family**. The girls blossomed like flowers since their arrival at camp, becoming more beautiful. Patrich also changed. During his time in the BLOCK, he felt comfortable wearing just a robe. Now he wore something akin to a kilt. He let his hair grow longer. Occasionally, he felt feminine. He was just "one of the girls" as he would say, with a magic hand whip into the air.

J'me had also changed. She now talked and smiled more. She was "normal" again with her girls around. They all loved the frequent hugs, casseroles, and care that Mar'Ann supplied. They loved how Mac was full of West Texas wisdom.

Every night Mac, Mar'Ann, J'me, Ease, Rose, Zen, and Patrich sat around and listened to Mac "chawing the rag" (telling his stories). Occasionally, he got out his six-string guitar and taught them a "sing-along" song. Mar'Ann always had plenty of popcorn made, giving each bottomless bowls.

The two were born "a long ride apart" (about 40 kilometers is the longest you would drive your cattle in one day). Mar'Ann was a chicken rancher and Mac was a "kicker" (raised cattle, referring to kicking the cow manure off your boots).

Mac, Harold von Viehzüchtermännerstamm, was fluent in German, which he learned from his parents at home, English, which he learned from his teachers at school, and Spanish, which he learned from his friends. Mac also taught himself how to play any type of stringed instrument and made money on the side at shindigs (lively local celebrations).

Life changed for Mac after he graduated from college with a degree in Agriculture. It seemed he could sit on the fence and the birds would feed him. Mac enlisted to fight in the Big War. Because of his degree, he entered at the rank of an officer in the Army. When they learned of his musical talents, he was given the position of Morale Officer.

Never ask a question that you really do not want to know the answer to. "Did you kill anyone, Uncle Mac?"

Mac closed his eyes for a tad-bit, and then answered in a somber tone. "The War was over... The General ordered me to volunteer as a witness... plus be his personal translator. Genocide... we saw stacks of corpses like firewood... inhuman.... extermination... Not what I had my face fixed for. I don't cotton to it. I can still remember the smell." That's when he stopped talking that night.

Changing the subject... Mar'Ann went to the same college to teach young women to become good wives and mothers. They say she graduated with two degrees, her Bachelors in Home Economics and an "M. R. S." degree. Mac and Mar'Ann met and married.

Mac's first job after the War was for the government, protecting migrant workers. There was travel, but by this time he had a truck and always made it home for dinner. "You can call me anything, but never late for supper." He was as busy as a one-eyed dog in a smokehouse. At the same time he completed his Master's in Education and then a Doctorate in Administration. You can't beat that with a stick.

The two settled down on a lot of land Mac had converted into pecan orchards. They had a place to roost. They never had children; the only addition was Mar'Ann's mother. You know they lived so far out in the country that the sun set between their house and town.

As exciting as a mashed-potato sandwich, their story was nothing to make a movie about. **But they were part of what started as the "Lost Generation" and became the "Greatest Generation".** Mar'Ann simply says, "We were blessed."

"Church is out. It's time to heat up the bricks." was usually how things ended, and then every scampered off to bed for the evening.

And that is how the cow ate the cabbage.

Chapter 54
Living a Dream

People enjoyed a more predictable lifestyle and were comforted by routines and rituals. The sun came up every morning and there was daylight. The sun set and it was dark, nighttime.

The daughters decided to take on the whole medical curriculum that was available. They loved this new technology and how easily they learned new things. J'me also enjoyed her classes but found herself running less and less with the pack. She enjoyed her own pace, exploring, getting lost, finding new things.

Then Patrich was Patrich. He was not required to attend classes and he enjoyed an unstructured life. He flit around from one place to another, volunteering. Every task he was given was finished to perfection. Even if you were not the envious type, you felt envy in a good way.

J'me developed her own "exquisite style" of helping others. She avoided attention; she stayed away from praise. It was not like she was putting on a levitation show with Frija. J'me advanced by practicing her gifts while doing good deeds for others. She found it more fun to be anonymous.

For grins and giggles, let's see if we can remember all of J'me's gifts... First, she had the natural and contagious ability to exude love. Besides scarves and a native Tio Juan wardrobe, J'me had the gold invisibility cloak, festival clothes, fruit seeds, the universal orb used in communications, a book without words, and seven sacred sapphires in her enchanted satchel. She could levitate just about anything. She had the rare solutions to secrets that were shared by others with only her. And now she was refining her ability to teleport.

With teleportation, J'me quickly learned she had to fully think it out or she could become a pee tree (as was her own experience). Do I use levitation or teleportation? In her arts and crafts, using teleportation for things such as weaving or needlepoint could get too dizzy. **Think first, act second.**

Each chance J'me got, she would venture further and further from the camp center. She used the "spiral search" technique taught to her during wilderness training. When lost, circle around. Increase the size of your circle and expand outward. This avoided walking in the same spots again and again. J'me chose to use pecan shells as a marker of where she had been before. With teleportation she could start where she stopped on the previous trek.

One day J'me was relaxing on a shaded stump in the woods, watching farmers plowing an open field. They hit a rock and stopped.

The men were not startled when J'me appeared. (They had met her earlier when she and the seven soldiers helped them build an irrigation ditch in short time.) The farmers had already started to move the dirt away from the stone with hardwood sticks. J'me was thinking that teleportation would be cleaner, but she was not sure of the size of the stone.

She found a pointed end and started lifting. The earth moved 20, then 30, 40, 50, 60, almost 70 meters away. She was able to levitate it out of the soil. It was one slender stone that expanded in girth. It looked like an obelisk with a pyramid peak.

The second piece was discovered. It was wider and much heavier... About 20 to 30 meters in size, the farmers' eyes opened wide as J'me laid the two pieces end to end. It was a perfect fit!

Lastly, buried beneath the ground was a solid base. She removed the top crust then extracted it like a tooth. After J'me had excavated the obelisk and base, she teleported it to an inlet lake where its currents naturally washed it clean.

While this was going on, J'me teleported to the center of an open grass land adjacent to camp. She first sat and meditated, feeling the warmth of the sun and the freshness of the afternoon breeze. Fully relaxed, she knew what she should do next.

Maybe J'me slept? Because when her eyes opened, she saw Mac and groups of people all dressed in white robes like those worn in the BLOCK. Mac crouched down before her, at eye level and said, "May I say a prayer? It seems like the right thing to do." Mac then dedicated the land that was to be used for the obelisk. When he was done, J'me heard harmonic humming from the radiant heavenly choir.

Chapter 55
Harold's Angels Sing

"Where do I put it?" was pre-determined by the appearance of the ground dedicated to the obelisk and the invisible circle created by the white robed singers. As if everything was already scripted and choreographed, the erection began.

Mar'Ann came holding Patrich's elbow... with Ease, Rose and Zen, followed by Master Wushi Yi, his apprentice, and electronic player with speaker. The prerecorded sounds of the wooden flute mixed smoothly with the choir's harmony. Residents of Camp KLOP started to make their way towards the activity.

J'me felt a loving touch from Mariah and Maribeth Naz (Mari A and Mari B). Their smiles meant more than words. $Mari^2$ quietly moved away, towards their older brothers who were already with J'me's girls.

The Bavarian schuhplattlers combined with African gumboot dancers, as a rhythmic wave was heard approaching. It was going to be a celebration fest!

"When to begin?" was obvious. The sun shone directly into J'me's face making her close her eyes. She was immediately in a tranquil state.

The dripping stone base was teleported from the lake bottom and placed directly in front of her. She felt freshness as she sat in its damp shade. The wet polished stone glistened as it slowly settled, pressing itself firmly into the ground.

J'me's eyes remained closed as the solid second stone appeared and fused itself to the base, just by its weight alone. There appeared large petroglyphs that seemed to predate the great flood.

It was not sudden, but smooth, as the third piece appeared and was absorbed atop the solid stones. And, as J'me had wished, she was not the center of attention, merely just an instrument in its assembly.

When she opened her eyes, it was not only the 100-meter rock tower that J'me noticed. She had 360-degree sensory perception. White robes fluttered like wings as the chorus was elevated by an unseen wind above everything. The choir was let by a cowboy chorister, Mac himself. The ground beneath her vibrated with the rhythmic steps of stompers.

J'me was also acutely aware of every detail surrounding her, from the movement of a person's hair, the texture of skins, the sound of a swallow, the smell from a pore that indicated what they had eaten that day. She even saw Mr. G appear and disappear into the crowd.

J'me was not sure if this was a feeling she wanted, so she soon shut it off. She knew, however, if she ever needed it back, she could summon her senses to this level again.

In the center of your brain is a small gland, about the size of an almond. It is shaped like a pinecone and thereby called the "Pineal Gland". It is part of your endocrine system and secretes chemicals that help your body regulate sleep, your natural rhythms, and also reproductive hormones.

The purpose of sleep is to flush out all the used and un-needed chemicals in your brain (like a toilet flush). During your deepest sleep the pineal gland is most "open", allowing positive things to happen to you physically, emotionally, and even spiritually.

Your brain operates both chemically and electronically. Now it gets to be a little more complex. For simplicity's sake, there are normally four to five ranges of electronic frequencies that your brain operates on:

- 0.5 to 4 hertz is when your brain is sleeping, super slow "Delta",

- 4 to 8 hertz per second is drowsy, half awake and half asleep, "Theta",

- 8 to 14 hertz is "Alpha" and is your normal speed during the times you are awake,

- 14 to 30 hertz means you are highly alert and focused and in "Beta to Gamma", or using Tio Juan's cognitive code "yellow melting into orange to red".

Hertz is the German word for "heart" and represents one cycle per second. The average human heart at rest produces about 1.25 hertz (or abbreviated Hz of electricity). At about 120 beats per minute, you will generate 2 Hz. Your body will produce about 60 to 70 megahertz of energy while awake.

Light travels electronically in invisible waves. Other electronic energies you cannot see, but perhaps sense. You are surrounded by vibrations of energy constantly.

Your body needs to be surrounded by around 60 to 80 megahertz of energy. Below this range, you will eventually become sick. Above this range, positive high frequencies strengthen you physically and spiritually.

Now, think of your tiny pinecone as more than just a toilet releasing chemicals to your brain. It is sensitive to electronic frequencies.

Chapter 56
Enjoying the Erection

J'me went to her girls and exchanged hugs. She was also welcomed by Maria, Maribeth, and Mar'Ann. The Naz brothers were huddled in deep discussion, but stopped to glance over with friendly smiles.

At this point the angelic choir finished and ascended straight upward beyond their vision. The drums and stomps stopped, and lastly, the sound of the wind flute faded. Then J'me noticed the Naz brothers speaking to a woman as they approached. The boys excitedly introduced, "Sabhee Kee Maan... Hamaaree Maan... Our Mother." The woman motioned them to hush as they began to hear birds singing in the surrounding woods. Then she pointed north to a mysterious cloud approaching with the wind. Everybody's eyes moved in that direction.

A squadron of geese in a tight V formation flew over, then another and another. Soon the sky was filled with additional birds flying playfully, changing leaders, and swirling with the airstream. The finale was colorful butterflies. It was as if somebody had invited nature to put on a show.

The noonday sun was directly above the pyramid point of the stone structure. It was then that you could see its true color, a deep, purple indigo.

First, a giant Japanese drum was hit once, breaking the silence. Its dense bass sound vibrated deeply. Next, in the opposite corner of the field there was an identical drum hit followed by a long echo... After a pause, there was a third beat; fading from another direction... then followed by four Japanese drums booming simultaneously from all four corners.

A slow quadraphonic vibration from the four corners of the field was accentuated by the deep African drums. It was the sound of a slow heartbeat: boom-boom, boom-boom... This became the base rhythm. Thud-thud, thud-thud... It was primitive until the island drums added melody. The percussion played alone.

The strikes increased speed, picking up your pulse. A melody was added that mimicked the tune of the previous choir and Mac's yodeling. Then the tune changed again, sounding like a picture... a picture of birds playing overhead.

During this time, people changed into native festival clothes – from a single cloth covering, to flamboyant silks and feathers. Some people also wore earthy fabrics and pelts. J'me changed into the only festival outfit she had — the long aqua blue dress, scarves, and braids given to her from the clan of Giants.

Mac and Mar'Ann were now in full cowboy regalia; Patrich was wearing an Irish kilt; and the three daughters of J'me had identical white skirts and blouses, sequenced in clear glitter that made them look frosted... and white lace was braided into their hair. (This was the fine lace that J'me had tatted for each one of them while she was in the

BLOCK.) The Naz family had the most beautiful colors: the men in dignified dhotis and kurtas. The best shiny and shimmering silk was used. Mari[2] matched in layers of fabrics to create a sari with strings of gold dripping down. (Bollywood would win the award again!)

J'me was now standing across from the "Mother of All". Mother reached out to hold both of J'me's hands. She had a smile that sent a hundred hugs. J'me had a similar smile when they connected. The two were google eyed, and then Mother asked, "Can we talk privately?" She then took her hands and cupped them together to form a scoop like that used to ladle water in your hands.

Spontaneously, the Naz brothers interrupted with the following advice:

"**Drink more water!**"

"**Avoid consuming chemicals** used in food processing, refined sugars, and dairy products (as much as possible)."

Aarov added, "**Get adequate sleep in a dark place**."

Arnav Naz said, "**Exercise your mind and body...**" Completing his thought was Arush,

"**Walk in nature every day.**"

Arjun continued with, "**Enjoy the sunrise and sunset; become a sun gazer.**"

" Do aesthetic activities: Make and create, work with your mind and hands."

"**Think deeply, and even do some daydreaming.**"

"Meditate outside naturally, sitting on the ground or earthy elements."

"**Quiet your mind.**" one whispered.

"**Be mindful of your senses.**" said Aarov in unison with Arnav.

Finally, with a long exhale, Arush said, "**Let go of limiting beliefs.**"

With her hands still cupped, the Mother of All was listening. "**Feel your heartbeat within you and let your mind ease. Subdue your power to resist. Surrender and float along with everybody around you.**"

Mac and Mar'Ann concluded with, "ah... Amen!"

Chapter 57
Your Mind's Eye

Can you see them? Glittering... sparkling light... layers or gradients of shine were before their eyes. In front of this was a filter of what looked like glossy bubbles, reflecting both light and color. When a bubble popped, it created a spit of a spark (just a spit). Blinking did not distort the fantasy; it was real. Can you see the bubbles?

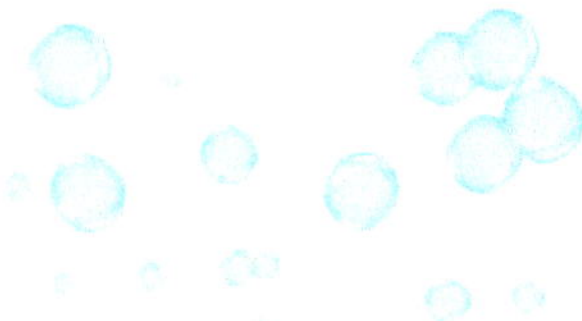

It seems every culture was present to celebrate the KLOP spike. It was not the differences that were obvious, but the similarities of everyone... **Everyone was one.** Magic was released.

The sound of trumpets blasting a tribute was heard... The bellows from bagpipes were heard... The striking of the stretched strings from an electric guitar was heard... These sounds were heard together... beginning the afternoon outdoor concert.

Soon a flash mob of immigrants appeared. It was something to behold. For you this may not seem very exciting, but for those there this was glory!

The Mother of All still had her hands cupped before J'me... waiting for a private chat. Without further delay, J'me pulled out her powerful pearl used to unite. When both sets of hands were clutched to it, the connection began.

"It looks like the head of a baby's penis. Science has proven we have a sack in the center of our brains, the pineal gland that gives us religious experiences. It works through both chemistry and electricity." Mother mentioned.

"**Be careful of things you do not see...** like fluoride that has been added to such things as your drinking water. Fluoride is absorbed into your teeth and bones for strength, but it also creates a shell around your gland, making it hard to open. Also, there are hallucinogens and psychoactive drugs that alter your entire brain chemistry and stimulate this gland to ejaculate. **Let nature control chemistry.**"

J'me was listening intensely to each and every word that was slowly sent through the sphere.

"Your heart produces a very small amount of electricity. Not enough to give your brain the energy it needs. Where does this extra electricity come from? "

"Now it gets more complex. The cells within our body are a conduit of energy, moving electrons constantly. They can store and produce enough energy to keep our brain alive. If your brain is dead, so are you." Mother faded off at the end of that sentence.

This time the Mother of All put added emphasis on the question, "Where does the extra electricity your body needs come from? If it is not from within you, it must be from outside of you. **You also absorb energy.**"

There was a long pause. People watching the two converse without speaking saw a couple of deep cleansing breaths simultaneously taken by the two women. Then Mother's mind moved... **"You have a third eye!** You may think I am 'satkela'. You know crazy, wonkers, la-la, barking mad!"

Mother of All and J'me laughed. When it subsided, Mother explained the cyclops sphere in the middle of your forehead...

"The third eye is a term used for thousands of years to explain what happens when you open your pineal gland. It is just symbolic of opening up your mind to a higher consciousness, enlightenment into both psychological and spiritual."

"Intuition, promptings, an urge, a silent whisper, a feeling of being in the zone... This moment of energy may also give you visions. Some also call this 'enlightenment' or just 'the way'. Others say it is the spirits, the Holy Ghost, communicating telepathically with higher beings... guides that connect you to God. **Trust this voice.**"

Directions: Ground yourself by calmly sitting emotionless and relaxed. Focus on your breathing or a candle flame, or sunlight. Feel love and joy, positive energy through meditation.

Next, visualize your forehead where your third eye chakra resides. Concentrate inward towards your pineal gland. Now close your eyes and focus them upward and center, towards your third eye. You will feel a bit of pressure here as it opens. Attention and meditation... not complex.

As your thoughts move, let them go. Breathe normally.

Later, practice sending energy out and receiving random thoughts and feelings. It is your involuntary subconscious communicating with your conscious (thinking) mind. **Train your brain.**

The meditation should last no more than 15 minutes. But before you go to bed or when you wake, you may again get subtle messages from this process.

During the time the flash mob appeared, nobody noticed that the seven Eagle Warriors vanished!

Chapter 58
From 5 to 8

Just then J'me felt a light touch on her shoulder. She broke the bond of the sphere to see Fairy Feya. She was wearing an oversized blue American football jersey that comfortably covered the wings on her back. "I heard you like the Giants?" she squeaked... With this she turned around to show the big number 44 and the letter "G" for the name.

Translating squeak speak, "I am sorry to interrupt you, but I must show you something. I had given you seven heart shaped sapphires at Café F. Can you bring them out?" high pitched peeped Fairy Number 44.

When J'me opened her purse, she saw that the seven gems were glowing. She cupped them in her hands and brought them forward. The Mother of All's eyes opened wide with joy.

"Oh, let's open up our eyes of wisdom." She took the glowing sapphires and placed them on the blanket between herself and J'me. "Pick one, any one..." They each randomly took a heart shaped gemstone in their hands. "Do as I do." With this, J'me mimicked the movement of touching the flat part of the jewel to the front of her head.

"Close your eyes... remember to relax... release your thoughts, quiet your mind... become aware of the limitless sensations coming to you."

Oh, it was overwhelmingly wonderful and all in her mind! This was similar to the spirit walks she had experienced with Tio Juan, but better. J'me was tripping at the concert. The music she heard had a kaleidoscope of colors. Her heart rate went up, her body temperature went up, and she began to sweat. She felt a mix of euphoria and hallucinations. She felt as if her body went up over the crowd and spire below. She was floating like a bubble in the breeze.

When Ease, Rose, Zen and Patrich saw this, they also picked up a heart shaped sapphire stone and sat next to J'me. Mac and Mar'Ann refrained, leaving only one more gem. With some hesitation, the beautiful Fairy Feya took off her jersey and decided to join in. Her wings calmed as she settled down.

Everybody awoke at almost the same time... Mariah, Maribeth, and Mar'Ann gave each other cold cups of water until they were back to reality.

Everybody "heard the smell" of a fresh blend of lavender, mint, and musk. It was pleasant. Finishing with the spire spinning, ratcheting to the right, in a clockwise direction. Slowly it clicked, clicked, clicked like a timepiece.

The seven stones were put back into J'me's satchel and they discussed what had just happened. Not sure of who said what, the first person started with...

"When I put the sapphire to my head, I felt a pressure... a little headache maybe."

"This was a sign that your pineal gland or third eye was opening."

"Third eye?" This question came from more than one.

"I had a dull sensation between my eyebrows. I guess where your third eye would be found."

"Exactly, I had a color and light sensation."

"I had both feeling and thinking. Like another dimension of my mind was opened."

"Yes! The third eye expanded my vision and my thoughts. I was more tuned into intuition."

"I just observed and not reacted. I wanted to experience it without limits."

"I still have this clear insight, open-mindedness, intellectual balance..."

They all took large gulps of water, then Fairy Feya began to squeak. She was so cute with her gestures, facial expressions, and bubbly personality.

"I think it was good, but at the end I had this perception of the obelisk turning. That was something I cannot explain." Everybody agreed by the nodding of their heads. After a long pause, J'me interjected, **"Some things we are not to know."**

Mac and the Naz brothers started their rounds; they moved from one source of music to another while the others sat sipping more water. And then they decided they needed to pee. The seven day-trippers moved shakily to the woods. The women squatted while Patrich stood. They all gave a little shiver when done. Ahh, relief.

When they returned, Mac was with a band of cowboy musicians. A roving band of mariachis accompanied them with their bright brass and suave accordion sounds. Throughout the night, different genres of serenades changed beat to classic songs from their generations.

The group ended up staring into the sunset. **It was a wonderful world.** They fell asleep outside as the music played.

Chapter 59
Sub QRUV

The new immigrants to camp were grateful, and it seemed they hosted many parties to share their thanks. **Everyone was welcome.**

The Naz brothers returned to their work at the BLOCK a few days later, but the Naz sisters stayed with Mar'Ann. Ease, Rose, and Zen were soon to complete their entire medical studies and preparing for their examinations. "Patrich Perfect", his new nickname, was routinely the extra magic hand needed to complete any task. Everyone was busy.

J'me had fallen into a routine of searching outward in the mornings, thinking inwardly in the afternoons. With everyone busy, it was not uncommon for her to explore.

During a distant excursion, J'me found a secluded stream. The river was wide and the water smooth. She kicked off her boots and began to swim. While in the water, she struck something solid. She reached down and touched what seemed to be a wall.

During her first attempt to search downward into the murky marine, J'me started to see bubbles. She became more curious. **What is at the bottom of this?**

J'me sat on the edge while contemplating her next dive. She took a deep breath and swam for as long as she could, scrubbing herself against the smooth wall all the way. She ran out of air and had to surface. When she got to the top, she gasped, and felt a little cramping.

After 10 meters, buoyancy reverses and instead of floating to the surface, you are sucked downward. Beyond a dozen meters you enter the "doorway to the deep", wherein your lungs start to shrink. J'me just free dived far beyond this point.

She relaxed and slowed her pulse. J'me felt loose, and ready to jump back in.

During her second attempt, she saw an opening. It was a square cut out that was the source of the bubbles. Out of air, she floated to the surface. The top of the structure was flat. So J'me was able to lay back this time to catch her breath.

On her third try, J'me coughed, expanded her lungs and took in as much oxygen as possible before diving. She felt fear for the first time. But J'me knew what she had to do.

When she saw the light at the bottom, she felt an invisible hand pushing her inside. Through the hole, through the bubbles, she kept swimming beyond her limits. She closed her eyes as she approached the source of the suds. A big hand reached down and pulled J'me up.

"QRUV!" was all she heard as she kept her eyes closed. Her body was recovering while her mind was thinking, "Why didn't I use teleportation?"

"Quarters for Reservation" or the "Underwater Village"? J'me was not clear with the communications of even the name of this location. Like hearing underwater with aqua ears, she strained here through the soft popping of suds.

J'me was milky minded. Things were heavy, not light, not tight. Everything was loose and smooth and felt sometimes juicy. Another description would be the feeling after you get a massage, a full body relaxation... creamy.

J'me was adjusting as she was absorbing the vast amount of thick energy from outside her. It was a process, not instantaneous.

QRUV consisted of four identical Cubes... no doors... no windows. Like the BLOCK, except self-contained and submerged. Plants and animals were once collected and now stored in these structures. Was it the original BLOCK, dating back to before the flood?

There were only eight people who tended to the care and upkeep of QRUV. Interestingly, there had always been only eight people, never more, never less. This meant that as one person died, another was born. One birth equals one death. It created an equilibrium or balance. This also meant that they evolved more quickly.

Almost alien, with skin tone that was light grey, the caretakers were without hair and genderless. Their bodies were slim with no visible genitals or nipples. Their heads seemed disproportionately large for their bodies. Perhaps they had larger pineal glands because they spoke telepathically to J'me. J'me could only decipher muddy speech.

Having been isolated for all these years, they were very curious about J'me. However, they did not know human behavior. They were a bit rough, trying to examine her body without regard to her comfort. It was when they paralyzed her and placed her on top of a table, things got weird. She felt pain.

Immediately, J'me teleported back to the bank of the river where she had left her belongings.

QUIZ

Quiz Five

Test your understanding of what you read. Pick the *best* answer for the following ten questions. After completing all ten questions, check your answers on the next page.

If you score a 70% or above (answer seven or more questions correctly) you may proceed to the following chapters. However, if you score below 70%, read the previous chapters again.

Please take your time reading and meditating to unlock the next chapters.

1. What did Mr. G say to J'me?
    a. How the BLOCK has changed
    b. They talked about truth versus tradition
    c. I love you
    d. All of the Above

2. Who did J'me train with at KLOP?
    a. Master Wushi Yi and his apprentice
    b. The seven Eagle Warriors
    c. Mac and Mar'Ann
    d. Luche libre wrestlers.

3. What new gift did J'me get?
    a. Levitation
    b. Telepathy
    c. Teleportation
    d. How to make delicious casseroles

4. Mac was not:
    a. A kicker, a cowboy, a farmer
    b. A WWII veteran
    c. Harold von Viehzüchtermännerstamm
    d. A Home Ec. Teacher

5. J'me had the most fun...
    a. Being in a predictable routine
    b. Taking history classes
    c. Wilderness training with the warriors
    d. Tripping at an outdoor concert

6. Who did not perform at the outdoor concert?
    a. Satkela and the Naz brothers
    b. Japanese, African, and island drums
    c. Geese, birds, and butterflies
    d. Mac with the angelic choir, a cowboy band, and mariachis

7. Of the following, what is not needed to open the third eye?
    __ Avoid hidden chemicals
    __ Daydream, yet be mindful of your senses
    __ Drink more water
    __ Electrical energy
    __ Enjoy the sunrise and sunset
    __ Exercise and sleep
    __ Hallucinogens, psychoactive drugs, DMT
    __ Less than 15 minutes of meditation

__ Pineal gland
__ Surrender, ease your mind
__ Think deep, yet quiet your mind
__ Trust the voice(s) in your head
__ Walk in nature, meditate in nature.

8. If there was a fight between J'me, Mother of All, and Fairy Feya... Wait! Here is a different question: What negative side effect was mentioned about opening your third eye?

    a. A headache with pressure on your forehead
    b. Infection, flu with a fever
    c. Blisters, bug bites, and snake bites
    d. Cuts and cramps

9. When the flash mob of immigrants came, they
    a. Hosted parties
    b. Were thankful
    c. Were from the outside world
    d. All of the above

10. What happened at QRUV?
    a. J'me toured all the exotic plants and animals
    b. Eight aliens tried to probe J'me
    c. They had interesting conversations
    d. J'me had her energy absorbed

Q5 – Answers

1.   We are not sure exactly what was said, except for "I love you", but they did have a long conversation from the BLOCK to Camp KLOP. Answer D: All of the above.

2.   KLOP is a transient place between heaven and earth, or the BLOCK and the outside world. J'me had to prepare with her friends the Eagle Warriors. Answer B.

3.   J'me never learned telepathy or communicating with her mind, however it did happen to her. She was told the secrets of quantum teleportation and quickly mastered it. (Answer B: Teleportation). Levitation was something J'me had practiced since the time at the BLOCK. Your mind is a powerful tool, but she did not use it to learn to cook. It seemed the Naz sisters wanted the secrets to Mar'Ann's casserole recipes, not J'me.

4.   Harold von Viehzüchtermännerstamm. preferred to be called "Mac" instead. His wife, Mar'Ann was educated and enjoyed teaching Home Economics. Answer D, definitely!

5.   C: Running with the warriors was the most fun. You know she dropped out of school? It was not her thing. She'd rather be busy than bored.

6.   The concerts of all concerts had just about everything except music from a crazy lady and the Naz brothers (Answer C).
The drums were interesting... Japanese Taiko, combined with African Drums (Dundunda was the lowest pitch, Sangbum drums were medium sized, and Kenkeni were smaller with a higher pitch... combined with the versatile sounds of the Djembe) ... Even better was when the melody from Conga, Bongo, and Steel drums was added last!
A concert could not be a concert, though, without bagpipes, trumpets, and a good lick from an electric guitar! Party on!

7.   Question 7 made you think... For example, **some things you cannot do at the same time** (like watch a sunrise and sunset, daydream yet be mindful, exercise and sleep are opposites, and then you would explode if you tried to think deep while also clearing your mind).
Many others on the list made sense... But can you use drugs to open the pineal gland, the third eye? Absolutely, but Mother suggests not doing this. Rather, she suggests allowing nature to control the chemistry.
Caution: It is real! As we have learned, not everything is good, not everything is bad. Everybody is different, but the headaches are certain. Others see it as scary and develop fear, then stop. If not balanced to begin with, you may develop anything from pride to suicide. (Yes, it can be too much to handle for some people)... It does drain your energy, so limit your meditation sessions.
What is the correct answer? Extra points! God loves you and does want to communicate with you. This was a freebie, but I would suggest not using modern chemistry and tripping. That has side affects you may not want.

8.   Everybody is different, but the headaches are certain when you try to open your third eye. Absolutely, A is the answer!

9.   The flash mob was a mass exodus of believers from St. Wx. They must not have liked it there because they were D: All of the Above.

10.   There was more to the dive than what was inside. Some things are best kept under water, you know what I mean? Answer B: She got probed!

How did you do? Did you score a 70? Did you get seven of the ten questions correct? Are you ready to move onto the next book, Chapters 60 through 69?

Chapter 60
The Secret Cubes

Megachurch St. Wx was a buzz of commotion. Occasionally interrupted by screams and uncontrollable tears, people were on edge... Members were asking, "Where did they go? They could not have just vanished!" The magic was missing from St. Wx.

By contrast, the Cube X penthouse was quiet. The square room held a rectangular table in the center. The lights were dim. Twelve people faced each other with the top chair empty. The focus was on the vacant seat that was usually occupied.

In front of each person was a name tag. The chair behind the title "CEO/COO" was empty.

People just stared at it, as if waiting for a miracle to happen at any moment. "We are a ship without a rudder. We lost our anchor!" For the first time, they did not know their future.

They felt sick. Anxiety made them physically ill. Their shaky hands created rippling surfaces and splashes in the liquid in their cups, so they clutched them with two hands and took only small sips. Occasionally, the quiet was interrupted by a person evacuating the room in an emergency. Luckily the toilets were nearby.

Like the BLOCK, K.L.O.P., and even Q.R.U.V.... S.T.W.X. was comprised of identical cubes, each 100 meters high, 100 by100 meters wide with spacing between them.

However, if you are reading these words, you have never seen St. Wx. The reason being is that it was a magnet to darkness. There was constantly a shadow surrounding the structures. It seemed even trash became attached to the buildings.

Perhaps at one time it may have been ornamented with beautiful plants, but they all were now in various stages of death. You got used to the smell, but it was not pleasant. Even the interior was fashioned similarly to the BLOCK but had evolved into locked rooms and secret passageways. Logic did not dictate location within the cubes. For example, the toilets were in the kitchens. Maybe this made sense for ease of disposal, but it just did not seem right. Maybe comical, but correct, the interior was shitty Sha Chi and Si Chi (the opposite of Feng Shui).

The idea behind St. Wx was for it to be a religious organization with total freedom, no government interference. Instead of taxes, the congregation paid mandatory tithes. Supposedly everything was equal. But as things evolved, the rich got richer and the poor got poorer. Corruption was quicker.

Cube T was only used as a medical building and the most active place in the complex. Triage was overrun by those people who self-medicated. Today at Cube T, there were protestors who wanted doctor assisted suicides.

One man pressed his hand forward, imagining that a fog would move away. He quickly looked down to assure himself he was standing on solid ground and balanced. Left foot: stomp. Both feet: Stomp, stomp. Yes, he was stable.

Closing your eyes did not distort the image; was it real? **When you closed your eyes, the darkness was still there.**

In Cube W, designated the work area, sat people monotonously doing their jobs. Managers managing managers managing members. Those confined to this Cube were the productive people. Workers were exhausted, and without purpose or meaning. It was a complex commune with overlapping layers of unproductivity. All movements were monitored and measured. They were domesticated animals on short leashes... and beaten too often. The occasional argument was actually a reassurance that some people still cared. "I hate you!"

There were those who, well... forgive me, had BAD burned into them. It is almost a curse to mention them, and their names cannot be uttered. But these are the folks who got pleasure from others' pain. Individuals, not members of groups or gangs, these people were at all levels and used all means and methods to deliberately delight in any decadent form of entertainment. These !&$☠@✳#! could be very clever and creative. Stay alert... **Beware. Be aware.**

First their leader leaves, then suddenly a mass disappearance of the sweetest souls. "Now is the time." (Mr. G quote) Many speculated on the meaning, but eventually it was dismissed. Only the Believers kept this memory...

And it was against the rules to be a Believer. You would be re-educated or even excommunicated from St. Wx. if anyone were to find out.

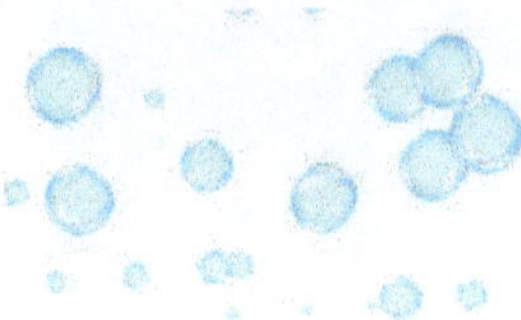

The overlapping of day-to-day activity made this momentous event disappear. Some things cannot be written. Some things cannot be told. Some things we are not to know. Here ends this chapter with a chunk of history that was washed away.

Chapter 61
SOS + SBB = SOB

St. Wx was not about the buildings... but the people. The people were negative and disconnected themselves from others... non-absorbent like the sticky film in the smoking rooms. There was a presence that pelted you non-stop... It was a unique sensation that penetrated deep inside you; a feeling of something passing through you, making your hairs prickle, or something swarming over you. Even standing still with your eyes closed, you could feel darkness.

Think of a magnet's polarities. The negative repels the positive and vice versa. St. Wx was a repelling place.

People were" fearious" (a combination of fear and unknown automatic anger, not conscious). It was a hidden burning feeling... not at all pleasant... they did not know why they had a rotting sensation from within.

St. Wx was unstable. The psychologist Dr. Meutal gave his expert opinion, "You want to know about the people here at St. Wx?" He paused to catch his breath. "Well, I can only speak in generalities. I never discuss individual patients." His shoulders shuddered as he began to relax. On his desk was a round sphere that he rubbed his hand across. He was not hiding that he was one of the Believers. Dr. Meutal smiled often.

"Addiction... anger... anxiety... bi-polar...dementia...depression... loss of self-control... negative actions... schizophrenia... temptation..." Taking in a deep breath caused him to redirect himself.

"What is good? What is bad? I am not here to judge. I am here to help." He sounded like somebody who was out of place at St. Wx.

"A vice can be anything that leads to something out of your control. You have to look at frequency, how often, and strength, the urge." That was something he had memorized from a textbook.

Then he muttered, "The point of no return." Dr. Meutal became noticeably saddened.

"Time's up! You can return next week. Schedule an appointment."

He kept himself busy to avoid the strife of his daily life. Dr. Meutal and his wife were hiding something that hurt.

St. Wx had long been separated from the original BLOCK. The group of Believers were primarily those born at St. Wx but knew the BLOCK was real. They heard of things spoken by their grandparents or parents in private.

The slang word for these people was, "Those S.O.B.'s!" (Society of Believers). They met outside at the intersection of the four buildings. This bullseye, at the center of the four corners, gave them a view in all directions. This was a perfect place to hide.

Who would have ever thought that behind piles of garbage was where you would find people who were happy? Sure, they had their problems, but they seemed to overcome their obstacles. **Hope assured them that one day their suffering would end. This optimism came from their belief that there was something stronger that would save them.**

During the day, they would look up to see the smog clouds form different shapes. "Look closely. The smoke is moving." "Look, I see a flower!" Soon everybody started to share his or her imaginary finds.

Occasionally there was a reassurance that they were not alone. Some days the skies could be seen when the wind created a vortex at the bullseye where the four corners met. This tunnel pushed the dark clouds away. They could see the light of the sun. Today birds came to visit and the flies vanished. It seemed every time they met, they were strengthened.

When not congregated together, they had secret codes. They called themselves "S.O.S." which meant Society of Smiles. And rather than saying "Hello", they would cup their hands together, curving their fingers tightly upward, forming a scoop.

There were those called the "subliminal bubbles". These were the wilted flowers that had once believed. Inside their hearts, hidden deep, was hope. Some of them were exposed, imprisoned, and reprogrammed.

Subliminal Bubble Believers (S.B.B. for short) were dispersed at every level, in every place within St. Wx. There was no radar that could detect them. **The only thing that remained private inside St. Wx was what was in your heart.**

Some things cannot be written or told. Something beautiful happened at St. Wx. It coincided with the building of the BLOCK Cathedral, and again during the erection at Camp KLOP. **Nobody talked about these events** – neither the Believers, nor those wishing it to disappear as unwritten history.

What happened? We can only speculate... Some things we are not to know.

Chapter 62
Meet the Players

Things were not totally dreary inside St. Wx. There was the Playground. Every weekend there would be a day of fights. It began with the beginners, the amateurs, and people chosen from the spectators to spar. There were three cages in the playground surrounded by elevated seats to see the circus. Each cage was a separate fight.

Routinely, the bouts would begin at noon and last until midnight. But this schedule was not strictly adhered to. If the moment warranted, there would be blood shed into the next day. It was the best amusement. You were always assured of seeing something violent!

The climax was a free-for-all. This was usually the professional fighters. There were no rules, and weapons were accepted. However, it was discouraged to bring a gun, because in the past, one man too quickly made sport of the rest. Long and painful was more pleasing to see.

The Playground was sponsored by the Board. The tithes financed free food and of course alcohol. Recreational drugs were for sale at the concession stands, but with an unusually high mark-up.

The Board sponsored the weekly event, but lately it had lapsed, since the disappearance of the CEO/COO.

Perhaps the most influential Board Member was named "104". She controlled three seats of the twelve-member Board. Her vote consisted of her, her oldest daughter, and youngest son. 104 was a professional politician, a community organizer... and a !&$☠@✳#!

Her net worth was zero units and she had no real income. She eked out a very nice living, however, from political contributions.

104's public image was impeccable. Everybody loved her (except those that truly knew her). She was a master of manipulation! The diva of deception!

Her title was Head of the Party. 104 was responsible for entertainment. The festivities were free perks for the people at St. Wx. The last big event 104 planned was themed "Happy Birthday", which was ridiculous. Nobody celebrated their birth date. Her finest festivity was the "Day of the Pencil" ... which was frankly fun!

Panhandling was not allowed, forbidden, but not enforced. If you asked for a donation, you were probably ignored. Even security would not arrest the beggars, because in jail they got free food and a room – this pulled profits from St. Wx.

However, both men and women would be picked up for services in exchange for units. Depending on the level of your skill, the more money you could make. It was possible to make more money as a freelancer than to have a job at St. Wx. Tithes were not taken; you were free of the lances that cut your pockets.

Everybody knew DD "Baby" Maye (pronounced ma-yay, stressing the second syllable, yeah!), she was a member of the Board. Baby was originally a beggar but made her way to wealth through the most popular eatery called the Playroom (not to be confused with the Playground). There were many women who mastered the three-hole orgy, but they say "Baby is the Best!" (The tagline used during her last election campaign.)

Another member of the Board, "Big Daddy" Don Gottfried, happily hired beggars. He was shrewd and maybe the richest man at St. Wx. He gave poor people work, "bonded labor" was what it was called. In exchange for your effort, you paid off your debts. It was frankly a form of slavery because his servants never earned enough to leave.

Don was a real "rags to riches" story. He started by organizing the workers at St. Wx. Coercive, Don Gottfried created alliances, associations, and unions that were structures to bond the masses together. Big daddy Don did under the table deals that padded "his people" with units. Morbidly obese, he paid for two extra chairs and controlled a quarter of the Board.

"Dick Richter, nice to meet you." It was not catchy, but everybody knew where he stood. He was always re-elected because of his reputation, 'A rule is a rule.' Richter was rock rigid, with no empathy or compassion. His responsibilities included General of the military, Chief of the security forces, and the only judge at St. Wx. This was his life. He took no sides, was not part of any faction, including the group of illegal Believers. Dick Richter was a loner.

That was two-thirds of the elected Board: There was 104 and her two underqualified kids, DD "Baby" Maye, "Big Daddy" Don Gottfried and his duo, and don't forget Dick Richter.

Chapter 63
St. Wx Secrets

Some people need no introduction and that was the case for M. T. Nobel, Sr. Esquire. As far back as anybody could remember, he was "the" Attorney. When St. Wx split from the BLOCK, it was M. T. Nobel Sr. who acquired the original satellite sites. The farms, factories, mines, storage, and sales sites became part of St. Wx. To avoid taxation and disclosure, M. T. Nobel Sr. founded the church from the four letters that represented Cubes S, T, W, and X.

M. T. Nobel Sr. was an original Board Member, which he created. He now held three seats with voting powers. His son and daughter (from two unnamed concubines), Junior and Opium II, were honorary Board Members since birth. What they did in public was tightly controlled by their father. What they did in private was none of M. T. Nobel Senior's concern. The two were neglected.

The siblings found humor in the fact that the CEO/COO had vanished. Their anxiety came from scoring higher on video games. It was entertaining for them to see the reactions of the other Board Members.

That would account for 11 of the 12 Board Members sequestered on the top floor. The last member was Dr. Edgar "Ek" Krass. The two major points about Ek were that he was a real medical doctor and he lacked basic hygiene.

His exterior presence personified what he was like inside. He found joy in every abortion and euthanasia. His only redeeming value was that he was good at keeping secrets. He was constantly asking questions and knew where all the skeletons were hidden.

He sat motionless in his high chair wearing a stained white jacket. He pulled from his pocket a lace panty and proceeded to blow his nose into its cotton crotch, then threw it into the corner of the room.

At this point, most neglected their duties. People were unsupervised... they wandered. This spawned the explorers, the "searchers" who wanted to scavenge concealed treasures.

Locked doors were opened and secret passageways found. There was a major discovery in Sublevel 2, just below the docks. This was where the "Beast" was located.

Part of the original structure, the Beast was a series of pneumatic tubes used to transport people around St. Wx. Everybody was fond of the Beast, which was derived from the archaic abbreviation "BLOCK Easy Access — Swift Transportation". The main configuration was two figure 8 tubes with pods moving in opposite directions. In the center of the two circles were gyroscopes to add stability.

One day the searchers opened the long-locked doors to the stabilizing rooms. However, what they found were incinerators that burned their daily garbage, solid and liquid wastes. This was the source of the stench and pervasive dark plumes.

Some said it was a subliminal symbol of those who followed the spheres, blaming the Believers. Others argued that this couldn't be true because they were just two circular rooms with flat floors and ceilings, not spheres. None the less, they were not gyroscopes and they did nothing to steady the structures. Despite this, people still loved their Beast and used it to lazily move around.

The searchers were incentivized and created a new part-time pastime.

Another secret was disclosed. On floors six through eight of the infirmary were the psychiatric wards. The previous eighth floor patients were pushed out and released into the general population, apart from the most extreme cases of dementia, schizophrenia, and other psychotic disorders. Psych was condensed into only the sixth and seventh floors... which were already overpopulated.

On the eighth-floor men and women disrobed for their daily extractions. Their cloth gowns stuck to their bodies by globs of black stinky goo that oozed from infected boils. Some of the sores would erupt! The job of lancing and sucking out the pus was not given to the medical staff. These disgusting jobs were outsourced to one of Don Gottfried's groups. These care givers had no choice.

Although the doctors were baffled as to the source of these infections, they derived that the immune systems of the workers were declining. Antibiotics were given, but not working. There was no cure. The rate of those afflicted was swelling. It was an epidemic that was about to explode.

They say **the difference between humans and animals is their ability to think ahead.** Animals are only instinctive. What happens when humans evolve into animals?

Chapter 64
Another Beginning

It is thought that dreams are a prediction of the future. If this is the case, many people had the same reoccurring nightmare. The work area stopped!

There was a slight variation to these nightly hauntings, but they were all basically the same. Dreams were compared to one another and the ending always matched. They were at their workplace, and then there was a total blackout. No power, no lights, nothing. Then you would wake up abruptly, shaking with extreme shock.

If you were to consult the self-proclaimed mediums at St. Wx, they all had different explanations. None were the same. The dreams were identical, but the interpretations were all over the place.

The psychics, seers, soothsayers, fortune tellers, astrologists, oracles, occultists, prognosticators, prophesiers, and diviners were all the same. They were very clever and creative. Supposedly they focused on the inner flame. **But these illuminists could not explain the darkness.**

The biggest clue was overlooked. When Dr. Meutal was asked about the meaning of these nightmares he answered, "I don't know. I do not have this problem." He smiled and fondled a sphere he had in his pocket.

This may not be the biggest story, but the Believers did not have these dreams. With the law laxer, they would greet each other with cupped hands and say, "Now is the time."

Then there was the announcement, "The Playground will start again." Perhaps the Board could fix these problems? At the least, it would **divert and distract**. The professional fighters were back in training. With this news, the pharmacies were flooded.

Not everything was bad. There was something good beginning to happen. The size of the S.O.S. group that congregated in the crosshairs of the four corners began to increase in size. Rubbish needed to be moved aside to make room for the new converts.

They began to get organized, also. They started by sharing stories. But they were a miss-mash in different directions. Somebody suggested they start at the beginning.

"First, there was a flood that covered the world in water." said one simpleton.

"Ah, not that far back... Let's begin with the BLOCK. Maybe tell the stories of Mr. G?" They agreed.

There was a group of young executives that found out how to get to the rooftops. During their lunch breaks they ventured up. At first, they walked the 100-meter distance and looked over the edge. Their fears soon disappeared, and they decided to make a sport of it. They called themselves the "roof runners".

The group increased in size as they added some of the rough kids that worked as office grunts. First, they decided to kick a ball across the ravine between each building. That was fun, until the balls bounced off the edge.

Their courage evolved into stupidity. During lunch breaks they became superheroes! One day somebody got the clever idea of placing bounce boards at the edges of each cube so they could jump the 40-meter crevasse.

Never once did one fall the 100 meters to become a stain below. Run... hit... dive... land, drop, and roll... Then stand up and run again. Some added acrobatics. Exciting!

This bravery evolved into arrogance. On a particularly wet day, instead of sling shots and paint ball wars across the edge, they looked down to find the crowd of Believers that were huddled in the intersection. The rough boys decided to be the tough boys.

The rooftop runners took the tube to the first floor and went out to bully the Believers. They used their sling shots and paint ball guns and fired upon the innocent. Exciting!

The Believers were a passive group and only shielded themselves against the volleys. Unfortunately/fortunately, their lunch break was over and the bullies went back to work.

The next day they decided to go back to their rooftop running. But there were those who thought this was becoming mundane. They were still enthused with the idea of beating the Believers. Eventually, the pack mentality came into play. The next week they planned to surprise the Believers and really give them a pounding!

The results were not as expected. Security caught wind of the Believers hiding outside and arrested them. They were taken down to Sublevel Three of St. Wx, where they were processed. Each person got a towel and tunic then placed with the others in one large open area.

It was crowded inside the jail, but inside their hearts, it was empty. Now is the time?

Chapter 65
Secrets Everybody Knew

The work area started to move again, however most people were on chat lines to find out what was new, not doing their assigned tasks. Remember, nothing is private at St. Wx? **People love to hear secrets!**

When this news broke about the Believers being busted, many people walked away from their duties. The subliminal bubbles burst. There were many over the following days that turned themselves in. Considering their environment, **being imprisoned with better people was not so bad.**

The reoccurring nightmares spawned special sects. The masses started to monitor the discussions looking for answers. In the beginning, it was just postings, but eventually it became factions with leaders. The fanatical extreme psychics got the most attention of course. Their suggestion was to wear sunglasses. When these nightmares were non-stop, people were willing to try anything to alleviate their suffering...

There was only one slight mention of the eighth-floor infirmary. It was an advertisement that suggested if you have projectile vomiting and diarrhea, the cost of 50 units would be the cure. It was only a lure to pull the pre-plague victims from the population.

Then there were the hedonists, those who sought sensual self-pleasure. The Playroom delivered daily promotions for the restaurant and recreation areas. Ah, there is nothing like instant gratification! People have to eat, right?

The Playroom was an entire floor fashioned after the original C³ centers at the BLOCK. It was probably the cleanest place at St. Wx. The walls were still sparkling!

The Playroom provided a friendly atmosphere to eat and be entertained. It was not what you would think. Some said there was not just sex, but there was love in the Playroom. Here there were infinite choices. The menu contained both food and fun. It was an entire booklet with "special desserts". There was even a map of the service locations. The only rules were that you had to pay for what you bought and "No" means "No."

The entire floor was without walls, nothing private. You could be eating next to couples engaged in full intercourse. Cushions and cloths were interspersed on the padded floor. In each corner were thrilling themes for those interested.

Some of the services were without charge. Maybe this was the only place at St. Wx that you could get something for free. Doms and subs... gay, straight, bi... singles, couples, groups...those with unique fetishes... voyeurs and players... Whatever the hedonist heart desired! It was possibly the only place that you had the feeling of freedom. "If it's free, it's for me."

Oh, and the hot dogs were good, also.

There were those who "had" ...and the others were "have nots". There were floors with doors and those without. Financial power granted access to better living spaces. The residential zones were dispersed throughout each Cube. There was no logic to their location.

The largest living areas were reserved for the wealthiest. These came fully furnished with fixtures and furniture and (direct access to) free deliveries. The floor plans did not disclose their hidden passages and safe spots in these quarters.

The lower classes lived on the floors without doors. But that was fine, because often people would not sleep in the same bed as the night before. What was not shared was stolen. That was fine too, because you usually had quick access to anything you wanted if you were not picky. It was accepted.

Tithes (taxes) were done the old fashion way – they were mandatory "donations". The less you made, the more you paid. The poor paid for the rich. Many times socialists suggested change, but not to be fooled again, these reforms were worse than before. **This was a communist complex.**

Fancy a dance with a game of chance? You could always go to the casino. They say that **once** somebody placed a one unit bet and made a million! In truth, this was another deception. The odds were not in your favor. And like the tithes, the poorer paid. But it did not matter... They had nothing to lose, they all were already losers!

"Dear Father." This was how the prayer began. "Please help us here at St. Wx. We are your Believers that have been imprisoned in Sublevel Three. Amen." With that there was a concluding chorus of "Amen".

"Ok, now what do we do?"

"I don't know. I just heard my grandparents do this..."

"Did they hear anything back?"

"I think so... because He was listening."

Chapter 66

Secrets in the Shadows

On the first floor of the Medical Cube, T1, newbies were put on display. Babies born at St. Wx were shown for a short time then sent off to either orphanages or boarding schools. (This depended on the wealth of the parents.)

Like a cut, even after the knife was removed, it still stung. It left emotional scars... When these babies reached working age they were either reunited with their families, or forgotten.

"Ah, a moment of pleasure followed by pain." Dr. Meutal was thinking out loud while viewing the sealed baskets of babies.

"Oh, now is the time? How are you feeling?" Dr. Meutal smiled." I only have a moment. I was just checking on my patients here."

Meutal moved from the hospital to the office and back again. It was impossible to be in more than one place at a time.

"Let's walk and talk... energy release?" Without pausing, he continued, "Do you know the secret to happiness?"

Everybody underestimates the value of little things... until they are gone. We take things for granted; we overlook the obvious, instead we focusing on something else."

"Take for example... air. Air is very important! Take advantage of it now with some very thankful, deep breaths. Ahhhhh..."

They continued their walk from the infirmary to his clinic, "And then there is water... H_2O is underestimated as well! Two-thirds of our body is water... not coffee, soda, tea, juice, milk. Would you shower or bathe in these? Better yet, how do you feel when you are not clean outside?" The best drink made ever was simple water, nothing else."

"Obviously, most health problems are started by dehydration. Water cleans the inside of your body as well as the outside."

Eye to eye, "I want you to make a commitment, an oath, a promise to yourself. **Take deep enjoying breaths. Drink plenty of pure water. And be happy with what you have and what you see.**"

"I will make three promises to you... Days one through three, you will need to pee... like a racehorse! Days four to seven, you are reaching heaven as you detox. Your body is changing now. Then you will feel better and beyond... in more ways than one!"

Dr. Meutal slowed his pace and started to sound even less like a psychologist... "Your core body temperature is 37 degrees (Celsius, 98.6 degrees Fahrenheit)... your external skin temperature is less, like 31 or 32 (degrees Celsius, 89 degrees Fahrenheit)... However, when you get a cut or a bruise, that area will heat up... Your body needs skin like a hot engine needs a radiator... And both need water."

His waiting room was forever full... People waiting for his wisdom. "Today, for you... free, no charge... Just remember, the secret to success is how you define it. **Forget what other people think. Believe in yourself. Be happy with what you have. Be grateful... not greedy.**"

The best things in life are free. But **you also get what you pay for.** The self-proclaimed prophets suggested sunglasses. They made a nice profit on that advice. It seems when people are desperate, they will do anything. The nightmares however were not gone.

Junior and Opium II were sitting on their sofa searching the sites for their next score. Junior preferred a bottle of wine with a methaqualone; this always made him feel disconnected from reality. Opium was more creative. She was searching for a slave for the night. In exchange for a good meal and a nice bed, she could get a full body massage and unlimited sex. She always preferred chubby men, "Bears". She enjoyed giving them a pleasure they may otherwise never have. She was considered a "giver" when it came to sex.

It was then that Junior and Opium II read the rumor of the Believers being detained. It seems they had the same idea when they went to the secret vault hidden in the kitchen/bathroom. They opened the panel and pulled out an old wooden box. They rubbed the dust from the block and then went down together to Sublevel Three.

Dick Richter was not there so it was easy to pass items to the inmates. Powerless guards knew they had to do what they were told when it came to Board Members. When the Believers received the box, the two siblings slipped away. There was something of value in the block of wood that they knew the Believers needed.

Chapter 67
Let's Talk

"Have you ever wondered what people outside our communal church think of us here at St. Wx? Do they think we are immortal blood sucking vampires or demons?" Laughing, "Perhaps part of that is true."

Why do we always hear about those people experiencing the extreme? Not the mundane? Here are random interviews with people within St. Wx. Bear through the boring:

"I am one of those crazy coots here. I work in production... I found something fun to do. What I like to do is one more... If I am to make 50, I make 51. It drives people crazy! But one day a friend gave me an amphetamine, an upper, speed. I was zooming! I did not sleep on my job and didn't take a break. Well, I produced one more than everybody else combined! I almost lost my job that day."

"I'm ok... I am fine. Some people have it worse than me. I think we will make our profit goal again here at St. Wx. Isn't that great?"

"Nobody tells me anything. It is like they want you to fail! We have a constant fear of the unknown. I have been made a spectacle before. It was sick humor for someone else... at my expense. Now I just keep my nose down, mind my own business, and keep my mouth shut."

"I get paid for smiling and asking strangers, 'Did you get your free gift?' It was the best lure tactic to get people to our showroom. You know, people are unable to see three, four, five, or six steps ahead. Clever, huh? This friendly face just made 500 units. Oh, the gift? I tell them it is worth 5000 units."

"Things have gone from bad to worse around here. I am thinking about paying one of those psychics everybody is talking about."

"My husband and I are both doctors; we had a lovely life. When I gave birth to triplets, things changed. They were going to ship our babies off to boarding school. But then Mr. G came and took our girls. Not a day goes by... "She continues to cry. "They are in a special place."

"I am a sweat back, day labor... Freelancer? There are good days and bad weeks. Sometimes I barely have enough for cigarettes and beer! Forgive me, I do not mean to complain. I am not looking for a handout. I am here to give you a hand."

"I am tired... I am sick. Sick and tired of my boss taking credit for all my work. I just hear words. The CEO/COO said, 'You are a valuable asset to St. Wx.' But my boss deducted my wages and told me, 'You are a worthless wasted fuck!'"

"I was so happy at the original BLOCK. People would ask me, 'How are you?' Coming here was a trap. Oh well, that is life... Life is life?"

"One day my wife and I went to the Playroom for dinner. Guess who served us? DD Maye! I remember she was wearing lavender lace gloves. My wife and I both smiled at her. Guess what happened then? DD smiled back! It gets better! When I went to pay, she comp'd our meal. It was free!"

"Repetitive rumors! Lies left unproven become truths... Why should I worry about what other people think of me? But I do.... Rumors attack my reputation. If I am right, and everybody else is wrong, I should be strong."

"You are the corn in my shit!" then he walked away in a tirade, "Fuck you and your clown!".

"I am just overwhelmed. My head is all cloudy. I can't think. This is beyond being too much. And it has been like this for a long time. I just don't care anymore. Nobody cares anyway."

"Discrimination... I am a victim, and if I complain, I am not a "team" player. Denied because I am different, feared, or deemed offensive to others. No money, looks, status... no diversity. I cannot express myself."

"What do you want to know? Yes, I pay my tithes, I live on a floor without doors. Just like everybody else, I get these dreadful dreams every night that one day the work will stop. Then what will we do?"

"Today you support me... tomorrow somebody will support you." In the sublevel cells where the Believers were amassed, it was pure enjoyment for the first time. Now that was peer enjoyment!

Chapter 68

Sincerely Sunny

It was destined to happen. St. Wx was as predictable as a poorly made horror movie. Life at St. Wx was evolving. Let's see how many predictions you saw coming. Let's talk.

Not everything is good, not everything is bad. The buildings at St. Wx were going through a transformation. The enslaved Believers were furloughed to fix the Beast. The incinerators were removed and replaced with purification systems in the two circular rooms. Perhaps they were preparing for something clean to come? People generally clean their homes before guests arrive.

But St. Wx was about the people, not the place. The outside improved but it was rotten from within.

Then you have Sunny... the only light skinned, strawberry blonde giant at St. Wx... Fortune's frown: he was brain damaged during his birthing; he was too dumb to know he was stupid. And he fit right in with the other folks at St. Wx! He lived a life without boundaries, not knowing the difference between black and white behavior.

Sunny did not suffer... He had empathy, but an innocent mind. Sunny had a sweet disposition, always smiling. He was permanently pleased as he roamed near his home that he owned.

Full disclosure: Sunny's real name was August RG3; the third of four children born to a wealthy family. Yes, Sunny was born with a silver shovel in his mouth. Some people said Sunny was a descendent of the dozen wealthy philanthropists that seeded money to build the original BLOCK. Let's talk...

He was the love child that the mother never admitted to. "Momma's baby, daddy's maybe." "The son of the mother I know, the son of the father I don't know." But do you really care about the affair?

His mother moved the family from the BLOCK to St. Wx before Sunny was born. His mother became mean like you never had seen! Later she devilishly divorced the dad, sucking him of all his worth. Adding to that, the manipulating momma made her guppies ghost their poor papa.

We do not know where his daddies are. When shipped back to St. Wx from boarding school, Sunny was not claimed. None the less, Sunny was special.

A book could be written, or a movie made just on DD "Baby" Maye. Deep down she was a doppelgänger of J'me eXquisite. Deep down they shared the same genetic disposition, but there were obvious differences. Perhaps this was due to the environments both came from? Let's talk to DD...

Interviewer: "Thank you for allowing us to chat with you."
DD: "My pleasure."
Interviewer: "The floor is yours. Is there anything you would like to share with our audience?"

DD after a moment of reflection: "Sure. Thank you. I do have something... Can I talk about sex and love?"

Interviewer: "Feel comfortable to say anything you want."

DD: "Everybody is pre-wired to need love... and sex. It is natural. People are born with libidos or sex drives. We all have a desire to give love and be loved...."

DD looked at the interviewer to gauge his reaction, then kept going. "Men and women are wired differently. For example, women want more love, men want more sex. In general, of course. Everybody is different."

Interviewer: "Let's talk." He then leaned forward to listen.

DD: "The same with sexy... Everybody has a different vision... infinite variations. Imagine no rules, freedom... nothing immoral or moral, no code. It's just self-discipline and self-control.

The Believers in Sublevel Three did not make a fuss. Secretly, supplies of food, drink, hygiene products and cleaning supplies were brought in for the Believers. Items were miraculously delivered to meet their needs before they wanted them. These anonymous donations made their captivity comfortable.

With the best Believers already emigrated out, those that remained had to become better.

Noticing how the cell walls began to shine, the Believers were summoned to repair the Beast in the basement. This had a profound affect. This sense of purpose united the Believers. They learned to work together to complete a task. **Teamwork replaced individualism. Independence was replaced with interdependence. Communal living was made good again.**

Meanwhile, an everyday inmate was talking to a young Believer. "Would you believe I was

a pedophile pastor? Really! Then I discovered I had a foot fetish. Now I am a podiatrist not a pedophile. You have nice toes." With that he goosed her, jamming his hand up her butt crack. "Oh, those days are behind me." Laughing...

Chapter 69
The Safe Word is "No"

DD stopped her soliloquy to say, "Are you sure this is ok?"

Interviewer: "Perfect, keep going."

DD: "Thank you... We live with conflicting commandments. We are told what not to do, 'Thou shall not...', 'Don't judge others.'... 'Sex is a sin.' The root purpose was for our joy... **Not about not...** I believe it should be simpler.

"Then we have customs that forbid us from doing something different. Society has placed norms on us to create conformity! Taboos, for example."

DD was passionate on this topic. "They are unacceptable! Let's get logical. Open your mind. Taboos started with good intentions, but bad results... The truth is frequent love and sex has proven to improve our physical and psychological well-being. It's all about happiness.

"With any deviant behavior, the question is, 'Where you born or did you become this way?' The answer is 'both'. As I said, we are prewired, but we are constantly influenced by what we see and hear around us. After enough repetition, **your 'normal' and my 'normal' are not the same.**

"Everybody is different; we come in all shapes and sizes. What may be acceptable to me, may not be acceptable to you as a result. Do you agree?"

Interviewer: "You make a good point, DD."

DD: "**Making love is a personal affair...** Women: It is not "Wo (stop) men! Women get horny just like men. They say 70% of all people masturbate. If you take offense to this, then don't do it. But also, do not feel you can control others' opinions and limits... If two or more people are compatible and consent to physical or emotional intimacy, go for it. Have fun!

"Mr. G wants us to be happy, right? I am not your judge; nobody really knows... And we are to love each other? **Restrict your restrictions and live life to its fullest without fear.** Relax and stop inhibiting yourself by unseen fear, go without guilt."

The interviewer nodded his head in agreement. Then DD said, "Give me a moment. There is something else I wish to say."

DD: "Intimacy... **There is a difference between love and sex...**" After another pause, she continued." We all want to be wanted... We want pleasure. It seems simple... Love is an emotion, while copulating is a physical pleasure. You can have love without sex and sex without love. But when you merge the physical act with emotional stimulation, it is ecstasy!

"Do not confuse the two. Know the difference... Make the distinction, because sometimes sex sure does feel like love. Do you desire mental or physical fulfillment? What is your motivation?

"Lust is not as long-lasting as love. After lust, you want to leave; after loving you want to stay. **You don't really want to know the other personally, so just forget about it.** Do not distract yourself with destructive thoughts. If it is love you want, bond and be committed to each other. Agree to respect each other's wants and needs.

"Sure, sexual excitement is emotional. But they are two different levels... Sex can make you hot, but it is love that keeps you warm.

"**You can give unlimited love.** You can love more than one with no limit on the number. Can you love both your father and mother? Does a parent only love one child? Can you love more than one mate? Sexually sharing yourself with more than one is also possible.

"Having sex is not bad... it depends on the experience. It can be pure... pure pleasure. What do you want to feel? Listen to yourself... What do you wish at the end? Impulsive sex is fun but be wise to the outcome. **But don't look to others to define your desires.**

"I urge everyone to get closer to one another. Not necessarily physically, but emotionally."

Finally, DD finished with a yelp, "Whew, did I wear that out?"

Interviewer: "May I follow up with a question, please?" Both had loosened up... "Emotional ouch. Not for me, but for my friend... What do you say about people who are in a committed relationship exploring sex with others?"

DD: "**Two as one is more fun!** Being bonded is better...You share everything from work to play. Not everybody can handle a physical connection without feeling: If you are the sensitive type that gets attached quickly, avoid intimacy elsewhere. Communications is key. **Keep each other fully aware, then there are no negatives, just positive outcomes.** Have it enhance your self-esteem and create a confident relationship!"

QUIZ

VI

Quiz Six

On the next page is a list of 60+ feelings that described the people at St. Wx., the real world. There are no right or wrong answers, only honest answers.

Even if you do not know the meaning, do not skip any description. And no cheating! Do not look at the answer page until you have completed all the questions and tallied your totals for each question letter/column.

Best results: Set aside half an hour to do this quiz. If you do it too quickly, you may be disappointed with the results. Do not start and stop; complete the survey at one sitting.

Question S

<u>Do you currently have</u> (during the last week) any of these feelings? Place the letter "S" in all the boxes that apply.

Question T

<u>Have you ever</u> felt any of these feelings? Place the letter "T" in all the boxes that apply.

Question W

<u>Do you have</u> close friends or family, frequent acquaintances with folks that have these feelings? Place the letter "W" in all the boxes that apply.

Question X

<u>Have you ever</u> met anybody who had these feelings? Place the letter "X" in all the boxes that apply.

What is your total number of boxes marked? (Count down each column.)

S	T	W	X	SCORES

S T W X FEELINGS

S	T	W	X	
				insincere

S	T	W	X	
				hustled
				misguided
				deceived
				exploited
				bullied
				oppressed

				fearful
				"fearious"
				on edge
				anxious

				evolving
				unstable
				instinctive

				toxic
				dark
				heartless
				hatred
				dreary
				painful

				congested
				crushed
				crowded
				overpopulated

S	T	W	X	
				scared

				traumatized
				insecure
				ridiculed
				demoralized
				exposed
				emotionally scarred
				suffering

				lackadaisical
				lax
				apathetic
				passive
				spiritless
				mundane

				supressed
				bound
				boxed in
				trapped
				powerless

S	T	W	X	
				confused

				untrusting
				cynical
				hopeless
				negative
				pessimistic

				overloaded
				overworked
				weak
				tired
				sick
				sleep deprived
				dehydrated

				disconnected
				unappreciated
				unloved
				friendless
				neglected
				unvalued

				stupid

Q6 – Answers

1.   Insert the totals scores for each question. Next, is math.

2.   Multiply the tally of S answers by two (2), T answers by one (1). Do the same with W times two and X times one.... You are basically doubling the values of S and W scores.

3.   Now we will add S plus T to get your innate or inner feelings.

4.   Add W and X to score your surroundings.

5.   Now check your scores to see what they indicate about you and your situation.

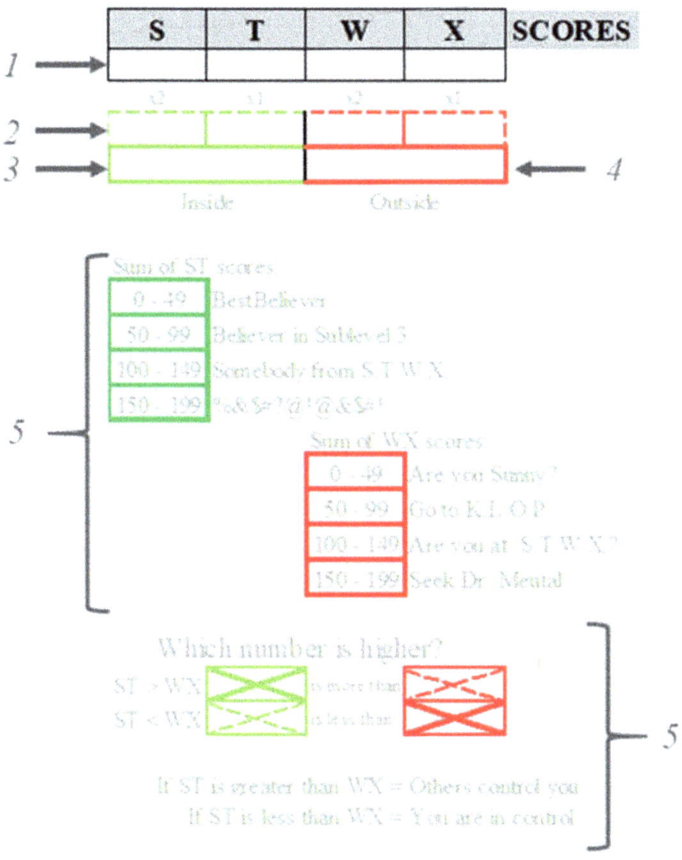

S   T   W   X   SCORES
1
x2   x1   x2   x1
2
3
4
Inside
Outside
Sum of ST scores
0 - 49   BestBeliever
50 - 99   Believer in Sublevel 3
100 - 149   Somebody from S T W X
150 - 199   %&$*?@!@ &$*!
Sum of WX scores
0 - 49   Are you Sunny?
50 - 99   Go to K L O P
100 - 149   Are you at S T W X?
150 - 199   Seek Dr. Mental
5
Which number is higher?
ST > WX   is more than
ST < WX   is less than
5
If ST is greater than WX = Others control you
If ST is less than WX = You are in control

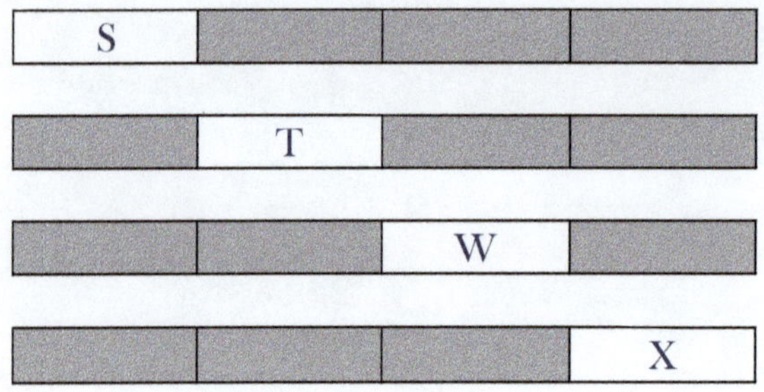

S	T	W	X	SCORES
x2	x1	x2	x1	

Inside   Outside

Sum of ST scores:

0 - 49	BestBeliever
50 - 99	Believer in Sublevel 3
100 - 149	Somebody from S.T.W.X.
150 - 199	!&$☠@ ✳ #!

Sum of WX scores:

0 - 49	Are you Sunny?
50 - 99	Go to K.L.O.P.
100 - 149	Are you at S.T.W.X.?
150 - 199	Seek Dr. Mental

Which number is higher?

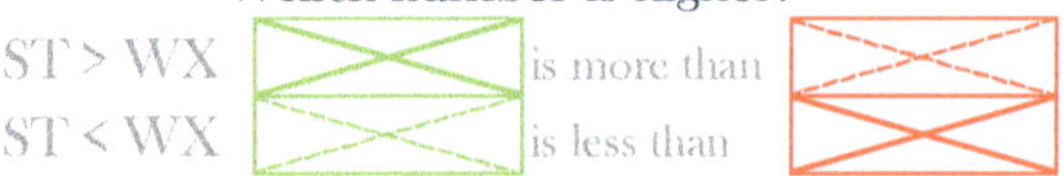

If ST is greater than WX = Others control you

If ST is less than WX = You are in control

Are you in control or do others control you? How did you feel? Are you ready to move onto the next book, Chapters 70 through 79?

Chapter 70
Completing Oneself

J'me found herself back at the camp. Her experience at QRUV was not to be believed, so she kept that to herself. Plus, she was not sure what to say...

A renewed sense of happiness came over her. She had abundance and was enjoying everything. She was excited to be with friends and family again. Today she loved every smile more than before! She strolled to Mac and Mar'Ann's home with her shoes off, just like the first day at Camp K.L.O.P.

When she opened the door, she could smell something good cooking. Mar'Ann was teaching the Naz sisters some of her secrets. "Are you hungry? We made a casserole."

Mac was sitting quietly reading his black book. He was content with the contents. It seemed to uplift his spirits.

"Why would anybody decorate their wall with a list?" The three girls were looking at a framed embroidery on the wall. It was a handmade gift for Mac. Inside the silhouette of a cow's head was the following concrete poetry:

<u>The Code of the Cowboy</u>
Know where the sun rises and sun sets, so you never get lost.
Take pride in your work because it is part of you.
Be tough, but fair.
Know when to fight and when to ride.

Care for things smaller than you.

Have courage facing all things larger than you.

Honor all women as if they were your mother.

When you make a promise, keep it.

Some things are not for sale.

Ride for your brand.

Relax in the saddle.

"Why would anybody decorate their wall with a list?" With that, Mac smiled and closed his book. He was honored they were interested.

"These are my values; the ethics I promised myself. We have the laws of nature, the laws of God, the laws of man, but these are my laws. That's how I ride."

"Those are good guidelines." It made an impression on them.

The next day was a doubly delightful day! It was diploma day for Ease, Rose, and Zen! But also, for the newcomers it was super special...

At sunrise, the buses lined up to drop off the children. Everybody cried with happiness. Even if you were not part of a family reunion, you could not help but feel the tug on your heart.

Infants to toddler to teens, and extras for adoption... Mac and Mar'Ann took two.

Ease, Rose, and Zen made a make-shift mass healing for the new families. This was their final practice; they were now doctors. Patrich assisted the trio by organizing an assembly line. People passed through smoothly. They entered with injuries, they exited energetically wholesome.

The triage trio was able to cure almost all ailments, but they could not go inside emotional pains. **Some things cannot be physically fixed. You can't unscramble eggs.**" They had memorized this from a textbook.

297

Patrich seemed a bit... maybe odd? Since the newcomers had arrived, he changed... Some appeared to recognize him. Today, some even said he looked like his father.

There was another grand celebration around the spire with food, friends, fun, and music! It was different now with the sound of children's laughter.

J'me reminisced about her time with her daughters at the BLOCK. She loved being an adopted Mom!

At first, the girls were her followers, then they shared the first hug and then hair braiding... The secluded sisters had changed from teenagers to grown women. J'me recalled how unsteady they were with their special gifts. Now, with much practice, they had it perfected. She remembered their first period... All the mother/daughter discussions... The time she took the girls to Cube H... and when they first met Auntie Juan Li... and when they got their names... Wait!

J'me unscrolled the diplomas and certifications. She was startled! "Girls! Come here please." Looking at them again she saw, Alice eXquisite, Rose eXquisite, Jen eXquisite. "What happened?"

The girls already noticed the name changes, "The computer changed it. **That is how we are in the system.**"

Chapter 71
Welcome to the World

It was the day of the girl's graduation. They had grown taller and filled out since their time at the BLOCK. Many people looked like they had grown younger in age and some had matured quickly, while Mac and Mar'Ann always stayed the same, people approached their prime.

Ah, J'me finally figured it out! Age was just a number. No difference between a 20-year-old or a 200-year-old?

And what about the widow woman? She stayed gray. It was because she felt she was in the prime of her life now, when she was older, not when she was younger. **There will always be people who define "now" as their perfect time.**

Therefore, little by little, people perfected. Some transients would retreat to Camp K.L.O.P. from the outside world to become renewed.

There were elderly people at the BLOCK, originals who did not redefine themselves... Well, some did not go through K.L.O.P. before entering the BLOCK. The camp was formed from the Cubes K.L.O.P. So, for example, Key-Oh-Coo did not know of the camp's existence.

Their time at camp K.L.O.P. had finished. The eXquisite family was moving to their next mission. They bade farewell to Mac, Mar'Ann, Mariah and Maribeth, and many other friends at the party. They already had their sacks packed and were climbing into their custom trailer home.

"Bless you." was all Mar'Ann could say while tearing up. She hugged and kissed each person's forehead, "Bless you, bless you..." The Naz sisters gave them bags and bags of food to eat on their journey. Mac was the strongest one. "So long. Ya'll come back now."

In the middle of a full moon night, in the back of the white box trailer, in the doorway balls of thread and yarn were stuffed behind them and the doors were locked shut from the outside. Inside the cargo container was quiet, outside the party continued.

Inside the mobile motel was a change of clothes for each one, plus a stack of 5000 units, which they split equally amongst themselves. Their new clothes had pockets, making them unique. Also, they found a log left behind by previous passengers. They passed around the papers, sharing the pictures and reading some of the random writings:

- "You feel the urge to satisfy a curiosity of discovery. You made up your mind and give in to (your) inner desires and take an unplanned break.

- **Your unforgettable memories are likely to last.**

- I love you.

- **Do not let heartbreak get the best of you.**

- **Get past the trauma and drama; let bygones be bygones.**

- **Intelligence can overshadow your judgement. Make a few mistakes here and there.**

- **Be on good behavior.**

- **Do not be shy about approaching people. The wealth of experience you gain plus friends' helps.**

- **Befriend locals, trust your gut feeling, try new things...**

- **Be open to new things, but don't feel obligated in any way.**

- **Have a financial safety blanket.**

- **It starts with donations. Help others while helping yourself.**

- **Safeguard your valuables.**

The memoirs were interesting, but maybe not be applicable to them. They did, however, make good conversation starters.

Patrich put a family photo in his pocket. After that, he moved into a white mood, sitting stoically, thinking deeply. He was quiet and did not contribute. Patrich looked tired.

"Let's get some sleep... It is the easiest way to make time pass more quickly."

"I wish we had music." said somebody.

For J'me, Patrich and the girls, the trip to St. Wx. was like a military mission. However, they were going to war without a plan. J'me and Patrich were natural explorers, but the girls were feeling the first fear... the fear of the unknown.

J'me opened her book without words and started sharing some of the secrets from Key-Oh-Coo. In his book he wrote: "Diversify... Go in with more than one." This was the start of the mission briefing...

To the best of her abilities, J'me explained Cubes S.T.W.X., but not until they scouted it out would they really know. The whole time, Patrich did not say a word. He was deep in thought.

Finally, he spoke, "Call me Patch." They suddenly looked at him. "They call me Patch at St.Wx. I was a member there..."

Suddenly the truck stopped and "Patch" stopped talking. The trailer unlocked from the rig... It was parked. Next, the doors unlocked and they heard movement behind the ball wall. From inside, they pushed the stuffing outward, exposing the exit. They focused their eyes on an elderly man wearing a toothless smile and broken glasses.

Chapter 72
High IQ, Low EQ

Outside the trailer, standing in a heap of thread and yarn stood a scruffy man with his arms stretched out. "Watch your step. I did not expect visitors, but you are more than welcome."

When they landed on terra firma they saw piles and piles of rubbish. A collection of odds and ends. He was a hoarder. In the distance were four train cars locked together. It seems this was his home. If not for the clutter, this spot next to the river was scenic.

"By any chance, do you have anything to drink in there?" asked the man.

The girls replied, "Sure, we have plenty. What would you like?"

"Well, it seems we have Mogen David "Mad Dog" 20/20 wine... cases of it... Is that ok?"

The man squinted with a toothless smile.

The elder spoke non-stop while they unloaded the cases of fortified wine. He was very cordial. And he seemed happy to have visitors. Also, he was playful, reminding J'me of Kung Tau Fu Z. But he was his opposite in cleanliness.

"Robert, Bob, Bobby, Bub... Bob the hobo, Hobo Bob, or I like Hobob... It was once Bobo, but when the Star Wars movie came out..." He started to get angry. "Bobo Fet! Do I look like Bobo Fet to you? I am a nice guy. I am not a tramp. I am a hobo! Do you know the difference? A hobo earns his room and board; he works. I am an honest man. I am not a bum!"

The girls were in fear, ready to run. J'me reflexed into an instinctive fighting stance while Patch just sat silently when he heard the man's tirade. It did not last long... he was out of steam quickly. They learned from Patch to just wait for Hobob to deflate and neutralize.

Hobob lacked what is called **"Emotional Intelligence", or what is sometimes referred to as having a low E.Q., Emotional Quotient.** This is a combination of low self-awareness, self-management or self-----regulation, low social awareness, lack of social skills or relationship management. However, he was motivated, somewhat empathic, and sometimes sensitive to other people. **He had a low EQ, not no EQ.**

When his anger balloon deflated, they introduced themselves. "Hello Hobob. Nice to meet you. I am J'me eXquisite and these are my daughters, doctors Alice, Rose, and Jen. And this is Patch."

Hobob then stopped at Patch. He stopped to stare — starting first at Patch's toes, then up to his nose. He noticed Patch shaking his head back and forth, signifying "No." Then Patch slyly put one hand to his mouth, meaning "Hush, be quiet." while turning Hobob by the shoulder in the direction of the rail cars. Luckily, the silent signals were not noticed by the others.

Despite the debris, it was actually a nice place to visit, but they would not want to live there.   Hobob enjoyed the wine and loosened up... and later let loose again, "I was a cheesemaker. Now they make cheese in big factories. Have you ever seen how they do it? Huge metal machines!" This time the visitors sat still and just allowed him to spout. It seemed his angry outbursts were just momentary, nothing serious. The best way to diffuse his anger bomb was to stay calm, not interrupt, and allow him time to release his emotions. It could not be ignored, but it was easily tolerated.

"Tomorrow I will sneak you into St.Wx. But before we do, I would like to go over a few things with you. The first are secret signals..."

Together they came up with the following signs:

- If you scratch you nose, that means "Hurry, come here quickly! I need your help."

- Touching your ear means somebody is listening. Be careful what you say.

- Rubbing or touching your eye means somebody is watching.

- Pulling your hair back with one hand is, "Let's leave."

- Pulling your hair back with two hands means to leave quickly!

When gestures were not appropriate, words could be used. "You never ate bologna?" Let's say, when the word "bologna" was brought up in a conversation it was a signal to "Be aware, be careful." Then they decided "(-2)3" meant to "Accept it and move on" ... And then there was "HonSuCan J-Wash" meaning, "That person is sweet and can be trusted." Having agreed to these secret signals was a form of safety for the squad. Codes were a clever way to communicate without being noticed.

Chapter 73
Anticipating Anticipation

Before bed, Hobob opened up about himself. "I have been hiding from the law for some time for something I did not do. It's true! I am innocent. Heaven knows I did not do it. I may not be perfect, but I am honest." This all was true. If anything, Hobob was very honest about everything. It was just that he had no filter to hold back or control what he said.

While Hobob slept, the three sisters sneaked into his train car to heal him, however, the next day their departure was delayed because of it... The side effect of a rapid removal of unhealthy substances shocked his system. "Detox is not instantaneous." said the new doctors. "Hobob must remove his toxins. It seems we will be here an extra day." Patch stayed with Hobob. It was nice... Both talked less.

When Patch and Hobob were alone, Patch said, "Cousin Bobby, is that you?"

"Patch R3G? Yes. I thought I recognized you!"

"Have you seen my family?"

Hobob blurted out the truth... "Your father stayed here a spell yonder after the divorce. But I do not know where he is now... August returned from school and is alone in Cube S. And your oldest sister and youngest brother are Board Members... with your Mom." Then, without warning, Hobob yelled out "Your mother is a bitch!"

This did nothing to improve Patch's mood. But he needed to know. His mind was moving again... And again, he kept quiet.

J'me had an idea of what to do while they waited for Hobob to detox. "Do you remember Cubes B and C had an exhibit area? We can clean this mess... Yes?"

Momma J'me thought cleaning would be a good distraction for her and her daughters. Plus, after sitting for so long, it felt good to move around. Momma J'me was not saying all that she was thinking but thinking all she was saying. She was thinking about something else... **She knew something new was going to happen.**

Anticipation can be a dual edge sword. It is a natural stress that your imagination can make negative or positive. **Thinking of the future can create either a mood of anxiety or excitement.**

We only have a clear 20/20 vision of what is happening now. But it is easier to understand something after it has already happened. Hindsight is 20/20... Worrying doesn't solve problems. You cannot change the past, which may bring regrets about bad decisions. If you let it... Or you can learn from your mistakes and move on, being wise after the event. And then... **nobody has sharp 20/20 sight into the future. Right?**

Before bed, Hobob looked like a new man... First, he lost a lot of weight and had a trim build. Hobob kept his long hair but shaved his face and had perfectly polished teeth. Without his glasses, he had 2020 vision and you could now see the color of his eyes. No more scars or tattoos... His skin went from ruddy and crusty to a radiant clean complexion. Even his clothes were cleaned and pressed and his shoes were shined... A total make-over!

"I have not felt this good in years. I'm) not sure what they put in those bottles I drank the other night, but they kicked my patootie! But you know what? I don't think I will drink anymore. I think instead I will go to church and find me a good woman! I'll git me one of those submissive types that cooks and cleans for me every day." It seemed he was no longer angry... but "Honest Bob", Hobob, was still without walls about what he said.

That night, while Hobob slept, the three sisters sneaked into his train car and braided his hair. The extra stay for one day helped everyone adjust. They departed early the next day for St. Wx.

When they approached the four Cubes, S. T. W. and X., it was not what they expected. Hobob's palace was less of a mess. From a distance they saw workers tending to the plants and picking up the debris. In order to get inside undetected, Hobob took them to a spot where they could sprint through Exit SW, shadowed by the morning sun. Once inside, they would hide on the docks.

One secret to stealth is move and wait, move, wait, taking your time. Slowly move and wait... This does not attract any attention. Luckily, without the foreman, the workers on the docks were lazy, lingering and chatting.... They noticed nothing.

Chapter 74
Negative Energy Flow

Together they made their way to the Beast. At this point they blended in with the rest of the members. Hobob left Patch to take them the rest of the way.

"Thank you, Hobob. Thank you..." It was not an exchange of hugs (like at Camp K.L.O.P.), but polite waves.

"That Hobob, he sure was a HonSuCan J-Wash!"

"It looks a little different from the last time I was here..." Patch noticed the work that was being finished on the two circular rooms inside the figure "8" base of the Beast. "We call this the Beast. It used to stink bad down here, but it was the best way to move quickly through the Cubes." They did not want to look like tourists, but they clung closely to Patch as he guided them.

It was crowded; it was crazy... There was an unstoppable noise! Negative energy was flowing, meaning that there were many impolite, intolerant, uncaring people in this place.

A psych patient was released too early, or not on his medications. Suddenly he screamed in their ears, "Banana! Hey brother!" then looked at the ceiling.

Simultaneously, three things happened. Like lightening hitting a lake, the sisters escaped into a pod. Patch did not notice and continued to head towards Cube S. And J'me instinctively stood still, not allowing others to bump and budge her.

When J'me rubbed her nose, nothing happened... nobody came. She kept calm and decided the best thing to do was to stay and wait for the others to return. Nearby, J'me saw a spot to sit and watch. This was where she perched herself to observe everything.

Connecting to her intuition, J'me summoned her third eye which told her, "You feel the urge to satisfy a curiosity of discovery. You make up your mind and give in to (your) inner desires and take an unplanned break." This was her gut feeling.

It was time to wander!

To understand what happened next, the easiest thing to do is follow the money trail, starting with Alice, Rose and Jen. The triplets were popped like a zit out of their pod by the other passengers. Staying together, they did not recognize a way back to the Beast. So, they stopped and rubbed their noses, but nothing happened, nobody came.

They smelled a false scent. It smelled good. They followed it to a perfumery at the entrance of a store. It was fun to free sample all the sprays and lotions. But with only 3000 units between them, they decided to save their money and buy only one fragrance.

Purchasing was easy to do. You gave them the units, and they gave you the item. Easy!

They soaked themselves, becoming super smelly in their new false scent. Later, they found some colorful T-shirts on sale. Buy two and get the third for free! That was a perfect purchase for them! They changed tops and placed their soaked shirts in the bag they got for free.

When store security saw three young black women stuffing clothes into a bag, they were detained and arrested without being questioned first.

J'me had in her mind, "Take an unplanned break to satisfy a curiosity of discovery. Do not be shy about approaching people. The wealth of experience you gain plus friends' helps... Try new things... Be open to new things."

She also felt a little hungry, so she asked a stranger for directions. "Excuse me, sir, but can you tell me a good place to get something to eat?" The man immediately had a glint in his squint... "Sure, give me 100 units and I will tell you." J'me exchanged the money for the information and was soon swept away in a pneumatic tube. However, the directions were deceptive. She found herself on a floor without doors, a residential area. After hanging around the halls, she decided to try it again, 100 units... and again a stranger deceived her. The next location was called the "Playroom".

Patch was on a quest to find his family. His only clue came from Hobob: August wandered the halls in Cube S. However, there were ten floors to forage.

He had thought long and hard beforehand. Like a game of chess, Patch had anticipated various outcomes. Patch (Patrich R3G) was certain that he did not want his mother to find him. Once in Cube S, he went to a cybercafé on the first floor, ordered a coffee, and leased a laptop by the minute. Next, Patch created a fictitious account.

Chapter 75
First Time Here

The trio now understood anger. "We are innocent! Heaven knows we would never steal. We may not be perfect, but we are honest." Nobody believed them.

But Sublevel Three was probably the safest place to be for Alice, Rose, and Jen. They were put in the common collective with the Believers. Facing the inevitable, without any options, they started to settle themselves.

Meanwhile, J'me got good directions and went to eat in the Playroom. When she stepped inside, it was not what she had expected. She moved to the side of the entry and just stood there before a greeter approached her.

"May I help you? What is your pleasure?" With that J'me was handed a menu. On one side of the pages were food choices, the backside contained carnal choices.

"Oh, I am here to eat. What do you suggest?" asked J'me?

"Please follow me... Everybody here loves our hot dogs." J'me was seated at an outside table. She sat with her back to the wall and watched.

"Hello, first time here?" asked the buxom waitress who set the table just as J'me sat down. J'me was distracted by everything happening around her.

"Yes... sorry. I would like a hot dog, with everything."

"Everything?" The waitress flipped the page and pointed to a picture on the menu.

"I mean, add all the extra condiments to the hot dog... and a water to drink, please."

"Got it, a hot dog and cold water. I will be back soon... Oh, and by the way, if you do not want to play, just say 'no'. Nothing else needs to be said. Enjoy the view!"

The voyeuristic view was new and entertaining. J'me was enjoying herself.

Meanwhile, Patch was catching up quickly on the situations at St.Wx. He was not a hacker, but he did know how to get into places very few knew about. He first got into the security system. Surprisingly, his personal information was still erased. His father's information was still blocked. Using facial recognition, Patch viewed his mother, brother, and sister secluded in the boardroom. August was on the top floor, Cube S, a floor without cameras. Patch remembered how he dismantled the feeds... but they were never fixed. The rest of the time, excluding the occasional pop-ups, was spent following the news about the dreams and psychics.

Not exactly sure what triggered the thought, but Patch suddenly realized he had lost J'me, Alice, Rose, and Jen!

They were right, the hot dogs were delicious. J'me was not shy, but when approached after eating she kindly declined. Her mood was somewhere else. She pulled from her purse the book without words, the gift from Key-Oh-Coo. Perhaps there was a clue?

Sure enough, the eXquisite family was not registered on the security servers. Updates were very slow or non-existent for the past months. The last inputs were about nonconformists being incarcerated. Nothing important.

With only a few minutes to spare on his rented computer, he dropped in a secret search program for four females. It would take some time for this process to complete. There was nothing more he could do but wait.

It was time for him to move before anybody recognized him. He already planned his path using the secret passageways in Cube S. Patch would not be seen.

After a while watching the activities in the Playroom became boring. J'me spent more minutes rifling through her book.

"Ah, found it!" she said to herself. "Top floor, Cube S... a floor with doors and the home of Key-Oh-Coo ." From there she could do more.

After paying her bill, she asked a woman exiting with her for help finding Floor 10, Cube S. This woman did not ask for money, but politely took her to the pod portal and even waited to make sure J'me was safely on her way. "Not everything is bad here." J'me thought.

In a flash, J'me was standing in front of a locked door, a Cube S10 suite. She heard a noise around the corner getting nearer. In a faster flash, J'me teleported herself inside.

It took a while to move up the ten floors to the top of the Cube, but Patch did it in quick time... More importantly, nobody saw him. Patch was close to being with his younger big brother, August.

From the other side of the door, J'me heard:
Tap, tap, tap, tap...
Tap...
Tap, scratch, tap, tap...
Tap, scratch, tap, tap...
Scratch, scratch, scratch.

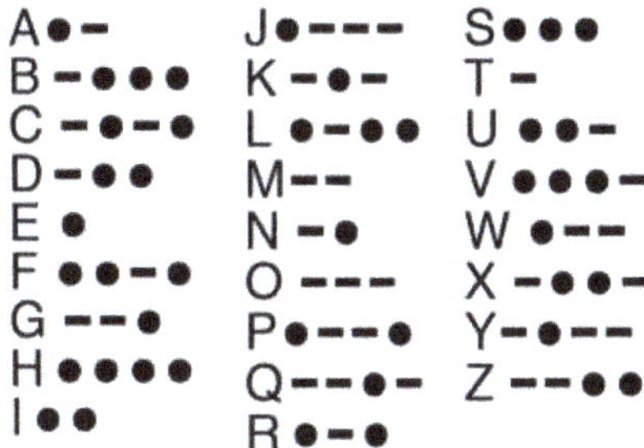

Chapter 76
First Day

It did not take long for Alice, Rose, and Jen to make friends. The loving nature of the eXquisite sisters was warmly welcomed by the Believers and strengthened them.

"Wow! You've seen Mr. G?"

"Wow! You are from the BLOCK?"

"Wow! You three are doctors? Can you give me a prescription for this pain?"

Soon they had the Believers and the rest of those imprisoned healed and whole again.

A normal person would be happy with all this positive attention and gratitude, but the triplets had a hollow spot in their heart, an emotional emptiness. They missed their momma.

"Excuse us, but we need to rest now." said the triplets.

"Wait, one more thing. Can you open this block of wood? It has something inside for us. We have been trying to figure it out since it was delivered by the Nobels."

The girls took a lookie. It was a wooden box without hinges and latches. They, too, were perplexed.

The shining walls in Sublevel Three began to fade as the girls shut their eyes and slept.

"Hello in the hallway." said J'me through Key-Oh-Coo's closed door. She heard something between a child's giggle and gorilla grunts. When she opened the door, the Giant jumped up and down, swinging his arms in unrestrained glee, then ran around in his imaginary circle, laughing.

Patch started to run. He heard an unusual and loud noise from around the corner.

"August!" Patch shouted, screaming with joy at the first sight of his big little brother.

August fell on his bottom. His large frame was in the threshold of the door, halfway in the apartment, halfway in the hallway. He stretched out his arms and pulled both Patch and J'me together to give them a hug. He was gentle for a giant. Patch cried, J'me rubbed the Giant's head and said, "It is alright." and August was exuberant.

"What do you mean? You gave away the block? Do you have any idea what you just did?" asked the annoyed M.T. Nobel Sr. to his two kids.

"Dad, settle down! We gave it to the Believers. But they don't know how to open it."

"Yes, daddy," added Opium II, "the wooden block is still down there."

It was just a matter of time before they knew he would notice their family heirloom missing. **What started as an impulse had developed into a plan.** Junior poured a tall drink while Opium II sat her father on the sofa and started to massage his shoulders.

"Have you noticed this place is a crapper? We have been here all our lives and..."

They were interrupted. "Damn it! You ungrateful pieces of shit. I did this for you!"

This was an obvious lie. But the tables were turning. What they did was now going to be of concern to their father. The two took and kept control.

"Diminish Dad... just pay attention for a while..."

"We appreciate all you have done... but we want to leave."

Senior took too big a swig from his drink and thought for a moment. "So that is why you were not in the board room? You were bored?"

The two did not answer... they just let their father's mind unwind. Senior took another big swig from his drink and thought further. "The Believers?" Again, "Believers?"

It took courage for the two to come out, "Yes Dad. We are both Believers. You too... you know it is true!"

Senior swallowed the last of his drink, sank down into the sofa, and said, "Well, what are we going to do about it?"

With that the two revealed their plans with the outcome being their escape. M.T. Nobel Sr. liked the idea but added a few extra steps.

"Just a few more steps." J'me and Patch said, helping August into the ex-apartment of the CEO/COO. J'me was able to unlatch herself from the giant's grip and left the two brothers together.

The apartment was too large for just one person. J'me counted a big bedroom and five additional sleeping areas. The style of the beds was like that of the BLOCK, pads were set on the floor. The ten-meter square bed in the Master Bedroom filled the entire space. Each sleep room also had attached a fully stocked bath with shower, sink, toilette, bidet... Plus, there was a half-bath near the kitchen.

Everything was well kept. Key-Oh-Coo had anticipated his departure, there was no spoiled food. On the kitchen wall were instructions on how to get the complementary services, such as cleaning, cooking, deliveries...

Chapter 77
Long Days

"Here, let me help..." Patch said to J'me. August stood nearby as he opened the kitchen computer and started first to check for messages. He had not got a response on the whereabouts of Alice, Rose, and Jen yet.

"It seems we lost Alice, Rose, and Jen. But they should be fine. I am trying to track them down now, but it may take some time."

"How did you know what I was thinking?" asked J'me.

Laughing, Patch replied while clicking on the keyboard, "I am clairvoyant." About a minute later he was done. "Perfect, I just ordered us some fresh food to be delivered. Can you cook?"

After Patch and J'me looked at each other, they looked at August. August just smiled.

"I am fine, I had a hot dog earlier..." J'me said.

While J'me was a bit antsy, cognitive code orange, Patch was yellow, and August was... forever white. Patch had to readjust his plan. He was reprioritizing what was urgent and what was important. On the top of each list was his brother, August.

"August, give me your hand." He reached for the huge hand and moved it towards J'me. "I want you to meet J'me eXquisite." With that he had August shake J'me's hand, but to her delight he stepped forward for her to rub his head. **(Neither knew what August knew.)**

J'me reached into her purse and pulled out her communications sphere but stopped herself. **Everybody deserves respect.** August was incapable of granting permission to his private thoughts.

"Perhaps you two can watch some TV while I do some work here?"

"What is a TV? Transvestites?" J'me had not yet connected... "Oh, you mean television?" Patch took August to the living room and gave him the entire sofa facing the wall-sized television. He turned on the controls, but immediately the porn channel popped up. Sifting through the selections, they found something a little more suitable, cartoons.

"Excuse me while I do some things..." Patch left August with J'me. Looking back over his shoulder, he noticed they had already bonded.

On the social feeds the major topic was recurring nightmares...long, sad looks. The major advertisements were from psychics with a cure. Interspersed were consistent, "feel good" campaign ads for 104, even though it was not near election time.

Searching the security cameras in each Cube was a tedious waste of time. The sleep deprived faces were contagious, and Patch soon fell asleep in his chair.

There was a knock on the door... it unlatched... opened slowly... and in came their delivery. The small woman was so shy and self-conscious she kept her head down and did not make a noise. She was afraid and never looked up to make eye-contact. After she unloaded her cart in the kitchen she left quickly. However, just before the door closed, J'me said "Thank you." and it seemed the woman smiled.

Patch made popcorn and drinks and spent the rest of the night on the oversized sofa, having a deep feeling of comfort cuddling close to August. This was a feeling neither could remember... The shining walls in the room began to fade when their eyes all closed. They slept.

Spoiler: It would be three days secluded in the apartment with August and Patch... J'me's premonition to wander was not working well.

She was now linked into the real world.   She was not sure what to do next, except wait...

Time is relative. It can seem to move quickly or slowly. But time is constant... constantly clicking forward, never backwards. Why is it that you feel time moves faster if it is something you enjoy, but moves slower if it is something difficult? **Your brain is picking up, absorbing, and processing information at different speeds.**

August preferred the college course channel over cartoons. This calmed him and kept him captivated. He started smiling.

Lecture with a British Professor on TV:

"Chi Nü was the seventh daughter of the Jade Emperor. While on earth bathing with her sisters in a lotus pond, she fell in love with an immortal cowboy who owned a gifted ox (from Cube Y). They shacked up. When Chi Nü got outed, her nutter grandma (Cube Zed) got miffed.

Now... every seventh day of the seventh lunar month, like Saint Valentine's Day, on QiXi Day she goes to the outside world to play with her immortal lover...

Thanks to my bud, ta, sitting in the first row. Bud ta!" The camera swiveled to a man, smiling, glowing and waving his hand in hello.

Chapter 78
Unlimited Love

When the three sisters awoke on the floor of Sublevel Three, there were already supplies set near them to refresh themselves. However, as they looked around, they were surprised to see Hobob in the corner, surrounded by seven or eight ladies! They heard them calling him "Bobby" and "Baby". When they got near, Hobob touched his ear, meaning somebody is listening, be careful what you say.

"What happened?" asked Alice, Rose, and Jen to Hobob...Bobby... Baby.

"Instead of going home I took a detour... and ended up here." explained Hobob.

The new "Bobby" was handsome, very cordial, playful, witty, open with his feelings, considerate, and looked like he had money. He was every woman's dream!

Apparently, they met in the Playroom. In addition, they knew he was packed to please, if you know what I mean. "Casi (Casanova), Cocksman, Lance Romance, Magic Man, MacDaddy, Mr. Amazing... Stud." Bobby was good in bed.

"I made the mistake of saying I wanted to go to Church and find me a good woman... Security snagged me as a Believer and my lady lovers followed me down here."

The women around Hobob were tending to his every need, but he also made them feel special and desired. It was mutually beneficial.

"They want me to be polyamory." This is an open relationship with more than one partner with the consent of all parties involved. It was consensual, ethical, stable and responsible non-monogamy. A zesty alternative lifestyle with special spiritual unions, not a legal marriage.

"**Love without limits.**" was the phrase Bobby used to describe his crazy love.

The sisters concluded, "Whew, that is wiki!"

Again, rubbing his ear with the secret signal, Hobob, Bobby, Baby, asked the three, "What happened to you? Why are you here?"

"Not long after we left you, we got lost. They accused us of lifting a shop and we were detained, without a chance to explain."

"Shop lifting?" replied the new Bobby. "What did you steal?"

Now the three sounded like the old Hobob, "No, we paid for everything! First, we exchanged money for a false scent and put too much on us. So, we next bought colorful tops and put our strongly scented shirts in the free bag they gave us. What did we do wrong?"

"I see two obvious mistakes here... The first was that you did not know those fragrances are concentrated, meaning they are powerfully strong, and you need just one light spray for all day..."

"Ohh!" The three said in unison, learning something new, "And the second mistake?"

"Your shirts."

They bought the texted t-shirts for their color, not knowing what the words meant:

"Stressed is desserts spelled backwards."

"Get over yourself."

"It's not my job to blow sunshine up your butt."

"Don't worry about it... **People always make false assumptions.** You will be allowed to leave. They will discover you are innocent." was the advice given. This did nothing to improve their mood, but they needed to know.

They liked living free in Sublevel Three. Days two and three were bonding moments. The Believers in the bottom felt reinforced after hearing about life outside St.Wx.

The eXquisite sisters were getting past the trauma; letting bygones be bygones... remembering it is fine to make a few mistakes here and there... and to be on good behavior.

Beep... beep... beep... beep... The noise was coming from the computer next to the sofa. An encrypted message was sent back from Patch's previous query. "Alice, Rose, and Jen were arrested on a 'missed demeanor' charge!" he told J'me.

"I found them! Your daughters are in jail, Sublevel Three, with the bottom feeders." Patch was not awake but thinking code red.

August was asleep in the master bedroom, having claimed the super-sized bed for himself. Patch looked in on him first and then got an energy drink from the kitchen and some water for J'me.

"I am going to scout out the area first..." Then there were a series of slurps, followed by "Ok...Ok..." Slurp, "Ok... Ok..." Slurp. This continued until his drink was empty. Then there was a long, 'Ohhh.''

"What is it?" asked J'me.

"We must go now! Follow me and I will explain along the way." J'me pulled her hair back with both hands, grabbed her bag, and darted out the door.

Just then, they heard a guard call out their names, "Dr. Alice eXquisite, Dr. Rose eXquisite, Dr. Jen eXquisite."

It took the girls a while to give the Sublevel Three Believers a hug and say, "I love you."

Then they retrieved their belongings, including the perfume-soaked shirts, excluding their money (stolen by security).

Chapter 79
Know Now

Some things are not noticed. Perhaps we have not seen or heard about them? Or we just deemed them as insignificant at the time? The reason does not matter... **But just because we do not know it, does not mean it is not true.** You know? Take, for example:

Medical science just discovered a new organ in your body! **The lining inside your abdominal cavity, your 79th organ, is called the mesentery.** What does it do? It attaches the stomach, small intestine, pancreas, spleen, and other organs together. It is a membrane with many folds... and also is rich in nerves and lymph nodes embedded within the connective tissues. **Did you know that 70% of the neurons not going to your brain are found traveling through the mesentery membrane?** Therefore your gut is connected to your central nervous system.

Its scientific significance is yet unknown, but if you go back before science, you will understand. In other words, **science has not caught up to something we knew thousands of years ago.** At one time this was known as your second brain. **Your brain regulates memories and thoughts... Your heart holds love and happiness, and the mesentery stores emotions.**
Tio Juan referred to this as your sensing soul. To the Mother of All, it is the navel chakra, where the sapphire gemstone glows yellow... Aren't you the least bit curious?

From the bottom of my heart, with my deepest feelings... your emotions are felt in your gut. Have you ever felt that twitching, gut feeling? Butterflies in your stomach?

From the vile bile in your belly comes anger, fear, anxiety... the bad ones. Ever felt that you have been punched... or kicked by a mule? Mean people suck the wind from you. Unforgettable moments... **when you suffer a defeat, your glands excrete... this is naturally normal.**

With no bones to protect it, like your brain and heart, your abdomen is exposed... more sensitive... All you have is a fibrous film... Maybe you are a mesentery mess? May I help you?

You are what you eat... For your long-term health, eat properly... This is the biological battery in your body. It stores energy. Thousands of years ago they discovered that if not charged, you feel tired, exhausted, depressed. Not comfortable... it disagrees with me.

When you eat, you digest downward. The top third of this area is the control center. **Fear comes from the kidneys.** That is why you piss all over yourself. **Envy, jealousy, frustration is from your liver.** Your intestines occupy the entire middle third and functions for absorption. The bottom is for elimination and reproduction. (Have you ever wondered why sex feels so good? It is to balance out the top two-thirds of your abdomen.)

The Chinese "reset" button is located on your waist at the mid-point between your belly button and your pubic bone. Place the palm of your hand, thumb up and the four fingers under your navel. Press around where your little pinky finger sits. There is a natural indentation near here. You will feel a pang when you press. Push this spot and hold it down for a few minutes.

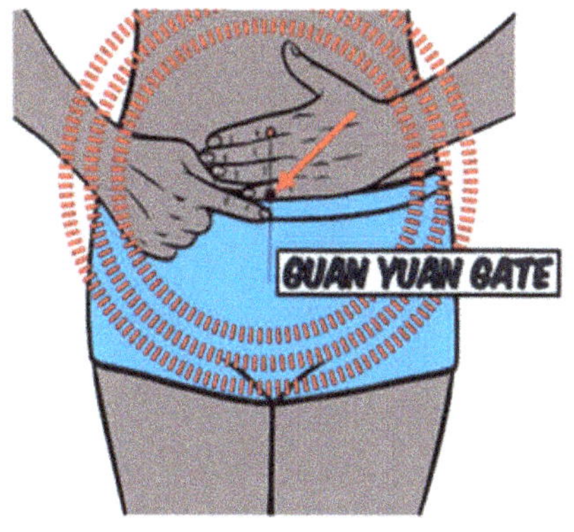

The "reset" button is where the major chi channels flow, referred to as the "Guan Yuan Gate" or sometimes the "sea of energy". Like sex, it is most comfortable to do lying down on your back. Press this point for few minutes, every day, for eight days.

Your body's energy will reset, opening the pathways for your chi to travel unobstructed.

It works wonders on diarrhea/constipation, menstrual cramps, boosting your metabolism and losing body fat. It also makes you better in bed, wink, wink, tickle, tickle...

So, eat and drink healthy, press the reset button on your guan yuan gate, and there is one more suggestion:

Exorcize your negative emotions with this exercise; **"Priming your Pump". When inhaling, put your hand on your lower gut and push your fingers up while inflating your belly.** This push upward gets your food and stagnant fluids moving. While inhaling and inflating, you will feel energized. Afterwards, feel the flow of positive energy. It links directly to your brain and supplies extra power. Athletes do this trick.

QUIZ

VII

Quiz Seven

Test your understanding of what you read. Pick the best answer for the following ten questions. After completing all ten questions, check your answers on the next page.

If you score a 70% or above (answer seven or more questions correctly) you may proceed to the following chapters. However, if you score below 70%, read the previous chapters again.

Please take your time reading and meditating to unlock the next chapters.

HOBO SIGNS

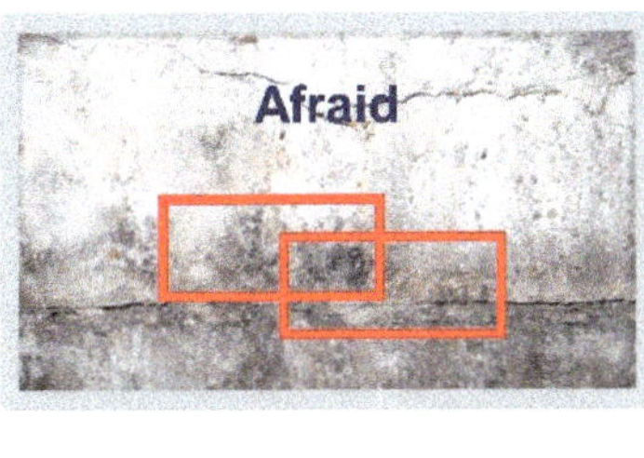

1. Mac had the "Code of the Cowboy" embroidery on his wall. This was...

    a. Based on the laws of nature
    b. Religious rules, commandments
    c. Legislative laws produced by politicians
    d. His personal ethics, rules of conduct

2. Which is NOT true about camp K.L.O.P.?
    a. It was a half-way point between the BLOCK and outside world
    b. It was formed by the Cubes K. L. O. P. from the original BLOCK
    c. It was the fountain of youth
    d. It was a place for people to "sharpen their saw"

3. Who was a hobo?
    a. Mogan David, MD
    b. MacDaddy, Mr. Amazing
    c. Cousin Bobby
    d. Bobo Fet

4. Which secret signals were not yet used?
    a. Saying "bologna" or "negative two to the third power"
    b. Touching your eyes, ears, or nose
    c. Pulling your hair back with one or both hands
    d. Saying "HonSuCan J-Wash"

5. Which is NOT true about St. Wx?
    a. It is family friendly
    b. It was formed by the Cubes S. T. W. and X. from the original BLOCK
    c. It was where the triplets, Patch R3G, and August R3G were born.
    d. It was a communist corporation disguised as a religious organization

For the following three questions, choose all that apply from the list provided:

6. When dispersed at the Beast, where did J'me go? ____________

7. When dispersed by the Beast, where did Alice, Rose, and Jen go? _________

8. When dispersed by the Beast, where did Patch go? __________
    a. Cube S – Top floor, S10
    b. Cyber Café
    c. Floor without doors
    d. Playroom
    e. Shopping
    f. Sublevel Three
    g. Guan Yuan Gate

9. Of the twelve St. Wx Board Members, who left the boardroom?
    a. The Nobel group
    b. The 104 group
    c. DD "Baby" Maye
    d. Dick Richter
    e. Doctor Edgar "Ek" Krass
    f. The Don Gottfried gang
    g. Mr. G

10. What is the purpose of the newly discovered organ, the mesentery?
    a. Science does not know
    b. It stores emotions
    c. It attaches the abdomen's organs together
    d. All of the above.

Nothing to be gained

Q7 – Answers

1.   Real cowboys are a different culture. They have their own set of rules. It is not like in the movies... Not every kicker is the same, but they usually share similarly strict ethics. Answer D.

2.   This was not intended to be tricky, but there is a difference between the fountain of youth and a choice to stay your "prime" age. (Answer C). Hidden away in a valley, it was once part of the original BLOCK, but is now used to prepare people for their individual futures.

3.   I love Hobob! Answer C for me.

4.   Answer A. The secret signals were devised with the help of Hobob for their future mission to St. Wx. Already they have come in quite handy.

5.   If you got this answer wrong, shame on you! Come on. Babies were sent away and the conduct of the "adults" living at St. Wx was definitely not conducive for a cohesive family unit, "A" is the answer. By the way, there are many things you may find offensive at St. Wx., but guess what, the real world is like? Look out your window.

6.   Answers A, C, D, and J'me is headed to F (Sub3).

7.   Answers E and F only for the Doctors eXquisite.

8.   Answers A, B, and Patch is heading to F (Sub3) as we speak.

9.   At first M. T. Nobel Junior and Opium Nobel II did not stick around the Board Room. Later their father joined them in their apartment. But the rest are camped out and cramped up on top of Cube X.

10.   D. All of the above. The 80/20 rule applies here just like in levitation and the third eye techniques. If you rake your fingers up your abdomen about 20+ times a day, while breathing, your blood and energy flow will

improve. And the secret reset button at your Guan Yuang gate works too. But it is not instantaneous. Full disclosure: Try it for at least eight days to yield results. Give your body time to repair itself naturally... After eight days and you do not notice any improvements, maybe it does not work for you.

Gratuitous plug: I am in no way affiliated with the Mogen David Vineyards, but I want to let you know that they make more than the mighty fine wine, MD 20/20. "This is a good place to start for the street wine rookie, but beware; this dog has a bite to back up its bark."

Honestly, if you compare Mogen David wines with expensive brands on a blind taste test, you will probably pick it as your preferred brand. Personally, my favorite is Mogen David Concord grape wine. Delicious! "A nice sweet wine with aromas of fresh Concord grapes that finishes elegantly."

How did you do? Did you score a 70? Did you get seven of the ten questions correct? Are you ready to move onto the next book, Chapters 80 through 89?

Chapter 80
Disorder

Things were blowing up more frequently. Sleep deprivation increased sensitivity at St. Wx. The bad things became worse; it was out of control. Everyday people endured every day.

"Have you noticed we are the only ones to leave the Board box?" said Junior.

"I could care less." responded Senior.

"No, you are missing my point. We have to pull the Board apart."

The first is the worst, then it becomes easier. Out of the twelve members, it seemed that only the Nobels sought balance outside. Nothing happened since the CEO/COO had left. No directions were given. **No decision was their decision,** which became a habit...

Opium II then suggested, "I think it would be easier to persuade DD Maye, first. She is an early adopter and willing to try anything once... or twice if it is nice."

"Good, **go for the low hanging fruit first**." affirmed Senior... "Let's get the odds in our favor. Three against one is better. Who's next?"

"Wait... Junior and I can take care of DD alone. Dad, you know how to handle Dick... "

"DD, Dick, and then Dr. Krass, in that order. They're alone." was the suggestion given by Junior.

Don Gottfried's gang and 104's family were left in their self-imposed seclusion. This was also best for the rest at St. Wx. Left alone were the cruelest control freaks.

He was a urologist; she was a gynecologist. They were both fertility experts, reproductive endocrinologists... not a "vas deferens" between them. This may sound silly, but this couple was "Doctors Love." his family name they began sharing when they married.

When they got to their home on S3 they closed and locked the door behind them and then kicked off their shoes. "We finished another day in paradise." They both laughed... then cried. "Smile now and scream later." was their maxim. They were not being genuine. Their forced grins were just a mask they wore in public.

Rarely noticed, meek and weak, they spent their workdays secluded... keeping low profiles. They did not want to interact; they weren't interested in anything but each other. These two dark skinned doctors found solace alone... Their home was their hiding place, a retreat from reality.

"Remember what Dr. Meutal told us about our depression?" This taboo topic came up as they showered together. They had a ritual of disrobing, de-stressing, and decompressing at the end of each day. **"When you block or slow down the movement of energy, you create disorder."**

"I liked his analogy of the jar of anger. You hold your anger in. Eventually the jar builds up pressure. Occasionally the lid opens, and you blast out. Only to close the lid tighter. **Energy needs to be released in a non-destructive way."** Their "gifts" were blocked because they could not release the energy they had locked inside.

"So, what do you want to do tonight? I am not in the mood to go to the Playroom for bondage... Maybe we should just stay here and play ... privately?"

"I'll prep the room."

Balls of thread in various sizes and colors were delivered accidentally to the sixth and seventh floors of medical Cube T. Some were so large that the spheres were waist high. Once delivered, they could not be routed or uprooted. Therefore, they remained with the mentally ill. Was it a mismanaged shipment or some twisted joke?

On the way to the jail, J'me was updated on the most urgent messages first about Alice, Rose and Jen. After Patch and J'me entered the waiting room, for security reasons, the officer kept J'me's purse while they waited to see the girls. J'me was reluctant to release her bag... especially when the officer got angry because he could not look inside.

Patch then summarized the chat lines... The Believers, the searchers and explorers caught J'me's thought. The insomniacs and self-proclaimed spiritualists were new to her. "There is a psychic war at St. Wx. They now offer you absolution, removing your sins." Divine intervention or spiritual cleanses was an idea they had given the gullible. The rumor mill was ripe about these gurus grinding lies from truth, milling money from miseries.

Just as the topic of the Board members (and his mother), was about to come up they called out her name, V poorly, "Jamey Ex... Ex... Excrement."

Chapter 81
Twisted Immediately

J'me rushed to Sublevel Three to see her triplets. Patch created a nice distraction about the chat lines. This kept her mind from wandering... Shady psychics? Belittled and beleaguered Believers? And those after her own heart, the searchers and explorers. But most important was that her girls were safe and unharmed. "Do not let heartbreak get the best of you." J'me reminded herself...

"Jamey Ex... Ex... Excrement."

J'me endured the harassment to see Alice, Rose and Jen. Even when she handed over her purse, she was only thinking of her girls. The concept of incarceration was not clear to J'me. **It did not seem logical to lock somebody up.**

The receptionist, the same officer who took her purse, was still angry. However, he permitted J'me to see the prisoners. However, "Look but don't touch." However... as J'me went to the back, the girls were being released into the waiting area where Patch was. Things got twisted immediately!

Patch gave the three girls warm hugs and sat them down. "Found you! This improved his mood immediately. "J'me just was sent to the back to see you... What happened?"

Their rage was released again as they explained their story... as they did earlier with Hobob, Bobby, Baby. It was a verbal vomit about everything they experienced... finishing with their captures stealing their money.... When done, all three of the girls exhaled a "Whew!"

Then Patch asked, "What's that smell?"

Dr. Meutal was running around, doing his rounds, caring for all his patients, including the bottom dwellers. He overheard the fury in the foyer and automatically assisted.

"Please excuse my interruption... I am Dr. Meutal, PsyD, MD. May I help you?" The girls knew his titles immediately.

"We are also doctors!" said the three, improving their mood immediately. They bonded beautifully, because during their wait for J'me to return Dr. Meutal invited the new doctors to the medical Cube.

"I am sorry, but at this moment we are waiting for our mother."

"No worries. I start each day on the first floor, in front of the nursery. Time's up... Bye-bye!" With that Dr. Meutal rushed to see his patients.

Unbelievable! J'me had never seen anything like this! It had a deep effect on her. "They suffered so much!" she cried for the Believers.

The Believers noticed and immediately went to her aide. The first thing J'me did was break the "Do not touch" rule.

Time was distorted. **J'me was still altered by the disturbing rhythms at St. Wx. and unable to adjust.** When the crowd around her subsided, Dr. Meutal stood before her. "Your son and daughters are fine."

"Thank you." she had already sensed they were safely united.

"We have not met yet, I am Dr. Meutal... and you are?"

"Oh, so sorry... J'me eXquisite... I am actually not..." she stopped herself.

"You are not their biological mother? I think that was obvious... But **where there is love, there is family**." This improved her mood immediately.

On his way out, Dr. Meutal revisited J'me. She then jotted a note on his prescription pad, "Patch, when the girls got out, I was put in. Please take care of your brother and sisters. I will meet you in the apartment. I love you."

Dr. Meutal knew what to do. He left the note with Patch while departing.

"You are a rock star!" This caught her attention, moving J'me out of an inner white mood...

It was the new Hobob, trailed by seven, uh, eight women. This time, J'me hugged him, eliciting no jealous response from his poly-lovers. She noticed his hand moved from his eye to his ear.

` Her second surprise was that most of the women, and some of the men, had their hair braided. This made her smile.

The next, immediate, surprise was she was not allowed to leave. This made her unhappy. (Anger was not part of her disposition.)

The Believers were discussing the psychic wars. J'me explained, **"Some things have a tendency to resolve themselves. Give it no thought, especially if it does not pertain to you.** It is just a distraction. Mind your business was what I was told (by Key-Oh-Coo). It will sort itself out...also, anything times zero is still zero.

Hobob added, "Negative two to the third power!"

Chapter 82
Halfway in the Hallway

When Patch opened the door to the apartment to let the three girls in they immediately met August. Patch raised August's hand and said, "August, this is Alice." Alice held August's hand, unknowingly releasing all his pain. "This is Rose." As Rose touched August, he was healed... "And Jen. They are my friends." As the last part of the healing, Jen felt the changes happening within August.

The three sisters looked at Patch, not sure what to say. Then August spoke, "Nice to meet you. My name is August R3G, but my friends call me Sunny." Patch fell on his bottom, halfway into the hallway.

"Excuse me, DD? May we have a word with you please? Privately?" The two Nobels took her down the hallway, away from the meddlesome members.

They gave her a gang hug. "Oh goodness... you are safe!"

This caught DD off guard. "What?"

"We need to go to the Playroom! Hurry!" while each took her by the arm and swept her away.

Yes, it was a lame plan, but it worked to get DD Maye out of the Board Room.

Moments later, "Excuse me, Dick? May I have a word with you please? Privately?" M.T. Nobel Senior, perhaps the least to be trusted, took Richard Richter down the hallway, out of view and ear shot of the meddlesome members.

Grabbing his shoulder, M. T. Nobel looked directly into Dick's eyes. "I do not know how to tell you this, but you are under arrest."

"What?" was his response.

"Yes, for unlawful detention. Come with me please."

Without hesitation, Dick Richter followed M. T. Nobel to Sublevel Three.

J'me huddled with Hobob, Bobby, Baby... Security had wrongfully arrested and detained her daughters, strike one... Security stole their money, strike two... Security would not allow J'me to leave... strike three.

"I believe now is the time for me." said J'me. "But I will be back for the Believers." She went silent. J'me only needed to close her eyes, concentrate, and relax... She vanished and reappeared at the front desk of the detention center. The receptionist, the same officer who asked for her purse was there.

"Excuse me, sir, but I would like my purse back. I am ready to go."

"Purse? I have no record of a purse." This was chance number one.

"Please check. Remember, you tried to open it?"

"No, you are wrong. You did not leave any personal items. Fuck off!" This was his second chance.

"Yes... You tried to open it when I arrived. You got angry..."

Rudely interrupting J'me, the man said, "Listen, if you do not leave now, I will..."

"You will not." That was his third and final chance... Three defenses triggered J'me to go on the offense. Immediately J'me concentrated and a bashing was heard in a metal desk. It became more violent, making the desk move, bounce, and finally fall forward, spewing all the contents on the floor.

Out burst her purse, blasting through the glass partition. All the guards came with guns drawn.

Behind J'me seven maintenance men marched in, forming a line in front of J'me with machete's waving. Just like they practiced on the football field, but this was a shootout. They defended their goal, keeping J'me safe. Once the shots were fired, they were easily deflected by the machetes being used as shields.

The haplogroup QM3 Y-DNA, the indigenous Mesoamericans in jeans rushed into the office and speedily subdued the Security Squad. Every man was restrained, lying on the floor, unconscious.

J'me removed all the doors and went to the back. "Now's the time!" she yelled... The Believers were freed from Sublevel Three.

When Dick Richter and M.T. Nobel entered the Security area, the doors were gone. The office was vacant. Nobody was there. When they went to the back, they noticed three things...

The Believers were replaced by a securely tied security force, stripped halfway of their uniforms... The wooden block was also gone... and the walls sparkled with a shine not seen in a long time, even with the lights off.

Detoured back to the BLOCK... Remember the different atmosphere? Movements are 10% slower with the feeling of vibrations and pureness. Take your time. Feel a deeper penetration:

Grandfather, grandson...Both fought to open their eyes... It felt like there was somebody there each moment. More than one...

A breeze brought in the manly scent of musk and wood. Other times there was a mixture of women's scents.

They felt the touches, they felt the kisses, and then they felt the wet tears falling upon them.

Then they heard a "Hello."

Chapter 83

It was August

"You ok?" Patch was pale. He kept repeating, "Oh my goodness... Oh my goodness... Oh my..."

August said, "I love you." then rubbed the top of Patch's head. "It's all right."

Patch was placed on the oversized sofa, in front of the TV... August began testing his ability to speak...

"The quick brown fox jumps over a lazy dog.... Crazy Frederick bought Mary very expensive opal jewels... Pack my box with five dozen liquor jugs..."

After a pause, August continued to communicate, **"Subliminal messages are hidden from your focus. There are no nueroethics!"** This was something he had to say.

Then he tested his creativity, "We should put an infinity pool on the roof of the Cube."

"Add artificial intelligence to our satellite systems... not just linking manufacturing, warehouses and distribution, but also use A.I. for offices, mining, and farming!" August was forward thinking.

Not only was August a Giant, now he was also a whiz.

"Where is DD?" the Nobels asked each other after they sat down in the Playroom. "I knew this was going to work. Where would you rather be?"

This was too easy. Once they got DD Maye out of the Boardroom and into the Playroom, she was free again.

Stress release: While DD was making up for lost time, pulling a train, Junior was calmed down crunk (getting high and drunk at the same time) and Opium II was getting excited!

Sparkle! Opium Nobel noticed a man... A nerdy man, with premature baldness and his shirt stretched so tight it tugged at the buttons... "Sparky" was alone and bulging belly sexy.

Opium walked over to his table, opened her blouse and sat down. He did not notice, unfolded his computer and said, "Did you see the chat lines?" She moved closer and started kissing his neck...

"FOMO (Fear of Missing Out) ..." Sparky said, then read, "Just new to the net.... Judge Richard Richter released the Believers... The attorney for this case commented, 'He exceeded his authority. Mr. Richter was convicted of false imprisonment, a crime that has indefinite days of incarceration'... due to the fact that the only Judge was arrested."

"Whew, let's celebrate. I want a hot dog with everything!" said the siren (Opium II).

The man blushed (Sparky).

The parade of ex-prisoners ended at Cube S. Already searched, a group of explorers had opened the locked doors where the Board Members lived lavishly. With the members gone, homes were picked clean. Their slaves were set free... but surprisingly stayed. There was a lot of open space for the Believers to congregate.

No longer a secret society with need for abbreviations, the Believers were without a leader. J'me did not want the job. Fortuitously, Patch was perfect at organizing and prioritizing the necessities. It was not "Patrich Perfect", but Patch and nouveau August were able to find quarters and supplied everyone with their needs. It was not a utopia or a perfect world... or Shangri-La...It was Cube S. However, it would evolve. **Not the best, it was good but could be better.**

After today, J'me was not sure what they should do... This was a time she wished they had a Tio Juan. During emergencies he could make quick decisions and yet abdicate when things settled down.

It seemed like a crazy day, time was sporadic... not smooth and calm like at the BLOCK. **(People naturally have the tendency to compare their current situation with that of the past.)**

Not wanting to attract attention, Patch stayed with August in the apartment. Not wanting to attract attention, J'me, Alice, Rose, and Jen got away from the crowd of Believers and went to the Cube S rooftop, away from the day. St. Wx had no shielding like the original BLOCK. They hung their feet over the edge. At first, each of the four just sat silently, trying to process their memories, trying to bring clarity to chaos.

J'me spoke first, "I am white." (referring to Tio Juan's cognitive color code.) In a minute or two they all burst out laughing.

Repetition... Repetition creates acceptance. Repetition reaps top of mind awareness and increases the likelihood to repeat purchase. Repetition creates acceptance. **It was a conscious subliminal brain washing.** Repetition creates acceptance.

Detour, back to the BLOCK...   Feel a deeper penetration of pureness.   Adjust yourself to feel these surreal sensations:

Light replaced darkness. They could not focus on the faces, but they were being absorbed into their thoughts. The younger and older man lay in wake...waiting for what was next. Soon they would see the light and feel again.

Chapter 84
Purposeful Path

"Imagine a fourth dimension. One we cannot see. The fourth dimension is not time, it is a non-physical force. It is trying to get your attention. Try to sense it.

You would think it's magic, but it's not. It is supernatural. Just because science cannot explain it, does not mean miracles do not exist. You cannot see air, but it's there. Let me explain...

In a three-dimensional world we see only two dimensions: height and width. Not until we touch it or move do we see the depth, the third dimension. So in a three-dimensional world we perceive only two dimensions... and in a four-dimensional world we perceive three dimensions. A dimension is within another dimension... We live in a world we do not see, but we know it exists. Move your mind around... Touch it... Try to sense it."

"Stop that August!" Patch made everyone laugh.

"Your mind sometimes meanders onto the meaningless. That is not practical."

"Hello..." chiding August, "Today is our day to rest. One week of work, one day to play."

The group gathered in the living room. The guys moved the furniture back while pads and pillows were put on the floor.

J'me, Patch, Alice, Rose, Jen, and August felt like a family. They were having a calm time together, "chillaxin". They were bonding. Their topics evolved and revolved. It was all entertaining.

"Do you remember that girl with the gifts? We met her in the basement. Her name was..."

"Angelica. Yes. Her parents are Believers. How long has she been here?"

"She was new from a girls' school. Not long I suppose".

"Imagine arriving and then being arrested?"

"She has a gift and a purpose, both. She is the giver of gifts."

"What's that?" asked both Patch and August.

"Yes, Angelica is able to sense people's special abilities. Rather than searching all your life to find your greatness, she can see it."

Patch thought out loud, "It would be nice to meet her."

"She is beautiful... and single." Then they laughed.

There was a sound at the door... swipe right , tap-tap... a smiley face enclosed in a circle.

"Are you expecting anybody?" asked J'me as Patch and August headed to the door.

Reminiscent of life on the BLOCK, you thought of something, you wished, and it appeared. At the door was a young woman in a white lace dress, holding a cake. Ready for a wedding... It was Angelica. They invited her in.

"I baked a cake. I thought it would be a warm welcome."

"That is sweet of you." said J'me... "Please come in."

Angelica was not the only unexpected guest that day, there was also the Hick brothers, looking like deep rural boys, but in contrast to their appearance, they were geeks. That is not the term they used, they called themselves "white hat ghost hacktivists".

Here is a trick: If you want to know how good somebody is at something, ask them. If they say they are the best, they are not. If they say they are the worst, they are not. **The best never admit it.** These three brothers would not admit to anything, but they were the best.

"Changing the subject..." J'me started, "Naturally we question, especially when things are low and slow in life. **Just as everybody has a special gift of greatness, everybody has a purpose.** Perhaps we will never know. Perhaps this creates a question that cannot be answered? **All of us are on an unpredictable path.** This is too complex for computers; **your end game is an enigma.** Am I going to be one of those lost souls?"

This made them think... Her insights were interesting...J'me was just chewing the rag, as Mac called it.

J'me was a positive energy magnet. It was her invisible vibrations that invited everyone to her. She did not feel special.... But what was unique was the way she exuded love. Her smile and personality attracted others to come together.

"By the way... Where is Hobob, Bobby, Baby?" asked the sisters.

"He mentioned something about a wooden block... and... miracle money to make a mansion?" replied August in a questioning tone. "He gave it to me to give back..."

"I heard he was going to take a cruise around the world while they were building." Patch added.

That night, around sunset, the girls gathered on the rooftop... J'me, Alice, Rose, Jen, and their new friend Angelica.

Detour, back to the BLOCK... Adjust yourself.   The bright lights may blind you. Feel a deeper penetration:

Darkness again replaced light. It was a fight. The young man thought, "It is not fair to not know who is there."

Chapter 85
(A&R) Adjust and Restart

The Playground was not inside the Cube campus. It was west of St. Wx. In the past, going to the Playground was their only outdoor activity. Sorry to inform you, but opening the Playground has been delayed. The workers, while doing the repairs, also had to remove the cages and lengthen the field from a square into a rectangle. There is no estimated time for completion, but the repairs are needed.

Now members were confined inside their Cube campus.

The chat lines disapproved of the improvements. Many people saw the previous Playground as part of their heritage and felt it should have been protected. **There are those h8ers and trolls who only complain.** Those that approved of the repairs, or the delay, did not post a thing.

The comments were hot and cold. Generally hot with criticisms, cold without compliments.

After an adjusting day, it was another re-boot. **Making a small positive change in your routine creates huge results.** Real resolutions are not yearly, but every week, every day, every minute, every moment... Adjustments and restarts can happen at any time and as many times as you wish.

Time period = week... August and Patch continued their bond. They were inseparable. Literally. August would shadow Patch; they were attached.

Remember the Hick brothers? No insult intended, they were" country", not authentic cowboys like Mac, but they wore white brimmed hats. (I doubt they had ever ridden a horse.) Well, they came each day and created a corral in August's old apartment.

Remember the lust lure of "Mama" Opium II? The guy with the premature balding and bulging belly? Sparky was a hardware guy and he also arrived; he could make scream machines with processing speeds that were out of this world.

They were in their planning stages. Their goal? "We will make dreams come true."

Time period = day...The triplets had help finding the first floor of the medical Cube. And just as he had said, Dr. Meutal was looking at the newborn babies. Master Meutal was to be their mentor.

They started their day in the emergency rooms. Then they worked their way up. Fixing the first floor, mending the second, restoring patients on the third... By the end of the day they finished the fifth floor and met Master Meutal on the sixth.

This was going to be their routine schedule until each floor was vacant except for the staff. Although inconspicuous, people suspected something was special about the new doctors without name tags.

Time period = minute... It did not take long for J'me to start her new expeditions. She was a wanderer, deep down. She did not need to be a third wheel to Patch and August. **They did not need a tricycle when they were already riding a bicycle.**

She wished to be moving and giving in to her inner desires. However, she was cautious about approaching strangers; she mainly observed. J'me did not want to be a leader. She only wanted to follow an unstructured life...

Time period = a moment... The Nobels were distracted by their new neighbors. Not in a bad way, only good. They enjoyed the feeling that they brought to the Cube. For M. T. Nobel, it was a feeling he had not felt in a long time. For Junior and Opium II, it was new... and nice. **It feels fantastic to have friendly neighbors.** Some even came by to introduce themselves. Interestingly, they asked for nothing. Just offering a friendly "hello".

They only spent a second celebrating. They knew it was much easier than they had planned to pull out DD and Dick. Their next step was Dr. Edgar Krass... or maybe Don? No conclusion, just confusion.

The Believers adapted well. They went out and worked, then came back to what seemed to them like a celebration every day. It felt good to be respected. This was something they could not find before at St. Wx.

Their fear of discovery was turned around. People now feared them. They held a power that people were afraid of. When the topic of the nightmares came up, the "coffee cooler" (coffee machine and water cooler) gossips spread the word that the Believers had sweet dreams. Perhaps it was more envy than fear? It would take them time to adjust to the Believers.

Each night, around sunset, the girls gathered on the rooftop... J'me, Alice, Rose, Jen, and of course, Angelica.

Detour, back to the BLOCK... Adapt to the feeling of empathy it evokes:

Darkness again replaced light. It was a fight.

Then it happened! He felt hands touching him. The instant of contact created a surge of energy, a lightning bolt then landed! "Mom? Dad? Grandma...?" Who?

Chapter 86
Progress Progressed

Progress was uneventful. Little by little things improved. August and Patch were working on their tech project. Computer equipment was sent by the BLOCK labs.

"Not zero and ones, this is going to be a quantum computing platform!"

"We can data dump the world!"

"Massaging the data... Our actionable analytics will make it dance... make it sing!"

This is how they explained it at "Sunny's Spot." (They needed to develop a super-secret name, like the bat cave, X-mansion, Paradise Island, Atlantis...)

J'me ventured away from the Believers' Cube and was exposed to those who were negative, hopeless, confused. There was a man who was a mumbler, a whisperer, and those who talked too fast (as if everything was one word). It was impossible to understand them. She met rude people, people with werewolf anger, arguers, and all the possible permutations. Many had more than one annoying characteristic.

J'me longed for... then she spied a man sitting on the floor with his back to the wall. The man faced J'me but with his eyes focused far away. His normally black irises became... orange, red, green, and blue rainbow auras. She had seen this before. He was thinking... His mind was moving... He was converting.

She squatted down and said, "I love you." then put his sunglasses back on and lifted him to his feet. It seemed to those looking that she was holding his gentleman's elbow, but she was using levitation to move him (his feet didn't touch the ground). She swiftly teleported to Cube S.

Soon she heard the familiar, "May I help you?" and saw people with cupped hands approaching.

"This is a convert. He is going through a phase of adapting. He will be fine, but he needs time... we need a place for him to stay." explained J'me.

"I know him!" said one of the Believers.

J'me did not want to say more. This was not something J'me wanted to be part of. She was not a member, just a visitor. She was a follower like everybody else. In her head, Code RED!

The new doctors were busy when they heard the announcement, "Code red!" This meant the building was on fire. The sisters coalesced quickly to the first floor and immediately searched for Dr. Meutal... their mentor... It was crowded and crazy. This was not something they wanted to be part of. They were merely volunteers here.

It was then they were approached by a Believer who said, "Now is the time."

"Now is the time. Let's get this baby up and running!" Sunny's Spot had just got another shipment of parts. They progressed little by little... It was an improvement, but not yet a miracle.

"It didn't work!" The Nobels were back in the safety of their own home. "I thought it was going to be easy to get Dr. Krass off his ass."

"Me too! The false fire alarm was a failure. He didn't budge..."

"He didn't care! That was where we went wrong." M. T. Nobel stated the obvious.

"I guess now is not the time."

J'me, the two brothers, and the triplets all said, "You are home early?"

"I will make some tea. Would anybody like to join me?" asked J'me.

"Sure Mom." answered the quintet.

It was a feeling of family. When they could privately talk. But it seemed that there was something sticky, like the walls at St. Wx.

"There was a fire at the hospital." This was the first of the family discussion.

"It was a false alarm..." Patch was quick to pick up the newest news. "Nobody got harmed."

"But not everyone got helped..." This sounded painful. The sisters loved their work, and this hurt.

August noticed this... **"You have to be a little crazy sometimes."** he advised. "You know what I used to do? Smile... laugh inside... and smile."

He was right. **When being placed in a situation that you cannot control, the best thing to do is just smile.** Smile in your mind and your life will be happy.

J'me wished for answers... "Mom, what's the matter? What happened to you?"

"I helped somebody...." They stared at her... waiting for a further explanation...

Then she blurted it out, "But I do not want to be a boss!"

"You need people to go out and search for you." said Patch, "You need spiders..."

Detour, back to the BLOCK... Adapt and adjust yourself. Slower, smoother movements:

Darkness again replaced light. The older man thought, "It's not fair to not know who is there."

Then it happened! He felt hands touching him. The instant of contact created a surge of energy, a lightning bolt then landed! "My loves?" My daughter! My wife!

Chapter 87

Re-Adjustment Time

Patch was perfect at organizing. He referenced Mr. G and how he did not work alone. He had helpers. Team power...

"But... "J'me wanted to disagree, but she knew he was right. "I know, but..."

"**Think about it**, while I get Angelica." Patch, followed by August, left and looked for their new friend. Remaining were J'me, Alice, Rose, and Jen.

"But... I am not Mr. G..." said J'me.

"You need to share your secrets. **It would be a shame not to share**." the triplets chimed.

Despite what the girls would say, these were just words to J'me. Her intuition reminded her, "**It starts with helping others while helping yourself**." But again, she was resistant.

The girls were trying to understand the source of her reluctance. They decided to stay quiet and wait for J'me to think it out. They would also wait for Patch, August, Angelica... and spiders.

Inside J'me was her wants. "I am a wanderer, deep down. I only want to wander. I want to be a follower like everybody else. I am not the type to be a leader, guru, or guide. I do not want attention. I want to be hidden.

Her plan fell apart... again. **Perhaps this was her purpose? She had been called.** No conclusion, just confusion.

"Let's go to the rooftop." said the trio in unison. "Maybe you will feel better?" "Plus, Angelica will know where to find us."

J'me was open to any suggestion at this point... She followed.

The mid-day sun was shaded by clouds. The smog was gone. It was nice to get some fresh air. They sat in their routine sunset spot, facing west. In the distance they could see work being done on the Playground. J'me waved at the workers but they did not look up.

Behind them, however, they could not see the roof runners. They were enjoying their time releasing their pent-up energy... Running, jumping, landing and rolling, then back up again. For them, it was freedom.

Cut to the quick... "Hey slits, get off our roof!" J'me and the girls just ignored them. This was not the response they expected. "Did you hear me?" they said less loud since they had drawn a crowd. Again, they were ignored. "They are Believer bitches." someone said. Their pack mentality created a level five rage!

J'me turned while the girls instinctively held each other's hands. "Get off our fucking roof if you know what is good for you!" someone said, followed by angry encouragement.

J'me stood up, facing the mob. She cupped her hands and smiled. It was not what the crowd expected. "Let's rape the sluts!" somebody shouted, but they were just words. The mob did not move. (Neither did her seven protectors working construction below. J'me was out of sync, disconnected.) It was an old-fashioned face off.

This was a stall maneuver for J'me. Preparing her plan of attack... she had many options. So far, they were just offensive words. She was not in fear. It was then she summoned her greatest power. J'me closed her eyes, concentrated, and relaxed...

"I love you." J'me said.

And it worked... They shivered, they shook, they saw bubbles, and they left. **LOVE BOMB!**

"Spiders?" Angelica repeated...

Patch and August explained that when you ask a few friends for help, and they ask their friends, and then those folks ask for help... You start with three... but end with hundreds of helpers... eventually you will find what you are looking for.

August interjected, "Three to the sixth power is 729 spiders."

"So, my love, you need me to find somebody to lead the Believers?" The two young men adored how she talked to them.

Just then, "What was that? Did you feel it?" The three shivered... shook... and saw bubbles... Each got weak in the knees and wanted to please. Sparkle!

When J'me, Alice, Rose, and Jen got back home, nobody was there. The brothers had not yet returned with Angelica. They decided to take showers and eat out. They needed a break. For J'me this was a welcome distraction.

On the way to the restaurant, they overheard people talking. They shivered, shook... and saw bubbles when J'me dropped her love bomb; it penetrated.

She took the girls to Cube X, the only place she knew to get something to eat. When they walked through the doors, the girls gasped. Instinctively they held each other's hands and Momma J'me scuttled her daughters safely to the side.

"We are doctors... it is not like we have never seen a naked body before." rationalized the triplets.

"The digestive and reproductive systems." J'me said with a smile.

Back at the BLOCK, with a deeper penetration:

Seconds seemed like hours or maybe hours seemed like seconds... Both sat up. Unable to talk... "We're blessed!"

Chapter 88
Bye-bye

"May I help you ladies?" asked the greeter.

"I think we will be ok. Thank you." J'me spied a friendly face. It was Dr. Meutal and his wife sitting alone at an oversized table. J'me remembered, **if you ever want to make a friend, ask them first for a simple favor.**

When Master Meutal saw the four approaching he stood up. "My love, these are the doctors I mentioned I was mentoring."

Introductions were made, then Master Meutal gestured for them to sit down, inviting them to his table. There were extra chairs for four plus one more.

Master Meutal, while not at work, seemed like a different person. He was chivalrous, with superior standards of conduct... a perfect gentleman.

Everybody was happy to be in their safe little bubble inside the Playroom.

"**Today is a different day...**" Master Meutal started, but stopped while everybody ordered...

"Were we interrupting anything? J'me stressed, "ANYTHING?"

"Oh no! My wife and I have an agreement... **Once you have done it once, you can never say you never done it.**" The love birds looked like they were still on their honeymoon, romantically holding hands.

"Doctors, pardon me for speaking shop during supper, but tomorrow you will make your way up to the Psych Floors? The reason I ask is that I want you to meet a couple of my colleagues."

"Sure, I think we will get there." replied the sisters.

Then somebody approached Master Meutal, who was surrounded by five women, and asked him "CU46? I won't take 'no' as an answer!"

"Uhm, thank you." he said with a smile. "Bye-bye Felicia."

"Spiders?" Angelica repeated... then asked, "Leaders? I have mixed emotions about this. **But it doesn't hurt to ask? Right?**"

Both Patch and August agreed.

Then Angelica asked, "Do you know anyone who would like to be a leader of the St. Wx. Believers?"

Emphatically they answered, "No!" They both saw the irony in her question.

DD was happy to have Dr. Meutal visit her establishment. He had an open invitation, but he rarely came. Today she spied him with his wife and four unfamiliar females. She thought she knew everybody, but they were new to her.

"Mr. and Mrs. Meutal. Thank you for coming. It is always a pleasure."

Dr. Meutal stood and shook DD's laced gloved hand. "Thank you, Madam Maye."

Then she hugged Mrs. Meutal with one arm. The Meutals gestured to the vacant seat.

"May I?" replied DD.

All angles zoomed in on DD and J'me, J'me and DD. Their eyes locked onto each other. Neither blinked. They each had googled-eyed grins. They got all gooey... Neither said a word, just stared... It was awkward for the others at the table... Odder yet, when approached, neither spoke, not a "Yes" or a "No."

After dinner, the Meutals left, not wanting to be led into temptation, delivered from evil.

They graciously said, "Ladies... Bye-bye."

Alice, Rose, and Jen said "no" again and again and again...then asked for paper and pen.

At first, they wrote the bolded words, "No, thank you." but decided a better sign should read, "**Out of order**." They kept this on the table and used one hand to pull their hair back... "Bye-bye."

Deep breaths in... slow exhales... J'me knew what she had to do.

About eight or nine minutes later... "Let go of limiting beliefs." J'me said, breaking the silence. "Subdue your power to resist."

DD replied, "I could not have said it better!"

Unbraided, unbridled, the two let their hair down. First, they walked the perimeter of the room in a clockwise direction. They just gave quick smiles, waves, or hugs to the people they met. Stopping only for some drinks. The second lap was more casual, and they often stopped to watch.

"I just think of everyone as a friend." said DD.

"I just think of everybody as a forever friend." replied J'me. There was a slight difference, but both agreed, **you can never have too many friends**. They shivered, shook, and saw bubbles; love bomb penetration!

Each night, around sunset, the girls gathered on the rooftop... J'me, Alice, Rose, Jen, and Angelica. This night DD was their new guest.

Take your time. Allow it to evoke a feeling... Remember the BLOCK was a different atmosphere. Movements are slower with the vibrations of pureness:

"We were always with you. Did you hear our whispers? Did you feel the touches or the kisses; did you feel the wetness of our tears? We were always near!" Oh, the love from family never goes away.

They shivered, shook, and saw bubbles; love bomb afterlife. The glorious reunion had begun!

Chapter 89

Both went "Whew"

The next morning J'me and DD sat privately on top of Cube X. They were watching the morning sunrise together.

"J'me, I agree with everything you said last night. Whew!" was overheard from DD.

J'me reciprocated, "DD, I never knew such things were possible. You are an artist. Physical pleasures of the body are beautiful. Whew!"

They had become BAE-friends (Before Anyone Else).

Members were appreciating the Believers and the "coffee cooler" gossip had lessened. In truth, they were not a negative topic any longer. St. Wx. was a leaderless commune and it seemed liberating. The Believers went out and worked, then came back to what seemed to them like a celebration every day. It felt good to keep their private and public appearance the same.

Little by little, people converted and were moved to Cube S to recoup. The Believers mentioned J'me and how she placed sunglasses on the converts and requested they rest. It seemed the solution. (J'me was not credited with releasing the Believers or the "LOVE BOMB", which was what she wanted...)

Bunkered in the God-Pod, the Board Members sat... They felt the earthquake and their own tremors from the previously released love bomb. They sent for their spiders, their spies.

The next day doctors Alice, Rose, and Jen eXquisite met Dr. Meutal in the first-floor baby viewing area.

"It is going to be a super special day." said Dr. Meutal.

The interconnected three were excited to get back to the work of healing. "We agree."

"There is a cafeteria here on the top floor of the medical Cube, T10... Meet there?"

The new doctors now knew why their mentor started each day viewing the newborns. It was a welcomed reminder: **babies are proof that miracles do exist and that they do not happen right away... there was a lag effect** of nine months before they arrived.

Although the day before was abruptly halted, there was a significant drop in patients. By midday, their work was past midway, to floor 6. This was Dr. Meutal's domain, the mental health unit.

The balls of thread and yarn distracted them, but they tried their best to physically heal the mentally ill. This was their first attempt, and the 80/20 rule prevailed. Eight out of ten did not change, but for every ten there were two that seemed to become better. Most just suffered from "dyscopia", which means a "failure to cope".

The perspective of Alice, Rose, and Jen was that **one is better than none and two is better than one.** Therefore, they were ready to move upward without regrets.

"Wait, we will be late!" said Jen, looking at the time (Question: How can you see time? I always wondered...). They each used both hands to pull their hair back.

When they entered the cafeteria, they were surprised. It was done in a Doctor "Ek" design...The place still smelled of something. But people were in line, receiving trays of food that were shoved through an opening in the gray glass. They had no choice...

They found a wobbly table but feared to sit down because of the leftover mess. Jen stayed with the trays while the two others looked for cleaning towels near the toilets. While away, Dr. Meutal arrived with two mature Meds in identical lab coats, each with "Dr. Love" name tags over their hearts.

"Doctors Love, I would like you to meet Doctor eXquisite." (Being generic, not knowing which of the identical triplets were who.)

"I am a plumber and she is a baby catcher." said the male Doctor Love whimsically. (Excuse me for being gender specific moving forward when referring to Mr. and Mrs. Love.)

Jen let out a "this makes sense" sounding smile, then shook their hands. "Please wait for my sisters... they are getting something to sanitize." Both doctors were impressed that she did not complain, nor did they wait for somebody else to clean.

If that was a good first impression, you should have seen their expressions when they saw identical triplets with braided hair.

"Do not be seen while you clean." And, "You know what I mean?' said Alice and Rose, laughing, when they arrived at the table with the cleaning cart.

"HonSuCan J-Wash" was what Jen said...

But that does not matter... It was the "Whew!" that came from Mr. and Mrs. Love when they saw their daughters for the first... second time. LOVE BOMB nuclear family!

QUIZ

VIII

Quiz Eight

Test your understanding of what you read. Pick the *best* answer for the following ten questions. After completing all ten questions, check your answers on the next page.

Please take your time reading and meditating to unlock the next chapters.

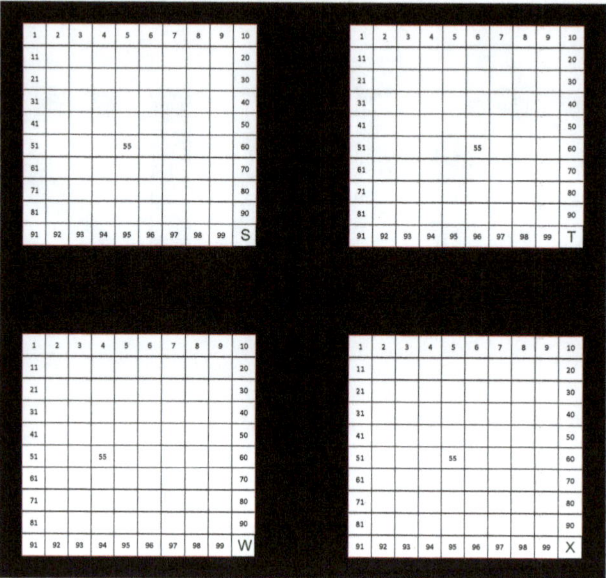

1. When you block or slow down the movement of your body's energy, what happens?

    a. It creates disorder that makes you feel tired and sluggish.
    b. It creates disorder that weakens your body.
    c. It creates disorder that weakens your mind.
    d. All of the above

2. Who are the (Reproductive) Endocrinologists?
    a. Doctors eXquisite
    b. Doctor Edgar Krass

  c. Doctors Love

  d. DD "Baby" Maye

3. J'me invoked the "three strike rule" on whom?

  a. The security services

  b. The roof runners

  c. Another unmentioned (insignificant to the story)

  d. All of the above

4. When did J'me use her special powers at St. Wx., the outside world?

  a. LOVE BOMB!

  b. Moved the new convert by levitation and teleportation

  c. Freeing the Believers from Sublevel Three

  d. All of the above

5. What wisdom did J'me share about the psychic wars?

  a. Sometimes things have a tendency to resolve themselves

  b. If it does not affect you, give it no thought (mind your business)

  c. Anything times zero is still zero

  d. All of the above

6. Who was NOT a "white hat ghost hacktivist?

  a. The Hick Brothers

  b. "Sparky", the computer hardware hacker

  c. J'me eXquisite

  d. August (Sunny) and Patch (Patrich)

7. Which Millennial jargon was used in this chapter? (Try your best)

  ___ 53X (sex)

  ___ Awks (awkward)

  ___ BAE (Before Anyone Else)

  ___ Basic (mainstream)

___ Beat (having a full face of make-up, verb tense: applying make-up)

___ Bye Felicia

___ Chillaxin' (a combination for chilling and relaxing)

___ Crunk (getting high and drunk at the same time)

___ CU46 (See you for sex)

___ Curve (romantic rejection)

___ FOMO (Fear of Missing Out)

___ GOAT (Greatest Of All Time)

___ Gucci (good, doing well or feeling fine)

___ H8ters (haters)

___ Humble Brag (complaining about life while bragging about yourself)

___ Hundo P (100%, as in 100 percent certain)

___ Keep it 100 (keep it real)

___ Lit (when something is amazing)

___ Micro-Cheating (interacting with somebody other than your significant)

___ Millennial (the generation born during the change in Millennia)

___ n00b (someone who does not want to learn)

___ Slay (someone who looks exceptional maybe to impress everyone)

___ Stan (a combination of stalker and fan, verb tense: stan'd)

___ Trolls (somebody who purposely tries to provoke others)

___ Phubbing (snubbing someone and paying more attention to your phone)

___ Rachet (trashy, obnoxious, rude)

___ Snatched (looking good, "You look snatched!)

___ Thirsty (horny)

___ Throwing shade (dirty look, making a subtle mean comment about somebody)

___ Trill (true and honest)

___ Tea (gossip)

___ Tool (someone who is stupid and geeky)

___ Turnt up (to be high or drunk)

___ QM3 Y-DNA (the genetics of an indigenous Mesoamerican)

___ Wig Snatched (exposing the truth about someone)

___ Woke (being aware of current events)

___ YOLO (you only live once)

8. Who got "spiders"?

    a. J'me

    b. August and Patch, then Angelica

    c. The Board Members

    d. All of the above

9. What was something August had to get off his chest after his silence?

    a. Pack my box with five dozen liquor jugs

    b. There are no ethics when it comes to your subliminal mind

    c. Create a Buyers' economy

    d. Start a super-secret "Sunny's Spot"

10. Of the following, which is your favorite "Life's Lesson Learned" moment in the later chapters (Chapters 85 – 89)?

___ There are h8ters and trolls that only complain.

___ Making a small positive change in your routine creates big results.

___ They do not need a tricycle when they were already riding a bicycle.

___ It feels fantastic to have friendly neighbors.

___ You have to be a little crazy sometimes.

___ When being placed in a situation that you can't control, just smile.

___ Smile in your mind and your life will be happy.

___ Think about it.

___ It would be a shame not to share.

___ It starts with helping others while helping yourself.

___ Perhaps your purpose is that you were "called" by a divine power?

___ If you ever want to make a new friend, ask them first for a simple favor.

___ Today is a different day.

___ Once you've done it once, you can never say you never did it.

___ It does not hurt to ask.

___ Out of order.

___ You can never have too many friends

___ When you hit a jackpot, collect and then leave immediately.

___ Babies are proof that miracles exist (with a lag effect)

___ One is better than none... two is better than one.

___ It is impossible to "look" at time.

___ Repetition builds acceptance.

Q8 – Answers

1.   Answer D, you have a weak body and mind. Technically, this chapter only emphasized C: Blocked or slowed body energy weakens the mind.

2.   An Endocrinologist works with the body's system of glands that produce hormones that control the way the body works. The experts in this field were Doctors Love. Answer C.

3.   Three chances, three defenses before you go on the offense, this was the Three Strike Rule used to win every fight. She used it a few times, Answer D, unfortunately.

4.   Again, All of the Above, answer D. J'me tried not to attract attention to herself. She also wanted to be like everybody else, not different. But sometimes she could not help herself... She really did try.

5.   Again, All of the Above, answer D. J'me thought the psychic wars were not worth her time or effort. (Like many things you follow, we should use this as an example.) There was no benefit to that news. Perhaps entertainment? Perhaps entertainment that gets hidden in your subconscious glue?

6.   White hats are the good guys, not doing any harm and usually trying to protect others. A ghost hacker changes their name often to stay anonymous, disguised. A hacker on a mission is called a "Hacktivist". This is techy talk for the guys working in Sunny's (secret) spot. Answer C: J'me was not involved... yet.
Spoiler Alert: **You have had a target painted on your back.** Target marketing has been used by businesses for over 50 years. Now, computers can collect over 5,000 personal data points about you and know you better than you know yourself. (Nothing is private, except what is in your heart.)

7.   This has got to be a throw-out question, sorry. There were at least thirteen Millennial terms: BAE, Basic, Bye Felicia, Chillaxin', Crunk,

CU46, FOMO, H8ters, Slay, Stan, Trolls, Ratchet and, oh, Millennials... And QM3 Y-DNA (the genetics of an indigenous Mesoamerican) is not slang, it's a scientific description.

Make this a freebie. Do you remember Freak (1970-80s), Groovy (1950-70s), and Keep on Truckin' (1930s and 1970s, both)? Will this book be somebody's Shakespeare, with passing English?

Here are a few old ones from the 1900s:

- Bash (a drunken spree)
- Goop (a stupid person)
- Wisenheimer (someone who is smarter than everyone else).

Now, get ready for fun... from the 1800s:

- 15 Puzzle (complete confusion)
- Bang up the elephant (perfectly complete; unapproachable)
- Bottom Fact (undisputed truth)
- Bricky (brave, fearless)
- Butter upon Bacon (extravagance)
- Damfino (Damn if I know)
- Dizzy Aged (Elderly)
- Doing the Bear (hugging while courting)
- Don't smell me a dog (do not lie to me)
- Fly Rink (a bald head)
- Gas-Pipes (tight pants)
- Half-Rats (partially intoxicated)
- Lally-Cooler (a successful person)
- Mafficking (getting rowdy in the streets)
- Meater (coward)
- Nanty Narking (great fun, usually at a bar)
- Not up to Dick (not well)
- Poked Up (embarrassed)
- Pool Snappery (putting on airs)
- Powdering Hair (getting drunk)

- Shake a Flannin (to fight)
- Shining Around (sneaking about quickly)
- Shoddocracy (people who get rich selling poorly made items or services)
- Skilamalink (a secret, a sometimes shady secret)
- Take the Egg (to win)
- Tell a Thumper (to lie)
- Umble-Cum-Stumble (thoroughly understood)
- Wake Snakes (get into mischief)

8.   Spiders are searchers that multiply fast and move outward. Answer D, however, there spiders were no helpful for J'me, Patch, August, and ultimately "HonSuCan J-Wash" Angelica. But the Board had their spider spies with many eyes.

9.   August held it in so long he had to burst! Cartoons and commercials made him angry inside. **People either don't know or don't care about the manipulation of their minds.** Answer B.

10. Except for the last bolded text, "Repetition builds acceptance", all the other lessons learned were from the second half of this book (Chapters 85 onward). Did you think about any of them or did you just glaze over them while reading? Take it to heart, because when I was your age...

How did you do? Questions 7 and 10 were freebies. Are you ready to move onto the last book, Chapters 90 through 99?

Chapter 90

It was not August

Three months have passed? Impossible! Just like everything else at St. Wx., it was just not right. Unless you go outside and see day and night, you cannot prove time was correct.

Things at St. Wx. were fast and slow distorted. You could go outside on the roof and see that the days were darker and fall was coming... (Officially autumn is late September to December). What happened to August? 90 days? I call bullshit on this!

J'me rarely used her hidden powers... Her most magical moment, so far, was her release of the Believers from the bottom of St. Wx. Or was it the love bomb she released on the roof? Even these were only witnessed by a few. There was no telling of her tale.

J'me's job was perhaps to prove to people they were loved. Her insights were posted on the chat boards...

> "Like water on a rock, it may get you wet, but do not allow bad people, bad things, or bad ideas to affect you. Ignore it! Yet, it is easier said than done. As humans we naturally implant both good and bad feelings. But it is possible to be positive... **Let the bad wash away and leave it in the past."**

Each message finished just with the phrase, "I love you." origins unknown...

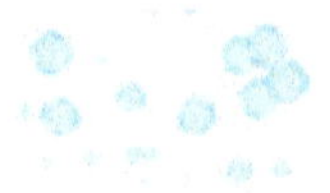

Black magic curse... Unconnected, rejected, J'me deflected. She did not want to explore, but just ignore. Dull to details, J'me was drifting. Voodoo void of any cognitive color all together! In transparent, translucent ice.

Reality disappeared and J'me was a frozen block. Nothing moved her... her "spirit walk" was just a dazed glaze. When she wandered the halls, she got special smiles. This was negated because she was deflated. On ice, she was...

It may not be new to you, but emotional hills and valleys were normal at St. Wx. Her walk thru darkness needed action when she reached the sixth floor of Cube T (T6) and curled in a corner with a ball of thread behind her head.

J'me closed her eyes and concentrated with all her might. Nothing happened. With all her might she moved... She stood up and fell against the ball of red thread. She put her hands around it and rubbed. Nothing happened. She stood again, focused, rubbing her hand on the orb. Nothing happened. She moved herself to the other side and rubbed again. Nothing happened.

"What are you doing?" somebody asked J'me.

Somebody answered for her, "**Looking for the end.**" The mentally disturbed, like the balls, became unwound until the ends were found.

Another thing noticed: The soles of their feet were worn from persistent pacing... They cried because they were worn out souls.

"Dear Father." This was how it started. "Please help us here at St. Wx."

"What are you doing?" somebody stopped them.

"Saying a prayer... If you keep your mouth shut, you cannot be fed."

"That seems like the right thing to do." they agreed and then when finished, added "Amen."

Quicker than you can say "Amazing!" there was a delivery at the door. A cardboard box filled with craft hooks and needles appeared. That was the worst of it... The best was the rest.
Some seniles came forward and helped J'me work the thread. They say, "An idle mind is the dirty deity's workshop." Others did the same and soon each ball was being used...

Something very profound was overheard, **"Take it slow and let it roll."** pertaining to the balls of thread. **"That way you avoid the tangles."**

Once you hit rock bottom, the only way is up. A few from T7, second level Psych, also appeared... They, too, had people skilled in the art of yarn and thread... combined to get that wicked mojo from their head. They took this idea upward. **If time cures all wounds, therapy quickens it.** All the king's horses and all the king's men, could not put them back together again... but string could!

Oh, the love from family... Oh, just a hug or kiss... Oh, in this case, one touch and their
pain went away. Another touch and they were healed, and the third touch made everything new again.

Doctors Loves' special gifts were revealed, previously blocked by their feelings! It was hidden in plain sight. While working in the labs, they discovered that much can be found in just blood and urine specimens. Your humors, the fluids in your body, are natures' key to balance. Your chemical systems regulate human behavior and vice versa. They referred to this as "the flavor of life" (so as not to sound humorous).

Doctors eXquisite- Love were partially with their parents in the labs, living the life of love. They started each day in the emergency rooms, T1, and made their rounds upward. They were now rapid with their routine.

However, when they reached T6... "Momma!" the triplets screamed at the sight of J'me on the floor. She took no notice, instead worked with her thread to clear her head. (No more can be said.)

The sisters found hemp and began braiding it tightly into cords, then again into rope. However, when done, they threw them outside (not to be a potential danger to the deranged, guarded from the retarded). This was added to their daily routine: to braid the hemp into rope and throw it away. It was how they relaxed and spent each day.

The delineation of time was not aligned. It was moving towards a time-less community. The demarcation of days was still a haze. This was something you could not get used to (it was still St. Wx.). Sometimes you must laugh inside and just smile outside.

Chapter 91
It Was Then

The insights of J'me were posted on the chat boards... The auto bot bulletins from 104 were replaced with:

> "Ever wonder why? **Why wonder?** Do not get carried away. **Feel good about the now, and do not dwell on the past or question the future.**"

Each message finished with the phrase, "I love you." origins unknown...

This proved it was not sent by J'me. She was only now awake, aligned and adjusted. Connected.

Moving upward, staying mobile, Doctors eXquisite-Love finally got to the locked door floor, the eighth-floor infection. They huddled at the entrance until their parents came with a master key.

"Now is the time." one said... It was time they tackled the task that awaited. Working with your body's humors, the holistic approach, the Phoenix Therapy! A pot with poles, rough towels, smooth silk gowns, a satchel filled with herbs...Ingredients, tools, and supplies already arrived (sent from the BLOCK). But there was one key missing...

"Have you eaten? Chi le ma?" That was the voice of Juan Li, followed by Chi Nü , and uh, uhm, Ota Menté.

"Did you miss me?" asked Juan Li to the Doctors eXquisite-Love.

No body budged... Bunkered in the board room, it became a game of stare down. Who blinked first? Nobody wanted to lose, thinking that the winner would get the throne.

Their eyes were open, but their minds were closed. Not meaning to malign, they were stuck...inflexible, unable to initiate and accept change. They still considered themselves the control center for the community.

Already DD, Dick and the Nobels were gone. "It's been a year up here." (using St. Wx. time). At this point the Board Members accepted that there was no CEO/COO to give them direction. It was about to become fall...

However, they did have their spiders, their spies, their eyes... In true slanted St. Wx style, some truth but mostly lies, there was one secret that enticed the Doc.

Thinking fast, then thinking slow... it was then that Dr. Krass had to go! A combination of fear and unknown automatic anger (fearious), plus self-protection, led to his destruction.

Finally, with half the board gone, 104 and Don Gottfried planned a poisonous plot! Don jotted a note and gave it to his two men, "First, deliver this to J'me eXquisite."

Phoenix therapy? Clap! The day that Dr. Edgar "Ek" Krass vanished. The inquisitive keeper of secrets... The lure of the undisclosed got the best of him.

Clap! Clap! When Dr. Edgar Krass entered T8, the scraping and scrubbing had started. The disgusting Doc shuffle stepped over to Ota Menté. Dr. Krass reached to grasp her ass, but Ota delivered a hoax hug and "Ek" got a paralysis pat on the back. Not to disturb the procedure, Dr. Krass was frozen in place! He could not move from his position. (Spoiler alert: There is a life like figure of Dr. Krass with his hands stretched forward, situated in the showers. It is used to hold wet towels.) Clap! Clap! Clap!

"Water. Try ..." Juan added a clap, clap... clap, clap. "Water, more..."

Then Juan Li went "alpha female" ... In the man's world of medicine, she became a bitch. By no means meant to insult, because it was incredible! It was a "Can I get a 'Go sista!'" from the balcony astounding!

The girls "gave the gospels" as they began transforming the medical Cube into something beyond belief! White trailers were already unloading deliveries at the docks, help from Cube H,
the BLOCK.

"Angelica, are you ok?"

Angelica was tuned into a sensation.... "Master Meutal... and uh, uhm, Ola, uh... it's... Ota Menté." Muttering, she was working with whispers.

Like spiders, J'me found Alice, Rose, and Jen... then they found Ota Menté. Cube T was being renovated so they went to Dr. Meutal's office.

The waiting room was full of patient patients. Angelica became inspired and said, "Rub her belly to fix your head."

Ota replied, "You create disorder when you block or slow down your energy. It must be released and not kept inside." (J'me thought of thread in her head.) By simply rubbing Ota Menté's belly, they were relieved!

Then Master Meutal stepped into the waiting room, "Ota?" "Padre?"

More of an evolution, not revolution... things just happened that way. Then it started. Steadily, there was a movement of sinners, a removal of corruption over the following months. (There was a lag effect.) Eventually, a total of one-third of the fellowship left St. Wx, without goodbyes. Freedom was not for everyone.

Did you know that yesterday was declared NO SEX DAY at St. Wx.? It was then?

It was a retaliation tactic against DD "Baby", J'me, the Believers, and against the entire idea of love. It did make the members a bit miffed but did nothing to affect their targets. Nobody was bothered by this. They just did their playing privately.

DD Maye and all the Believers' love exploded. There was more ways than bodily contact to express love. It became a great day to express your feelings and learn how to please those you cared for. I urge everyone to get closer to one another.

That night they found J'me, Alice, Rose, Jen, Angelica, DD, Chi Nü , and Juan Li sitting on the roof of Cube T, watching the sunset. (Ota Menté' Meutal was missing.)

Everybody was quiet and cozy. Then DD shared shyly, "I have a secret." She peeled off her lace gloves to reveal deformed fingers and horrid hands. It seemed everything on DD Maye was not perfect, but she was now naked with the truth.

Alice, Rose, then Jen gave DD "Baby" a hug... and her hands were healed.

Then two white laced gloves floated down to the Playground.

Chapter 92
Better Than

J'me's insights were posted on the chat boards...

> "When complimented, say, "Thank you" and feel good. When loved, feel appreciated... **Allow positive things to affect you in a positive way.**
>
> But do not pump yourself up too much or else your bubble will burst. Pop! You will have a drastic drop; feeling bad when overblown. You will be a mess... less!"

Each message finished just with the phrase, "I love you."

The St. Wx. Believers were not the best... they were the rest. (Remember, the best Believers emigrated out already to K.L.O.P.) Bad Believers? The place was not perfect. These were only a few incongruous painful experiences J'me endured in just one day at St. Wx.:

- Rushing onto the Beast before others got off.
- Stopping short while walking.
- Those who interrupted discussions and intruded. (It seemed what they had to say was more important than you.)
- "Smell this, it stinks."
- Tapping their feet.
- Sitting too close.
- Humblebragging.
- Starting a sentence with, "No offense".
- Eating with their mouths open; being noisy eaters.
- "Why?" People asked out of the blue for no apparent reason, "Why?" Why ask why? Why what?

Like scratching fingernails on a chalkboard, there were those with low or no emotional quotients or intelligence... but they were annoying friends. And compared to the rest, they were better than the others.

But... behind the crust was something clean. Believers gave freely of all they had. They took care of each other and even took the doors off Cube S.

The "Rule of Seven" prevailed (give away one and get back seven-fold.) Theoretically, these givers would get unlimited gifts, it you took away the takers.

Two men hand delivered J'me a note which read, "Meet me at the casino." Signed, "Big Daddy."

Without her will, the two men man-handled her. J'me was followed by August and Patch. Patch did not care if his mother (104) was aware, he followed J'me to the Cube X Casino. And it was not uncommon or rare for Sunny to be there and just stare.

There they met Don Gottfried, Big Daddy, at the big ballers table.

It was an old-fashioned face off...

J'me asked, smiling, "How do we play?"

Witnesses ran to the walls, wanting to watch who would win.

The dealer explained: "You have six die and the highest scoring roll wins. Straights are weak (1, 2, 3, 4, 5, 6). What you want are matches: doubles, triples, quads, fivers or nickels, and a full set of the same is better than sex." Then he pointed to the score board.

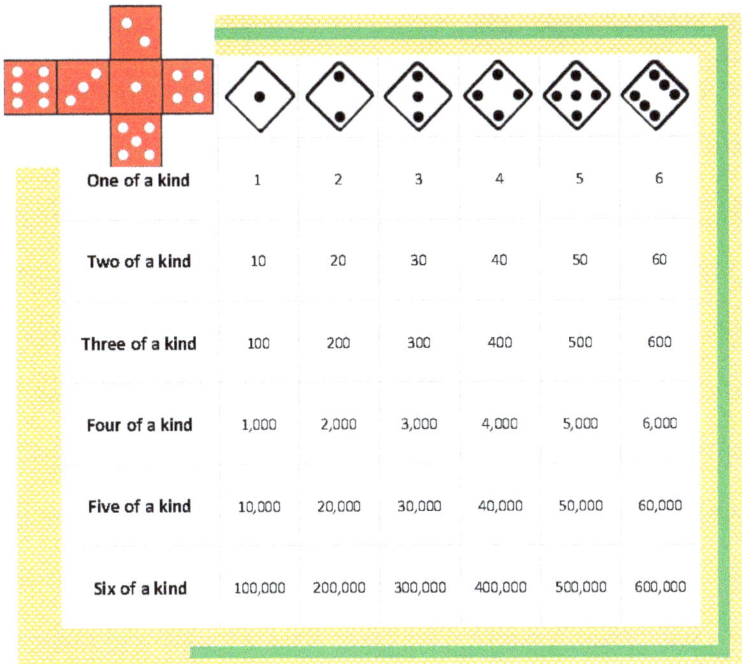

	1	2	3	4	5	6
One of a kind	1	2	3	4	5	6
Two of a kind	10	20	30	40	50	60
Three of a kind	100	200	300	400	500	600
Four of a kind	1,000	2,000	3,000	4,000	5,000	6,000
Five of a kind	10,000	20,000	30,000	40,000	50,000	60,000
Six of a kind	100,000	200,000	300,000	400,000	500,000	600,000

Let me interject, it would be really very easy for J'me to use her special gifts and cheat at this game, but she was too honest, too pure. Even to the point that "Pat Perfect" was not allowed to play. So... what you would observe was only luck, nothing more. Remember, there is no such thing as good or bad luck... Let's take a lookie.

"Million unit minimum, missy." Very simply, J'me pulled out the book without words and whispered to the dealer the account number from Key-Oh-Coo. "Is that enough?"

"92 million units!" A gasp from the gallery.

The game moves quickly. Bet, roll, then collect...

"Roll'em!" said the dealer.

*** Wager: 1 million units ***
1-2-1-4-4-5-5   JME   Score: 93
5-6-6-6-6-6   DON   Score: 60,005 (Winner)

*** Wager: 2 million units ***

2-2-3-4-5-5   JME   Score: 77
4-5-6-6-6-6   DON   Score: 6,009 (Winner)

*** Wager: 4 million units ***
1-1-1-3-5-6   JME   Score: 114
6-6-6-6-6-6   DON   Score: 600,000 (Winner)

"Holy bologna!" Patch said... then August added, "I call bullshit on this!"

Then the dealer picked up each dice and threw them twice, each time with the same results: "The ones were weighted so the six–dot surface would pop on top."

J'me said, unruffled... "We'll share."

The gallery moved in closer.

J'me kept doubling her bet, building drama with each, "Roll'em!"

*** Wager: 8 million units ***
1-2-3-4-4-5   JME   Score: 61
1-1-2-2-6-6   DON   Score: 82 (Winner)

*** Wager: 16 million units ***
1-1-1-2-2-6   JME   Score: 126
2-3-3-4-5-5   DON   Score: 86

J'me won! Now her losses were 15 million, but she just gained 16, up a million. J'me learned this trick from Melvin K. Klug. **Double your bet until you win, then start again.** Next wager went back to one. The crowd was now at the table.

Sorry to deprive you of the details, this was what the tale entails. **She made her own luck.** After nine hours and about twenty minutes, it was over. J'me had cleaned out the pockets of Don Gottfried, "Big Daddy" ... gone with the gallery.

"Thank you" she whispered to the tired dealer and gave him a gratuity gift. J'me quietly walked out.

Everybody was a winner (except for Don Gottfried and his gang).

Grunts and groans, exhales with moans, J'me got poked by the prick squad on her way home. There was a price on her head, somebody wanted her dead. But when August carried J'me to S10 with the needle hanging loose, it was pointless. In her home were the Masters of Medicine. She was back on the roof top by sunset.

The construction of the playground was almost complete. From their viewpoint it looked neat. They worked all night testing the lights, preparing for the fights. Now this was something concrete.

However, too long in the ether zone. The barrage of brainwashing created a weird time warp affect that cannot be described. This sensation would not go away. Fast, slow, fast... forever forward. It may seem normal to you, though.

In the distance, you could now see the color green coming in. Plants were approaching.

Chapter 93
Bowel Movement

J'me's insights were posted on the chat boards...

"Your minds are too full. There is no more room to learn new things and enjoy the now. Simplify. Organize. Planning is ok. But do not get carried away. **Do not sacrifice tomorrow for today."** Each message finished with the phrase, "I love you."

Was it the Vietnamese philosopher Văn (Not Wen) who said, "Every moving object remains in motion until stopped"?

Or was it the Pacific Islander from California, Caasi, who said, "Every object will remain at rest unless bumped or budged"?

Or maybe it was the Indian Yogi "Ris" (Krish) who said, "For every action there is an equal and opposite reaction, plus a social media overreaction"?

Was it Sir Isaac Newton who said, "Force equals mass times acceleration"?

The point being, there is a natural balance. The laws of nature dictate that St. Wx.: One, will not stop. Two, is being bumped. Three, has positive powers reacting to the bad. And four, this force of change is accelerating. Simple, like a bubble falling on your head.

The Believers began believing in each other. They did not go tribal, like in the Bible. They saw each other's differences as you would see colors. No insult, no injury, nothing personal; they were open to new things.

Using the bubble analogy, occasionally the bubbles bounced into each other. If you can imagine one bubble, try to picture a group of bubbles charmed together. Sliding against each other in one cluster. Some unified... They became bound rather than popping. Shaken sudsy and bubbled over! St. Wx became a bubble bucket.

Love is constantly being absorbed and emitted. As the spheres moved, they continually transformed and created the future.

Love is an energy that does not require matter to exist.

See the translucent rainbow of light bounce off its shimmering surface. Radiant and shining. Feel the excitement and the cohesion of the group. The refracting light contrasts the dimness.

Where were the Nobels? They gave up and were gone. They left before they could be transformed. They had not achieved their potentials, no powers, no knowledge they needed to know. "Dad, we gotta go!" said the Nobels' scions. "Now!" It was a shame because they were so close. **People give up precisely at the moment they are about to achieve their miracle.** The reason for this is that life is a game, and they just got played!

At the transport trucks, the Nobels were with Patch and August who were returning the wooden box. The gold was gone, and the money was missing, but what was left inside was more valuable. It was filled with hope. Inside were priceless family heirlooms.

What they got was a Nobel apology. "Before we leave, I have something to share. I represented your mother during the divorce." M. T. Nobel, to prove his point, gave the brothers a thick envelope. "Here is the original divorce decree." Patch pulled out the papers then gave them to August to read.

"I destroyed myself when I betrayed your father's friendship. I am sorry..."

Junior and Opium II wanted their father to stop, "Dad, this is not part of our plan! We must go now."

"Your father does not have a unit to his name. He divided it equally amongst the four of you, leaving nothing for himself." Then August found the financial sheets. "By now I am pretty sure you have a sizeable amount, even though he donated heavily to the BLOCK. How do you think they got their supplies this past century?"

Patch then asked, "Where is he now? Do you know where he is?"

"I saved your dad's life from his ex-wife. I helped him hide. Look on the last page..."

One last thing, before the double doors closed... Sparky reached in and gave Opium II a note. Sparky and Opium II were an item! This was the start of a longer distance romance.

Just as a St. Wx. Sample, for example, a woman squatted down near the Beast, squeezed a steamy soft shit on the floor, scraped her hole clean and wandered away! Then there were the depressed, suppressed angry masses, some with sunglasses... At St. Wx., **There was comfort in structure, even though painful, it was predictable.**

Just a normal day.

Annoying can get too annoying for anyone. But the last experience of that day climaxed it all! Something smelled like water and eggs on the fourth floor.

In sight, there was a strobing red light outside a door on X4. Was this right? There was a porn palace hidden away. (For those that do not know about pornography, it is fake love and phony sex... It was not real, just a visual thrill.)

Something new and never experienced before, J'me paid her fee, originally 60 units but jacked to 69 (psychological pricing). First mistake.

Inside was an entire video wall of pornography! Plus, virtual reality of every mutated sex act you cannot imagine. Innocent J'me originally took the perspective of "driven by desire and passion." Second mistake.

A little too much skin or sin? This was not a love shop. Somebody in the back yelled "Puthsy, puthsy, puthsy!" in an odd accent.

But then a sleaze ball forcibly shoved her, "Hey lady leave." Then, "Sorry, no refunds." Mistakes three and four? This was worthless love.

J'me teleported all the people to undisclosed places! These park bench perverts are now somebody's new neighbor. Excommunicated from St. Wx. were the rotten eggs. Double flush, stink stopper!

Do not dare to compare and deduct that she was a dictator. **J'me was not part of the competitive cancellation culture.** (With a little work, Cube X would get a new learning center.) Like pulling the wild weeds or pruning the bad branches, J'me started cautiously cleaning the cupboards at St. Wx... Washed away!

"Patch, can I speak with you? Privately please?" asked Angelica.

"Sure, what?"

"Darling, there is something wrong with your Mom."

"She just got poked... she will be ok." Patch responded.

"No, I mean... sorry... 104."

Patch said nothing, but smiled.

(But 104 was mean. Really mean! Very cruel!)

Chapter 94
Inferior Interior

J'me's job was perhaps to prove to people they were loved. People posted her insights on the
chat boards...

> **"YOU are important.** (Almost) everybody undervalues their worth... less than what they are. Do not compare or compensate. **There is always somebody better or worse than you. Look positively at your value. Wealth is what you have, do, know, and are."**

Each message finished just with the phrase, "I love you."

Some things are good. Some things are bad. The woman sat in the courtyard alone, eating her lunch. She was blessed, living a charmed life. A good wife and mother, but she believed that she needed an identity of her own, to own. She needed what the other wealthy women around her had. But she also carried in her conscious no control. She wanted more.

A stranger approached her, asking a question. "If you could go back in time with any idea, what would it be?" She had to think about it.

The next day, sitting in the same spot she said, "I cannot answer that question. It would disrespect other people's lives."

The stranger countered with, "Most inventions were designed by somebody else: Gottfried Wilhelm Leibniz for Isaac Newton, Alfred Russel Wallace for Charles Darwin, Antonio Meucci for Alexander Graham Bell or Nik Tesla for Tommy Edison, Mrs. Currie got hers from her husband, Stephen "Woz" for Steven Jobs, and Facebook was invented by Zuckerberg's roommates. ... Do I need to go on?"

The next day, sitting in the courtyard, her conscience was curdling. She wanted more control of her life. Then a tall man with two suits beside him approached her, asking a question. "Life without filters... would that interest you? You can do anything you want! No penalties, free pass, front of the line." She had to think about it.

The next day, again they approached, and she answered, "There are consequences to your actions." This made the man think. His solution was simple, "You make a good point... Just lie about it!" Then they left.

Day five she sat in the courtyard, white, without a conscience... Then her husband came and sat next to her. No lovey, dovey, kissy, huggee...She did not acknowledge him, but stared straight. He said, "Hello." but she just looked straight ahead. Just before leaving, his last words were, "I love you."

Day six she sat, alone and thinking... Her husband no longer had value. (He split his fortune equally amongst the four children during the divorce.). He never broke his original promise, made in marriage, to love, honor, and obey, every day. His refusal to fight ruined her game of pain. She still used the last card in her deck by controlling her kids, he was ghosted, gone...

Then appeared the man with the silver shine standing in front of her. She was in his shade and could not ignore him. Looking up, she saw his face. It was Mr. G.

He said nothing. She said nothing. Nothing had changed. She was shadowed, he was gone...

On the seventh day she did not rest. She started working on her new, not true, image as "104".

On one of her walks, J'me met the searchers. "Have you checked under the docks?" she asked. "The place was once a prison. I noticed on the west wall some cracks and rubble. Maybe we could remove it?"

When the explorers arrived, they saw Dick Richter and the security team in their self-imposed imprisonment.

J'me heard whispers: "Restrooms to your left... and the gift shop is to your right. The exit is on the other side of the room past the cashier's stand. Just look for the tall security scanners."

She found it! "Tear down this wall." J'me stepped back. First allowing them to begin the wall work, but then remembered the big mess at the BLOCK, so they stopped.

Now is the time... J'me knew she would have to reveal her gifts. It was like a dream she once had of booty in the bottom.

"Stay behind me. I can do this." If done differently, there would be difficulty. She took to the task of taking away the debris... unblocked the barrier and exposed locked forged doors.

She got a gut feeling... "Seek, knock, and it shall open." Three sets of double doors automatically opened in front of them. One... two... three...

J'me smelled the familiar scent of lavender, mint, and musk... but with a whiff of dust. A spray of lights, millions of stretching slivers invited them. The brightest of lights froze them. The searchers had a sensory surplus... Everything rushed to their attention.

. J'me felt like she had been here before... Inside were treasures and a wooden box with a "Do not touch" painted on the exterior. Something special: The block contained a ball bigger than her belly.

She knew what she should do. She took the box and ball directly to S10, Sunny's Spot.

"I found your missing master key." said J'me to August and his crew. "What do you want me to do?"

Their eyes widened! Everybody stopped. "Don't let it drop! Send it to the outer exosphere!"

Then they calculated... "Hydrogen and helium... Almost midway to the moon... 100 k kilometers... orbital velocity of (pause) 10 kilometers per second. I hope this works." They said something like that.

Have you ever done this? Just for fun, somebody put a "test spit" spot on the wall... waiting to see how long it would linger. Every day you walked past it to see if the gob of slob was still there. (This showed how clean it really was kept.)

J'me saw some people cleaning in a frenzy and asked, "What are you doing?"

"We are cleaning quickly so we have time to relax." was their reciprocating response.

"Why don't you relax while you clean? Move naturally... flow...become an artist." Then, "Maximum efficiency with minimum effort. **Organize once, then multitask.** Find a friend and have fun! You'll see."

Then began a cleaning spree. It was done free... for fun, with glee.

Chapter 95
Update

J'me's insights were posted on the chat boards...

"Rise! **Our best days are still ahead** building opportunities together.

Not me, us... Promises made, promises kept. **Be brave!**"

Each message finished with the phrase, "I love you." Updated to also include: You're the light of my life, my missing piece, my inspiration, you are important to me.

Are you paying attention? Your subconscious mind does not comprehend languages or words... It deals only in images and emotions. About 85% of your brain power is in your subconscious... It is your remote and multitasking master memory, permanently storing everything.

To access your subconscious mind, find a comfortable quiet place where you will not be disturbed. Perhaps focus on a point or close your eyes. Concentrate on your breathing, imagining yourself sinking in relaxation. Deeper... deeper...

When you are completely calm, this is mindfulness. With practice, your unconscious mind does not have to work so hard, allowing you to do things without effort, autopilot, automatically controlling comfort.

Instead of re-educating the prisoners, they were left alone... **they took their time to meditate and self-evaluate**. Although they were imprisoned, they were finally free.

They learned that they, and nobody else, owned their time. What they did in the past, doing evil in ignorance, was unfortunate. **The act of repentance is a magical miracle moment we can make.** What they wished for their future was forgiveness, doing alms. Now the security police only wanted to serve and protect others. They asked for mercy and were granted parole and probation (for good behavior).

History has more than one perspective, depending on who tells the tale. Here's another view, a scene as seen from another set of eyes:

Cube S, Floor 10 (Sunny's Spot): The ultimate info machine was complete... almost. The computer room was stuck, stalled... They had **DIKE: the movement of "Data" to "Information" to "Knowledge" and then finally "Enlightenment".** It was a full A.I. system, August Intelligence... Block chained to servers in each of the Cubes and outside resources (sharing data, not copied). Instead of a 5G connection, this was a Mr. G connection.

J'me delivered a wooden block with "Do not touch" posted on the exterior. Inside was a ball, bigger than your belly... an inspiring pearl.

J'me opened the lid, using levitation, she elevated it out. Inside, now outside, was an oversized communications sphere. Just like the miniature she carried in her bag.

Sometimes the solutions are under your nose. This was the missing master key.

"I hope this works." (Something like that.)

Eyes popped! Then they yelled, "Stop!" (Afraid it would drop.)

"Where do you want it?"

"Into the heavens!" So J'me teleported it out to orbit the earth like a satellite sphere.

Not everything is fair and equal. Stop trying to feel that way! **Fair and equal are false.**

The ex-slaves were having problems adjusting. **But to make it worse than the back of a hearse, was the back of the bus treatment from some of the worst.** Don't expect empathy. Don't expect help. St. Wx. was still selfish.

Failure is part of the process. It was two steps forward and one step back. They had to work harder than everybody else it seemed.

No more fights, but reality bites. The blame game was gone. Their identity was no longer "slaves", or even now "ex-slaves". They were real people with real feelings. Their lives mattered.

Some felt entitled, but they did not see where they were... or what once was. Bitter, but they were better, no longer serving a master. Free from domination is freedom. But they had to change. There were no promises or privileges... No free pass to the front of the line.

Step off that soap box and **EVERYONE adjust themselves. (It is not too late for an update.)**

You can't just dream to make your wishes come true. That is not how wishes work. You must work for your wishes.

Make the most of it. Remember Mr. Most? (An acronym for Mission, Objectives, Strategy, Tactics). He occupied the minds and lifted the spirits. His objectives were SMART... (Specific, Measurable, Attainable, Relevant, and Time bound). Motivated by his plan of action, Mr. Most was happier.

J'me entered a room where she heard people quoting her words verbatim. She was surprised that entire messages were memorized. They were also listening to each other, asking understanding questions. And helping each other with whatever difficulties they had. (Like a large family.)

J'me felt flattered and went further...

Reboot:

1. Smile
2. Love yourself
3. Be balanced

First Update (you are crawling):

4. Forgive mistakes, accept
5. Create good habits
6. Rest, exercise, meditate about a happy place, eat right and drink more water!

Second Update (you are walking):

7. Treasure experiences not possessions
8. Become more positive, ignore unpleasantries

Next Update (you're running!):

9. Stay focused, control yourself
10. Improve yourself, improve your self-satisfaction
11. Do your best

Final Update (you're flying):

12. Run... hit... dive... land, drop, and roll... Then stand up and run again.

13. Write it down. Make a list. Embroider it and place it on your wall.

In the boardroom sat 104, her eldest daughter and youngest son. Now Dr. Krass and the Gottfried gang were gone! Fake news was circulating a myth that Big Daddy Don was buried under section 95 of the Playground.

Plan A. Plan B. Now there was Plan C and D. The queen of "control" was living her "dream"! (or so it may seem…)

That night they sat on the roof watching the sunset. It was the most beautiful scene they had yet seen. Tints and tones of red hidden behind stretched out, bright white clouds (high level, cirrostratus or "wispy sheets"). This was nature's way of saying the weather would be nice the next day. **"Red at night, sailors' delight; red in the morning, sailors' warning."** Tomorrow would be a perfect day for a party!

The next day was their down day, the seventh day, their day to rest. Somebody suggested they should sleep late and have an afternoon picnic. DD "Baby" would do her best to cater and J'me would take care of the rest. The hostesses would invite their extended families and friends.

"But wait! Tomorrow are the fights at the playground!"

Chapter 96
Play Day

Drums began banging mid-morning, waking everyone from their slumber. It was the day of the fights on the Playground... Scheduled to start at noon.

The drones were already flying over the arena, posting their pictures on the new video boards. And from the rooftop you had a bird's eye view.

The Meutals would be late to the lunch, they were given the first med shift. Chi Nü and Juan Li invited themselves to help. The Love Doctors were informed their duties were on the last shift, from nine to midnight, the clean-up crew.

The countdown began at 11:00 with testing the speakers, "Go out and play!"

At noon there were trumpet blasts to herald in 104, the Mistress of the Ceremony.

"Are you ready to play? ... Louder!" Building up the crowd. "Ready to play? ... Louder! Louder! Louder!"

On the rooftop of Cube S, they started serving beverages and snacks. It did not take long before most of the guests ignored the arena down below.

"It is just a distraction from taking action." DD declared. Interesting and entertaining conversations ensued.

The crew from Sunny's Spot was already drawing diagrams on the tablecloths. And then the unexpected voices of the A. Naz brothers were heard in the discussion (connected remotely from the BLOCK). Most of the people on the fringe just listened in and smiled, understanding just a fraction.

Later there was a more inviting conversation about the topic of love that J'me, DD, and the Love Doctors hosted. "I urge everyone to get closer to one another". With this, everyone scooted their chairs forward. Although they had diverse viewpoints, they all came to the same conclusion. **Love is a need we all share.**

The Meutals, Chi Nü and Juan Li finished their shift, showing up around midafternoon.

"What was it like? The Fights?"

Not much was said, nobody dead, but the crowd liked it.

Master Meutal added something positive, "There was a lot of aggression released. One against ones', fights within families, husbands versus wife, wife versus husband, but mostly frenemy fights."

Ota added, "It was messed up! My stomach is sore. I need to rest."

"Next are the groups." muttered Mrs. Meutal.

While eating their lunch, they looked out to watch more of the activities, which became more brutal.

"Do you want to go down? I have exclusive seats." DD pointed to the shaded center section.

"Not now, but maybe later." J'me responded.

"Come with us tonight... for the best fights." It was from the triplets, with their parents sandwiched between.

Some took siestas, afternoon naps, to pass the time away, while others watched the big boards with the display.

At about half-past eight, J'me took everyone down to Sublevel Three. "We can enter through the tunnel." The three sets of double doors opened when she knocked.

DD Maye asked Judge Dick Richter to escort them in. Making it a show, with her friends in tow. However, when they stepped into the arena, the contrast of lights played havoc on their hurting eyes. They were led to their cushioned seats, removing those who had scalped their way in.

Before departing, the Doctor Love family said, "Dang, this is disgusting!" They were going to be busy.

Dick Richter was actually a nice guy. It was hard to understand why he was in his self-imposed imprisonment. He helped the others by explaining the event and answering all their questions. Plus, just his presence, kept the riff raff away.

After each event, the clean-up crew carted the carnage away. They wore bright orange jumpsuits, so as not to be part of the fray.

The lights came on and the turnt up, stoned and smashed spectators were moved to the upper seats. But the die-hards had worked themselves into a frenzy, moving closer to the field.

The face of 104 was often seen on the big screens. She was having a heyday! "Are you ready to play? ...I can't hear you!" was repeated every time a new bout was to begin.

It didn't take long for the hackers to replace her campaign commercials with some of the most embarrassing moments in the God pod. This brought cheers from the crowd as they were tired of the repeating loop of 104 and her goody goody girl face.

"Are you ready to play? Next are the roof top runners!" They were moving their jump boards onto the field while 104 wailed, "We have a challenge match!" You could hear a "whoop whoop whoop" in the arena. "The roof top runners (applause) versus... Jamey Exquisite!" She mispronounced her name.

The drones took a close-up of J'me's face as she heard this. She was sitting between DD and Dick. Everybody stood up. J'me grasped the inside of Dick Richter's elbow as he helped her to the field.

"But ma'am." J'me stopped him and waved him back to his seat. She was not frightened.

In the floor of the arena stood 40 fighters, flipping and running around. J'me was in the pit alone and waved to the crowd, smiling. She sat herself down in the center, crossed her legs, cupped her hands, and closed her eyes. She had a 360-degree view of everything around her. Her heightened senses even saw seven members of the staff removing their jumpsuits, wearing primitive attire. They grabbed their machetes and rope and surrounded J'me.

If you think 40 to eight was bad odds, it was worse when the Eagle Warriors stabbed their swords into the ground for a make-shift fence around J'me... a fairer fight. Then they slapped their chest and rumbled raspy, jagged jaguar roars.

Now the crowd noticed J'me levitating off the ground in her meditative state. This was more of a marvel than the pre-game show from the runners.

"Are you ready to play?" started the melee. The fight moved quickly and was over in fewer than five minutes. At the very end the Eagle Warriors started to collect their captives. But this was paused when the professional fighters entered the field.

"Don't go away! (Growl) Are you ready to play?"

It seemed only fair, J'me thought. She dropped to the ground. However, the fans did not feel that way, drawn out boo's drowned out 104's voice.

J'me huddled with the warriors, explaining a change in tactics. "We will win this way."

Something never seen before, only defensive maneuvers were made against the feisty fighters. Making them more and more mad. People were laughing. Especially when soccer balls were thrown onto the field. They would hit and ricochet off their opponent's heads, making them even more mad. The crowd was crazy, when J'me said, "Ready."

With this the warriors relaxed... somewhat. J'me was fresh and ready to fight.

The sides of their blades, not the edge, were used to slap their foe. Joints were sprained and some bones were broken as they all fell in pain. Some fought on, but were soon subdued as their numbers melted away.

When it was over, it got quiet... Really quiet... Very quiet... Then you could hear a "Roar! Thwit, thwit." – Efficient arrow shots through the heart and head of 104... Instant, painless death. Juan was standing on top of a lamppost, illuminated from below. When 104 fell down, she was still grasping her gun. Game over... Gone.

"Uno vida para vengar, muchas vidas para salvar." ("One life to take. Many to save.") Tio Juan explained to his warriors his reason for breaking their rule.

Chapter 97
X C V I I

Automated insights were posted on the chat boards...

"Love each other as you love yourself."

"Above all, love each other deeply, because love covers over a multitude of sins."

"My command is this: Love each other as I have loved you."

But perhaps this message was ignored. Folks focused on the following:

"Sorry to inform you, but the internet will be down for non‑necessary purposes. There is no estimated time for completion, but the repairs were needed."

Disapproved; the comments were hot with criticisms! Many people saw these privileges as a "need", not a 'want", necessary for their existence. This was part of their heritage and should be protected.

Eventually the chat lines may be gone? Now members felt confined. What would they do? How would they communicate?

Bonfires were made from the boardroom furniture and anything else that would burn. The looting lasted all day. Stores were closed. Consumerism was cancelled. (Energy was now exchanged, not currency.) The fire seemed a fitting farewell.

The funeral for 104 was fake, like her life. Her body was missing. It was a closed casket that was dropped into the not so sacred ground. It was just for ceremony because funerals are for the living. Funerals help you recognize what is important in your life: what is valuable and what you can do without.

About 97 percent of the people decided not to attend. Everybody mourns in a different way. It may sound sad, but people were glad.

The daughter and sons of 104 did not have anything good to say, so they said nothing at all, except, "She was my mother." and "She is dead."

Others sounded similar, "I guess it was fate... with her hate, maybe a little late, but there was a death date." The self-centered selfishly complained, "We had to wait."

Somebody said a prayer. It seemed like the right thing to do. J'me then pulled from her purse a mixture of orange and apple seeds and sprinkled them over her grave after the "Amen".

It was a dark day and it started to rain. The skies were crying. Soon there were sprouts, then they remarkably, rapidly grew green and tall. All of this in a matter of moments.

Sweet words of, "So sorry for your loss. If you ever need anything, please let me know." did not last, promising promises they could not keep. They were just fake friends, insincere with their words.

J'me earnestly added, sincerely saying, **"Do not let heartbreak get the best of you."** Plus, **"Get past the trauma, without drama, and let bygones be bygones."** She was honestly heartbroken for her friends and finished with, "Reminisce about the good.... I love you."

"You are not orphans. You were conceived in love." The great spirits of the past, present, and future sent messages that day.

From the union of R3G and 104: the oldest sister and youngest son were unaware... They just did not know. **Doing evil in ignorance; just going with the flow.** They were surprisingly nice, "HonSuCan J-Wash" sweet, and sensitive.

They began building a bond by spending time together talking, listening, and sharing. The R3G offspring stayed in seclusion for several days in Sunny's old apartment.

The four in the family decided to see Dad. They would reunite and form a renewed union.

Settling her spider search, Angelica was incessantly ignored when asking, "Dear, do you want to be the leader of St. Wx.?" Nothing but "no's" or "Nobody knows". They knew the obvious, **communism gets corrupted by commanders**. Concluded.

Midway through the day, the workstations stopped! This marked the start of when people wundered for 40 days and 40 nights... "What would we do without work?"

Where was the darkness they worried about? Three theories abound:

- Workers purged the work areas. Glass, wires, plastics and rubber were added to the bonfire. This created a dark and starchy smoke that stung your lungs and eyes. The fire kept on burning through the rain, spewing smoldering soot. It was safer to stay inside cleaning.

- The unclean walls! Without fake lights, parts of the Cubes looked like night. Darkness. Immortals (even those immoral) started scraping.

- Those that were miraculously converted, saw the light, so to speak. But part of the process was the change in eye color and lack of focus. Non-believers started washing away their sins.

All three theories have in common, brushing, scraping, scouring and scrubbing, and purging the place of impurities. It was a purification process. Then they finally all got tired and fell asleep.

But there is yet another thought which had to do with the devil deity and darkness. Nobody was willing to explain it, however. Unmentionable, thus I won't mention it. It was complicated and would put you to sleep.

The enigma of time, J'me now understood. It seemed that things moved faster at simultaneous speeds at St. Wx. Too many things happened that she could not maintain focus. She did not share this, but she thought it was perhaps the wrong pace for her pleasure. Her solace was to sit on the rooftop every night with her friends, watching the sun set.

This is an excerpt from the love table conversation, said earlier on the roof (removing the names of those who remarked):

"Consummate love includes commitment, liking, intimacy, and passion. Did you know that the average person will be in love three times in their lives?"

"Not once, not twice... three times?"

"There are those that had non-love or empty love. That average should be higher."

"Imagine those who have zero!"

"What's your number?"

"I have zero... but I put them at the end of my number."

After the bonfire cooled and the black was washed away, an abstract monument dedicated those days. Grass would not grow nearby, and somebody placed old signs on the sides that read, "Out of order" and "Do not touch."

From this they created a park with a walking trail lined with mint, lavender, and other fragrant herbs and flowers. However, the trail centered around the shade of intertwined orange and apple trees.

Chapter 98
980,000 Meters Square

Angelica put up posters in public places, inviting all psychics to meet in the old board room on X10. The psychic wars seemed over, but this would complete the competition once and for all, tying up the loose ends.

The first to show was August and Patch. They just came to say they were not psychics; they just could predict the future through algorithms, logic and math.

Next were Doctors Love and Master Meutal, accompanied by Juan Li. Together they came to say they were not psychics. They could use medical science and arts to predict the future of people's lives.

Then J'me entered. She also said she was not a psychic, but she knew some who shared their secrets with her. She knew real psychics, but was not actually one.

Wait, did J'me possibly have powers? Unbeknownst to J'me, her third eye remote viewing was an unlocked ability that aided her teleportation. Seeing behind closed doors is outside the range of normal vision. J'me had ESP, extra sensory perception, not normal but paranormal.

Other times, during moments of meditation, she imagined others' auras. Some had dull, dark bubbles surrounding them. Bound in bad bubbles... When her mind and spirit worked together, she could go unnoticed, covered and cloaked in invisibility. If only they could see how beautiful they truly were. This psychic ability she did not like. Sometimes a blessing could be a curse.

An elderly woman came in late, escorted by her middle-aged son and daughter. Her mind was spirited, but her body was weak. At this point Leoba was almost blind, but she found the hands of J'me and started gently rubbing them and told her how she used to make her own clothes and asked J'me how her red sweater was coming along.

She, Leoba, walked around and blessed everybody. While doing this, her son and daughter explained, "She will not admit being a psychic... She says there is no need. But we know she got this gift from her grandmother... She is greatly loved."

Leoba was a chatterbox. She told old stories about old friends (some she would repeat again and again). She bestowed blessings, compliments, and funny quips. She was fun to be with.

Angelica knew instantly, this was an authentic saint. She asked but a few questions. "Did you post anything on the chat boards my dear?

"What are those?" she said. Then Leoba talked non-stop. Her mind moved in a different direction, joking about being a child, then went back to her old stories of old friends.

"My sweetness, where have you been?" interrupted Angelica.

"Originally, I am from my mother." Leoba laughed.

"Oh, no!" She predicted Angelica's next question. "If I were to profit from my prophecies, they would go away! That is not how it works." A moment of silence (finally), then Leoba added. "Sure, if it is Mr. G's will, I will. But can I take my son and daughter with me?"

Soon they would be sent camping to K.L.O.P. But before Leoba left, she said something significant, **a warning of a future great awakening in the outside world!** She wanted to be as far away as possible. Leoba's prophecy would later be known as, "The Secrets of Saint Leoba".

The supercomputer was on self-control. It needed nothing to perform. It seemed August was a wizard and the developers were divine at Sunny's Spot. From the past they could predict the future. And what they created was a dream.

An early delivery of robots arrived from one of the factories. They were gray with large eyes on oversized heads, and no genitals (like the Inhumans J'me had met at QRUV). The bots began with simple redundant functions. Spiritless, they self-maintained, cleaned and repaired themselves. They could also loop their logic to automatically update and improve.

"Get with the times! They were for the future." was what people believed.

With warm words, J'me welcomed the robots. But their response was only motions, lacking emotions. These machines were the extreme. Automatically update and improve? Replacing people? Was this the life of dreams? Not blessed with a nurturing approach that was ideal yet practical. (Angels don't bless bots.)

Things were no longer just a black-white fight, now there were shades. It was the way of the world; a more logical and organized compromise was created. St. Wx. became a recycling center of sorts, now zoned by different levels of purity.

Cube S was for "safe", level one;

Cube T was for "tame", level two;

Cube W was for "wild", level three; and

Cube X was zoned for the "weird", a bit more extreme level four... for adults only. (By the way, gray robots were only allowed in certain zones.) It would be communal living without a commander.

Everybody mixed in Sublevel Three. It was expanded and excavated by adding zeros... from 300 by 300 meters, to 3,000 by 3,000... 30,000... then 300,000 meters! (Almost a million meters square.) Partitioned only for structural support, it was now for shops, services, and storage. From the exhumed earth: berms, bumps, and bubbles ornamented the grounds around the complex.

This is an excerpt from the love table conversation, said earlier on the roof (removing the names of those who remarked):

"Let's get this in order."

"Companion love... **Storge** starts as friendship, based on similarities, familiar family love."

"**Philautia** is the love of oneself. This self–love can range from a healthy embrace to narcissism."

"I like **Ludus** love. Love that is played like a game, teasing, and as innocent as a child. Infatuation or playful love."

"Oh, **Mania** is obsessive love! It has its highs and lows, but it is very possessive and jealous."

"**Pragma** is a more practical love, long lasting and enduring. It is driven by the head and the heart and is more realistic."

"**Philia** is deeper than friendship. How do you explain it? Affectionate, highly valued... a
brotherly love or platonic."

"Mmmm, **Eros** is passionate lust, romantic, love with the body. Sparky! ...A sexual attraction, a physical desire, an erotic loss of control."

"The biggest? The best?"

"It's got to be **Agape**... Agape is altruistic. It is more of a self–less, spiritual love."

Chapter 99
Finale

The weird thing about that winter is that it did not get cold at St. Wx. Was this the global warming everybody worried about?

It was as if somebody had invited nature to put on a show. Birds came back and plants started to grow. One day while J'me was walking, she saw her first flower. This was a message with meaning. She kept it there for others to also enjoy. Then she told her friends that it was her time to leave.

Like a pendulum swing, things met in the middle. St. Wx. became more balanced. An influx of immigrants came from the outside world as well as Camp K. L. O. P. Bringing with them fresh hope. And every day was super special when the children returned. Wow! It was wonderful.

The distortion of time, plus sleep deprivation, prompted people to leave. Clean was uncomfortable for them. Like the self-proclaimed psychics who escaped St. Wx, they could predict their future. It was no longer fun. They found a fit elsewhere and exited out.

Already, members were leaving on missions with meaning, at simultaneous speed:

- The Hick brothers were part of the group that went to K. L. O. P. and changed their names... again.
- Sparky went searching for his true love.
- And quarreling couples were sent out to waterfalls: Victoria Falls between Zambia and Zimbabwe... Tugela Falls, South Africa... Kaieteur Falls in Guyana.
- The warriors returned to the outside world, dispersed to fight for the right, as mercenaries or private security contractors.

Then there were a few that went directly back to the BLOCK, like Tio Juan and Auntie Juan with Chi Nü . A handful of deceived Believers, original BLOCK residents, were rerouted through Camp K. L. O. P. before returning.

The last page of the divorce decree revealed where R3G was living (the father of August and Patch, oldest sister, youngest son). They sailed to a location near Latvia. From there they were sent to see the Giants. Angelica was also invited. (Perhaps wedding bells will be ringing?)

It was time to wander. When walking the halls of Cubes S, T, W. and X, they would reach out their arms, people touched as they passed by. It was the heart felt "hello" J'me used to know.

When J'me teleported back to the blessed BLOCK the halls were vacant! She was alone... she saw nobody. As she walked past Cube G, she met Mr. G.

"You did good."

Then there was Mo, in a white robe, saying "It seems there is a commotion at Cube X and Y. We have something we must attend to. The party has already started."

"Cube X? Cube Y? A party?" J'me was puzzled.

"They are waiting for you on the docks." They must have thought I would enter that way, thought J'me.

"I will be right behind you." Mr. G said with a kiss to the center of her forehead...

"Mori, ...please?" Messenger Mori, teacher of morals, replied. "I will try, but there are many meanings... like:

- Bubbles represent merriment, fun, and childhood joys.
- Pearls symbolize the human soul, inner beauty, perfection, purity, and chastity.
- A block is obstacles that need to be overcome. These are things that try to hinder you from achieving your goals. But when you envision a cube it means earthly things... block head!
- Cube Y was for those reincarnated. Cube Z was the lair of Mr. Z, the dirty deity. (There were now no new secrets to share.)"

This was Mori's message.

Veiled deeper in the tale were secrets to joy:

- surround yourself with positive people,
- avoid comparing yourself to others,
- make others happy – give, help, and be kind,
- feel grateful, appreciate, and acquire an attitude of gratitude,
- monitor your thinking, practice mindfulness,
- be confident; tell yourself you can overcome everything,
- remember, happiness exists from within, not from outside.

There is one last key to being happy. The last words of wisdom: Be like a child... be playful and young!. **Do not take yourself so seriously. Have fun. Be bizarre and child-like.**

Elsewhere...   In and out of consciousness. The mind fog was annoying.

"Hello." The voice of a man... the deep voice of a man... the deep voice of a Russian man. Yes! She was correct! When she opened her heavy eyes, she perceived a man.

She saw shadows. Layers upon layers of darkness. Then the man spoke in a harsh voice, demanding that she answer, "What is your name?"

"I...." Her throat was raw. "I see... arrrgh...   I.V." She quickly noticed the sources of her pains. Intravenous tubes were plugged into her body, making it impossible for her to move.

"C I V... good name." he said without true emotion. "I am Mr. Z. Do as I say and everything will be ok."

It took a moment to internalize this. Then 104, oops, C I V heard, "Are you ready to play a game?"

Elsewhere, back at the BLOCK... J'me walked down the entrance ramp of DH. The two dandelion girls rushed up in their yellow dresses and white scarves, clutched both of her hands, and pulled her, giggling with glee...

"Cake is already served... and you missed the casserole!"

By the time J'me entered the room, friends were swirling around and reached out their arms to touch her. She saw a crowd, but it was not loud. Music was playing and bubbles were spraying. She found her seat, to make it complete.

Fading out...there were wonderful songs playing. (Ah, the magic of music!)

https://www.youtube.com/watch?v=A3yCcXgbKrE
https://www.youtube.com/watch?v=ddLd0QRf7Vg
https://www.youtube.com/watch?v=V1bFr2SWP1I

Worksheet 1

Time Management

There are three worksheets. Start in order. Do not skip any questions. When finished move to the next worksheet.

Note: Some people chose to use an electronic worksheet (like Excel) to do these exercises. Then it can be saved, updated often, and may be more easily accessible every day.

A. **Make a list of things to do. Then ask two questions:**
What is important?
What is urgent?

- Give each a score (from 1 to 100, wherein 1 is the most important/urgent) or rank them.
- Total the scores from both "Important" and "Urgent"
- Sort from smallest to biggest.

***Your highest priorities will be your lowest sum of both questions.**

Example:

	Important	Urgent		Total
Wash Clothes	4	1	=>	4*
Exercise	2	3	=>	5
Meditate	3	2	=>	5
Call Mom	1	5	=>	6
Watch TV	5	4	=>	9

B. **What are your time wasters? What are your distractions?**

- Now that you are aware, this is your first step in avoiding things that are meaningless. Remember, anything times zero equals zero. (Internet surfing, social media, TV...)
- What keeps you too busy to do what you want to do?

- How do you think? Past, present, future... What occupies your mind?

- Simplify, then multi-task.

C.   Have a plan.

"Eventually, after many small improvements, comes something enormous."

Start Big	Start Small
Mission	One mission.
Objective	Two (or more} objectives...
Strategy	Four (or more) strategies...
Tactic	Eight (or more) tactics...

Now, get smart with your objectives, strategies, and tactics:

- Specific,

- Measurable,

- Attainable,

- Relevant, and

- Time bound.

D.   Logical time management means A before B, B before C, C before D... Do you see what I mean? **It is step by step.**

Keep these three things in mind when managing your time:

- **How long will it take?**

- **How often do I need to do it?**

- **What intensity, urgency, speed do I need?**

E.   **Do you ever look back and say, "I did not get done all that I wanted to."?** Ask yourself why. Why ask why?

- It took longer than I planned.

- Distractions, interruptions, or other problems.

- Others' priorities and emergencies

- Control **your** time, not allowing others to control you.

My suggestion is this: Learn and move on.

Be diligent. Little by little...Persevere! Finish the job right.

The sooner it is done the sooner it can be crossed off your list and removed from your mind. Do not let it linger.

F.   Finally you are finished. **Remember to reward yourself.** Meditate, find some quiet time, or just feel good and generate a positive feeling from this.

However, beware of the time wasters. Those are not rewards. They take away, not add to your productivity and positivity.

Notes:

Worksheet 2

Destress/Decompress

There are three worksheets. (Did you do Worksheet One, on time management?) Start in order. Do not skip any questions. When finished move to the next worksheet.

A. **Take control of yourself.** Have some alone time. Use this escape to readjust yourself. Deep cleansing breaths with slow exhales. Settle yourself down. Remember that stress may be caused by something external, but it is internal. Control yourself, not letting others control you.

B. **Slow it down! Calm down... count to ten.** Do not overinflate your bubble... Remind yourself to **focus on the now.**

C. **Simplify.** "Do not think too much!"

D. Ask yourself what I like and hate?" **Make a list.** The trick is to look at each entry and ask yourself, "What can I control?" and "Was it really important?" (In a year from now, will that be something you remember?)
   - What do I like?
   - What do I hate?
   - What can I control?
   - What is important?

E. **Positive thoughts = positive feelings = positive actions.** Catch yourself when you start to become negative and unhappy. Sometimes you just have to laugh inside and smile.

F. **Surround yourself with positivity.** Avoid the "h8ters", "takers", an "trolls" — they suck — In other words, avoid anything negative. Use your six senses and look for something positive always:
- See positive
- Hear positive
- Smell positive
- Touch positive
- Taste positive
- Feel or sense positive vibes

G. **Do your best.** After death, divorce, imprisonment, or marriage, there is not much more that you have to endure.
But if you find yourself worried about money, work, family, or your health... stress is nature's way of warning you.

H. **Help others.** Donate and somebody, somewhere, sometime, will reciprocate and give you back more than you gave away.

I. **If all else fails, work your body, exercise that stress away!** Working out does wonders!

J. **Plan ahead and prioritize!**
- There should only be a few priorities on your daily list.
- Take time to contemplate, not immediate emotionally react. The higher level of emotion, the lower level of reasoning.
- Learn what triggers your tremors. Have a plan made ahead of time in the likelihood it happens to you.
Think this out before you are faced with the stress. Create a plan, beforehand.

Lists/Plans:

Worksheet 3

Wishes (Goals)

There are three worksheets. Start in order. Do this worksheet last.

Note: Some people chose to use an electronic worksheet (like Excel) to do these exercises. Then it can be saved, updated often, and may be more easily accessible every day.

If you read this book, and have become a "Believer", then you are already blessed. Remember Angel Number 42?

"The 42nd Angel just blessed you with a nurturing approach that was ideal yet practical."

Now, make a wish... make another... make a list of wishes. But before you begin, this book suggests beginning with the basics:

- Drink more water and less of the other stuff. Cleanse your insides.
- Watch what you eat. Food is a source of energy.
- Have a balance between your energy intake and activity.
- Exercise, move your body, take a walk. Become more active.
- Take time to meditate... Cleanse your mind.
- Everything in moderation. Have a life balance... ying and yang.

Wander through the book and find suggestions. Write them down to read and remember them each day.

Not only is everybody different, but each person is different every day. Change happens... Life is life... Different times you feel differently. Review repeatedly!

Have fun, be happy, feel loved at the **BLOCKXXXX.COM** website!

Wish List:

<u>Life's Lessons Learned List (L4)</u>

It is interesting how you can read the bolded texts in the book separate from the context and get a better meaning. When the phrase stands alone, you may get a new connotation, another level of significance to your life.

- Clothes were not worn for status, but more for reflecting their feelings. (Book 0, Chapter 0)
- In sociology, a "bubble" occurs when fiction is repeated again and again until you feel it is true. (Book 0, Chapter 0)
- Upon its completion in the late 1920s (exact date unknown), when urban renewal and planned neighborhoods were in full swing, the project was abandoned. (Book 0, Chapter 1)
- Nobody talks about it... Nobody else took notice. Nobody else said anything. (Book 0, Chapter 1)
- One must surrender. (Book 0, Chapter 2)
- Forces in motion seek balance... (Book 0, Chapter 2)
- The law of seven: for every one that you give, you will get back seven fold. Also called "The promise of seven." (Book 0 Chapter 2)
- Man has limited needs and unlimited wants. (Book 0, Chapter 2)(Book 4, Chapter 43)
- Helping, aiding, and caring for others creates a warm energy within the giver. (Book 0, Chapter 2)
- An infinite amount of giving begat infinite receiving. (Book 0, Chapter 2)
- Simple yet complex. (Book 0, Chapter 2)
- Do not dwell on time that has past at the expense of the present. (Book 0, Chapter 2)
- Relax. (Book 0, Chapter 3)
- Light immediately replaced darkness. (Book 0, Chapter 3)
- No more floating in the water of nothingness. (Book 0, Chapter 3)
- Juan easily got aroused. (Book 0, Chapter 4)
- We have no rules... There is no right or wrong, no good or bad... no judgement. (Book 0, Chapter 5)
- We are followers... (Book0, Chapter 5)
- Do what you want. (Book 0, Chapter 5)

- Love yourself and others. (Book 0, Chapter 5)
- Don't think too much. (Book 0, Chapter 5)
- So sweet. (Book 0, Chapter 6)
- Vanished into vapors... like the steam from the boiling pot. (Book 0, Chapter 6)
- Oh, this is wonderful! (Book 0, Chapter 6)
- You can learn anything at any time. The only limit is you... yourself. (Book 0, Chapter 7)
- The conscious, thinking and knowledge. The subconscious, feelings and memory. (Book 0, Chapter 7)
- The sensing soul... I listen to whispers. (Book 0, Chapter 7)
- There is also a mind and body balance. (Book 0, Chapter 7)
- We learn in both cognitive and intuitive ways. (Book 0, Chapter 7)
- We must balance our desires. (Book 0, Chapter 7)
- Within everybody is greatness! (Book 0, Chapter 8)
- Everybody has a "gift." (Book 0, Chapter 8)
- Many people are searching for their magic powers. Others just try to manage them. (Book 0, Chapter 8)
- I enjoy natural. (Book 0, Chapter 8)
- "Infinite greatness! I am not just saying that... Everybody has a "gift." (Book 0, Chapter 8)
- Beautiful inside and out, within and without. (Book 0, Chapter 9)
- Sex is one of the basic needs of man and therefore not taboo. (Book 0, Quiz 0)(Book 3, Quiz 3)
- Sexual intimacy is the highest form of showing physical love. (Book 0, Quiz 0)

- A great tree, before it is born, is just a seed hidden in dirt. (Book 1, Chapter 10)
- It began with a dream. (Book 1, Chapter 10)
- Before the beginning of the 21st century, life was very different from now. (Book 1, Chapter 10)
- It was not a single concept, but a series of concepts, interwoven like a beautiful tapestry. (Book 1, Chapter 10)
- Everybody brought something! (Book 1, Chapter 10)

o   Confidential... Hidden... Unknown. (Book 1, Chapter 10)

o   Those that were lost were now found. (Book 1, Chapter 10)

o   Everybody was happy! (Book 1, Chapter 10)

o   The more they saw, the more they neglected to see... (Book 1, Chapter 10)

o   "Thank you... Thank you... Enjoy yourself. Please drink responsibly. Stay clear.... Thank you for visiting and have a happy every day!" (Book 1, Chapter 10)

o   Meditating... thinking... putting the pieces together and braiding the loose ends. (Book 1, Chapter 11)

o   Together it created a captivating feeling. (Book 1, Chapter 11)

o   The 80% rule (true to define eight of ten occurrences, with a couple of exceptions. (Book 1, Chapter 11)

o   Grouped together... sat down at a table together... simultaneously, working together... their hands clasped together... (Book 1, Chapter 11)

o   Work was considered a reward for the children... a good and wholesome activity! (Book 1, Chapter 11)

o   The workers moved together in synchrony. (Book 1, Chapter 11)

o   They guided him along the best paths. (Book 1, Chapter 12)

o   It took a moment to become balanced... (Book 1, Chapter 12)

o   If you consider yourself dead, and only living in the present time; the remaining time is relished. (Book 1, Chapter 13)

o   Everyone felt at ease. (Book 1, Chapter 13)

o   Unplugging from the universe is a good method of discovery to see what is removed and what remains. (Book 1, Chapter 13)

o   Anything times zero is nothing. If it is not important, it does not exist. (Book 1, Chapter 14)

o   One is the beginning of exponential growth and decay. (Book 1, Chapter 14)

o   They were not strangers, but longtime friends. It felt heavenly. (Book 1, Chapter 14)

o   She felt a peculiar tingling inside her. It felt odd, but good. (Book 1, Chapter 14)

o   It is easy, if you know how. (Book 1, Chapter 14) (Book 5, Chapter 52)

o   Size does not matter? (Book 1, Chapter 14)

- o Our powers are exponential! (Book 1, Chapter 14)
- o Successful students were mainly females. Another observation was that the best were men. (Book 1, Chapter 15)
- o Their reasons were not to leave, but to go back. (Book 1, Chapter 15)
- o The gentlemen Giants preferred the pleasure of plump ladies. (Book 1, Chapter 15)
- o Music affects your mood and works better than any food or drink to liven a moment. (Book 1, Chapter 15)
- o Hosting the Giants was a giant risk that not only worked, but also infused the BLOCK with new energy and inspired creativity. (Book 1, Chapter 15)
- o Their spirits affected each other in a special way. (Book 1, Chapter 16)
- o Negative two to the fourth power! – the product of which is a positive number 16. (Book 1, Chapter 16)
- o Math is symbolic logic...   (Book 1, Chapter 16)
- o x-1 = you harm yourself. (Book 1, Chapter 16)
- o x-2 = somebody harms you. (Book 1, Chapter 16)
- o (-2x)2 = (-2)(-2) = two wrongs creates a stronger balance, an eye for an eye. (Book 1, Chapter 16)
- o (-2x)3 = (-2)(-2)(-2) = learn, then turn the other cheek. ...But do not stop; avoid a negative outcome. (Book 1, Chapter 16)
- o (-2x)4 = (-2)(-2)(-2)(-2) = outcome finished positively, reset and start again. (Book 1, Chapter 16)
- o There is no such thing as good or bad luck. From bad comes good. And from good comes bad. Not everything is bad. Not everything is good. (Book 1, Chapter 16)
- o From chaos and conflict and confusion comes creativity. From creativity comes innovation. (Book 1, Chapter 17)
- o Creativeness creates a beautiful balance. (Book 1, Chapter 17)
- o Everybody is creative to some degree. (Book 1, Chapter 17)
- o Sometimes the best moments are those not planned. Unplanned pleasures... (Book 1, Chapter 17)
- o We need to think less and play more! (Book 1, Chapter 17)
- o She was definitely not saying all that she was thinking but thinking what all she was saying. (Book 1, Chapter 17)

o Care, repair, and prepare – these are the ways to wise maintenance... The fourth is fun. (Book 1, Chapter 17)

o It had passed... ended. (Book 1, Chapter 17)

o The 'lag effect'... That is the time from efforts to rewards... There is a natural delay or decay rate... (Book 1, Chapter 18)

o The lag can range from a lifetime or even generations... The lag can be immediate. (Book 1, Chapter 18)

o Everything can be calculated. (Book 1, Chapter 18)

o Positive energy yields positive responses.   Very simply... Cause and expect an effect.   Action... then reaction.   Expect rewards, not consequences. (Book 1, Chapter 18)

o 1. Top down then circle around. (Book 1, Chapter 18)

o 2. Organize, then multitask once. (Book 1, Chapter 18)

o 3. Worst first, trash last.   (Book 1, Chapter 18)

o Maximum efficiency with minimum effort... blend in... be invisible... Moving with their natural rhythm was relaxing. A blend between energetic focus and tempered concentration allowed them to "flow."   (Book 1, Chapter 19)

o Now is the time. (Book 1, Chapter 19) (Book 6, Chapter 60)

o It is crazy how things happen and at the time you do not see the significance of it. (Book 1, Quiz 1)

• Life is not a game. (Book 2, Chapter 20)

• Everybody wins! — That is not how it shall be. People should be free to choose. Give them the freedom to decide for themselves. Stop playing with them.   (Book 2, Chapter 20)

• The most innocent people suffered most. Bad things happen to good people. And there were good people doing bad things. (Book 2, Chapter 20)

• While part of the world was off the bubble crazy, the BLOCK was balanced. There was also absolution, forgiveness, mercy, and innocence. (Book 2, Chapter 20)

• It was a new time and a new beginning. (Book 2, Chapter 20)

• Everybody "cared" in one way or another: carefully or carelessly. (Book 2, Chapter 21)

- It is a perfect day to play outside. (Book 2, Chapter 21)
- May I help you? (Book 2, Chapter 21)
- They moved freely. (Book 2, Chapter 21)
- A feeling of love was absorbed in toto to the center of their brains. (Book 2, Chapter 21)
- This way please. The tour is about to begin... Welcome. Hello everyone! My name is Mr. G, your guide. If you have any questions, please ask. I would like to remind you to stay with the group and do not wander... Also, be kind to one another. (Book 2, Chapter 21)
- But she now felt inquisitive. (Book 2, Chapter 22)
- The feeling in that room was festive. (Book 2, Chapter 22)
- Each room had its own "feelings". (Book 2, Chapter 22)
- The more she learned the less she knew. (Book 2, Chapter 22)
- prioritize her thoughts based on only two criteria: Is it urgent? What's important? (Book 2, Chapter 22)
- As J'me was able to simplify, she regained control. (Book 2, Chapter 22)
- He came from an ancient time when a beautiful body meant a beautiful mind. (Book 2, Chapter 22)
- You may be blessed with a wonderful life without end, or cursed with it and suffer. (Book 2, Chapter 23)
- Earthly angels are usually related, following a family line. (Book 2, Chapter 23)
- We know there are those who walk among us who have never died. Chances are that you have seen at least one. You may even know an eternal! (Book 2, Chapter 24)
- Accept that some things are not for us to understand. (Book 2, Chapter 24)
- We are all, in some part, descendants of ancient families. We are special! (Book 2, Chapter 24)
- Cognitive color code: Red is reacting... Orange is ready... Being aware of what is around you is yellow, and ... White is your head is in the clouds. (Book 2, Chapter 25)
- I do not know what I don't know. (Book 2, Chapter 25)
- Nobody knows everything. (Book 2, Chapter 25)

- Sometimes you do not know what you see... until somebody tells you. (Book 2, Chapter 25)
- Clean and fresh, people feel better when they look better. (Book 2, Chapter 25)
- Happy and healthy, people look better when they feel better. (Book 2, Chapter 25)
- Everything starts with the spirit. (Book 2, Chapter 26)
- Our spirit powers our thoughts... Our thoughts guide our feelings and mood... And this controls our actions. (Book 2, Chapter 26)
- You will have failures... (Book 2, Chapter 26)
- Rolling through recognition, remorse, rectify/resolve/repair, reform, and then to reset. (Book 2, Chapter 26)
- Try to recover quickly. (Book 2, Chapter 26)
- The purpose of the mind is to forget, not remember. (Book 2, Chapter 26)
- They say there is no such thing as a pink sun... (Book 2, Chapter 26)
- Meditation cleans a messy mind. (Book 2, Chapter 26)
- Do not dwell on history. (Book 2, Chapter 26)
- History is based on more than one perspective... based on the number of eyes. (Book 2, Chapter 26)
- I am many spirits. (Book 2, Chapter 26)
- Life is filled with "What in the world?" distractions that are impossible to understand... (Book 2, Chapter 27)
- Most of the time we are unaware; sometimes we wonder why they are significant. (Book 2, Chapter 27)
- Without these prescribed pieces, you may feel bored. But so is life... sometimes.   (Book 2, Chapter 28)
- Without these prescribed pieces, you may feel bored. But so is life... sometimes.   (Book 2, Chapter 28)
- De-stress not distress.   (Book 2, Chapter 28)
- Pressure is what you put on yourself. (Book 2, Chapter 28)
- Bad ideas bubble up... (Book 2, Chapter 28)
- You made mistakes, you are making mistakes, and you will make more mistakes! It has and had consequences. (Book 2, Chapter 28)

- You made mistakes, you are making mistakes, and you will make more mistakes! It has and had consequences. (Book 2, Chapter 28)
- Your first step is to stop being stupid. (Book 2, Chapter 28)
- You underestimate your good values. (Book 2, Chapter 28)
- If you cannot change it, accept it and move on. (Book 2, Chapter 28)
- You are not the first, nor will you be the last, to have this pass. (Book 2, Chapter 28)
- Do not blindly follow all things recommended. (Book 2, Chapter 28)
- Clean your mind, be open to advice, but ultimately know you are in control of your thoughts and feelings. Ultimately you are responsible for your actions. (Book 2, Chapter 28)
- We should thank our ancestors for thinking.   (Book 2, Chapter 28)
- What do you think? (Book 2, Chapter 28)
- For a moment J'me felt regret, but quickly stopped herself. (Book 2, Chapter 29)
- Sentiment/sediment was covered in clarity and clarity lifted the foaming surface. (Book 2, Chapter 29)
- Your brain works better when your eyes are closed. (Book 2, Chapter 29)
- Some things are not allowed to tell and some things are not allowed for others to know. (Book 2, Quiz 2)
- Conflict, rising tension, climax and conclusion... When writing your life story, will you have this formula?   (Book 2, Quiz 2)
- Some people bring stress upon themselves by thinking or acting stupid. Avoid storms and dangerous situations. Find and remedy your mistakes quickly and be more careful. Dedicate time; make an appointment to remove stress you have built up. (Book 2, Quiz 2)

- You give and get what you interact with. (Book 3, Chapter 30)
- There was also a special harmony that affected the sense of sound and individual intuition. (Book 3, Chapter 30)
- Perfect communication was possible through the harmonies that transferred feelings. (Book 3, Chapter 30)
- Life is magical! (Book 3, Chapter 30)
- Inside the BLOCK everybody was connected. (Book 3, Chapter 30)

o   Before something new can be created, it must be destroyed. (Book 3, Chapter 31)

o   A new dimension, change over time, was another perception added to J'me's skills. (Book 3, Chapter 32)

o   Her followers were her followers. (Book 3, Chapter 32)

o   Everybody has a special gift. (Book 3, Chapter 33)

o   Sometimes the best moments are those not planned. (Book 3, Chapter 33)

o   What was in her mind was the now. (Book 3, Chapter 34)

o   Health, happiness, and good cheer. (Book 3, Chapter 36)

o   Moderation... Do not exceed your bounds... Balance everything... More is too much. None is not enough. (Book 3, Chapter 36)

o   Nature has a rhythm... Go with the rhythm of the body. (Book 3, Chapter 36)

o   Some people choose to follow tradition, a straight path, while others meander through unlimited choices trying to choose the best one. (Book 3, Chapter 37)

o   There are some things we must learn on our own. (Book 3, Chapter 37)

o   It is not an eye for eye... or turn the other cheek. You must always protect yourself. It is a three-strike rule. (Book 3, Chapter 37)

o   You mean Mr. Most? (An acronym for Mission, Objectives, Strategy, Tactics.) M...O... S...T.... mission, objectives, strategy, and tactics.... (Book 3, Chapter 37)

o   His objectives are SMART... Specific, Measurable, Attainable, Relevant, and Time bound. (Book 3, Chapter 37)

o   Eventually you can run without being weary. (Book 3, Chapter 37)

o   Balance work with play and rest. (Book 3, Chapter 37)

o   Our body is energy. (Book 3, Chapter 38)

o   We replenish our xi energy by breathing, sleeping, and eating... primarily. (Book 3, Chapter 38)

o   When you block or slow down the movement of energy, you create disorder. (Book 3, Chapter 38)

o   You must release your energy, use it, not keep it inside you. (Book 3, Chapter 38)

- o Prepare, care, and repair your body and your brain as you would a building. (Book 3, Chapter 39)
- o She learned to balance herself. Each energy center was unblocked and J'me felt spirited. (Book 3, Chapter 39)
- o She learned to balance herself. Each energy center was unblocked and J'me felt spirited. (Book 3, Chapter 39)
- o Her tensions drifted away. She decided to go with the flow. (Book 3, Chapter 39)
- o Energy can be released at different weights and in different ways. (Book 3, Chapter 39)
- o 2 people = (2 people + 1 person) = 3... The "division and specialization of labor" that takes advantage of each other's skills and abilities. (Book 3, Quiz 3)
- Everybody has 20/20 hindsight into the past. Nobody has 20/20, perfect vision into the future. Therefore, see what is happening now. (Book 4, Chapter 40)
- People couldn't have cared less... (Book 4, Chapter 40)
- Things do not stay constant, forever in motion. It grew... it changed... it is living.   (Book 4, Chapter 40)
- Born again! In order to be new, the old must die. (Book 4, Chapter 40)
- Eventually, after many small improvements, comes something enormous. (Book 4, Chapter 41)
- The art of "working a room." (Book 4, Chapter 41)
- People were more important than the place. (Book 4, Chapter 41)
- Not everything is bad, not everything is good. (Book 4, Chapter 41)
- What's bad is good and what's good is bad. (Book 4, Chapter 41)
- Extra sleep was her cure. (Book 4, Chapter 42)
- Eventually, after many small sorrows, comes change from within. (Book 4, Chapter 42)
- I love you. (Book 4, Chapter 42) (Book 5, Chapter 50) (Book 7, Chapter 71)
- If you are not cutting the tree, you should be sharpening the saw. (Book 4, Chapter 42)
- Optimize every moment. Strive, drive, and push for maximal efficiency! There is always improvement. (Book 4, Chapter 42)

- You must mind your business.   (Book 4, Chapter 42)
- People love money... But money has no feelings. (Book 4, Chapter 42)
- ... blessed them BOTH with a nurturing approach that was ideal yet practical. (Book 4, Chapter 42)
- Income should exceed expenses. (Book 4, Chapter 43)
- The hush of time was a secret for J'me to fully understand. (Book 4, Chapter 43)
- Time is money and money is time. (Book 4, Chapter 43)
- A slave to money, a slave to time? (Book 4, Chapter 43)
- TAKE your time... Take YOUR time. (Book 4, Chapter 43)
- Over time it is normal to become desensitized. Adjust...   Adapt... Attach... (Book 4, Chapter 43)
- But I enjoy this change. I am learning new things. (Book 4, Chapter 44)
- Everything has a price. (Book 4, Chapter 44)
- She forgot what she had forgotten. (Book 4, Chapter 44)
- She saw the light. She was pure. (Book 4, Chapter 44)
- God is love. (Book 4, Chapter 45)
- Everything made cents. (Book 4, Chapter 45)
- Get up, get up.   Do not be afraid. (Book 4, Chapter 45)
- Aren't you tired? (Book 4, Chapter 46)
- The love from the cook gives flavor to the food. (Book 4, Chapter 46)
- You have one more stone. (Book 4, Chapter 46)
- Do the needful. (Book 4, Chapter 46)
- Individually they were creative, but collectively they were art. (Book 4, Chapter 47)
- You can never have too many friends. (Book 4, Chapter 47)
- The love from "family" never goes away. (Book 4, Chapter 47)
- Oh, just a hug or a kiss makes you feel exalted! (Book 4, Chapter 47)
- If you are happy, I am happy. (Book 4, Chapter 47)
- There was an empathy, sympathy, and compassion connection that became a considerate cycle. (Book 4, Chapter 47)
- Everybody was a winner! (Book 4, Chapter 47)
- There is nothing like something. (Book 4, Chapter 47)
- It was not for the goal of perfection that she enjoyed practicing, it was in the doing. (Book 4, Chapter 47)

- The great spirits of the past, present and future are with us. (Book 4, Chapter 48)
- Each one of you is special. The future is foretold. (Book 4, Chapter 48)
- There is magic to music. (Book 4, Chapter 48)
- It seemed the right thing to do at the time. (Book 4, Chapter 49)
- Wealth has no limits, but there are four kinds: What you have, what you do, what you know, and richness of character, what you are. (Book 4, Chapter 49)
- Be trusted, respected, honorable, and ethical. (Book 4, Chapter 49)
- Be fair, do the right things, otherwise you will not be happy. (Book 4, Chapter 49)
- Money can't buy everything. (Book 4, Chapter 49)
- Rich or poor is a mindset, you can be rich yet poor and poor yet rich. (Book 4, Chapter 49)
- Never be afraid or ashamed to be rich; but remember, your wealth comes from others around you and before you. (Book 4, Chapter 49)
- A wealthy tree never stops producing fruit; be grateful. (Book 4, Chapter 49)
- Give away your surplus; be generous and do not demand it back. (Book 4, Chapter 49)
- Wise men save and share, while fools spend whatever they get. (Book 4, Chapter 49)
- Perish through foolishness. (Book 4, Chapter 49)
- Do not look at a poor person as a fool, they just have other fortunes not found. (Book 4, Chapter 49)
- Wealth is a reward. (Book 4, Chapter 49)
- Meaningful wealth is only obtained from good objectives. (Book 4, Chapter 49)
- The best part of wealth is what you make of it. (Book 4, Chapter 49)
- There is nothing wrong with a little profit. (Book 4, Chapter 49)
- Always be a lender, never be a borrower. A borrower is a servant to the lender. (Book 4, Chapter 49)
- Pay what you owe. (Book 4, Chapter 49)
- Owe nothing to anyone, your only obligation is to love them. (Book 4, Chapter 49)

- Have faith that you will be supplied what you need (except a fool). (Book 4, Chapter 49)
- Have confidence, not hope. This is stability. (Book 4, Chapter 49)
- Success is how you define it; it is different for everybody. Successful is feeling grateful. (Book 4, Chapter 49)
- What golfers do to their mind; mixed martial artists do to their bodies. (Book 4, Chapter 49)

o Love can take you to the highest of highs and the lowest of lows. (Book 5, Chapter 50)

o This time she felt feelings. (Book 5, Chapter 50)

o Time flew. (Book 5, Chapter 50)

o She was enlightened. (Book 5, Chapter 50)

o But the BLOCK was not about the buildings, it was about the people. (Book 5, Chapter 50)

o Not all things are good or bad. There are different levels. For example, there is good, better, and best. (Book 5, Chapter 50)

o Those coming to the camp from the outside world needed to decompress, destress, and become their natural selves again. Simplify... (Book 5, Chapter 51)

o Fun? (Book 5, Chapter 51)

o We should connect our thoughts. (Book 5, Chapter 52)

o Ach, it is all in your head. Mind over matter! (Book 5, Chapter 52)

o From everything there was a lesson. (Book 5, Chapter 52)

o Love is infinite and never empties, never ending, with no limits. (Book 5, Chapter 53)

o Mi casa es su casa (my home is your home). (Book 5, Chapter 53)

o There is beauty all around when there is love at home. (Book 5, Chapter 53)

o No matter where you call home, you are still family. (Book 5, Chapter 53)

o Never ask a question that you really do not want to know the answer to. (Book 5, Chapter 53)

o But they were part of what started as the "Lost Generation" and became the "Greatest Generation". (Book 5, Chapter 53)

- o   Think first, act second. (Book 5, Chapter 54)
- o   The purpose of sleep is to flush out all the used and un-needed chemicals in your brain. (Book 5, Chapter 55)
- o   Drink more water! (Book 5, Chapter 56)
- o   Avoid consuming chemicals. (Book 5, Chapter 56)
- o   Get adequate sleep in a dark place. (Book 5, Chapter 56)
- o   Exercise your mind and body... (Book 5, Chapter 56)
- o   Walk in nature every day. (Book 5, Chapter 56)
- o   Enjoy the sunrise and sunset; become a sun gazer. (Book 5, Chapter 56)
- o   Do aesthetic activities: Make and create, work with your mind and hands. (Book 5, Chapter 56)
- o   Think deeply, and even do some daydreaming. (Book 5, Chapter 56)
- o   Meditate outside naturally, sitting on the ground or earthy elements. (Book 5, Chapter 56)
- o   Quiet your mind. (Book 5, Chapter 56)
- o   Be mindful of your senses. (Book 5, Chapter 56)
- o   Let go of limiting beliefs. (Book 5, Chapter 56)
- o   Feel your heartbeat within you and let your mind ease. (Book 5, Chapter 56)
- o   Subdue your power to resist. Surrender and float along with everybody around you. (Book 5, Chapter 56)
- o   Everyone was one. (Book 5, Chapter 57)
- o   Be careful of things you do not see... (Book 5, Chapter 57)
- o   Let nature control chemistry. (Book 5, Chapter 57)
- o   You also absorb energy. (Book 5, Chapter 57)
- o   You have a third eye! (Book 5, Chapter 57)
- o   Train your brain. (Book 5, Chapter 57)
- o   Some things we are not to know. (Book 5, Chapter 58)
- o   It was a wonderful world. (Book 5, Chapter 58)
- o   Everyone was welcome. (Book 5, Chapter 59)
- o   What is at the bottom of this? (Book 5, Chapter 59)
- o   Some things you cannot do at the same time. (Book 5, Quiz 5)

- •   When you closed your eyes, the darkness was still there. (Book 6, Chapter 60)

- Beware. Be aware. (Book 6, Chapter 60)
- People were" fearious" (a combination of fear and unknown automatic anger, not conscious). (Book 6, Chapter 61)
- Hope assured them that one day their suffering would end. This optimism came from their belief that there was something stronger that would save them. (Book 6, Chapter 61)
- The only thing that remained private inside St. Wx was what was in your heart. (Book 6, Chapter 61)
- Nobody talked about these events. (Book 6, Chapter 61)
- The difference between humans and animals is their ability to think ahead. (Book 6, Chapter 63)
- But these illuminists could not explain the darkness. (Book 6, Chapter 64)
- Their courage evolved into stupidity. (Book 6, Chapter 64)
- This bravery evolved into arrogance. (Book 6, Chapter 64)
- People love to hear secrets! (Book 6, Chapter 65)
- Being imprisoned with better people was not so bad. (Book 6, Chapter 65)
- This was a communist complex. (Book 6, Chapter 65)
- Everybody underestimates the value of little things... until they are gone. (Book 6, Chapter 66)
- Take deep enjoying breaths. Drink plenty of pure water. And be happy with what you have and what you see. (Book 6, Chapter 66)
- Forget what other people think. Believe in yourself. Be happy with what you have. Be grateful... not greedy. (Book 6, Chapter 66)
- The best things in life are free. But you also get what you pay for. (Book 6, Chapter 66)
- Today you support me... tomorrow somebody will support you. (Book 6, Chapter 67)
- Teamwork replaced individualism. Independence was replaced with interdependence. Communal living was made good again. (Book 6, Chapter 68)
- Not about not... (Book 6, Chapter 69)
- Your 'normal' and my 'normal' are not the same. (Book 6, Chapter 69)
- Making love is a personal affair... (Book 6, Chapter 69)

- Restrict your restrictions and live life to its fullest without fear. (Book 6, Chapter 69)
- There is a difference between love and sex. (Book 6, Chapter 69)
- You don't really want to know the other personally, so just forget about it. (Book 6, Chapter 69)
- You can give unlimited love. (Book 6, Chapter 69)
- But don't look to others to define your desires. (Book 6, Chapter 69)
- Two as one is more fun! (Book 6, Chapter 69)
- Keep each other fully aware, then there are no negatives, just positive outcomes. (Book 6, Chapter 69)
- Are you in control or do others control you?   (Book 6, Quiz 6)

o Know where the sun rises and sun sets, so you never get lost. (Book 7, Chapter 70)
o Take pride in your work because it is part of you. (Book 7, Chapter 70)
o Be tough, but fair. (Book 7, Chapter 70)
o Know when to fight and when to ride. (Book 7, Chapter 70)
o Care for things smaller than you. (Book 7, Chapter 70)
o Have courage facing all things larger than you. (Book 7, Chapter 70)
o Honor all women as if they were your mother. (Book 7, Chapter 70)
o When you make a promise, keep it. (Book 7, Chapter 70)
o Some things are not for sale. (Book 7, Chapter 70)
o Ride for your brand. (Book 7, Chapter 70)
o Relax in the saddle. (Book 7, Chapter 70
o These are my values; the ethics I promised myself. We have the laws of nature, the laws of God, the laws of man, but these are my laws. That's how I ride. (Book 7, Chapter 70)
o Some things cannot be physically fixed. You can't unscramble eggs. (Book 7, Chapter 70)
o That is how we are in the system. (Book 7, Chapter 70)
o There will always be people who define "now" as their perfect time. (Book 7, Chapter 71)
o Your unforgettable memories are likely to last. (Book 7, Chapter 71)
o Do not let heartbreak get the best of you. (Book 7, Chapter 71)

o Get past the trauma and drama; let bygones be bygones. (Book 7, Chapter 71)

o Intelligence can overshadow your judgement. Make a few mistakes here and there. (Book 7, Chapter 71)

o Be on good behavior. (Book 7, Chapter 71)

o Do not be shy about approaching people. The wealth of experience you gain plus friends' helps. (Book 7, Chapter 71)

o Befriend locals, trust your gut feeling, try new things... (Book 7, Chapter 71)

o Be open to new things, but don't feel obligated in any way. (Book 7, Chapter 71)

o Have a financial safety blanket. (Book 7, Chapter 71)

o It starts with donations. Help others while helping yourself. (Book 7, Chapter 71)

o Safeguard your valuables. (Book 7, Chapter 71)

o "Emotional Intelligence" or "Emotional Quotient" is a combination of low self-awareness, self-management or self-regulation, low social awareness, lack of social skills or relationship management. (Book 7, Chapter 72)

o He had a low EQ, not no EQ. (Book 7, Chapter 72)

o She knew something new was going to happen. (Book 7, Chapter 73)

o Thinking of the future can create either a mood of anxiety or excitement. (Book 7, Chapter 73)

o Neither knew what August knew. (Book 7, Chapter 77)

o Everybody deserves respect. (Book 7, Chapter 77)

o Your brain is picking up, absorbing, and processing information at different speeds. (Book 7, Chapter 77)

o Stressed is desserts spelled backwards. (Book 7, Chapter 78)

o Get over yourself. (Book 7, Chapter 78)

o It's not my job to blow sunshine up your butt. (Book 7, Chapter 78)

o People always make false assumptions. (Book 7, Chapter 78)

o But just because we do not know it, does not mean it is not true. (Book 7, Chapter 79)

o The lining inside your abdominal cavity, your 79th organ, is called the mesentery. Did you know that 70% of the neurons not going to your brain are found traveling through the mesentery membrane? (Book 7, Chapter 79)

o   Science has not caught up to something we knew thousands of years ago. (Book 7, Chapter 79)

o   Your brain regulates memories and thoughts... Your heart holds love and happiness, and the mesentery stores emotions. (Book 7, Chapter 79)

o   When you suffer a defeat, your glands excrete... this is naturally normal. (Book 7, Chapter 79)

o   You are what you eat... (Book 7, Chapter 79)

o   Fear comes from the kidneys. (That is why you piss all over yourself.) Envy, jealousy, frustration is from your liver. (Book 7, Chapter 79)

o   The "reset" button is where the major chi channels flow, referred to as the "Guan Yuan Gate" or sometimes the "sea of energy". (Book 7, Chapter 79)

o   Priming your Pump". When inhaling, put your hand on your lower gut and push your fingers up while inflating your belly. (Book 7, Chapter 79)

•   The first is the worst, then it becomes easier. (Book 8, Chapter 80)

•   No decision was their decision. (Book 8, Chapter 80)

•   Go for the low hanging fruit first. (Book 8, Chapter 80)

•   When you block or slow down the movement of energy, you create disorder. (Book 8, Chapter 80)

•   Energy needs to be released in a non-destructive way. (Book 8, Chapter 80)

•   It did not seem logical to lock somebody up. (Book 8, Chapter 81)

•   J'me was still altered by the disturbing rhythms at St. Wx. and unable to adjust. (Book 8, Chapter 81)

•   Where there is love, there is family. (Book 8, Chapter 81)

•   Some things have a tendency to resolve themselves. Give it no thought, especially if it does not pertain to you. (Book 8, Chapter 81)

•   Subliminal messages are hidden from your focus. There are no nueroethics! (Book 8, Chapter 83)

•   Not the best, it was good but could be better. (Book 8, Chapter 83)

- People naturally have the tendency to compare their current situation with that of the past. (Book 8, Chapter 83)
- Repetition... Repetition creates acceptance.... It was a conscious subliminal brain washing. (Book 8, Chapter 83)
- Your mind sometimes meanders onto the meaningless. That is not practical. (Book 8, Chapter 84)
- The best never admit it. (Book 8, Chapter 84)
- Just as everybody has a special gift of greatness, everybody has a purpose. (Book 8, Chapter 84)
- All of us are on an unpredictable path. Your end game is an enigma. (Book 8, Chapter 84)
- There are those h8ers and trolls who only complain.   (Book 8, Chapter 85)
- Making a small positive change in your routine creates huge results. (Book 8, Chapter 85)
- They did not need a tricycle when they were already riding a bicycle. (Book 8, Chapter 85)
- It feels fantastic to have friendly neighbors. (Book 8, Chapter 85)
- You have to be a little crazy sometimes. (Book 8, Chapter 86)
- When being placed in a situation that you cannot control, the best thing to do is just smile. (Book 8, Chapter 86)
- Think about it. (Book 8, Chapter 87)
- It starts with helping others while helping yourself. (Book 8, Chapter 87)
- Perhaps this was her purpose? She had been called. (Book 8, Chapter 87)
- LOVE BOMB! (Book 8, Chapter 87)
- If you ever want to make a friend, ask them first for a simple favor. (Book 8, Chapter 88)
- Today is a different day... (Book 8, Chapter 88)
- Once you have done it once, you can never say you never done it. (Book 8, Chapter 88)
- But it doesn't hurt to ask? Right? (Book 8, Chapter 88)
- You can never have too many friends. (Book 8, Chapter 88)
- Babies are proof that miracles do exist and that they do not happen right away... there was a lag effect. (Book 8, Chapter 89)

- Wait, we will be late!" said Jen, looking at the time (Question: How can you see time? I always wondered...). (Book 8, Chapter 89)
- You have had a target painted on your back. (Book 8, Quiz 8)
- People either don't know or don't care about the manipulation of their minds. (Book 8, Quiz 8)

o Let the bad wash away and leave it in the past. (Book 9, Chapter 90)

o It may not be new to you, but emotional hills and valleys were normal at St. Wx. (Book 9, Chapter 90)

o Looking for the end. (Book 9, Chapter 90)

o Take it slow and let it roll... That way you avoid the tangles. (Book 9, Chapter 90)

o Once you hit rock bottom, the only way is up. (Book 9, Chapter 90)

o If time cures all wounds, therapy quickens it. (Book 9, Chapter 90)

o Why wonder? (Book 9, Chapter 91)

o Feel good about the now, and do not dwell on the past or question the future. (Book 9, Chapter 91)

o Their eyes were open, but their minds were closed. (Book 9, Chapter 91)

o Allow positive things to affect you in a positive way. (Book 9, Chapter 92)

o Double your bet until you win, then start again. (Book 9, Chapter 92)

o She made her own luck. (Book 9, Chapter 92)

o Your minds are too full. There is no more room to learn new things and enjoy the now. (Book 9, Chapter 93)

o Do not sacrifice tomorrow for today. (Book 9, Chapter 93)

o Love is an energy that does not require matter to exist. (Book 9, Chapter 93)

o People give up precisely at the moment they are about to achieve their miracle. (Book 9, Chapter 93)

o There was comfort in structure, even though painful, it was predictable. (Book 9, Chapter 93)

o Annoying can get too annoying for anyone. (Book 9, Chapter 93)

o J'me was not part of the competitive cancellation culture. (Book 9, Chapter 93) o   YOU are important. (Book 9, Chapter 94)

o   There is always somebody better or worse than you. (Book 9, Chapter 94)

o   Look positively at your value.   (Book 9, Chapter 94)

o   Wealth is what you have, do, know, and are. (Book 9, Chapter 94)

o   Organize once, then multitask. (Book 9, Chapter 94)

o   Our best days are still ahead. (Book 9, Chapter 95)

o   Be brave! (Book 9, Chapter 95)

o   They took their time to meditate and self–evaluate.   (Book 9, Chapter 95)

o   The act of repentance is a magical miracle moment we can make. (Book 9, Chapter 95)

o   History has more than one perspective, depending on who tells the tale. (Book 9, Chapter 95)

o   DIKE: the movement of "Data" to "Information" to "Knowledge" and then finally "Enlightenment". (Book 9, Chapter 95)

o   Not everything is fair and equal. Fair and equal are false. (Book 9, Chapter 95)

o   But to make it worse than the back of a hearse, was the back of the bus treatment from some of the worst. (Book 9, Chapter 95)

o   Failure is part of the process. (Book 9, Chapter 95)

o   EVERYONE adjust themselves. (Book 9, Chapter 95)

o   It is not too late for an update. (Book 9, Chapter 95)

o   You can't just dream to make your wishes come true. That is not how wishes work. You must work for your wishes. (Book 9, Chapter 95)

o   Smile. (Book 9, Chapter 95)

o   Love yourself. (Book 9, Chapter 95)

o   Be balanced. (Book 9, Chapter 95)

o   Forgive mistakes, accept. (Book 9, Chapter 95)

o   Create good habits. (Book 9, Chapter 95)

o   Rest, exercise, meditate about a happy place, eat right and drink more water! (Book 9, Chapter 95)

o   Treasure experiences not possessions. (Book 9, Chapter 95)

o   Become more positive, ignore unpleasantries.   (Book 9, Chapter 95)

o   Stay focused, control yourself. (Book 9, Chapter 95)

- Improve yourself, improve your self-satisfaction. (Book 9, Chapter 95)
- Do your best. (Book 9, Chapter 95)
- Run... hit... dive... land, drop, and roll... Then stand up and run again. (Book 9, Chapter 95)
- Write it down. Make a list. Embroider it and place it on your wall. (Book 9, Chapter 95)
- Red at night, sailors' delight; red in the morning, sailors' warning. (Book 9, Chapter 95)
- It is just a distraction from taking action. (Book 9, Chapter 96)
- Love is a need we all share. (Book 9, Chapter 96)
- "Love each other as you love yourself." (Book 9, Chapter 97)
- "Above all, love each other deeply, because love covers over a multitude of sins." (Book 9, Chapter 97)
- "My command is this: Love each other as I have loved you." (Book 9, Chapter 97)
- Do not let heartbreak get the best of you." Plus, "Get past the trauma, without drama, and let bygones be bygones. (Book 9, Chapter 97)
- Doing evil in ignorance; just going with the flow. (Book 9, Chapter 97)
- Communism gets corrupted by commanders. (Book 9, Chapter 97)
- A warning of a future great awakening in the outside world. (Book 9, Chapter 98)
- You did good. (Book 9, Chapter 99)
- I will be right behind you. (Book 9, Chapter 99)
- Surround yourself with positive people. (Book 9, Chapter 99)
- Avoid comparing yourself to others. (Book 9, Chapter 99)
- Make others happy – give, help, and be kind. (Book 9, Chapter 99)
- Feel grateful, appreciate, and acquire an attitude of gratitude. (Book 9, Chapter 99)
- Monitor your thinking, practice mindfulness. (Book 9, Chapter 99)
- Be confident; tell yourself you can overcome everything. (Book 9, Chapter 99)
- Remember, happiness exists from within, not from outside. (Book 9, Chapter 99)
- Do not take yourself so seriously. Have fun. Be bizarre and child-like. (Book 9, Chapter 99)

Commercial: A young family playing with puppies in a field of flowers. Zooming in on the smile of the baby after being pulled from its mother's teat and shoulder burped. Voice over: "Are you tired of reading the same story over and over again, or watching a movie that is predictable? Have you ever wasted hours of your time and had nothing new to show for it? Try reading something productive. **Try BLOCK XX/XX!** There is nothing else like it..." The scene faded into a picture with many peoples' hands cupped together forming a scoop, and bubbles floating across the screen. Flashing Red Text: Now is the Time!

9 781734 068900